"ANYONE WHO THINKS THAT THE ONLY THING TO FEAR IS FEAR ITSELF SHOULD MEET BRAD THOR."
—*Newsweek*

Praise for *ACT OF WAR*

"Thrill-a-page. . . . Thor's most ambitious, prescient, and wondrously realized book yet reads like the best of James Bond sprinkled with just enough of a Vince Flynn's Mitch Rapp–like edge. . . . A thinking man's thriller quilted in an action-adventure fabric that's Thor at his very best."

—*Providence Journal*

"For those missing Jack Bauer and his *24* exploits, Harvath provides a page-turning alternative with a no-matter-what determination."

—*USA Today*

"*Act of War* will keep you up at night."

—*Bookreporter*

"Thor has proven once again why he is a favorite of the genre. . . . *Act of War* is a suspenseful ride through the world of terrorism. . . . Thor keeps the action fast, furious, and full of the technical details his readers have come to love."

—*Nashville Scene*

"A heart-pounding thriller. . . . Thor creates a read that feels like the TV show *24* on the page."

—Associated Press

"Prepare for an all-nighter!"

—*Watch!*

"The reader v[. . .] while enjoying Brad [. . .]"

—[. . .]*Magazine*

"It's top-speed beach-read stuff—and the action is riveting."

—*The Day*

"The god of thriller writers."

—Phil Paleologos, WBSM

More acclaim for Brad Thor and Scot Harvath, "the perfect all-American hero for the post–September 11th world" (Nelson DeMille)

HIDDEN ORDER

"One of Brad Thor's best books to date."

—*The Washington Post*

"[A] great, great thriller."

—Rush Limbaugh

"Rockin' from cover to cover."

—Charlie Daniels

"One of the best writers you are ever going to read."

—WROK

BLACK LIST

"Intense, authentic, addictive."

—Glenn Beck

"Nonstop intensity."

—Associated Press

"A terrific read. . . . It has you right from the very beginning."

—Lou Dobbs

"Nail-biting."

—*Huffington Post*

FULL BLACK

"Thor has mastered thriller storytelling with fast pacing and plots that are relevant."

—*The Miami Herald*

"Gripping."

—*People*

"Enough adrenaline-charged adventure to fill several books."

—*Bookreporter*

FOREIGN INFLUENCE

"Frightening, illuminating, and entertaining."

—*Bookreporter*

"Intrigue, adventure, and adrenaline-rushing action."

—*New American Truth*

THE APOSTLE

"An out-of-the-ballpark homerun. You won't want to put it down."

—*Blackwater Tactical Weekly*

"Powerful and convincing. . . . A breathtaking, edge-of-your-seat experience."

—The National Terror Alert Response Center

THE LAST PATRIOT

"As close to a perfect thriller as you'll ever find. . . . Brilliantly plotted and ingeniously conceived."

—*Providence Journal*

"Wow, this guy can write."

—*The Atlanta Journal-Constitution*

BRAD THOR

ACT OF WAR

A THRILLER

WAR

POCKET BOOKS

New York   London   Toronto   Sydney   New Delhi

The sale of this book without its cover is unauthorized. If you purchased this book without a cover, you should be aware that it was reported to the publisher as "unsold and destroyed." Neither the author nor the publisher has received payment for the sale of this "stripped book."

Pocket Books
An Imprint of Simon & Schuster, Inc.
1230 Avenue of the Americas
New York, NY 10020

This book is a work of fiction. Any references to historical events, real people, or real places are used fictitiously. Other names, characters, places, and events are products of the author's imagination, and any resemblance to actual events or places or persons, living or dead, is entirely coincidental.

Copyright © 2014 by Brad Thor

All rights reserved, including the right to reproduce this book or portions thereof in any form whatsoever. For information, address Atria Books Subsidiary Rights Department, 1230 Avenue of the Americas, New York, NY 10020.

First Pocket Books paperback edition June 2015

POCKET and colophon are registered trademarks of Simon & Schuster, Inc.

For information about special discounts for bulk purchases, please contact Simon & Schuster Special Sales at 1-866-506-1949 or business@simonandschuster.com.

The Simon & Schuster Speakers Bureau can bring authors to your live event. For more information or to book an event, contact the Simon & Schuster Speakers Bureau at 1-866-248-3049 or visit our website at www.simonspeakers.com.

Manufactured in the United States of America

10 9 8 7 6 5 4 3 2 1

ISBN 978-1-4767-1713-5
ISBN 978-1-4767-1714-2 (ebook)

For Emily Bestler—
the world's greatest editor and publisher.
Thank you for everything.

"Let her sleep. For when the dragon wakes, she will shake the world."

—NAPOLEON BONAPARTE

PROLOGUE

The air was thick with humidity. *Oppressive.* Typical for this time of year. It was monsoon season and stepping outside was like stepping into a steam room. Within half a block the man was sweating. By the intersection, his clothes were sticking to his body. The Glock tucked behind his right hip was slick with perspiration.

Guns, money, and a bunch of high-tech gear. Just like something out of a movie. Except it wasn't. This was real.

Turning right, he headed into the large open-air market. It looked as if a car bomb packed with neon paint cans had detonated. Everything, even the luminous birds in their impossibly small cages, was aggressively vivid. The smells ran the gamut from ginger and garlic to the putrid "gutter oil" dredged up from restaurant sewers and grease traps by many street cooks.

There were rusted pails of live crabs, buckets of eels, and shallow bowls of water filled with fish. Men and women haggled over oranges and peppers, raw pork and chicken.

Like the first spring snowmelt snaking along a dry, rock-strewn riverbed, Ken Harmon moved through the market. He focused on nothing, but saw everything—

every cigarette lit, every newspaper raised, every cell phone dialed. The sounds of the neighborhood poured into his ears as a cacophony and were identified, analyzed, sorted, and stored.

The movements of his body, the functioning of his senses, were all conducted with calm, professional economy. The Central Intelligence Agency hadn't sent him to Hong Kong to panic. In fact, it had sent him to Hong Kong precisely because he didn't panic. There was enough of that back in Washington already; and along with it, the repatriated body of David Cahill.

Cahill had been an Agency NOC based in Shanghai. An Ivy League blueblood type, who knew all the right people and went to all the right parties. He saw things in black and white. Gray areas were for professional liars, like diplomats and men who lacked the testicular fortitude to call evil by its name when they saw it. For Cahill, there was a lot of evil in the world, especially in China. That was why he had learned to speak the language and requested his posting there.

As a NOC, or more specifically an agent operating under "nonofficial cover," he wasn't afforded the diplomatic immunity enjoyed by other CIA operatives working out of an embassy or consulate. Cahill had been a spy, a true "secret" agent. And he had been very good at his job. He had built a strong human network in China, with assets in the Chinese Communist Party, the People's Liberation Army, and even the Chinese intelligence services.

Via his contacts, Cahill had been on to something, something with serious national security implications for the United States. Then, one night, while meeting with one of his top assets, he dropped dead of a heart attack right in front of her.

The asset was a DJ out of Shanghai named Mingxia. Her parties were some of the best in China. Celebrities, drugs, beautiful women—they had everything. And it was those parties that had propelled her into the circles of China's rich and powerful.

She was not without her share of troubles, though, and that had made her ripe for recruitment by Cahill. But when he died, Mingxia dropped off the face of the earth. The CIA couldn't find her anywhere. They wanted answers and they had turned over every stone looking for her. Then, two weeks later, she had reappeared.

It was via an emergency communications channel Cahill had established for her—a message board in an obscure forum monitored by Langley. But since her disappearance, speculation at the CIA had gone into overdrive. Did the Chinese have her? Had Cahill been burned? Had the woman been involved in his death? Was this a trap?

She allegedly had information about a crippling attack being planned against the United States, but nobody knew if they could trust her. The Agency was desperate for information. And so it had called Ken Harmon.

Harmon wasn't a polished Ivy Leaguer like Cahill. He was tall, built like a brick shithouse, and he didn't attend fancy parties. He usually drank alone in the decrepit back-alley bars of some of the worst hellholes in the world. He was a rough man with few attachments and only one purpose. When someone somewhere pushed the panic button, Harmon was what showed up.

He had decided to meet the asset in Hong Kong. It made more sense than Shanghai and was much safer than Beijing, especially for a white guy.

Harmon had chosen the coffee shop. A Starbucks knockoff. It was busy, with the right mix of Chinese and Anglos. People chatted on cell phones and pecked away at keyboards. They had buds in their ears and listened to music or watched videos on their devices. *Whatever happened to a cup of coffee and a newspaper? Hell*, he thought, *whatever happened to newspapers?*

There was a front door and a back door, which meant two ways out, *three* if you counted kicking out the window in the women's bathroom leading to a narrow ventilation shaft. The men's bathroom was a death box. There was no escape if you got trapped back there. Harmon didn't plan on getting trapped.

A net of human surveillance had been thrown over the neighborhood. He'd picked out a couple of them. Men who were too fit and too clean-cut. They were Agency muscle, ex–special operations types. They were excellent with a gun and terrific to have on your team if things went sideways, but they were too visible and Harmon had requested no babysitters. His request, though, had been ignored.

He had also asked that they buy the woman a plane ticket so he could conduct the meeting in a nice, anonymous airline lounge out at Hong Kong International. It was a controlled environment. Much harder to bring weapons in. Easier to spot trouble before it happened. Tradecraft 101. That request had also been ignored.

Langley felt the airport was *too* controlled and therefore too easy for the Chinese to tilt in their favor. The CIA wanted a public location with multiple evacuation routes. They had cars, safe houses, changes of clothes, medical equipment, fake passports, and even a high-speed boat on standby. They had thought of every contingency and had built plans for each. That was how worried they were.

Stepping inside, Harmon scanned the café. The air-conditioning felt like being hooked up to a bottle of pure, crisp oxygen. He grabbed a paper napkin and starting at the top of his shaved head, wiped all the way down the back of his thick neck. He ordered a Coke in a can, no ice. He had learned the hard way about ice in foreign countries.

Paying in cash, he took his can over to the service station where he gathered up a few items, and then found a table. It was set back from the window, but not so far back that he couldn't watch the door and what was happening outside on the street.

He carried no electronics. No laptop, no cell phone, no walkie-talkie. He carried no ID. Beside his large-caliber Glock, spare magazines, and a knife, there was nothing on his person that could connect him to anything, anyone, or anywhere. That was how professionals worked.

Removing a small bill from his pocket, he folded it into the shape Mingxia had been told to look for. A heart. He could do swans, too, but everybody did swans. It was the first thing you learned. He normally did hearts when meeting female assets. It was something different. Some of them liked it. Some didn't. He didn't care. A heart was just a heart.

When it was finished, he set it atop a white napkin. It was unique, but low-key, nothing that could be noticed from the street. In fact, you might only notice it as you walked by the table on the way to the ladies' room—and even then, only if you were looking for it.

An hour later, the woman arrived and slowed as she

passed the table. It wasn't much, but it was enough to tell him that she had seen it.

While Mingxia was in the bathroom, Harmon scanned the café and the street outside. He sipped his second Coke and flipped through one of the free tourist magazines that littered every café and fast-food restaurant in Hong Kong.

When Mingxia left the bathroom and passed his table again, she found the heart sitting by itself. The napkin had been removed. *All clear.* She hadn't been followed inside. It was safe to sit down. Ordering herself a tea from the counter, she took the table next to his.

She was attractive. Better looking than the photo Cahill had included in her file. He could see why he had recruited her. According to the dossier, she had family somewhere that needed the money. They always did. Harmon didn't want to know about it. He wasn't here to date her, just to debrief her, and if necessary, help smuggle her out of China. He was glad she spoke English.

Reaching into her purse, Mingxia removed the glasses Cahill had given her and placed them on the bench between them.

Harmon had been shown how to use them before leaving the United States. He wasn't a fan, though they were better than the earlier versions Google had developed for the Agency. The Lego-brick-sized projector had been replaced with one about the size of a staple. Even so, the glasses were still too sci-fi for his taste.

It was a better method of sharing information, though, than trading briefcases under the table or being passed an envelope full of reports and surveillance photos. The glasses also had a one-button delete function that scrubbed all the data if it looked like they were about to fall into the wrong hands.

Slipping them on, Harmon turned his attention back to his magazine and pretended to read it.

As the information scrolled across the inside of the lens, his mind began connecting the dots.

"Are you positive about all of this?" he asked.

"Yes," Mingxia replied.

They would, of course, need more than just her word for it. But if this was true, the United States was in trouble. *Big trouble.*

"What's this bit in Chinese that keeps popping up?" he said. *"Xuě Lóng?"*

"It's the codename for the operation."

"What does it mean?"

"Xuě Lóng is a mythical Chinese creature said to bring darkness, cold, and death."

"What's the translation?"

"In English, it would be called a snow dragon."

CHAPTER 1

The Secretary of Defense cleared his throat. "Mr. President, with your permission, I'd also like to suggest we move some Fifth Fleet assets out of the Mediterranean and over to the Seventh Fleet in the Pacific."

"We should consider positioning additional bombers in the region as well," the Chairman of the Joint Chiefs added.

The President studied the array of images displayed throughout the room. He had expected to be tested during his presidency, just not this soon—and not to such a degree.

Paul Porter was a two-term governor who had won election by playing to the best in Americans. He was an affable man in his early sixties. A tall, trim outdoorsman with a weather-beaten face, Porter looked as if he would have been just as at home leading fly-fishing trips in Montana as occupying the most powerful office in the world.

He was known for telling the truth, *especially* when it was hard. He never took the politically expedient route of only telling people the parts they wanted to hear. America could no longer afford to be given half the story.

Porter had campaigned on helping to bring about

a brighter, more prosperous future for the nation. He had promised an America at peace with itself and the world. But those things, like anything worth having, would require work. The phrase *we must act today in order to preserve tomorrow* had become a hallmark of his speeches. He liked to paraphrase Founding Father Dr. Joseph Warren and remind Americans that the liberty of all future generations depended upon what they did today. It was an appropriate call to action, which, in light of what they had learned, had just taken on much deeper significance.

"First things first," the President replied, flipping to the page he wanted in his briefing book. "Who's our China expert here?"

All eyes shifted to the CIA's senior China analyst, a woman named Stephanie Esposito. "I am, Mr. President," she said, raising her hand. She was nervous. She had never briefed a president before.

"Agent Esposito, is it?"

"Yes, Mr. President."

"I understand you were quite insistent that this briefing include information on the Chinese concept of unrestricted warfare."

"Yes, sir. I was."

"Why?"

"Because I believe it is the single most important doctrine they've developed in the modern era. It informs everything they do, especially Snow Dragon."

The President agreed. "For those in the room who aren't familiar with unrestricted warfare, will you please explain what it is?"

"Yes, Mr. President," Esposito replied. "China sees the United States as its number-one enemy. The defense minister, General Chi Quamyou, has stated that war with the United States is inevitable and can't be avoided.

"At the same time, China understands that they can't defeat the United States on the conventional battlefield. We're too technologically advanced. But in the words of the People's Liberation Army chief of staff, General Fu Haotian, *the inferior can defeat the superior.*

"It can only be done, though, by throwing out the rule book, which is actually what two very dangerous PLA colonels did back in the 1990s. By abandoning the traditional concept of warfare, Colonels Qiao Liang and Wang Xiangsui completely reinvented China's view of warfare and of itself."

"How so?"

"In their doctrine of unrestricted warfare, Liang and Xiangsui rejected the idea that China was required to meet the U.S. on any conventional battlefield. Why fight in a manner in which you know you'll lose? Instead, the colonels proposed that China only fight battles they knew they could win.

"Merciless, unconventional attacks are at the very heart of their philosophy. In fact, Colonel Liang has been quoted as saying that the first rule of unrestricted warfare is that there are no rules. Anything goes. Bombs in movie theaters, collapsing America's electrical grid, taking down the Internet, poisoning our food or water supplies, dirty bombs, chemical or biological attacks—nothing is beyond the pale in their new philosophy.

"It also gives China the edge. We'll never see them coming. There won't be mass troop mobilizations or anything like that. In fact, unrestricted warfare renders planes, soldiers, and tanks almost totally unnecessary in the traditional sense."

"But someone still needs to carry out the attacks," the President's Chief of Staff interjected.

Esposito nodded. "Correct. While the PLA has millions of hackers who can mask the origin of their cyberattacks, physical attacks on the United States are different. That's why Liang and Xiangsui advocated funding, equipping, and deploying third parties whenever possible. They singled out Muslim terrorists as an excellent proxy."

Everyone around the table looked at one another.

"Understand that the key for China is to never be attached to any attack. A third party, that probably wouldn't even know it was doing China's bidding, affords China plausible deniability. The world would have a perfect bad guy to blame and China would be able to avoid any international repercussions. For any of our allies to take action, there would have to be rock-solid proof that China was behind the attack on the United States."

"And even then," the Vice President added, "some of our allies wouldn't have the stomach for it. It'd be the start of World War III."

"That's what China is counting on," Esposito replied.

The Director of Homeland Security shook his head. "I still can't believe China would risk everything to attack us. What for?"

Esposito looked at the President, who nodded for her to respond.

"The Chinese are extremely deliberate and pragmatic," she said. "They can see the writing before anyone else has even seen the wall. Mr. Director, they're dying. Their air is polluted. Their water is polluted. They have cut down their timber and have mined all of their minerals. Less than 5 percent of China has arable land left suitable for agriculture. The investments they made in North Africa have been a complete bust. In fact, they've taken substantial losses. The mines there didn't even produce a fraction of what they had projected.

"And during all this, China's population has continued to expand while its economy has continued to slow. Every day, China experiences riots and mass social unrest that never makes it into international news. There's not enough work in the cities and the peasants who return to the country are starving to death. In some desperate, lawless areas, reports of occultism and even cannibalism are starting to leak out. As conditions deteriorate, China, like North Korea, has become a hotbed of new, drug-resistant diseases that threaten the entire world. About which they routinely lie to WHO and other international health organizations.

"The Chinese know that it's not daylight they're seeing at the end of their tunnel. It's a train heading right at them."

"So their answer is to come steal our resources?"

"That's just it. The Chinese don't see it as stealing. They see it as surviving. Anything that assures China's survival is not only acceptable, it's imperative."

"Even if it means war?"

Esposito nodded and the President thanked her. He then turned to the Director of National Intelligence. "Against that background, let's address what the CIA learned in Hong Kong."

"Thank you, Mr. President," the DNI said as he turned toward the other members of the National Security Council. "As you all have been made aware, a CIA asset with access to high-ranking members within the People's Liberation Army and China's Ministry of

State Security has learned of a potential attack on the United States, codenamed Snow Dragon.

"While the asset was not able to ascertain the date or methodology, the attack is believed to be imminent. The Chinese have projected a 90 percent fatality rate within one year, which leads us to believe we're looking at something nuclear or biological in nature."

"Missiles?" the Attorney General asked.

The DNI shook his head. "We don't think so. According to the intelligence acquired by the CIA, the Chinese used a cutout named Ismail Kashgari from the Uighur region to approach an Al Qaeda fixer in Pakistan named Ahmad Yaqub. Our belief is that Yaqub was hired to staff the operation."

"The Uighur area borders Afghanistan, doesn't it?" asked the Director of Homeland Security. "Can't we get to this Kashgari character?"

"He's dead," the DNI replied. "We believe the Chinese killed him to cover up their involvement."

"What about Ahmad Yaqub? Can we get to him?"

"Yes," replied the President. "We have actionable intelligence on Yaqub's whereabouts. A mission plan is being developed as we speak."

"Do we have any leads beyond this Ahmad Yaqub?" the Attorney General asked.

"There's one more," replied the DNI. "According to the CIA's asset, the Chinese have been training some kind of special PLA detachment in North Korea."

"What's so special about it?" the Director of Homeland Security asked.

"We believe it is a landing force of some type, training to come in after the attack. As you can see on the screens, the area they are supposedly training in has been netted over. We can't see what they're up to. If we could get eyes on, we believe we might be able to learn more about the nature of the attack."

"How would you go about that?"

"We'd insert a four-man SEAL reconnaissance and surveillance team," the Secretary of Defense replied.

The Attorney General was a bit taken aback. "Into North Korea?"

He nodded.

Looking at the Secretary of State, the AG asked, "Where do you stand on all of this?"

The Secretary of State took a moment to collect his thoughts before speaking. "I stand with the President, but I have a couple of concerns."

"Such as?"

"We've been able to confirm some of the intelligence the CIA received, but it's still largely single-source. That's dangerous. We don't know if this is *officially* the People's Republic of China at work. It could be a rogue element from somewhere within their intelligence service, the military, or even the Chinese Communist Party. We just don't know."

"Which is exactly why the North Korea and Ahmad Yaqub operations are necessary," the Chairman of the Joint Chiefs stated. "If it makes it easier, consider them fact-finding missions."

"With guns and Spec Ops personnel."

"These aren't trips to Disneyland, Mr. Secretary."

The Secretary of State took in a deep breath, puffed out his cheeks, and then slowly exhaled in exasperation. "My job is *diplomacy* and I'd prefer diplomatic channels, but the President is right. We can't let the Chinese know we suspect them."

All eyes shifted to Porter. As great as the risks were, the greatest risk lay in doing nothing. Both operations needed to go forward. There was no other course a responsible leader could choose to take.

Nodding to his Director of National Intelligence and Secretary of Defense, he said, "I'm green-lighting them."

The men immediately reached for secure telephones.

"Blackbird is a go," the Director of National Intelligence said into his.

Moments later, the Secretary of Defense's call was answered. "We're go for Operation Gold Dust," he confirmed.

Blackbird and Gold Dust were codenames randomly created by the CIA and DoD for two missions that might save America from an unspeakable attack, or a deadly, all-out war.

After they had discussed what military assets could be repositioned without tipping their hand to the Chinese, the meeting was adjourned.

As his national security team filed out of the Situation Room, the President asked the Secretary of the Treasury to remain behind. There was an additional piece of intelligence the CIA had collected, but that had been excluded from the briefing.

Once they were alone, the President spoke. "Dennis, I want you to do something for me and you need to be very quiet about it."

CHAPTER 2

F our men in drysuits quietly broke the surface of the choppy, black water and scanned the rocky shoreline. The North Koreans were paranoid about invasion. They went to great lengths to defend themselves, even raking their beaches in order to make footprints visible.

A high-altitude low-opening (HALO) jump had been out of the question. No plane would be able to get them close enough to North Korean airspace. The insertion had to be done via water.

They had used a minisubmarine known as an Advanced SEAL Delivery System. Unlike the open SEAL Delivery Vehicles, which exposed SEALs to strength-sapping cold water, the ASDS was completely contained, warm and airtight. After a battery problem had caused an early prototype to catch fire, a rumor circulated that the SEALs had canceled the program. In fact, it had merely been put on hold until a student at MIT conceived of a completely new way to deal with the batteries. At that point, it was full speed ahead.

The minisub could be launched from any Virginia-class submarine and had a range of over 150 miles. For the insertion into North Korea, the ASDS had been launched from the USS *Texas*. Once the four-man team had exited the minisub via its moon pool, the ASDS left to rejoin the *Texas* and cruise the Sea of Japan for the next seventy-two hours until returning for the team's extraction.

What was to have been a four-SEAL DEVGRU reconnaissance and surveillance team ended up being three SEALs and an agent from the Central Intelligence Agency's Special Operations Group. The SEAL leading the mission hadn't been crazy about the substitution. Thirty-two-year-old Lieutenant James "Jimi" Fordyce of Lancaster, Pennsylvania, thought swapping out one of his shooters for a spook, even one with local contacts and language capability, was neither a good idea nor necessary for the successful outcome of the mission. The Pentagon, the White House, the Central Intelligence Agency, and the Joint Special Operations Command had all disagreed, and Fordyce had been overruled.

The other two SEALs on the team were twenty-eight-year-old Petty Officer First Class Lester Johnson of Freeport, Maine, and twenty-five-year-old Petty Officer Second Class Eric "Tuck" Tucker of Bend, Oregon.

Rounding out the team was thirty-year-old CIA operative Billy Tang from Columbus, Ohio.

Billy not only spoke the language, but he knew North Korea better than almost anyone else in the United States. Over the last six years, he had successfully infiltrated the Democratic People's Republic of Korea eleven times. Whether his teammates appreciated it or not, there was a host of problems they could end up facing in the DPRK that weren't going to be fixed with the business end of a gun.

Because the North Koreans had the ability to pick

up transmissions beamed out of the country, this was going to be a no-comms op. The men could communicate with each other via their encrypted radios, but even then they had been instructed to do so only sparingly. If they were compromised or captured, there would be no rescue. The United States would disavow any knowledge of the men and why they were there. That was why Billy Tang had been added to the team. If things went south, Billy was their insurance policy.

As soon as Jimi Fordyce had given the all clear, the men had begun swimming and the minisub had gone to rejoin the *Texas*. The ASDS had the capability to remain submerged for days without resupply, but the sooner it left, the better. Even along this remote, jagged strip of the North Korean coastline, a coastal patrol had passed right above them. Putting the minisub down in a depression in the sea floor had allowed them to just barely escape detection. Leaving the getaway car idling in the driveway would have been just asking for trouble and they were already going to have enough of it.

Nothing about the mission was going to be easy, but that's why Operation Gold Dust had been built around the SEALs. No matter what happened, they would see it all the way through. And things did happen. Even in a business this precise with men this well trained, Mr. Murphy, of the eponymous Murphy's Law, had a way of popping up at all the worst times. The SEALs had witnessed it during the Bin Laden raid and on multiple other operations. Sometimes, things just happened. But when they did, SEALs adapted and overcame. Failure in their culture was never an option.

The surface swim was made difficult by a strong current that tried to drag them off target. When they finally reached the shore and pulled themselves and their equipment out of the water, they had taken a few minutes to rest. They needed their strength. Towering above them was a cliff the height of an eighteen-story office building.

As if they could read each other's minds, the three SEALs rose in concert and began prepping their climbing gear.

Billy Tang had worked with SEALs before. They were smart, hard men just this side of machines. They embodied a toughness that very few possessed these days. No matter how bad things got—no matter how cold, how desperate, how dangerous, or how deadly—the SEALs pushed on.

Tang admired them for that and at the same time had a bad feeling that they were all going to be pushed to their limits and would need every last ounce of mental and physical toughness before this operation was over. What they had come to the DPRK to do would be almost, if not completely, impossible to achieve.

CHAPTER 3

Scot Harvath caught sight of himself as he checked the truck's side mirror. He was wearing the traditional shalwar kameez—baggy, pajamalike trousers with a long cotton tunic. His skin was tan from having spent the summer outside. He had sharp blue eyes, short sandy brown hair, and was in better shape than most men half his age. He needed a shower and shave, but for a former Navy SEAL in his early forties, he looked pretty good.

Sitting next to him, driving their white Toyota SUV, was twenty-eight-year-old Chase Palmer. Eight years ago, he had been the youngest soldier ever admitted to Delta Force, or the "Unit" as members referred to it. His hair was lighter than Harvath's, but their appearances were so similar they could have been taken for brothers.

Cradling an H&K MP7 submachine gun in the backseat beneath her burka was twenty-five-year-old Sloane Ashby. In her short military career, she had racked up more confirmed kills than any other female soldier, and most of the men. With her high cheekbones, smoky gray eyes, and blonde hair she looked more like a college calendar coed than a "kick in the door and shoot bad guys in the face" operator.

Harvath moved his eyes back to the taillights several car lengths ahead. The night was alive, *electric*. Motorbikes buzzed in and out of traffic. Trucks clogged the streets. Between the curtains of diesel exhaust, he could smell the ocean. They were getting close. Activating his radio, he said, "Look sharp, everyone."

With over twenty-three million inhabitants, Karachi was the third-largest city in the world and Pakistan's most heavily populated. It was an easy place to hide. *Staying hidden, though*, thought Harvath, *required discipline.* It meant not going to your favorite restaurant just because it was your last night in town. But that's exactly what Ahmad Yaqub had planned.

There had been debate over where to grab Yaqub. Should they do it in Karachi while he was under the protection of the ISI—Pakistan's Inter-Services Intelligence Agency—or should they wait until he returned to his stronghold in Waziristan?

The Secretary of State wanted to wait. He wanted to pay a rival faction in the lawless border region between Pakistan and Afghanistan to snatch him so there'd be no American fingerprints on the job. Hitting an ISI motorcade in Karachi was asking for trouble. *A lot of it.* The clock, though, was ticking.

Yaqub was an Al Qaeda–linked Saudi who had traveled to Afghanistan for the jihad and had married into a powerful Waziristan clan. From his mountain compound, he helped fund and coordinate terror operations against corrupt Pakistani and Afghan politicians, as well as anyone else seen as enemies of Islam and the Taliban.

His greatest coup had been the assassination of Benazir Bhutto in Rawalpindi. She was the American-backed "puppet" who had been predicted to win the election and become president of Pakistan. She had made no secret of the direction she would take the country and how she intended to crush the Taliban.

Yaqub knew there would be an investigation into her death and had left just enough clues to confuse everyone. Some believed a rival political faction had ordered her death. Some blamed the Taliban. Some swore it had come from deep within the ISI, whose continued hold on power was dependent upon chaos reigning throughout the region. Where these clues didn't lead, though, was back to Ahmad Yaqub. Or so he had thought.

But people in Waziristan talked, especially when money was involved. The Taliban often lamented that cash was the greatest weapon the Americans brought to the battlefield. Money frightened them more than the drones that killed without warning. American dollars were like a cold wind in winter. No matter how well constructed your house, the wind could always find a way inside. And a particular gust of American dollars had done just that.

The U.S. had made the apprehension of Ahmad Yaqub a top priority. They had moved heaven and earth to compile as much information on him as quickly as possible. The best intelligence on Yaqub had come from a private intelligence agency run by an ex–CIA spymaster named Reed Carlton.

As part of the Carlton Group's force protection contracts with the Department of Defense, they had developed unparalleled human networks throughout Afghanistan and Pakistan. Nobody collected better intelligence in the region than they did; not even the CIA.

Within twenty-four hours of being tasked, the Carlton Group had reached out to its networks and had assembled an impressive dossier on Yaqub. They knew exactly where he was, how long it would take him to do his banking and assorted business in Karachi, and where he'd be spending his last evening. But the Carlton Group's expertise didn't end there.

In addition to hiring top people from the intelligence world, Carlton also recruited the best talent from the Special Operations community. One of his greatest accomplishments had been landing Scot Harvath.

Harvath had served on SEAL Teams 2 and 6, with the Secret Service's Presidential Protection Division, and under a prior president who had successfully used him to covertly hunt and kill terrorists. Harvath and the President had enjoyed a simple understanding—if the terrorists refused to play by any rules, Harvath wasn't expected to either.

Carlton saw in Harvath a bottomless well of raw talent. When he hired him, he had not only honed Harvath's exceptional counterterrorism skills, he had also taught him everything he knew about tradecraft and the world of espionage.

When he was finished, Harvath had become more than just a talented hunter and killer of men. He had become an apex predator—a creature who sat atop the food chain, feared by all others.

There was one other plus Harvath brought to the current assignment—plausible deniability. The Carlton Group was a private organization. If Operation Blackbird went sideways, there wouldn't be a trail leading back to the White House.

In order to give the United States even greater insulation, Harvath had suggested using Kurdish Peshmergas instead of American operators for the hit. The Peshmergas had trained with U.S. Special Forces, were tough, and could be relied on no matter how bad things got.

The Peshmergas would be augmented by a couple of trustworthy Pakistanis from the Carlton Group's network who had supported delicate, in-country covert operations in the past. Harvath and his people would not get involved unless absolutely necessary. That was the best he could offer. The U.S. had to move on Yaqub. Time was running out. It had to be now and it had to be in Karachi. The Secretary of State had reluctantly agreed.

Once they had the green light, Harvath and Carlton began planning the operation. There was layer upon layer of detail to be covered—weapons, logistics, contingencies, and personnel chief among them. The key was to get Yaqub in transit. That was when he'd be most vulnerable. Harvath knew exactly who he wanted with him on the assignment.

Chase Palmer was smart, aggressive, and very talented. By twenty-eight, he'd seen more action than many Unit operators ever would and was already looking for his next adventure. Having worked with him on a previous assignment, Harvath had been quite impressed and knew he'd be perfect for the Carlton Group. That was all it had taken.

With Chase on board, there was only one other operator he had wanted along.

With the Taliban and Al Qaeda having put a price on her head for all her kills in Afghanistan, the Army had removed Sloane Ashby from combat. They had assigned her to the Unit compound at Fort Bragg, where she had become a trainer for Delta's all-female detachment known as the Athena Project. She was a good instructor, but she was far too young to be mothballed and she missed the action. When Carlton met her and offered her a position, she had jumped at the chance.

Noting the intersection they were approaching, Sloane said, "Khayban-e-Jami coming up."

They had driven the routes between Yaqub's safe house and his favorite restaurant multiple times. The team knew every intersection and had plotted multiple points where they could grab him. When they did, the Peshmergas would have to move fast. The key was incapacitating his bodyguards as quickly as possible.

Yaqub's destination was a popular restaurant called Bar-B-Q Tonight. It was close to the Karachi Yacht Club and just across the street, ironically enough, from Benazir Bhutto Memorial Park. Whether that provided an added sick appeal for Yaqub was anyone's guess.

"Fifteen meters to the intersection," Sloane called out.

"Damn it," Chase swore as the car immediately in front of them began to slow. "We're going to lose them. The light's changing."

Yaqub's two-car motorcade had already entered the intersection, trailed by the Peshmergas.

"Try to stay with them," Harvath replied.

Chase leaned on the horn. "C'mon, Chicken Little. Be a man. Move your ass."

"Easy with the horn."

"This guy's gotta be the only idiot in Karachi who doesn't push through a yellow light."

"We'll be okay," said Harvath. "Let's just not draw attention to ourselves."

Chase tried to steer around him, but there wasn't enough room.

"Not good," Sloane stated from the backseat.

"Everybody, stay calm," Harvath instructed. He

didn't like the idea of being separated from the motorcade or the rest of his team either, but there was no use blowing their cover. They'd been very careful and had made sure not to get too close, repeatedly switching positions. The ISI was well trained and would be looking for a tail. There was also no telling how many of the motorbikes or scooters zipping through traffic might have been spotters.

"We know where they're going," Harvath continued, "and we've got eyes on—"

Before he could finish his sentence, a massive truck came barreling through the intersection and slammed right into the car carrying the Peshmerga fighters.

CHAPTER 4

"G o, go, go!" Harvath shouted as Yaqub's motorcade began to speed away.

Chase rolled into the car in front of them and then stepped on the gas. The tires of their heavy SUV smoked as he pushed the smaller vehicle into the intersection.

"Contact left!" Sloane yelled as gunfire erupted between the Peshmerga fighters and eight armed men who had leaped out of the truck.

Picking up Chase's rifle, Harvath shouted out what he wanted. They weren't going to leave any of their team to die.

Chase braked and pulled the steering wheel hard to the left. The large SUV skidded sideways and as it did, Harvath and Sloane aimed their suppressed weapons out the window. Coming parallel across the intersection with the truck that had plowed into their Peshmergas, they began firing.

The compact MP7s Harvath and Sloane had brought were personal defense weapons designed for close-in work. They fired the HK 4.6x30mm round, renowned for its ability to penetrate body armor. In order to have further reach, Harvath had grabbed Chase's Hoplite. It was a lightweight, concealable "truck gun" built by a company called Citizen Arms. The extremely accurate rifle fired the 5.56 round and was made even more effective by its Aimpoint Micro T-1 quickfire red dot sight. Sloane took the attackers closest to them and Harvath focused on the ones farther away.

Harvath dropped the first man he fired on and then readjusted and took down a second. Sloane nailed one in the throat and a second with a headshot. The attackers moved to take cover behind their vehicle. As they did, Harvath and Sloane continued to fire. It gave the Peshmergas enough time to move to a better position. The last man on their team punctuated the fight by throwing a fragmentation grenade into the attackers' truck.

"Grenade!" Harvath yelled. "Go, go, go!"

Chase stepped on the gas and sped out of the intersection just as the grenade detonated. Windows shattered behind them and a massive column of fire raced up into the night sky. Within seconds, shards of debris rained down on the roof of their SUV like a metallic hailstorm.

Harvath and Sloane had cut the team who ambushed their Peshmergas in half and had helped them get out of the kill zone. If any of the attackers had survived the grenade attack, they were going to wish they hadn't. Right now, some very pissed-off Peshmergas would be enacting their revenge. They wouldn't stop until all of their attackers were dead. Once they were, the Peshmergas would disappear into the night. They'd split up and regroup at their own safe house outside the city. Within twenty-four hours they'd be out of the country. Harvath had no further use for them. They were compromised. He was moving to his contingency plan.

Somehow, the Peshmergas had been spotted. Did the ISI also know about Harvath, Sloane, and Chase? Did they have another ambush planned? There was no way to know. They had to remain ready for anything. Better yet, they needed to spring their own trap before Yaqub's ISI handlers could get him to safety. No doubt, they were already on their cell phones summoning reinforcements and putting the entire city on alert.

Harvath radioed his motorcycle team and plotted their location on his map of Karachi. The ISI wouldn't be taking Yaqub back to the same safe house. They'd use an alternate. Not that it mattered. Harvath planned to hit their motorcade within the next three blocks. They couldn't let Yaqub get away.

They were headed away from the water, deeper into the city. Not a good thing. Too many one-way streets, back alleys, and warehouses where the ISI could vanish. Yaqub would go to ground and the ISI would help keep him hidden. It would be a long time, if ever, before he returned to his compound in Waziristan. Harvath and his team were only going to get one last chance. He decided to throw everything they had at it.

Pronouncing the name of the street as best he could, Harvath radioed his Pakistani assets to tell them what he wanted them to do. What they carried in their backpacks was now critical to the survival of the United States.

Harvath pointed to the street coming up on their right and said, "This one. Here."

"Hold on," Chase replied.

The tires of the big SUV screeched in protest as it swung around the corner and Chase punched the accelerator once more.

They were on a parallel street to Yaqub's motorcade, but they were still behind. Harvath could see traffic in front of them beginning to slow.

"Hold on," Chase instructed again.

Jumping the SUV up onto the sidewalk, he honked his horn and yelled for people to get out of the way.

As Harvath squinted at his map, the voices of the Pakistanis could be heard over the radio.

"We're here!" they replied in unison.

"Don't do anything until you see their vehicles. Understood?" he ordered.

"Understood."

Turning his attention to Chase, Harvath said, "Two blocks down we make a left turn and we go hard. Got it?"

"Got it," Chase confirmed.

Two blocks later, Chase jerked the SUV back into the street, pulled a hard left turn, and sped toward their rendezvous with Yaqub's motorcade. The key was to get there before the ISI agents could get out of their vehicles.

"They're coming," said one of the Pakistanis over the radio. "Very close. Almost here. Almost here," he continued.

There was complete radio silence for several moments until one of the Pakistanis commanded his colleague, "Now! Now! Now!"

Harvath could envision what was happening. Both of the men would have taken off their backpacks. The first man would remove what looked like a large black wheel of Swiss cheese. Inspired by the Spider-Man character, the SQUID—or Safe Quick Undercarriage Immobilization Device—deployed sticky webs of netting from its holes that would entangle a vehicle's axles and bring it to a complete and almost immediate stop.

It was safer and far more effective than strip spikes and could stop anything from a Mini Cooper to a Chevy Suburban.

The second Pakistani was carrying two magnetized explosive devices developed by the Israelis to kill Iranian nuclear scientists. While the scientists sat in traffic, an operative on a motorcycle would pull up alongside, affix the bomb to their vehicle, and speed off just before it detonated.

According to the Carlton Group's intelligence, Yaqub was accompanied in his vehicle by two of his fighters from Waziristan, plus an ISI driver. Two more ISI operatives followed in the second vehicle. As far as anyone knew, both vehicles were thin-skinned and not armored. Nevertheless, Harvath believed in the SEAL motto that two is one and one is none. He would rather do too much damage than not enough.

As Yaqub's vehicle passed, the first Pakistani would activate the SQUID, bringing it to a halt. As the ISI chase car following behind slammed on its brakes, the second Pakistani would emerge from hiding and affix one bomb to the chase car's undercarriage and another to the side. The Pakistanis would then retreat to cover and Pakistani number two would detonate the devices.

Chase, Harvath, and Sloane were less than thirty seconds away when they heard the first explosion, followed by the second.

Skidding into the intersection, they could see everything had worked. Netting was twisted around Yaqub's axles and behind it, the chase car was on fire, the two ISI agents inside either dead or dying.

As Chase brought their SUV to a screeching halt, Harvath was like ice. He felt nothing for the ISI operatives or the fighters from Waziristan. They were giving aid and protection to a terrorist planning to help murder hundreds of millions of Americans. The men had made their bed, and now they could burn in it.

Harvath and Sloane jumped out of their SUV, MP7s up and at the ready, followed by Chase, who had reclaimed his Hoplite. Together, they rushed Yaqub's car.

From the front passenger seat, one of Yaqub's fighters produced a short-barreled shotgun. As soon as Harvath saw it come above the line of the dashboard, he yelled, "Gun!" and fired multiple rounds through the windshield, killing the man instantly.

The ISI driver tried to unholster his weapon, but Sloane was already at his window and fired two shots at his head, shattering the glass and killing him.

When the fighter in the backseat on the passenger side made himself known, Chase had almost been on top of him. The man didn't wait to get the door all the way open before firing. He sent heavy 7.62 rounds from his AK-47 slicing right through the door panel. Chase had to lunge between two parked cars to take cover and avoid being hit. Had they not been taking such great pains to make sure Yaqub didn't get shot, he would have fired and nailed the guy.

The Waziristani fighter had been trained well and took advantage of Chase's predicament to keep firing and move to cover. Gunfights were louder than most people realized and the reports from the AK-47 were deafening.

The man had Chase pinned down and was about to fire at Sloane when Harvath appeared. He had maneuvered behind the burning follow car and, taking aim, pressed his trigger.

There was a spray of blood, accompanied by an explosion of bone and brain matter as the rounds entered the back of the man's head and blew out an eye, teeth, and half of his face. He looked like he'd been hit with a missile.

Harvath picked his way forward, using a parked car for concealment. He couldn't see Yaqub. He assumed he was crouched in the backseat and likely armed. "Hands up!" he yelled in Arabic.

Yaqub didn't comply.

Harvath fired a three-round burst through the rear window, showering the backseat with broken glass. He then yelled his command in Arabic again.

Slowly, Yaqub sat up and raised his hands.

Keeping his weapon trained at the man's head, Harvath approached the rear passenger door. He nodded at Sloane, who slung her MP7 and transitioned to her Glock. Removing her flashlight, she sent a blinding beam of light into Yaqub's eyes, illuminating the entire backseat.

"Gun!" she shouted. "On his lap!"

Chase repeated in Arabic for Yaqub to keep his hands up. *"Raweenee edeek. Raweenee edeek!"*

Slinging his MP7, Harvath said, "If he moves, kill him."

Both operatives nodded.

In Yaqub's lap Harvath saw a 9mm Beretta pistol. Keeping his eyes on Yaqub and his hands, Harvath reached through the shattered driver's window, unlocked and then slowly opened the rear passenger door. Yaqub never moved.

Fixing him with his gaze, Harvath reached in and retrieved the weapon. Making sure it was on safe, he tucked it into his waistband at the small of his back and ordered in Arabic, "Get out of the car. Do it now!"

Slowly, Yaqub complied.

He was big and ugly. While Harvath stood five-foot-ten, Yaqub was at least two inches taller. It looked like the doctor had delivered him with ice tongs. His face was a roadmap of pockmarks and scars.

Harvath spun him around, bent him over the trunk, and patted him down. He found the Arab's cell phone and tossed it to Chase. Police klaxons could be heard in the distance.

Removing a pair of FlexiCuffs, some duct tape, and a black hood from his pocket, he told Sloane and Chase, "Secure everything. We're out of here in forty-five seconds."

After securing Yaqub's wrists behind his back, he stood him up and turned him around. "Do you know who I am?" he asked in Arabic.

The terrorist studied him for a moment and then responded in English. "A dead man."

Harvath smiled. "Wrong," he said, before whipping his head forward. There was a crack of cartilage and a spray of blood as he shattered the man's crooked beak of a nose.

The Saudi's knees went weak as a wave of agony swept through his body.

Harvath held on and steadied him. As he did, he leaned forward and whispered into his ear, "I'm the Angel of Death, and I'm taking you back to hell where you belong."

CHAPTER 5

The USS *Florida* was an Ohio-class ballistic missile submarine just off the Pakistani coast. Fitted behind its sail structure, piggyback style, was a pressurized garage called a dry deck shelter, or DDS for short. It was capable of launching not only SEAL Delivery Vehicles, but also the SEALs' fast, highly maneuverable inflatable Zodiac boats known as combat rubber raiding craft, or CRRCs. These boats could be launched or recovered regardless of whether the *Florida* was on or beneath the surface.

Harvath would have loved to have brought Ahmad Yaqub aboard the *Florida* via a subsurface recovery. It would have scared the hell out of him and made him even more pliant to interrogation. Trying to get him to calmly breathe air from a SCUBA tank while dragging him underwater, though, was a disaster waiting to happen. Instead, Harvath had another plan.

A SEAL team from the *Florida* had rendezvoused with Harvath and his prisoner near Karachi's Clifton Beach. After hog-tying Yaqub and placing him facedown in the CRRC, Harvath hopped in with the SEALs and headed out into the open ocean. Chase and Sloane would link up with the rest of the team who had hit the ISI safe house, review any materials they had found, and prepare a report to be transmitted back to the States. After that, a private plane would return them to the United States.

Powered by its fifty-five-horsepower outboard motor, the black, fifteen-and-a-half-foot-long CRRC skipped over the top of the water, but landed hard off a couple of particularly large waves. Each time it did, Harvath heard Yaqub grunt as the terrorist took the brunt of the impact via his face and his already broken nose. That was nothing compared to what was coming.

With a spray of water, the USS *Florida* broke the surface. It was an impressive sight to behold even through the gray-green of the night vision goggles Harvath and the other SEALs were wearing. Prepping the team, the SEAL helming the CRRC signaled for everyone to make ready. Adjusting his throttle, he aimed right at the massive vessel.

Seconds later, there was the whine of the outboard's engine as the rubber boat came up out of the water and skidded to a stop atop the *Florida*. Instantly, there was a flurry of activity.

Pulling out his knife, Harvath cut Yaqub's feet free. Two SEALs grabbed him under the arms and lifted him out of the boat. There was the distinct *clank, clank, clank* as the heavy locks of the DDS were released and its large hatch began to open.

Members of SEAL Delivery Vehicle Team 1 hurried out to help drag the CRRC inside. As they did, one pointed Harvath to the gear he had requested.

Once the boat was inside, they began to rapidly deflate and dismantle it as the hatch closed.

The DDS was shaped like an airplane fuselage. It was nine feet high, nine feet wide, and thirty-eight feet long. It consisted of three separate compartments, all capable of being pressurized. The compartment they were in now was known as the "hangar." This was where the SDVs and CRRCs were stored, and could be flooded to launch SEALs and their equipment from underwater.

At the other end, opposite the hatch, was the "bubble"—a Plexiglas booth that came halfway down from the ceiling. It was pressurized, and as water filled the DDS, it would only come up waist-high for those inside the bubble. It was where the controls for the DDS were located and where a member of SDV Team 1 communicated with the crew down inside the *Florida*. When everyone in the DDS was ready, the SEAL in the bubble relayed the message to the *Florida*.

Moments later, the chamber operator passed the warning that the *Florida* was preparing to dive. Harvath reached over and removed the hood from Yaqub's head and ripped off the piece of duct tape covering his bearded mouth. The tape was covered in dried blood and pulled a lot of hair with it. Yaqub grimaced.

Even though the lights inside the DDS weren't particularly bright, it took the Saudi's eyes a moment to adjust. The first thing he noticed was that everyone around him was suiting up in SCUBA gear. Harvath nodded and the two SEALs who had walked Yaqub into the DDS took turns minding him as they also suited up.

Harvath remained silent as the *Florida* dipped beneath the surface and the submarine began its descent. As he climbed into his own drysuit, he could see the fear building in Yaqub's eyes. He had no idea if the man could swim or not, but it didn't matter. It wasn't the swimming part Yaqub was going to have to deal with.

Opening up the valve of his tank, Harvath depressed the purge button on the regulator. It made a loud hiss, indicating that air was flowing.

Harvath signaled the SEAL inside the bubble to begin flooding the hangar.

"What are you doing?" Yaqub demanded as the water started rushing in.

Harvath looked at him as he spat into his face mask. "I told you. I'm taking you back to hell."

The terrorist glanced down. Harvath had removed the man's shoes and socks back in Karachi. The cold water was already covering the tops of his feet.

"What do you want from me?"

Harvath ignored him and held his mask up to the light to judge whether he had fully coated the inside.

"Answer me," the Saudi demanded.

Picking up his tank, Harvath carefully slung it over his back and slowly adjusted the straps. Finally, he addressed his prisoner. "How long do you think you can hold your breath, Ahmad?"

Yaqub nervously looked around the narrow, cramped space. Despite the chilly temperature, he had begun to perspire.

The dry deck shelter hadn't been Harvath's first choice. What he had wanted to do was get onboard and drag Yaqub straight down to the torpedo room, stuff him in a tube, and flood that. The sensation would have been much more unnerving. The problem had been getting him past the *Florida*'s crew. There'd be too many witnesses, so the plan was nixed back in D.C. Whatever Harvath intended to do with Yaqub, it had to be done in the confines of the dry deck shelter.

That meant either threatening to drown him, or locking him in the forward hyperbaric chamber and keeping him there until his ears bled or his eyes popped out of his skull. One way or another, Yaqub was going to tell Harvath everything he wanted to know.

Each of the SEALs who were present had been read in on the prisoner and the imminent threat to the United States. Not only would they never reveal whatever Harvath was going to do, they'd *help* him with it. The President himself had pulled out all the stops. Harvath's instructions had been perfectly clear—do whatever needed to be done to neutralize the threat. And that's exactly what he would do.

He had no reservations about torturing a scumbag like Ahmad Yaqub if he had to. He had done it before.

While the politically correct crowd was against any form of coercion, Harvath appreciated its merits. The uninformed often confused enhanced interrogation techniques like loud music, sleep deprivation, and open-handed slaps with torture. Those weren't torture. And they didn't bring America down to the terrorists' level.

What would bring America down to the terrorists' level was if the United States had the same callous disregard for human life. Life was cheap in the eyes of the terrorists, not so for America. The United States revered human life and therefore would do everything it could to protect it. Using enhanced interrogation techniques, or even torture in some cases, demonstrated the high value America placed on the lives of its citizens.

People liked to talk about the Geneva and Hague conventions, but very few had read them. Not only were terrorists not signers to the conventions, but they also didn't wear uniforms to identify themselves on the battlefield—a key provision. They hid in the general population, behind women and children, and therefore were not entitled to any of the Geneva and Hague protections.

In any other time in history, terrorists would have been shot on sight, not shipped off to some Caribbean island for religiously sensitive Halal meals including dates, honey, olive oil, and fresh-baked pita bread, along with access to lawyers, newspapers, unlimited DVDs, a library, and soccer games.

The terrorists had chosen to not only go to war with the U.S.A., but to keep that war going through attack after deadly attack. Their convoluted religious ideology was beyond reasoning with. It was impossible to convince them, facts be damned, that America had been the greatest force for good in the history of the world. They would slaughter innocent men, women, and children to impose their will on the entire world. As far as Harvath was concerned, America and its allies couldn't kill these people fast enough.

The water in the DDS was now up to Yaqub's knees. "If you had wanted to kill me," the terrorist said, feigning bravado, "you would have done it in Karachi."

Harvath thought he heard a slight tremor in the man's voice, though it could have been from the cold.

"That's right," Harvath replied. "I don't want to kill you. I want to watch you suffer and *then* I want to kill you."

The expression on Yaqub's face tensed. Just for a moment, before turning defiant again. It was a micro-expression, something Harvath had been trained by the Secret Service to detect. It was a subconscious indicator given off by a subject when under stress. It normally meant the subject was lying or intending to do harm. It could also mean you had him scared shitless.

Yaqub was anxious, but tried to cover it. He looked around. "All of this for just one man?"

Harvath's visage was like stone. "Not just any man,

Ahmad. This is for you. This is what happens when you kill Americans. We come for you. We never forget. We never stop hunting. Sooner or later, we find you."

"I don't believe you," he said, the frigid water nearing his genitals. Yaqub tried to rise up onto the balls of his feet.

The SEALs holding him by the arms forced him back down. His body began to shake from the cold. It was time for Harvath to increase the pressure.

"I want you to remember my face, Ahmad. For the few minutes you have left alive, I want you to study it. After you're dead, we're going to defile your body and dump it into the ocean, the way we did to Sheik Osama, in order to make sure you don't go to Paradise. Then I'm going to visit your family."

He paused to watch the expression on the terrorist's face before continuing. "Your wives, your children . . . I'm going to torture them and then I'm going to kill them. *All* of them," said Harvath. "And then I'm going to visit your father, your mother, your four brothers and your two sisters and their families in Saudi Arabia. They'll meet deaths even more horrific than yours. And as each of them writhes in pain, as they beg death to come and take them, I'll make sure they know that it was you who brought that misery upon them."

Yaqub's lips were beginning to turn blue and his teeth had started chattering. "I curse you and your entire country. You and your American arrogance. You are doomed."

Harvath stepped forward and drove his fist into the terrorist's chest. When the Saudi doubled over in pain, Harvath signaled for the SEALs to release him, and then he grabbed the back of his neck and plunged Yaqub's head beneath the water.

CHAPTER 6

arvath held the terrorist there until the air had left his lungs and he was struggling for his life. Breaking Yaqub meant breaking his ideological willingness to die. He had to want to live more than he wanted anything else.

When Harvath finally yanked the man's head out of the water, the Saudi terrorist drew in huge gulps of air and then started vomiting. Harvath waited for the vomiting to stop, and then shoved his head back under the water.

A few moments later, he pulled him out, allowed him to partially catch his breath, and then plunged him back down. He repeated this process several more times.

When he next pulled the Saudi's head from the water, he did so with a demand. Once the man quit heaving and could hear him well enough, Harvath said, "I'm going to give you one chance, Ahmad. If you don't tell me what I want to know, we're going to open the valves all the way, fill the rest of this compartment with water, and we're all going to watch you drown."

Yaqub shook his head as he coughed and sputtered.

"Then, just as I promised, I'm going to visit your family."

The terrorist shook his head even more vigorously before vomiting up more seawater.

Harvath waited, his blue eyes like two cold pieces of ice as he bored his gaze into Yaqub's. "You have something I want," he said. "If you give it to me, I'll let you live and no harm will come to your family. Do you understand me?"

Yaqub nodded.

"I know about the coming attack, Ahmad. All of it. And I know you're a part of it." Harvath watched the man again for a moment before continuing. "I know Ismail Kashgari came to you for assistance. Correct?"

Yaqub nodded.

"Why?"

"Men," the terrorist mumbled.

"How many men?"

"Six," said Yaqub.

"To do what?" Harvath demanded.

"I don't know."

Harvath slapped him. "You're lying to me, Ahmad. You know what happens to your family if you lie. Now tell me about the attack."

"*I don't know,*" he insisted, the water now up to his chest. "It was a trade."

"What do you mean *trade*?"

"I helped him get men and he paid me."

Harvath studied him. "You know the target, though, don't you?"

"America. Yes."

"That's why you helped him."

"Yes," Yaqub replied.

"But you never asked about the attack? You weren't curious? I don't believe it."

The man vomited again. The water was nearing his shoulders. His teeth kept chattering and Harvath had to strain to understand him. "He would not tell me."

"Why not?"

"I don't know. He told me not to ask him again. I don't think he knew. I think he was working for someone else."

"Who?" said Harvath.

"I don't know."

"Who do you think?"

"I don't know. He is a Uighur. Chinese Muslim. We knew each other from the jihad. I don't know who he worked for."

Harvath changed tack. "Where are these six men?"

"It's too late."

"*Where* are they?" he repeated.

"They are already inside the United States."

"How?"

"I don't know," Yaqub answered. "I didn't handle that part."

"You don't seem to know very much, do you, Ahmad? You know what? I don't believe you."

"Kashgari requested special men," the terrorist clarified. "Smart men. Engineers."

Engineers. The word sent a chill down Harvath's spine. Terrorists recruiting engineers could mean only one thing—*bombs.*

"Where did these engineers come from?"

"I don't know."

He was playing with him and Harvath didn't like it. He forced his head beneath the water again.

Yaqub was weak and he didn't fight for very long. Harvath knew he was taking a risk.

Pulling the man's head back up he yelled at him, "This isn't a game, Ahmad. You tell me now. Who are they and where did they come from?"

Yaqub, his body suffering from the cold and repeated oxygen deprivation, was trembling wildly. "*I don't know,*" he repeated.

"Which of your children, which of your wives do you want me to kill first?"

"Khuram Hanjour," he muttered. "Khuram Hanjour."

"Who is Khuram Hanjour?"

"Khuram Hanjour," the terrorist repeated, his eyes glassy and unfocused.

Harvath slapped Yaqub again. He looked like he was going hypothermic. "Ahmad, *who* is Khuram Hanjour? Ahmad. *Ahmad.*"

Harvath slapped him once more, and for a moment, the man's eyes met his. "Ahmad, tell me who Khuram Hanjour is."

"The recruiter," the man said.

"Khuram Hanjour recruited the men?"

Yaqub's head lolled to the side, the water now up to his chin.

Harvath slapped him again. "Ahmad, where do I find Khuram Hanjour?"

Nothing.

"Who was Kashgari working for? Tell me."

It was no use. Yaqub had lost consciousness.

CHAPTER 7

Colonel Jiang Shi hated politicians. Few possessed analytic minds. Fewer still understood the tenets of warfare. It was why he had wanted the politicians kept out of it.

But the nine-member Politburo Standing Committee was the supreme decision-making body of the Chinese Communist Party. Nothing in China was done without their permission. Shi had been left with little choice, especially when his superiors secured an invitation from the General Secretary for him to make the presentation himself.

Depending on whom you asked, the meeting had either been a success or an utter disaster. Shi believed it fell in the latter camp.

A thirty-five-year veteran of the Chinese military, Colonel Jiang Shi worked for the PLA's intelligence division, known simply as "Second Department." Second Department was home to some of China's greatest strategic thinkers, including Shi, who headed the PLA's unrestricted warfare program. Snow Dragon had been his idea.

With good reason, the Politburo Standing Committee was highly resistant to any talk of attacking the United States—even if carried out by third-party nationals. If China's involvement were ever exposed, the repercussions would be devastating. It would mean nuclear war. No matter how many times Colonel Shi repeated his deepest held belief that the United States would be made to bow to China, the answer from the PSC was an unequivocal and emphatic *no*.

Shi had been disappointed, but far from surprised. Politicians lacked not only vision, but courage. He had returned to his office, opened his walk-in safe, and relegated Snow Dragon to the stack of other rejected plans he and his people had developed over the years. At some point, China would wake up and realize that war with the United States was inevitable. When that happened, his phone would ring. Two weeks later, it did.

The General Secretary, who was a supporter of Second Department and its unrestricted warfare program, had lobbied continually in favor of a strike against the United States. He presented them with fact, after fact, after fact. China was running out of time, and options. Either China would dictate the terms of war or the terms of war would be dictated to it. War, though, was inevitable. Eventually, the PSC agreed. Permission was granted, but with one caveat. The Politburo Standing Committee wanted essential Chinese personnel evacuated from America beforehand.

There was absolutely no way such a thing could be done without risking exposure. The plan's success depended upon the United States and the rest of the world believing that the attack had been committed by Al Qaeda terrorists. If anything at all hinted at China's involvement, the entire operation would be undone.

There were two key reasons Shi and his people had picked September for the attack. The first was the most obvious. A strike on the September 11 anniversary would automatically be blamed on Al Qaeda. It would be the only evidence most people needed in order to levy blame.

The other reason was that the strike Shi had planned would create absolute chaos in the U.S. But to maximize that chaos, they needed to hit before America's crops were harvested. If they did, famine would take hold over the winter and the die-off of American citizens would be accelerated.

Despite these excellent reasons, the politicians on the Politburo Standing Committee had convinced themselves of a "better" idea—postpone the attack until Chinese New Year.

It was one of China's biggest national holidays, and millions of Chinese from around the world returned for the event every year. The United States wouldn't think twice about influential Chinese doing the same. Shi disagreed.

While it might not draw attention before the attack, it definitely would afterward. It wouldn't matter if the United States government was in a shambles. Every intelligence agency around the globe would be trying to figure out what had happened. The timing of the attack would be one of the key things they'd be looking at. That it had taken place during Chinese New Year and so many of China's America-based VIPs had been miraculously spared wouldn't go unnoticed. In the intelligence business, there were no such things as coincidences. They were always signs of something more sinister afoot.

Because the men and materials would already be in the United States, postponing the attack until midwinter also meant more time for the attack to be uncovered. The PSC was unswayed. The General Secretary delivered their decision.

Even though the PSC planned to abandon many high-level Chinese executives and diplomats in the U.S., Shi still didn't like it. Knowledge of the 9/11 attacks and the significance of the anniversary were burned into global consciousness. Using any other date was a mistake. The PSC didn't care. Shi was ordered to make a New Year's strike a success.

No matter what time of year, attacking America on its own soil posed special challenges. Security was always elevated and American law enforcement was getting better and better training on what to look for. Even if men and materials could be smuggled into the country and could remain hidden, one American patrol officer could undo everything. In fact, once in the United States, terrorist operatives had more chance of being discovered by a beat cop or state trooper than they did by an FBI or CIA officer.

Shi had studied the histories of the Al Qaeda members sent by Bin Laden to carry out the 9/11 attacks and was fascinated by their brushes with the law and how many clues they had dropped in the run-up to that dramatic day. Examining all of the pieces in the aftermath, he was stunned that the United States hadn't uncovered the attack. Bin Laden had been extremely lucky. Shi's plan would also require a certain amount of luck. He decided to set the attack for two days after Chinese New Year.

Once the date had been fixed, he arranged to meet with his colleague who ran one of the PLA's best hacking units—Unit 61398. It was based out of a twelve-story building in a run-down neighborhood in Shanghai. Their job would be to populate key jihadist websites with chatter in the run-up to the attack. Anyone investigating afterward would believe all of the signs had been there. Hindsight could always be counted on being twenty-twenty.

As he put the rest of the wheels in motion, Shi worried about the early February attack date. He was concerned about the weather. Snow Dragon was designed as multiple attacks that would be launched simultaneously. If one cell launched before the others, or if any one of the cells simply failed to launch, the entire operation could be undone. He kept wishing there was a way that the Politburo Standing Committee could be made to reverse its decision and agree to his earlier attack plan. Then, something had happened.

CHAPTER 8

Wazir Ibrahim wasn't stupid. Only a guilty man would ask for a lawyer. If they had anything substantial on him, they would have arrested him already.

"You know what this is, Wazir?" the young detective asked, holding up an official-looking piece of paper. "This is a police report. Your wife claims you roughed her up. What do you have to say about it?"

The Somali man took a deep breath and replied, "It is not true."

"You're calling your wife a liar?"

"She does not speak the truth."

"You didn't beat her?"

"I did not beat her," Wazir replied.

The detective smiled. "I think you're full of shit. You know that?"

The Somali had seen this man's type before. He was angry, coiled tight inside like a snake. He had become a police officer so he could lord his power over others. He had an inflated sense of self. He held himself out to be a protector of the weak when in reality he had pursued his badge so he could prey upon a sea of others with impunity. Insecure men with a patina of authority could be annoying. Give those same men actual authority and they could be deadly. Wazir had seen it time and again in Somalia. America pretended to be better. Wazir knew different. Men were men no matter what country they called home.

This man named Hoffman possessed a bearing beyond that of a simple police officer, one that he couldn't immediately place.

"Does it make you a tough guy to beat your wife, Wazir?" Detective Hoffman asked.

"I did not beat my wife, sir."

Hoffman placed the piece of paper he had been holding back into the folder and removed another. "Does Islam condone the beating of wives, Wazir?"

It was a rhetorical question. The Somali man understood that well enough to know that the detective did not expect a reply.

"For an infidel, I thought I was pretty squared away when it came to Islam and wife-beating."

Infidel. It was an interesting choice of words. The detective didn't refer to himself as a Jew or a Christian. He referred to himself the way Muslims would have referred to him. Wazir could now place the officer's hostility, his bearing. He had served in the U.S. military and had probably seen combat in a Muslim nation. Maybe he had been shot. Maybe he had seen his comrades die. If so, he was much more dangerous than just an insecure policeman hiding behind a badge.

"The prophet Mohammed's fathers-in-law slapped his wives Aisha and Hafsa for annoying him, didn't they?" he asked.

The Somali paused for a moment before nodding.

"When Mohammed heard this, what did he do? He laughed. He thought it was funny."

Wazir Ibrahim didn't bother to reply. What the man was saying came from the Hadith.

"One night when Aisha left the house without permission, Mohammed punched her, right in the chest, didn't he? His *favorite* wife. He struck her so hard that she claimed it gave her great pain. Correct?"

The Somali didn't answer.

"The Qur'an specifically gives husbands permission to beat their wives, doesn't it?" Hoffman asked. "So if you beat your wife, you're only doing what the Qur'an gives you permission and the Hadith supports you in doing, right?"

"I did not beat my wife, sir."

"Is the wife-beating subject a little boring for you?" the young man said, setting the paper down. "Why don't we talk about something else? Let's talk about what the Prophet Mohammed thought about nine-year-old girls."

Wazir Ibrahim's cool expression, along with his confidence that the police had nothing to charge him with, suddenly melted away.

The detective noticed the change instantly. "What's wrong, Wazir?"

Panic began to build in the Somali's chest. "We're not talking about the Prophet Mohammed anymore, are we?"

"No, we're not," said the detective. "We're talking about a group of Somali men from Minneapolis and the underage girls they brought to Nashville for sex. What do you know about it?"

Wazir looked away and replied, "I think I am done answering questions."

CHAPTER 9

Placing the hood back over his head, Harvath and the SEALs transported Ahmad Yaqub from the dry deck shelter down into the USS *Florida*.

While they moved him, crewmembers were kept out of the gangways. This way, if ever asked, they could testify that they never saw a thing.

Yaqub was put in dry clothes, cuffed to a bunk in a private berth, and covered with blankets. A SEAL corpsman monitored him. When he started to come around, he was given warm soup and hot tea to help bring his core body temperature back up. Once the corpsman gave the okay, Harvath began to interrogate him again from the beginning.

He focused on Ismail Kashgari, the Chinese Muslim who had approached Yaqub for help in staffing the attack on the United States. He was probing for inconsistencies in Yaqub's story. He pushed him for every detail he could remember: their means of communication; where, when, and how often they had met; how money was exchanged; how much money was exchanged—all of it. Harvath filled half a legal pad with notes.

An hour later, he changed the subject and asked about Khuram Hanjour, the recruiter. He now wanted to know everything he could about him—where he lived, how to contact him, who he associated with, what mosque he went to, anything that could help them paint a better picture.

When he had exhausted the salient details about Hanjour the recruiter, he handed over the interrogation to a SEAL named Scobell, and stepped out into the gangway.

His mouth was dry and his head was pounding. He needed a handful of aspirin, a bottle of water, and a cup of coffee.

Harvath stuck his head inside the berth next door and asked if any of the SEALs had any Vitamin M, slang in the SEALs for Motrin. One of the men tossed him a bottle.

Harvath shook two pills into the palm of his hand and tossed the bottle back. Thanking the SEAL, he headed down to the submarine's mess hall.

Entering the mess, he asked for a bottle of water. On the wall was a plaque commemorating the *Florida* for being the first Ohio-class sub to ever fire a Tomahawk cruise missile. At the other end of the room, a group of sailors were watching one of Harvath's favorite westerns—*The Magnificent Seven* with Steve McQueen. He remembered someone telling him that it was the second-most-shown film in U.S. television history, second only to *The Wizard of Oz*.

In the Navy, you ended up watching any and every movie ever made. There wasn't much else to do if you were under way and not on shift. While Harvath had seen *The Magnificent Seven* plenty of times in the Navy, the first time he ever saw it was with his father.

It was playing in a small movie theater in San Diego that occasionally revived popular Westerns. He and his father had driven across the bay from their home on Coronado one Saturday afternoon to see it. Harvath had been about nine years old at the time.

The film followed a team of gunslingers hired to protect a small Mexican village from marauders. The villagers were farmers and didn't know how to fight. The gunslingers taught them.

Harvath's father was a SEAL and the movie was a great metaphor for what they did. It helped Harvath better understand his father. It was full of great dialogue, with more than a few poignant lines.

Sitting there in the dark, Harvath watched his dad silently recite line after line by heart. It had a profound impact on him.

They returned together over the next three Saturdays. It was the happiest he could ever remember being, sitting alone in the dark with his dad. They weren't sports guys and they couldn't talk very much about what his dad did for a living, but they had movies, and especially, this movie.

By the time Harvath was seventeen, he had seen *The Magnificent Seven* more than two dozen times. He now knew all of the lines by heart as well. Some took on greater meaning for him as he grew older, but one in particular resonated with him after his father had died in a training accident and Harvath had become a SEAL himself.

Many of the villages he passed through around the world reminded him of the one in the movie. There were always children and they were always fearless. They gawked at the weapons he and his teammates carried and wanted to touch all of their equipment. *What's this do? What's that do?* The questions were always the same and the children sported smiles that seemed outsized for the squalid conditions they were living in.

While the SEALs were indeed a novelty in most of the places they were dispatched, the children in particular were drawn to them, often to the exclusion of their own families. While this was problematic for obvious operational reasons, there was also a balance that needed to be maintained. If not careful, the SEALs could have been seen as stealing the thunder of the village men, which wasn't their intention and could have disastrous consequences. The SEALs needed their cooperation, not their resentment.

In one village, a young boy had told Harvath that he wanted to be a brave warrior like him someday, not a coward like his father who was *just* a farmer. Via his interpreter, Harvath admonished the little boy right in front of all the others. Just as Charles Bronson had done in the film, he told the little boy that carrying a gun wouldn't make him a man; carrying responsibility was what would make him a man.

He explained that the men of their village were truly brave. They cared for their families, they went out to their fields and worked hard every single day, not knowing if they were going to be able to provide enough to eat, yet they worked their hardest nonetheless because their families were counting on them. *That* was courage.

The boys were ashamed of themselves, as they should have been, and they sulked off, leaving Harvath to contemplate his own courage, particularly as it related to relationships.

He wanted a family, but he knew what he did for a living would make that difficult. Having to disappear in the middle of the night, not knowing when or if he would be coming home was almost too much to ask of the people you loved.

He had watched SEAL marriages fall apart left, right, and center. But almost to a man, those SEALs had chosen incompatible women. There were SEALs who had solid marriages and they were always the envy of the rest of the men. Harvath had always wanted to be one of those guys, but the rigors of his career had made personal relationships difficult to establish, never mind maintain.

For the people of the United States to enjoy the American dream, someone had to protect it. Harvath saw himself as one of those protectors. In his worldview, there were wolves, there were sheep, and there were sheepdogs. He was a sheepdog—he always had been, even as a child when he befriended a mentally impaired kid next door who had been plagued by bullies. Harvath had never tolerated those who preyed upon the innocent or the weak. That wasn't in his DNA. For better or for worse, he always did the right thing even if it cost him, which sometimes it had.

But his greatest fear was of failing. Failing his team, failing his country, failing himself. It drove him and was why he pushed himself as hard as he did. It was why he had become so good at what he did.

At some point, though, he knew he would have to dial it back. Not today, not tomorrow, but at some point he'd have to hand over the watch to someone younger, faster, and able to rebound in less time. He wasn't twenty-two anymore. What's more, he had met someone. She was a wonderful woman with a wonderful little boy and he had begun seeing the possibility of a life together with them.

Twisting the cap off the water bottle, he popped the Motrin in his mouth and stepped closer to the TV. Yul Brynner was about to deliver a great line. When asked by one of the village leaders how there could be a gunslinger who didn't care about money, Brynner explained that men who carry guns for a living aren't all alike. Some don't care about money at all. Some, for their own reasons, simply enjoy the danger.

Harvath mouthed the words just as his father had done sitting next to him in that darkened theater in San Diego when he was a little boy. Then, grabbing a paper cup, he filled it with coffee and walked back to check on Yaqub.

Scobell stepped out of the berth to debrief Harvath on what he had learned. There were details about Yaqub's organizational structure and how they moved men and supplies in and out of Waziristan. It was low-hanging fruit.

Harvath thanked him, told him to keep at it, and, coffee in hand, went forward to file his report.

After the submarine came up to periscope depth and his encrypted transmission had been sent, Harvath grabbed a quick shower and a shave before finding an empty bunk where he could get some sleep. It was cramped quarters, but it was warm and it was dry. This was the Four Seasons compared to some of the places he had been forced to sleep over the years.

Having left word with Scobell to wake him if Yaqub revealed anything that could be of value to their operation, he closed his eyes and, willing himself to relax, concentrated on slowing his breathing in order to help fall asleep.

As he did, his mind drifted to the four-man reconnaissance team the President had sent into North Korea. He tried to envision where they would be at this point in their operation.

He had conducted only one operation ever in North Korea and it had been harrowing. He said a prayer for the men on the ground that it would be successful. They were going to need all the help they could get.

CHAPTER 10

Every freedom in the DPRK was restricted, especially freedom of movement. Over his years of infiltrating the communist country, CIA operative Billy Tang had organized a loose underground railroad that had helped shuttle him around. He learned quickly that the only North Koreans who believed in the government's communist vision were the bureaucrats at the very top—and even then, the majority were only giving lip service to it in order to avoid being executed.

Human beings were hardwired to act in their own self-interest and the North Korean people were no different. Almost all of them were on the lookout for any opportunity to earn extra money. Even the smallest amount could make a huge difference in their lives and the lives of their families. Everyone did it. The key was doing so at a level that didn't draw the attention of government officials.

Citizens in the oppressive communist state, though, were also wary of entrapment and Tang hadn't built his network overnight. Favor by favor, envelope of cash by envelope of cash, he expanded and tended his relationships like a garden. Some of them had grown to be as strong as family ties. In fact, so many families relied on him that Tang had more than once smuggled his own money into the country when the notoriously bureaucratic CIA had been late disbursing his operating capital.

Born in the United States of South Korean parents, Billy Tang was not only of Korean extraction, but he spoke the language fluently. The North Koreans he bankrolled had no idea he was American, much less an operative for the CIA. They believed him to be a South Korean journalist aligned with a human rights organization in Seoul. He snuck into the DPRK, or so they thought, to chronicle its abuses and help expose them to the rest of the world. It was dangerous work, but for the risks they took, his North Korean assets were rewarded handsomely.

Each time he visited, he brought not just money, but also medicine. Cholesterol lowering drugs, blood pressure medication, insulin, EpiPens, and even Viagra—he was seen as an angel of mercy and in some cases a literal lifesaver. The more Tang did for his network and their family members, the more loyal they grew. And the more loyal they grew, the greater the risks they were willing to undertake on his behalf. Some risks, though, were too great to ask even of his core people, so he had begun branching out.

Unlike the rest of the world, where organized crime tried to infiltrate the government, in North Korea the government worked hard to infiltrate organized crime. Even at the top of the totalitarian food chain, life in the "utopia" of the Democratic People's Republic of Korea was so destitute that many high-level officials searched for ways to augment their own meager incomes and improve the standard of living for themselves and their families. To do that, they turned to organized crime.

They trafficked internationally in methamphet-amine, opium, heroin, counterfeit currencies, and knock-off luxury goods. The illicit trade was esti-mated to contribute upward of a billion dollars a year to North Korea's coffers. But while much of the orga-nized crime was geared toward distributing products into foreign markets, there was still a certain amount of organized crime conducted within the DPRK it-self. Tang's challenge hadn't been infiltrating one of these groups, but rather finding one that wasn't al-ready shot through with government officials. The last thing he needed was to be directly doing business with members of the state's armed forces, diplomatic corps, or intelligence service. If he ever could turn one of these people, it would be best to do it through a cutout.

When Tang identified a low-level smuggler he wanted to recruit, he posed as a representative of the Jopok, South Korea's mafia, and made the young man an enticing offer. In exchange for drugs, Tang offered him something very hard to acquire in North Korea—real American products, not knock-offs. The young man had jumped at the chance.

The CIA purchased iPads, MacBooks, Xboxes, Jack Daniel's, American cigarettes, and smartphones, among other coveted items. Tang made only limited quantities available to the smuggler. He didn't want to turn him into such a big player that he drew the attention of the larger syndicates—only enough to make him reliant on Tang and hungry for more.

The kid wasn't some country bumpkin, but he wasn't a criminal mastermind either. Not yet. That might come at some point in the future. For now, he had just the right combination of guts and smarts to make him both useful and dangerous. Tang had made up his mind to fully exploit both qualities.

There were only two types of people who could afford the prices Tang's American products would fetch in the North Korean marketplace—organized crime figures and DPRK officials. The young smuggler, named Hyun Su, didn't have those kinds of contacts. He would sell the goods to the next person up the criminal ladder from him. From there, they might pass through two more rungs, their prices doubling and tripling, until they were sold to the final customer.

Knowing the electronics were destined to end up in influential hands, the CIA and NSA had made sure that all of them contained the most advanced spyware available. Thanks to Tang and his young smuggler, U.S. intelligence had been welcomed into the homes of some of the DPRK's most powerful families and none of them had a clue.

It was a brilliant operation and one the Agency began replicating in other parts of the world. But there was an additional benefit that Tang didn't uncover until two years into their relationship. While all North Koreans hated the DPRK government, Hyun Su's hatred of it was *very* personal.

Highly distrustful of everyone, the smuggler had kept Tang at arm's length. Over time, though, remarks had begun to slip. Finally, after Tang had spent the better part of an evening getting him drunk, Hyun Su's walls had come all the way down and the truth had poured out.

Six years prior, his family's village had been near an army barracks—a particularly unsafe place for North Korean citizens to live. One evening, there had been pounding on their door. Hungry soldiers were out looking for food. When his father told them that the family didn't have any extra food, the soldiers beat him with the butts of their rifles. His mother and older sister begged them to stop. The soldiers did, but only long enough to brutally rape them both before moving on to the next house.

The attack left his father paralyzed—a death sentence for a family forced to physically eke out its daily existence. After a string of indignities that followed, his sister committed suicide. Shortly thereafter, his mother stopped eating. Then she stopped getting out of bed. Soon she began having fevers. When she died, it was blamed on pneumonia. Hyun Su knew better. A broken heart could not be expected to pump life-giving blood through the body.

He had only been thirteen and his world had completely crumbled. The final straw was when his father begged the boy to kill him. It was a request no parent should ever make of a child. Hyun Su couldn't do it. As hard as it was to find food and take care of his father, he couldn't kill him. He loved him. His father was all he had left in the world.

Then one day, he, too, was gone. Someone, Hyun Su never knew who, had done what he couldn't do. What he *wouldn't* do. Someone in the village had waited for the boy to go out and had then smothered the father, putting him out of his misery.

Others in the village told Hyun Su to take it as a blessing. His father had begged to die. He was now released and so, too, was Hyun Su. He would not have to "suffer" the burden of taking care of his father any longer. He was free.

That life could be seen as so cheap disturbed him beyond words. He couldn't live in the village any longer, especially not knowing who the murderer was.

Hyun Su gathered what few possessions were of value to him and disappeared. He left behind his innocence, his childhood, and any grudging respect he might have had for authority. The military, and the country at large, had become his enemy.

Back in the United States, Billy Tang had two small children of his own. He couldn't begin to fathom the pain Hyun Su had been through. It did, though, explain a lot about his personality. It also meant that Tang could bring him deeper into his operations and use him for more than just feeding NSA-rigged electronics into the local pipeline. If anyone had told him that the young smuggler would eventually become his most valuable asset, Tang wouldn't have believed it. But at this moment, that's exactly what he was. Hyun Su was their lifeline.

The team had hiked five kilometers in from the coast and had dug into a hide site just before daybreak. They rotated the watch. As the team leader, Jimi Fordyce went first. No one spoke and they kept all movement to a bare minimum. When Hyun Su arrived at the rendezvous point that night, he was right on time. Only after Tang had checked everything out and had given them the all clear did the camouflaged SEALs reveal themselves.

After they had been secreted in the back of the truck, Tang and Hyun Su climbed into the cab. They were both dressed in the peasant clothing seen throughout the country—a black Mao cap, baggy cotton trousers, and a loose-fitting tunic.

Hidden beneath his tunic, Tang carried a four-and-a-half-inch-long, razor-sharp CRKT knife called the Otanashi noh Ken, which meant "Silent Sword" in Japanese. It was a deep-concealment folding blade that had been created for the Special Operations community by famed knife-maker and close-quarters combatives expert James Williams. Designed for maximum penetration through clothing, it was small enough to be hidden, but long enough to reach critical organs and finish the job. The Otanashi noh Ken had one purpose and one purpose only—to kill as quietly as possible.

While firearms were excellent tools for rapidly killing one or multiple targets, there was no way to totally silence a firearm. Even a suppressed pistol emitted a muffled *pop* when fired. That was why Billy Tang preferred knives. They were completely silent. Only the victim made any noise, and that could be mitigated if you knew what you were doing.

That didn't mean firearms didn't have their place in Tang's toolbox. Tucked into the door pocket next to him was a full-sized 9mm SIG Sauer P226 Tactical Operations pistol with a SWR Trident 9 suppressor. The five-hour drive would take them into parts of the country he had never been before. They had no idea who or what they would encounter.

In addition to his weapons, Tang had come armed with a stack of currency, a bottle of Jack Daniel's, a carton of cigarettes, and three *Playboy* magazines. In the DPRK, those items were equivalent to a small fortune. If they found themselves in a tough situation, Tang's goal was to bribe their way out of it. They were behind enemy lines. Shooting was to be avoided at all costs. The minute one police officer or soldier went missing was the same minute the alarm bells would start ringing.

Their objective was to get in and get out without the North Koreans ever knowing they had been there.

As Hyun Su fired up the engine of his truck, Tang

looked him over once more. He was transporting foreign soldiers—a death penalty offense—yet he appeared completely calm. *No*, Tang thought. *Not calm. Content.* This was his way of getting even.

The young smuggler had no idea who the men were or why they were here, but judging by their appearance, he had probably guessed that they weren't friends of the regime in Pyongyang. That was all that mattered to him.

Hyun Su's only job was to drop them off and pick them up. *So far, so good,* thought Tang. If everything else went this smoothly, they'd be back in the United States in a matter of days.

But Tang knew all too well that the best-laid plans of mice and men often go awry. In the darkness of the cab, he reached for his SIG and wondered if this would be the trip where his good luck would finally run out.

CHAPTER 11

Harvath had been asleep for about four hours when the communications room sent for him. He could feel the submarine ascending toward the surface. "We picking somebody up?" he asked the young sailor maneuvering through the narrow hatchway in front of him.

"No, sir," the sailor replied. "Dropping off."

Something told Harvath he didn't need to ask who was getting dropped off.

Moments later, via a secure satellite uplink, he had his answer.

"I hear you are looking for Khuram Hanjour," said a voice from CIA headquarters in Northern Virginia. It belonged to the Agency's Deputy Director, Lydia Ryan.

Believing the Agency needed more overhaul than could be handled by one person, President Porter had originally tapped Ryan to be a codirector, along with her CIA mentor, Bob McGee. It had been a bear trying to get that through the confirmation hearings. The CIA was highly protective of its turf, as well as its long-standing way of doing things. It didn't like change and it had some key allies on the Hill. The unprecedented idea of two DCIs, especially one only in her early thirties, was more than the bureaucracy at Langley could abide.

It became clear pretty quickly that it wasn't going to pass. To help the President save face, and also to save McGee's candidacy for Director, Ryan had graciously stepped aside and agreed to accept the deputy directorship.

In her opinion, she had gotten the better end of the deal. For the most part, she'd be free from having to deal with the politicians on the Hill and could focus on day-to-day intelligence operations, as well as helping to clear out the deadwood at Langley that prevented the Agency from being the absolute best it could be. There was plenty of time left for her to become Director of Central Intelligence—if that was even what she wanted. Right now, she liked where she was. She believed in the CIA and its potential to be even better. She also liked serving a president who was determined to give those on the front lines anything and everything they needed to succeed.

Harvath had worked with Ryan before and he liked her. She was a tall, striking woman with dark hair and green eyes who was half Irish and half Greek. She had been a highly adept field operative who also knew how to navigate the Agency's personalities and inner workings. "What do you have?" he asked.

"Khuram Pervez Hanjour, age fifty-seven, current base of operations Dubai. Suspected of recruiting for Al Qaeda and other Islamic terrorist organizations. He's also done recruiting for sundry criminal enterprises in Russia, South America, and Asia."

"Where in Asia? China?" Harvath asked, hoping there was a connectable thread.

"No, Thailand mostly. Which doesn't mean that he

hasn't done work for the Chinese, just that prima facie there isn't any direct connection."

"And his ties to Yaqub?"

"Based on the phone you took off Yaqub in Karachi, we were able to trace some calls back and forth to Dubai, but we don't know yet if any of the numbers belong to Hanjour," Ryan replied. "The NSA is working on it."

"How about financials? Any indication that money has moved between them?"

"I wish we had something concrete, but you know how murky the transactions usually are with these guys."

Harvath did know. Following the money used to be a surefire way to build relationship trees in order to see who was working with whom. The problem now was that traditional banking transfers had been abandoned in favor of what were known in the Muslim world as *Hawalas.*

Hawalas were networks of Muslim money brokers. Money was left with one Hawaladar somewhere in the world and it could be picked up from another anywhere else. It was based on the honor system and was described as money transfer without money movement. There weren't even any promissory notes involved. It was all done via personal relationships, which made it virtually impossible to track. Only informal records were kept, and the Hawaladars settled up accounts between themselves, sometimes doing so by exchanging things other than cash, such as precious stones, property, even employees. The system was confounding for law enforcement and counterterrorism agencies.

"So nothing conclusive connecting Hanjour and Yaqub?" said Harvath.

"Not yet, but a week ago Emirati intelligence rolled up a Hawaladar in Dubai on a narcotics charge. He was having synthetic cannabis, also known as Spice, along with crystal meth, shipped to him from abroad. The UAE has a zero tolerance policy on drugs and he's looking at anywhere from four years minimum to a max of fifteen in prison. The authorities haven't rushed to get him a lawyer, but he's been rushing to make a deal. He's telling them anything they want to know. He's already named all of his clients, legit or otherwise, including a Khuram Hanjour."

"He listed Hanjour as a drug client?"

"No," Ryan replied. "From what we understand, he ID'd Hanjour strictly as a Hawala client."

"Do we know for sure if this is *our* Hanjour?"

"We're talking to the Emiratis now."

"Where is this Hawaladar being held?" Harvath asked. "Dubai?"

"We think so. We should have more information soon."

"If his client is our guy and he's in Dubai, how fast can you get eyes on him?"

"Our local people are working on it."

"What about leverage? Is there anything we can use against him?"

Ryan flipped through some notes before replying. "The French and the Brits also have files on Hanjour. We're going through those now, but there do seem to be two interesting items that could be useful."

Once she explained to Harvath what they were, he told her what he needed and then asked, "How soon can you get me to Dubai?"

CHAPTER 12

Forty-five minutes later, Harvath was standing topside on the *Florida* along with a squad of SEALs and a hooded and bound Ahmad Yaqub.

It took over fifteen minutes to get everyone winched up to the U.S. Navy Seahawk helicopter hovering above the submarine. Once everyone was aboard, the helo banked and took off for the USS *Abraham Lincoln*.

The Nimitz-class aircraft carrier was the flagship of Carrier Strike Group Nine and home to the United States Navy's Carrier Air Wing Two. In addition to its Growler, Hawkeye, and Greyhound fixed-wing aircraft, Air Wing Two boasted four strike fighter squadrons. Strike Fighter Squadron 2, aka the "Bounty Hunters," flew the F/A-18F Super Hornet.

The almost $70 million aircraft had a range of more than twelve hundred nautical miles, a top speed of 1,190 miles per hour, and—best of all for Harvath—a second seat.

By the time the Seahawk touched down on the deck of the *Abraham Lincoln* and the SEALs unloaded their prisoner, Harvath's flying taxi was already fueled, hot, and ready to take off.

In all of his time with the Navy, Harvath had never flown in a Super Hornet. He was given a rapid briefing, during which the ejection seat was explained and he was told not to touch it. After he changed into an anti-G flight suit and put his helmet on, he climbed into the aircraft and was strapped in.

The pilot made a joke about there not being a beverage service because of the short duration of the flight, then after communication with the air boss, the yellow-shirted catapult officer gave a series of signals and the pilot throttled his engines to military power. Twenty seconds later, the steam catapult fired, shooting the plane down the deck of the *Abraham Lincoln* and out over the Persian Gulf.

While a special request could have been made to allow the Super Hornet to land at Dubai International Airport, Harvath wanted to keep his arrival in the UAE quiet. The United States 380th Air Expeditionary Wing was already stationed at Al-Dhafra air base outside Abu Dhabi, and that's where he was flown.

When the pilot landed at Al-Dhafra and slid the Super Hornet's canopy back, the cockpit was instantly enveloped in desert heat. Waiting on the tarmac was one of Ryan's people from Dubai, a sharp-as-nails case officer named Anne Reilly-Levy. She was an attractive blonde in her forties with a distinct Texas drawl. "Welcome to the United Arab Emirates," she said, extending her hand.

Harvath shook hands and followed her to a waiting SUV. Levy had left it idling with its air-conditioning on full blast. "It's so damn hot," she said as they climbed in, "I saw two trees fighting over a dog."

Her comment made him smile. "What part of Texas are you from?"

"Dallas."

"So you're used to the heat."

She shook her head. "You never get used to this kind of heat."

Harvath agreed. "But at least they make up for it with the culture, right?"

Levy chuckled. "Yeah, in spades." She pointed to a large shopping bag on the backseat as she put the truck in gear. "There are shoes and a couple changes of clothes in there. If they don't fit or you need something else, let me know."

Harvath glanced at the bag and thanked her. "How long have you been here?" he asked.

"In the UAE? Almost a year now. Before that I was in Iraq. And before Iraq, Saudi and Yemen."

"Somebody back at Langley must hate your guts."

She smiled. "My father was in the oil business. I spent most of my childhood in the Middle East. I'm good with languages. Arabic in particular."

"You're lucky the CIA got you and not the Navy. With language skills like those, they would have sent you to South America."

"They're that screwed up?"

"I've seen some dumb stuff."

Levy turned onto a service road and increased her speed.

"If you're not a fan of the culture," Harvath asked, "what are you doing here?"

"This is where the fight is. Yemen, Saudi, Jordan, Syria, Iraq, every Muslim country is rotting with jihadists. This isn't a vacation, this is work, and I go where they send me. Fortunately, I enjoy what I do."

She was right. The Middle East was definitely where the fight was. He was also glad to hear her say that she truly enjoyed her work. The war on terror had exacted a heavy toll. In addition to those who had been killed or wounded, it had destroyed marriages and broken families both in the military and in the intelligence community. It was just wave after wave that never relented. There was only so much people could handle.

Harvath, though, had yet to reach his breaking point. He enjoyed his work, too, and Levy's comment reminded him of the wooden sign that hung near his front door at home. The property had once belonged to the Anglican Church. In the attic he had discovered an old wooden sign engraved with the motto of their missionaries—TRANSIENS ADIUVANOS. *I go overseas to give help.* It was strangely fitting for the career he had chosen for himself.

Levy drove them to a squat, sand-colored building on the base that the CIA used for planning and operations. Its narrow windows were covered with reflective film meant to keep out the sun and also mitigate blast damage should a potential bomber ever get inside the wire.

"We sweep it daily," she said as she pulled into a parking spot marked by two sun-bleached stripes. "My team just went over it forty-five minutes ago. It's clean."

Harvath grabbed the bag out of the back and followed Levy inside.

She led him to a midsized conference room lined with maps of the UAE and other countries in the region. A large flat-screen monitor hung on the wall at the front of the room. Waiting for them were three other CIA operatives.

Harvath wasn't thrilled with the welcoming party. He had asked Ryan to keep his arrival off the books. All he wanted were the items he had requested and any additional intelligence they had available. After that he preferred to be on his own.

After the introductions had been made, one of the operatives, a man named Cowles, pointed to the back table and said, "We've got coffee, water, and sandwiches. Whatever you want."

Harvath nodded and helped himself to a bottle of water and what looked like a turkey sandwich before grabbing a seat at the nicked-up conference table.

As Cowles worked on hooking up his laptop to the flat-screen, Levy removed a small cell phone and a black U.S. diplomatic passport and slid them across the table. "The phone has been programmed with several numbers listed as belonging to our embassy in Abu Dhabi or the Consul General's office in Dubai. All of them will be answered by Agency personnel if dialed. The number listed for the economic advisor's office rings to my cell.

"Now, the passport we created for you should succeed at shooing away any local law enforcement flies, but the higher up the chain you go, the less chance it'll hold water. Hopefully you won't need it, but if you do, be careful how you use it."

Harvath flipped it open. The Carlton Group had provided the Agency with one of his recent photos. He familiarized himself with the name, date of birth, and country stamps, then scrolled through the numbers on the cell phone and nodded. Levy signaled for the lights to be turned out.

After firing up their PowerPoint presentation, Cowles handed her the remote and she narrated. "I know Deputy DCI Ryan gave you a partial briefing, but we've been able to gather some more details since then. We only have a handful of photos of Khuram Pervez Hanjour, none of which, as you can see, are terribly good." She cycled through them slowly, stopping when she reached a photo of an obviously different man.

"This is twenty-six-year-old Najam Fahad," Levy narrated. "Fahad is the Hawaladar being held by the Emiratis. He has identified Hanjour as one of his clients. The NSA has also just confirmed phone calls between Fahad and Ahmad Yaqub's Hawaladar in Karachi. At this point, we're operating with an 80 percent certainty that we've got the right Khuram Hanjour, so everything is a go."

Good, Harvath thought. "What else?"

Levy moved to the next slide in her presentation. It was a satellite photo. "Hanjour is known to frequent the historic district west of Dubai creek, known as Bur Dubai. It has several mosques," she continued, advancing through her slides. "Including the Grand and Iranian mosques.

"It has a lot of shopping streets, outdoor souks, cafés, and restaurants, which makes it popular with tourists. Fahad says he has no idea where Hanjour lives. Whenever they meet, it's at a restaurant called the Silk Route."

She advanced to a surveillance photo of an outdoor restaurant and Harvath studied it. "Is that at some hotel?" he asked.

"It is. It's called the Arabian Courtyard, but I want to show you something else, first."

Harvath nodded his assent.

"The Emiratis let us examine Najam Fahad's cell phone."

"Did you get anything off of it?"

"We got *everything*," said Levy. "His entire phone. We cloned it. That's how the NSA was able to link him to Yaqub's Hawaladar in Karachi."

Harvath smiled. "Good job. What did you learn?"

"Fahad was using a quilt."

"A *quilt*?"

"It's a layer of perfectly legitimate apps like Google, Twitter, and Yelp that hide apps underneath you don't want anyone else to see."

"What apps was he hiding?"

"You want the whole list?"

Harvath shook his head. "Just the important stuff."

Levy advanced to her next slide. It was a screen capture from Fahad's phone. "Do you know what Snapchat is?"

"It's an app used for sending nude pictures that self-destruct once viewed."

"You must have teenage kids," she said.

"No kids."

When he didn't elaborate beyond that, Levy let it go and continued. "Snapchat can send still photos, nude or otherwise, as well as video. The sender decides how long the photos or videos can be viewed before they're deleted from the Snapchat server and hidden from the recipient's device."

"Meaning they remain on the sending device."

"Yup. And our friend Fahad was fond of taking selfies."

"Fully clothed, I'm sure," Harvath joked.

"If only. I omitted them from the presentation, but we've brought the phone if you want to scroll through them."

"No, thanks," Harvath replied. "I'll pass."

"Smart choice," said Levy. "Okay. You're one for one with the Snapchat answer. How about Grindr? Do you know what that is?"

"No, and I can't wait to find out."

"You asked for it," she said, advancing to her next slide, another shot from Fahad's phone. "It's a geo-locating app. It allows gay and bisexual men to find sex partners in their area who are looking to hook up discreetly."

Homosexuality was a death sentence in many places in the Middle East, so gay Muslim men had to operate in absolute secrecy. The lengths they went to in order to cover their activities rivaled—and in many cases neces-sarily so—the techniques of the law enforcement agen-cies in their countries.

Because of their expertise at covertly meeting, com-municating, and transmitting illicit materials, many gay Muslims had actually excelled in the Hawala industry. That they were now learning this about Fahad didn't surprise Harvath.

"What else did you find?" he asked.

"Do you know what the acronym PnP stands for?"

He shook his head.

"It stands for party and play, also known as a chemi-cal session or *chem* for short. It's when two or more people get together to do drugs before engaging in sex-ual activity."

"And Fahad—our Hawaladar and part-time drug importer—liked to PnP," Harvath stated.

"He did," replied Levy, "and you'll be quite inter-ested with whom." She advanced to a new slide that had the same picture of the outdoor restaurant at the Arabian Courtyard Hotel. "Remember, this is the Silk Route restaurant where Fahad said he and Hanjour would meet. Now," she said, advancing to the next slide, "look at this."

The slide showed a man's body from the neck down, naked. His head had been cropped out of the shot.

"This is the Grindr avatar for one of the men Fahad was communicating with. Do you see his handle?"

Harvath did. "1234KPH. Khuram Pervez Hanjour?" he said. "Not very creative."

"It's probably lazy and clever at the same time. The speed of sound is 1,234 kilometers per hour."

Though Harvath knew better than to underestimate the people he hunted, he was still going to chalk the handle up to laziness. "We've got a headless body with our guy's initials. That's it?"

Levy shook her head. "He's standing near a window."

"With the curtains closed."

"Let's talk about the window first. Look at the shape, how it comes to a point."

Harvath looked and then Levy went back a slide to the façade of the hotel with the restaurant.

"See how the hotel's windows are all done in Arabian style, pointed at the top?"

"Unless these are the only pointed windows in Dubai, we're going to need something more than that."

Levy went back to the picture of the man standing in the room. "You mentioned the curtains are closed, but not completely. Look over the figure's left shoulder, there's a sliver of curtain open."

Harvath leaned forward to get a better look.

Levy used a laser pointer. "Right here. This area."

"You're being generous with the word 'sliver.'"

"It doesn't look like much until you enhance it. Like this," she said, advancing to the next slide. "This is how we know the picture was taken from inside one of the rooms at the Arabian Courtyard."

"What am I looking at?"

"Across the street from the hotel is the Dubai Museum. They have a traditional Arab dhow in the court-yard. What you're looking at is the tip of the mast through the hotel room's window."

She advanced to her next and final slide. It was a split screen of the enhanced photo along with a photo of the ship across the street. There was no question. They were a match.

"So it looks like KPH uses the hotel for more than just the Silk Route restaurant."

"And based on the texts we pulled from Fahad's phone, they get together to PnP on a pretty regular basis."

"Then the Brit and French files were correct about Hanjour's extracurricular activities," said Harvath. "Do we know if he travels with any security?"

"We don't think so. And it wasn't in any of the files. So we're going with no."

Harvath agreed with the assessment. Even if Hanjour did have a security detail, he couldn't see him dragging them around for drugs and gay sex. Security details were also expensive. Hanjour did strike him as a big enough player to warrant that type of thing. Having some means of self-defense, though, was different. "Do we know if he's armed?"

Levy shook her head. "We don't know for sure, but the UAE has very strict laws against firearms. One year in prison for every bullet you're caught with."

"The UAE supposedly has strict drug laws, too, so we'll assume he's armed," said Harvath. "What about prior military experience? Any arrest record or outstanding warrants?"

"Not that we know of. At this point, you know everything about Khuram Hanjour that we do."

"Which leaves us with only one issue. How we're going to break him."

"Whenever you're ready on that," the operative named Cowles interjected, "we've got what you requested out back."

Harvath looked at Levy. "Anything else I need to see? Or are we all done here?"

"We're done," she said and signaled for the lights to be turned back on.

Harvath took a bite of his sandwich and followed Cowles and Levy out the rear of the building to an adjacent Quonset hut. It had a large roll-up garage door. Cowles opened it up. Inside was a black 7 Series BMW. Producing a key fob, he depressed the trunk release button.

Harvath looked inside and studied the contents. Everything that he had asked for was there. "Excellent," he said, shutting the lid and pocketing the fob. "Safe house?"

Levy removed a map and pointed to where it was and recited the address. "We plugged a bunch of decoy addresses into the car's GPS system. One is for a Dubai temp agency that's at the end of the block on the opposite side of the street."

"What about the Emiratis and their intelligence division?" Harvath asked. "What do they think we're up to?"

"They know we've begun looking into an Emirati suspect named Khuram Hanjour, but we told them it was in relation to a Russian organized crime ring."

"And they bought that?"

"For the moment, yes. We've buried them with requests to run down a ton of leads. We also gave up two high-end Ukrainian call girls out of Dubai who we know are working for the FSB and who were sent here to seduce influential Emiratis. That alone should be enough smoke to keep them busy and cover us for the next twenty-four to forty-eight hours. If we need more to throw at them, we have it."

"Sounds like our bases are covered."

"There's one last thing," said Levy. "The assistant DCI wants a countersurveillance team on you. Just in case."

Harvath shook his head. "No way. We don't want to spook Hanjour. If the wind even blows the wrong direction, he's going to bolt."

"I understand that, but there are too many unknowns here. We don't know if he has a team of floaters that follow him. We don't know if we've accidentally piqued the Emiratis' interest in him, even though we've tried to downplay it. We don't know if Al Qaeda is watching him to make sure no one else is. We don't know much of anything, except that he's the only lead we have and if he disappears, we're *all* in trouble."

"But if we flood the zone," Harvath replied, "he's going to pick up on it. That's what matters."

"We're not going to flood the zone. We'll use a very light footprint." She paused for a moment, trying to choose the right words to make the Agency's case. "I can't force you to do anything. I've been told this is your operation. We just want to make sure that as you're going after Hanjour, nobody's going after you. Make sense?"

It did make sense, but it didn't make it easier for him to accept. He preferred to operate alone, or at the very least with professionals he knew. He didn't know any of these CIA people.

He knew he could roll Hanjour up on his own, but if anything went wrong, it would be on his head. And a lot could go wrong. Karachi was a perfect case in point.

They had been successful, but only because they had involved other people. Rule number one if heading into a gunfight was to bring a gun, preferably two, and all of your friends who had guns. Harvath didn't know what he was headed into, but he knew that he didn't want to be taken by surprise again.

It was not an easy decision, but he made what he hoped would be the right choice. "All right," he relented. "Let's go over how we're going to handle this, including if anything goes bad."

CHAPTER 13

Colonel Shi knew who was at his door even before he heard the knock. General Yi Ming Wu's cigarette smoke usually arrived before he did. "Come in," Shi said.

Wu opened the door and stepped inside. He was a large man in his early sixties with a round face, nicotine-stained fingers, and a growing spare tire around his middle. Wedging himself into one of the narrow chairs in front of Shi's desk, he removed a pack of cigarettes and offered one. The colonel shook his head.

The general took it between his lips and used his old cigarette to light it. After taking a deep drag, he crushed the old cigarette into the ashtray Shi kept on the corner of his desk. "You should go back to smoking," he said. "It'll help your mind work better."

Shi was now running five times a week and feeling healthier than he had in years. As much as he respected the general and his directorship of the Second Department, the man was one of the last people who should be dispensing health advice.

Shi had been waiting several hours for his boss to return from his meeting and was eager for the man to get to the point. "How did it go?"

The general exhaled two tendrils of smoke from his

nostrils that twirled up toward the yellowed ceiling tiles above the desk. "Not good."

The colonel had expected that. "*Not good*, how?"

"The general secretary is still particularly upset that you have lost one of your assets."

Shi shook his head. "You of course explained that *I* didn't lose the Somali?"

Wu shrugged. *Semantics.* "It's your operation. You're responsible."

"Fine. *I'm* responsible. I'm responsible for the Emirati engineering students, as well as the Somali accomplices we teamed them with. Now what was the Standing Committee's decision?"

"They discussed many issues. In anticipation of America's collapse and the global economic shockwaves, China has been quietly stockpiling food, fuel, and medicine."

"It has also not-so-quietly," Shi added, "been stockpiling gold."

The general dismissed the concern with a wave of his hand. "Gold goes up in price, gold goes down. Everyone is buying. There's too much debt everywhere and no one trusts paper currency anymore. Some countries have even begun repatriating their gold from third-party vaults abroad because they want it closer to home. Our gold purchases are not that unusual."

Shi believed that China was buying too much, too fast. He had expressed his concern, but it had fallen on deaf ears. None of that mattered at this point. "What did they end up deciding?"

"You know, there are some who think you orchestrated this problem."

"*Me?*" the colonel replied, taken aback. "That's ridiculous."

"The timing is quite coincidental, wouldn't you say?"

"Do you think I wanted a cell member to go missing so the operation and our national security could be thrown into jeopardy?"

"No," Wu replied, "but I know you. What I'm telling you is what *they* think. They wanted the attack to take place over Chinese New Year. You argued for September. Suddenly, they're being forced to accept your position. Wouldn't you be suspicious?"

"I'm paid to be suspicious," Shi said. "They're paid to be politicians."

"But they are in charge and they have decided."

"So do we launch the attack now?"

"No," the general replied.

"*No?* Don't they understand what's at stake? We've lost contact with a cell member. We have to assume that his cover has been blown and that the Americans are wringing every ounce of intelligence out of him that they can."

"None of which will point to us."

Shi threw up his hands in disbelief. "All six cells trained together. They know how the attack is to be carried out."

Wu nodded. "They know the delivery method, but not the means."

"From just one cell member, a skilled interrogator could paint a bigger picture."

"With broad brushstrokes," Wu clarified, "anyone can paint a big picture. But without the details, the Americans have nothing."

"They will have enough. That's why we need to strike. If we don't do it now, we're going to lose our chance. And if the Americans figure out what is happening, they will have cause to strike us. We *have* to move first."

Wu took a deep drag on his cigarette and, exhaling a whorl of smoke, replied, "The PSC agrees."

Shi's eyes widened and his mouth was agape. He was being whipsawed. "I don't understand. They agree, but they *don't* want to launch the attack? That doesn't make any sense."

"They have suggested a different path."

"A *different path*? What different path? There is no different path. There is either attack or wait to be attacked."

"They want to be absolutely sure that the missing cell member has been compromised before agreeing to launch the attack."

Shi shook his head. *Politicians.* "He has missed four communication windows. He has not accessed his email and he is not answering his cell phone. We have no way of knowing what has happened to him. We have to assume that—"

"The PSC wants us to send Cheng," the general interrupted.

Shi's eyes widened once again. "How does the Politburo Standing Committee even know about Cheng?"

"From the General Secretary. He quietly likes to refer to Cheng as China's James Bond."

"He's not James Bond," Shi replied angrily, "and the General Secretary shouldn't be referring to him *at all*—quietly or otherwise."

"I agree with you, but what's done is done. The General Secretary and the PSC want us to use Cheng."

"Even after what happened?"

"Don't be so dramatic," Wu insisted. "They have *no*

idea what happened. As far as they're concerned, it was an accident."

"But you and I know better. We know a Communist Party official blackmailed Cheng's wife into bed and when Cheng found out, he killed him. He only made it look like an accident."

"Has Cheng ever confessed this to you?"

"No," Shi replied. "But when I put it to him directly, he didn't deny it either."

"We should never ask questions we don't want the answers to."

"Regardless, he's not ready to go back out."

"Do we have another operative as familiar with America and with such a well-backstopped cover?" asked Wu.

It was a rhetorical question. Shi answered it anyway. "We have several."

The general looked at him and smiled. "None of them are as good as Cheng. He will get the information we need and he will do what needs to be done. Which brings me to this," he said, removing a slip of paper from his pocket and sliding it across his subordinate's desk.

As soon as Shi began to read it, he shook his head. "Impossible. No way."

Wu had anticipated this reaction. Orders were orders. He pressed on. "Of the nine Politburo Standing Committee members, five have a child or grandchild currently attending school in the United States. All of whom would have been home for Chinese New Year."

"Princelings," Shi said with contempt. It was the derogatory term used for offspring of influential Communist Party leaders.

Wu ignored his sarcasm. "They are willing to sacrifice the Chinese diplomatic corps and the other Chinese VIPs within the United States. Their children, though, are another matter. If Cheng confirms that Snow Dragon has been compromised, you may launch the attack, but only after the names on that list are safe."

"Define *safe*."

The general paused for a moment before responding. "Their relatives would like them immediately brought home. Obviously, we can't do that."

"*Obviously*," Shi stated. "The Americans would know something was afoot. How are we supposed to round up all five when—"

Wu had his answer ready. "The Americans have them under intermittent physical surveillance. Their FBI doesn't have the manpower to watch them 24/7. We assume there are informants in their social circles and that their electronics are being monitored. None of this, though, will prevent Cheng from getting to them."

"Wait. They want Cheng used for this operation, too?"

"Nothing is more important to them than the safety of their children," Wu replied. "They want the best. That means Cheng."

Shi and his wife had never been able to have children. With the hours he worked, he had always looked upon that as a blessing. Even so, he understood the human urge to protect one's children. It was one of the few human traits he was willing to cede to China's politicians, even though far too many lavishly spoiled their offspring while publicly espousing Mao's revolution and the glories of communism.

"Assuming Cheng is able to locate all of them—" Shi began.

"*Once* Cheng has located all of them," Wu corrected.

"Okay, *once* Cheng has located all of them, then what? The doubles program doesn't exist anymore."

The general took a slow drag off his cigarette. It was well known that the Americans tracked the visas of all Chinese nationals who entered the United States, especially those connected to the higher-ups in the Chinese Communist Party. Because the U.S. put special flags on these visas, China had created a doubles program.

At every university a princeling attended, the MSS enrolled a similar-enough-looking Chinese national. When princelings needed to be recalled for disciplinary action or any other reason that China wanted hidden from the U.S., a princeling borrowed the travel documents of his or her double, while the double stepped into the princeling's shoes at school until the princeling returned. The adoption of sophisticated biometric devices by America's Immigration and Customs Enforcement had rendered the doubles program obsolete.

If the five princelings tried to leave the country on one airplane, or even five different airplanes, the United States was not only going to know about it, they were going to start connecting the dots and soon thereafter questions would begin. China couldn't risk that. The Second Department would have to come up with another way.

After a couple more moments of thought, Wu said, "What about Medusa?"

Medusa was the codename of an asset the PLA maintained in the southeastern United States.

Shi thought about it. "We'd use him to get them out of the country to the plantation?"

The plantation was China's intelligence division based in Havana.

Wu nodded. "We could have a plane waiting for them there."

It was an interesting plan, except for one thing. "Medusa has disappointed us in the past. If any of this goes wrong, the PSC and the General Secretary will hold you and me responsible."

"That's why we need Cheng. He will not disappoint us. He'll make sure nothing goes wrong."

Shi wasn't as confident. There was not just the question of whether Cheng could handle the assignments; if the Americans did have the missing Somali and they had broken him, they would have a two-day head start.

Tasking Cheng with both operations was wasteful and it was Shi who ultimately would be held responsible if Cheng failed. Looking at his boss, he said, "You are placing a lot of confidence in one man."

"No," the general replied. "I am placing my confidence in two men—you *and* Cheng."

"If this fails, and the PSC also uncovers what we know about Cheng, you and I are both dead men."

"Then you had better make sure this doesn't fail, and that you complete your assignment before the Americans have any idea what's going on."

CHAPTER 14

It was after five o'clock and the dusty Bur Dubai neighborhood was still crowded with tourists. Businessmen were headed home or out for drinks. Taxicab drivers, immune to the heat, drove with their windows rolled down, picking up and dropping off customers in front of shops emblazoned with brightly colored Arabic script. Clothing, jewelry, and electronics competed alongside prayer rugs, hookah pipes, and antique furniture for buyers' attention. The scent of the Gulf mingled with the aromas wafting out of restaurants up and down the neighborhood streets.

One of the first things Harvath had noticed about Bur Dubai was that it wasn't as security-conscious as other parts of the city. There weren't cameras on every single building and street corner. He was glad. It would make his job a lot easier.

He had gone around and around in his mind as to the best way to grab Khuram Hanjour. What about an invitation from Fahad? Would he respond to something like that? Would he respond on short notice? From what Harvath had seen over his career, particularly in his training with the Secret Service, people who engaged in risky behavior were extremely compulsive. The risk alone delivered its own high, and they were constantly trying to top the last time. It was a reasonable bet that if Hanjour was in town, he'd drop everything to come PnP with Fahad.

Based on Fahad's Grindr account, as well as the questions Levy's colleague had asked him in the prison, Fahad and Hanjour had had no contact for over a week. All Harvath had to do was properly bait the trap.

He and Levy studied the previous messages back and forth between the men. After a brief discussion, Levy crafted a short but seductive invitation. All they had to do was wait. Hours passed.

They had held off until after arriving in Dubai, sweeping the safe house, and checking into a room at the Arabian Courtyard, before attempting to contact Hanjour. If he was anxious to meet and they were still on the road from Abu Dhabi, they might have blown their opportunity. There was too great a chance that if Hanjour wanted to play, but Fahad was hours away, he'd simply scroll through Grindr and find someone else.

Despite that possibility, there was something about their communications that suggested the fifty-seven-year-old Hanjour had an affinity for the twenty-six-year-old-Fahad. Harvath assumed it was akin to older straight men who got their kicks dating women half their age. He couldn't be sure, but he hoped that if there was something there, it would work to their advantage.

When the chime sounded on the cloned phone, Harvath and Levy immediately stopped what they were doing and read the message. Hanjour wanted to meet. "SR@1800," he typed.

"Silk Route at 1800?" asked Levy.

Harvath nodded, "Six p.m. at the Silk Route."

It was on. Hanjour had taken the bait, but now the

real work would begin. The biggest problem with Bur Dubai, next to the traffic, was the fact that there was no parking. The Arabian Courtyard offered a valet service, but there was no way Harvath was going to place his operation at the mercy of how quickly valets could bring a car around.

Being able to devote someone from their team to remain with a vehicle was a big advantage. Harvath was reminded once more of the advantages of not always going it alone. Levy and her resources were worth their weight in gold.

In addition to leaving a man with the BMW, she placed a couple of spotters outside the hotel on Al Fahidi Street to watch for Hanjour. Once they saw him, their job was to figure out whether he was alone. Levy also put a man and a woman in the restaurant to have a long, leisurely dinner at a table where they could observe everyone who came and went.

It wasn't exactly the light footprint Harvath had envisioned, but it was the right thing to do and Levy more than knew her stuff.

Their biggest challenge was where and how to actually grab Hanjour. Bur Dubai was a lot like being in the French Quarter in New Orleans, but with three times the people. It was going to be impossible to pull up, stuff him in the trunk, and take off without anyone noticing. Even if they could slip him a drug like Rohypnol, it would be a tightrope act getting him out of the restaurant and through the hotel without attracting attention.

What they needed was for Hanjour to do their work for them. He needed to walk right into their arms, and that gave Harvath an idea.

When he presented it to Levy, the first thing she

said was, "What's Plan B?" It wasn't exactly a vote of confidence.

But as Harvath explained how it could play out, Levy came around to his way of thinking. That didn't mean they didn't need a Plan B. Harvath and Levy assembled one, as well as Plans C, D, and E. If all else failed, they'd go to Plan F—universally known as *Fuck it, we'll do it live*. Sometimes, no matter how hard you tried to anticipate and plan for all eventualities, things just went south. When that happened, it usually happened fast. At that point, you relied upon your training and did everything possible to secure the objective. A lot of times it got messy. Very messy. Harvath was hoping this wouldn't be one of those times.

At seven minutes to six, the call came in that a man fitting Khuram Hanjour's description had just pulled up in front of the hotel. He valet-parked his white Mercedes and walked inside. There was no one else with him.

As the spotter relayed what the man was wearing, Anne Levy told the rest of her team, particularly the couple she had sitting in the restaurant, that the target had arrived.

Turning to Harvath she said, "Now what?"

"Now we wait," he replied.

The Arabian Courtyard Hotel was built around a grand atrium with glass elevators you could watch ascend. That allowed Cowles, who was seated in the ground-floor lounge, to watch Hanjour cross the marble lobby, get into one of the elevators, and take it up to the Silk Route level. After relaying the target's movements, he sat back and pretended to enjoy a coffee as he continued to scan the lobby and the front door for any unwanted guests.

"We've got him," the female CIA operative said over her Bluetooth earpiece when Hanjour entered the restaurant. She watched him speak with the hostess and then be shown to a table near the windows.

Hanjour was a balding man of medium height with a thin build. He wore an obviously dyed, tightly cropped black beard and a pair of stylish, frameless glasses. He had paired his khaki trousers with a white, short-sleeved silk dress shirt and a pair of soft leather driving shoes. On his right wrist was a large gold Rolex and on his left pinky finger was a gold signet ring. He wore no other jewelry and carried nothing in his hands that they could see.

He ordered a gin and tonic and surveyed the room as he sipped, waiting for his companion to arrive. The young CIA couple kept him in their peripheral vision, pretending to be more into each other than anything else. The last thing they needed was for him to know he was under surveillance.

When the clock on his phone read two minutes past six o'clock, Harvath texted Hanjour a picture. It showed a pillow on a turned-down bed. Propped up against the pillow were two small plastic bags. One was filled with what looked like meth and the other with what looked like synthetic marijuana. There was a box of condoms and a red rose. The only text that accompanied the picture was the room number, 501.

Hanjour slid the phone from his pocket and read the message. Taking out his wallet, he left some money for the waitress and walked over to the hostess. He said a few words to her and she smiled as he tipped her. Then he exited the restaurant.

The female CIA operative rang Levy. "He just left."

Levy pinged Cowles down in the lobby and told him to watch the elevators. Raising his coffee cup to his mouth, Cowles turned his attention to the elevators and gave a play-by-play of what he saw, ending with, "The elevator is stopping on five. He's getting off. Headed in your direction."

Levy looked at Harvath and said, "Here he comes."

The door had been propped open using the swing guard lock. When Hanjour entered, he would walk down a short hallway with the darkened bathroom to his right. The bedside table lamps were on, but had been covered with pieces of red fabric to dim their brightness and add to the mood. A small amount of incense had been burned so that it would appear that perhaps Fahad was trying to cover up that he had already started partying and was ready to go right to play mode. The bedspread had been kicked off and dropped on the floor at the foot of the bed. The radio was playing softly.

Dim lights, a little bit of incense, the bedspread on the floor, and music. It was all designed to throw Hanjour off balance; to reinforce in his mind what he wanted to see.

All they needed now was for him to walk through the door, which was exactly what he did next.

CHAPTER 15

K huram Hanjour gently pushed the door open
and slipped inside room 501. He saw the bedspread up ahead on the floor. Turning, he
locked the door behind him.

He spoke in hushed Arabic as he kicked off his shoes
and began unbuttoning his shirt. He had dropped it to
the floor and was just unbuttoning his pants when he
stepped into the bedroom and saw Anne Levy standing
there. In her hands was a suppressed, Elite Dark SIG
Sauer P226, the same weapon carried by a lot of Texas
Rangers and Navy SEALs. It was pointed right at him.

Hanjour spun, as if to flee, only to see that Harvath
had stepped from the darkened bathroom and also had
a weapon pointed at him. This one, though, looked different, like something out of a sci-fi movie. Its barrel
was rectangular with a bright, white light and two inte-
grated lasers.

Before Hanjour was able to process that he was
looking at a new cutting-edge Taser, Harvath depressed
his trigger. The weapon delivered an incapacitating
electrical charge that caused Hanjour's muscles to
seize. His body went completely rigid and he cried out
as he fell forward. As soon as he hit the floor, Harvath
was on top of him.

"We're out of here in ninety seconds," he said, securing Hanjour's wrists and ankles with FlexiCuffs.

Levy placed a strip of electrical tape over the recruiter's mouth, then stood up and alerted the team to go to the next stage.

As Harvath finished trussing up Hanjour, Levy reclaimed a large, hard-sided Storm Case from the closet. Air holes had been drilled in strategic places and covered with a fine mesh, painted the same color as the case. It had sturdy wheels rated for over three hundred pounds of gear, far exceeding what Hanjour weighed. Kicking it over onto its side, Levy flipped open the latches and threw open the lid.

The effects of a Taser were short-lived. Once the subject was down, you had to move fast, which was exactly what Harvath had done. As soon as Levy opened the case, Hanjour knew what was in store for him and began to thrash around wildly like a fish on a hot summer pier.

It was estimated that anywhere from five to seven percent of the world's population suffered from severe claustrophobia. In their files, the French and the Brits had remarked not only on Hanjour's sexual proclivities, but also on the fact that he was likely a claustrophobic. His reaction upon seeing the Storm Case was the only confirmation Harvath needed.

He had very strong hands and grabbed Hanjour by the back of the neck and squeezed until the man stopped struggling.

Nodding to Levy, he stood and then they bent over, picked up Hanjour, and attempted to put him in the case. Immediately, he started going wild again—thrashing against his restraints, twisting his body, and screaming from behind the duct tape that muffled his mouth. Harvath signaled for Levy to put him down.

He got right up in Hanjour's face and said, "If you fight, if you so much as make a sound, I'm going to weigh this box down with rocks, cut a nice big hole in the corner, and dump you in Dubai Creek to drown. Do you understand me?"

Hanjour looked from Harvath to the Storm Case and back to Harvath. He began shaking his head wildly.

"Khuram," Harvath said. "This isn't a negotiation. You're going in that box and trust me, at this point, you've got much bigger things to worry about. Now, we can do this the easy way, or we can do it the hard way. It's up to you."

Hanjour continued to violently shake his head.

Harvath handed Levy the Taser and grabbed the duct tape. When he had a piece starting to peel away from the roll, he nodded for her to give him another charge.

When she did, Hanjour's body went rigid once more and he let out another muffled yell from behind his gag. When his body lost its rigidity, Harvath brought the man's chest to his knees, rolled him onto his buttocks, and began wrapping him with duct tape.

Almost immediately Hanjour was fighting him again. Harvath had to work fast. He had no idea if anyone in the hotel had heard his initial cry upon being Tasered and had possibly called security. They needed to get out of the hotel as quickly as possible.

With Levy's help, they forced his arms across his chest, and with a second roll of tape succeeded in mummifying him in the fetal position. He was harder to pick up this time, but they managed, and laid him on his side inside the Storm Case. He was rocking violently from side to side, but that would change once the lid was shut and his shoulder was pinned up against it.

Before closing the lid, Harvath reminded him one last time what would happen if he didn't cooperate. "Move or make a sound and you're going to the bottom of Dubai Creek. Understand me?"

Hanjour didn't respond. He didn't need to. The fact that he finally stopped thrashing was response enough.

Harvath closed and locked the lid as Levy quickly wiped down the room for prints. She tucked Hanjour's shoes and shirt into her bag and informed the team they were on the move. Once the hallway was given the all clear by the operative in the stairwell, they exited the room.

With Harvath pulling the case down the brightly carpeted hall, they made their way to a service corridor where another one of Levy's people was waiting with the freight elevator. After making sure the coast was clear downstairs and the BMW was at the loading area, they stepped into the elevator and depressed the button for the ground floor.

Once they were there, Cowles met them and helped Harvath wheel the Storm Case out the service entrance, down the ramp, and load it into the trunk of the waiting BMW. Harvath took the front passenger position, Levy got in behind him, and Cowles sat behind the driver.

Quietly they pulled away from the loading dock, down the alley, and disappeared into the deepening night of Bur Dubai.

CHAPTER 16

During the five-hour drive, the Operation Gold Dust team tried to catch some more sleep, but it came only in fitful snatches. The North Korean roads were terrible. No sooner would they fall asleep than the truck would hit another rut, or a mammoth pothole, and they'd all be slammed awake.

When they arrived at the drop-off point, which was nothing more than a kilometer marker and a sign for the next village over one hundred kilometers away, they climbed out of the truck. While Billy Tang discussed the pickup with Hyun Su, the SEALs fanned out and took up firing positions.

Once Billy was done talking, he said good-bye to Hyun Su and rejoined the team. Fordyce studied their position on his map and compared it to what his GPS was telling him. With a lot of ground to cover and limited darkness in which to do it, he was anxious to get going.

The team waited until Hyun Su had driven off and they could no longer hear the sound of his engine. And then they waited some more.

They let the pitch-black North Korean night close in around them as they familiarized themselves with every sound it produced. Finally, Fordyce gave his men the signal to move out.

Their course would take them up through a series of steep, forested foothills and over the back side of one of the mountains that bracketed their objective—the tapered valley that had been partially obscured from satellite view. They were expected to be dug in by sunrise and to spend the day collecting as much intelligence as they could before retreating to the pickup point, where Hyun Su would drive them back to the coast. There, they'd link up with the minisub and be delivered back to the USS *Texas,* where they could prepare a full briefing and securely transmit it back to the States.

So far, the forest floor was covered with soft pine needles and reminded Fordyce a little bit of Pennsylvania. If his Lab Bailey had been along, he could have imagined for a moment that they were out for a nighttime hunt. That was until the gradient began to change.

Even though the team was in top physical condition, the steep angle, combined with the eighty-plus pounds of gear each of them was carrying, made the climb more difficult.

They drank water from their Camelbaks via the hoses threaded through their pack straps and kept their suppressed rifles ready to fire. Fordyce, Johnson, and Tucker all carried H&K 417 carbines, while Tang carried an M4 by FN, which had been secreted in the back of the truck with the SEALs.

Their direction of approach had been chosen not because it would give them the best view, but because it was the most challenging and, they hoped, would be less guarded than the other ways into the valley.

As Fordyce checked their progress once again on his GPS, he reviewed the mission for the thousandth time in his head.

According to the intelligence the CIA had developed, China was training some kind of landing force on the other side of this mountain in rural North Korea. It hadn't been described as an invasion force, but rather a follow-on force that was supposed to land after a major attack on the United States took place. No one, though, seemed to know what kind of attack it was going to be. All Fordyce and his team had been told was that it was designed to wipe out at least 90 percent of the U.S. population.

Using the term "rural" in the mission briefing had drawn head-shaking from the SEALs. There wasn't much of North Korea that *wasn't* rural. There were virtually no modern conveniences in the entire country outside a very small handful of cities. The DPRK was another testament to the failures of communism. The entire nation was a horrific pit of misery and human suffering.

The DPRK was beset with starvation and malnutrition. Bodies fished out of rivers after floods or boys lucky enough to escape alive showed teenagers were now five inches shorter and weighed twenty-five pounds less on average than their contemporaries in South Korea. Mental retardation brought on by childhood lack of nutrition was estimated to have rendered a quarter of the DPRK's male population unfit for military service. Even in its largest cities, like Pyongyang, Kaesong, and Chongjin, North Koreans were starving to death.

While the "free" people starved, "enemies of the state" had it even worse. The tales of North Korea's savagery toward prisoners were brutal and legion.

Hundreds of thousands languished in hidden prison camps across the country—many sent without charge or trial. As part of a collective punishment system known as "guilt by association," relatives, children, and entire families were imprisoned as well. To "cleanse the bloodline" of evil deeds, the DPRK often targeted three generations of a transgressor's family.

Female prisoners were routinely forced to dig their own graves before being brutally raped by guards, and even visiting officials. The women would then be beaten to death with hammers or clubs, their bodies rolled into the graves and covered over with earth in order to hide the crime.

In addition to rape and murder, prisoners faced regular beatings, starvation, and other absolutely unthinkable acts of torture. It turned Fordyce's stomach, as he knew it did for the rest of his team members. Every assignment required restraint and self-control, but this one especially so. There was no question what would happen to four heavily armed Americans if captured by the North Koreans.

The propaganda embarrassment for the United States would be off the charts, and Fordyce knew all too well that he and his men would be subjected to torture worse than any POW had ever seen. The team had made an unspoken pact. If things went bad, they'd do all they could to make sure they weren't taken alive. Fordyce's job, though, was to see to it that things didn't go bad.

If the United States were to have any hope of deciphering the planned attack, it needed to know as much about the PLA's landing party as possible. What were they training for? Why were they doing it in North Korea and not China? Did anything about the training suggest what kind of an attack was planned? Were they using equipment or techniques that would be applied in the wake of a biological, chemical, or nuclear attack? The list of questions was endless.

What wasn't endless was the amount of time

Fordyce and his team had to complete their assignment. They had been instructed to get in, get whatever intel they could, and get out. There was very little margin for error and every moment was going to count.

The narrow valley that was the team's target was just under three hundred kilometers from the coast. As best any of the experts at the National Reconnaissance Office could tell, the North Koreans had shrouded parts of it with a series of overlapping nets suspended from tall poles. In order to hide what, though, was what the team had been sent in to discover.

Fordyce halted his men at the edge of the forest where the pine needles turned to scree. He wanted to give them a moment to grab a snack and rest before they went up and over the ridgeline.

He ate some cheese and sausage, the snack he liked to bring on operations, as he studied photos of the terrain. He was looking for the spot where he wanted them to cross over the top and then make their way down.

Part of the valley was being cultivated with crops of some sort, and a stream about twenty feet wide cut down the western side. The question no one had been able to answer back in the U.S. was how far they would have to descend into the valley in order to get a good enough view of what was under those nets. At some point they were going to lose the benefit of rocks and trees for cover and be left with nothing but high grass. And unlike trees and rocks, grass moved when you brushed past it.

Fordyce wasn't averse to taking risks. He would do almost anything if it was necessary, but he didn't want to place his men in any additional danger if he didn't have to. They were already way far out on the risk curve as it was. If everything the CIA had been told about this location was true, then they were going to start bumping up against North Korean foot patrols soon enough. His biggest fear was that they might have dogs. If that turned out to be true, they would be looking at some serious trouble.

Until that trouble showed itself, though, Fordyce wasn't going to worry about it. He had enough on his mind. Checking his map once more, he gave his team the signal to ruck up. When they were all ready, he led them out of the trees and up toward the ridgeline.

They moved slowly through the rocks and loose shale. It was like climbing a mountain of guitar picks. Time after time, their footing gave way and sent a cascade of stones sliding down behind them.

Fordyce adjusted their path and tried to pick a course through the green-gray haze of his night vision goggles that would give them firmer footing, but still allow them to summit in an area with plenty of natural cover. It wouldn't do them any good to arrive at the top, only to be caught out in the open and possibly spotted by the Chinese or North Koreans below.

As they climbed, Fordyce also kept an eye on their time. They needed to be over the ridgeline and down far enough on the other side before the sun came up. They had identified three potential locations via satellite for covered overwatch positions, but you never really knew how good a site was until you saw it for yourself. Concerned they were falling behind, Fordyce picked up the pace.

Just before the ridgeline, he stopped. Pointing at Les Johnson, whose face was covered in camouflage paint like the others, he signaled for him to crawl up and take a look.

Fifteen minutes later, Johnson came back. "Are you sure we're in the right place?" he whispered.

"Of course I'm sure," said Fordyce. "Why?"

"That valley is pitch black."

"They must be practicing light discipline."

Johnson grinned. "Or we're not in the right place."

Fordyce flipped Johnson the finger. They were in the right place, but that was Johnson—always a smart-ass. His father had been an executive with an outdoor clothing company in Maine. Had he followed in his father's footsteps, he'd be on his way to running that same company, but Johnson hadn't been cut out for the button-down corporate world. He'd been a hellion as a teen, a real troublemaker. In hindsight, his father probably should have provided more "wall-to-wall" counseling. It wasn't until Johnson got kicked out of his third private college and had a pretty serious run-in with the Freeport PD that he realized he needed to get his act together.

The police chief had coached Johnson in Little League. That was back before Johnson's parents had divorced and he had begun his spiral toward becoming a less than productive member of society. The chief painted an ugly picture of where Johnson was headed if he didn't apply some serious course correction. He capped it off by introducing him to a Navy recruiter in Portland, who also happened to be a SEAL. Whether it was his similar upbringing or his no-bullshit style, the SEAL, and what he had done with his life, appealed to Johnson. Within forty-eight hours, he had signed up, shipped out, and the rest was history.

After Fordyce showed him the spot on the map where the first potential overwatch site was, he signaled for Johnson to take point. It was easy for your senses to become dulled and for you to miss something if you didn't rotate out. It was time to put fresh eyes and ears up front. There was no telling what kind of intrusion or antipersonnel devices had been placed along the downward slope to prevent exactly what they were doing.

They moved much more slowly and deliberately now that they were on the valley side. They took great pains to make sure they didn't create a single sound or send any loose rocks tumbling down the slope in front of them. They needed to be ghosts—and that's exactly what they were.

When they arrived at the first overwatch site, they could tell right away that it wouldn't work. It had looked good on satellite, but there was one side that was too exposed. It wasn't even up for discussion. Fordyce showed Johnson where the next location was and they headed for it.

Site two was better, but not by much. If anyone popped up on the ridgeline behind them, the team risked being exposed. It wasn't worth it. Fordyce checked his watch. If site three was a bust, they were going to have to scramble. Showing Johnson the final location on the map, they headed out. Fordyce had to remind himself not to rush and to choose his steps carefully.

The third site was a major improvement over the other two, but halfway downhill and a little to their left was something that looked ideal.

Getting Johnson's attention, Fordyce pointed it out to him. It would give them an even better vantage point for observing the valley and, surrounded with more trees, it would give them more cover. Johnson nodded and led them to it.

Although there was no such thing as a perfect hide, this was the closest to one Fordyce had ever seen. As was his style, once they were installed, he took first watch. It had been a rough climb and everyone was tired.

While the other team members pulled food from their bags and ate or tried to nod off, Jimi Fordyce looked down into the valley through his magnified Aimpoint Comp M4 sight. Nothing was moving and it was still pitch black.

Laying his weapon across his chest, he checked his camera equipment. The Pentagon wanted as many pictures as possible. He had extra memory cards, an additional antireflective telephoto lens, fully charged batteries, and pieces of earth-colored burlap he'd use to camouflage the camera further. There were very few objects that created reflections in nature. If any of their gear bounced even a quick flash of sunlight, it'd be game over.

Restowing his camera equipment, Fordyce was quietly zipping up the case when he thought he heard a noise just downhill. Instantly, his hands went to his weapon. Bringing it up, he seated the stock in his right shoulder and tried to identify the source.

He swept his rifle slowly back and forth. For a moment, he wondered if his ears had played a trick on him. Then he heard the sound again. Something was definitely out there, and it was headed uphill, in their direction. Very quietly, he alerted his teammates.

Each one of them slowly raised his weapon, got into firing position, and powered up his night vision device. But while the SEALs went to their rifles, Billy Tang pulled out his suppressed SIG. For close work, he preferred a pistol, and with the 147-grain Special K rounds he had loaded, his SIG Sauer would make a lot less noise.

The sound was getting closer. They could all hear it now. It would move, then stop, and then move and stop again. It was erratic, going off in one direction for a moment before coming back and heading closer to them. It wasn't an animal. It sounded like a person, and whoever it was, he was looking for something. *Was he looking for them?*

Time stood still as the person out in the darkness got closer and closer. The team kept their heart rates and their breathing under control. Weapons were hot. Fingers were on triggers.

Inside their heads, they were all saying the same thing—*Don't stop. Keep walking. Just pass us by.*

When the figure finally came into view, that sentiment dramatically increased.

Fordyce signaled for his team not to fire. Johnson couldn't believe what he was seeing. The kid looked like he was maybe eight years old. What the hell was a kid doing in this valley, and in the middle of the night, no less? Tang quietly prayed that the boy would just walk past. Eric Tucker, the team's corpsman, was ready to do whatever needed to be done.

This wasn't a war zone like Iraq or Afghanistan. The rules about combatants versus noncombatants didn't apply here. But even if they did, most SEALs, Tucker included, had already decided what they would do in a situation like this. The topic had been discussed ad nauseam throughout the teams.

In 2005, a four-man SEAL recon team, under the codename Operation Red Wings, had been inserted into Afghanistan's Kunar Province to surveil and gather intelligence on a high-value Taliban target. During the surveillance, three goat herders—an old man, a teen, and a young boy—had discovered the SEAL team.

The SEALs apprehended them, but once they determined that the goat herders were civilians and not combatants, the rules of engagement dictated that they

be released. The SEALs let them go and paid the ultimate price for it. The teen sprinted to his village and
within two hours, the SEALs fell under a vicious ambush of mortars, AK-47s, PK machineguns, and RPGs.
A quick reaction force of eight more SEALs plus eight
Army Special Operations aviators was also shot down.
In the end, only one of the original SEALs survived to
tell the harrowing tale.

Eric Tucker had hoped never to find himself in that
kind of situation. You could say whatever you wanted
sitting in a team room half a world away, but killing
a civilian, especially a child, would be a tough call to
make. This op, though, was critical to the survival of
the United States and its civilians, including its own
children. The team's ROE didn't prevent them from
shooting anyone, including a little boy, if it meant pre-
venting their op from being compromised. Adjusting
his rifle, Tucker walled off his conscience, sighted in on
the child's head, and gently flicked off his safety.

Twigs seemed to snap as loud as firecrackers as the
boy came closer. He was making a beeline for them.
What the hell was he doing?

Two feet from their hide, the boy stopped. He
was so close that Fordyce could have reached out and
touched him. The team didn't even dare breathe.

The little boy had a cloth bag of some sort strung
across his shoulder. Something on the ground had his
attention and he bent over to examine it.

Bootprints were the words every team member was
thinking. But the little boy hadn't been examining
bootprints. Straightening up, he held a small loop of
wire in his hands—a *snare. He was out checking his animal
traps. But why now? Why so late at night?*

It was a question they would have all happily gone

without ever having to answer. As long as the kid just reset his trap and went back to wherever he had come from. They didn't need to know who he was or why he was out here. But once Mr. Murphy brought two bodies into the same orbit, he usually made sure there was a collision. And a collision was exactly what happened.

Preparing to reset his snare, the little boy must have decided to move back a couple of feet. There was no way he could have known what a bad decision that was. He had no idea that Jimi Fordyce was there until he stepped on him.

Whether it was a snake or some other animal didn't matter. What he had stepped on was alive, and his body instantly reacted.

No sooner had his thin sandal pressed down on Fordyce's body than his mind screamed *danger* and his body leaped backward into the air.

His eyes quickly focused on what it was. It was human—at least the eyes appeared to be—but he wasn't sure about the rest. He had been told the woods were full of demons and all sorts of monsters. He had no desire to stay and figure everything out. His flight mechanism had kicked in and he was already running.

For his part, Fordyce hadn't even had a chance to grab the boy. Right until the very moment the child stepped on him, he had hoped he would just move an inch or two to the side and walk right past him.

The boy had reacted so quickly, he was just out of arm's reach when Fordyce attempted to grab him. Now the kid had spun and was on the run.

As Fordyce leaped to his feet to chase him, he thought of reminding his team not to fire. Then suddenly there was a *pop*, and Fordyce watched as the boy fell to the ground.

CHAPTER 17

Had the safe house garage been soundproofed, Harvath could have carried out the entire interrogation right there. It had a drain in the center of the floor and a utility sink with a long hose connected to a plastic spray nozzle.

Harvath had debated whether to clean Hanjour up. He had soiled himself inside the Storm Case. Leaving a subject in his own filth was a powerful tactic some interrogators employed. It sent a solid message about who was in charge and how much mercy the subject could expect. Harvath, though, had never been a big fan of the tactic.

While he could be brutal when he needed to be, there was a line from Nietzsche that was never far from his consciousness. *Battle not with monsters, lest ye become a monster, and if you gaze into the abyss, the abyss gazes also into you.*

Harvath had no choice but to battle monsters. It was his job. He did, though, have a choice when it came to how deeply he would let the abyss stare into him. He had no intention of becoming like the monsters he hunted. Besides, a simple act of human kindness could also be a powerful interrogation tool, especially if the subject was already broken.

Feed their dreams and starve their fears was a mantra the Old Man had taught him. Judging by the looks of Khuram Hanjour, all the recruiter was dreaming about right now was gaining his freedom. His biggest fear was being locked back inside the psychologically suffocating confines of the Storm Case.

After wheeling the container inside the ground-floor bathroom, Harvath and Cowles had donned masks, butcher's aprons, and rubber gloves. They lifted Hanjour out of the case, propped him up in the tub, and turned on the shower.

Once he was as clean as he was going to get, they used trauma scissors to cut away the duct tape. Some strips refused to come loose and Harvath knew they'd be pulling away skin, so he left them on. They could be used later to inflict pain, but he didn't think that was going to be necessary.

They cut away Hanjour's soiled khakis and underwear, then put a hood over his head and dragged him out of the bathroom and down to the basement. The cell was at the end of a short cinderblock hall. Cowles removed a set of keys and opened the door. There were portable construction lights, a video camera, and a lone chair. Along the wall behind the chair, a sheet had been hung so that no one would ever be able to reverse-engineer where the video had been shot.

Harvath sat Hanjour down and secured him to the chair. He then nodded to Cowles, who left the room, closing and locking the cell door behind him. Harvath stood at the far corner for a few moments watching Hanjour. Placing the hood over his head had brought about a severe panic attack. Harvath walked over and removed it.

"Take deep breaths," he told him. "Breathe."

Harvath walked back over to the wall and watched. The mind was an incredible thing. It could help transport a person to incredible heights or reduce him to unfathomable lows. The range and breadth of personality traits, mental disorders, and capacity for good or evil in human beings was staggering. Harvath had watched interrogators break some of the toughest subjects he had ever seen in half the time it had taken him to break weaker men. Interrogation was an art form, and at its core was an understanding of how the human mind and all of its complicated components worked.

He waited until Hanjour's breathing had normalized and then turned on the video camera to begin his interrogation. "Khuram, you have something I want. If you give it to me, I'm going to let you live. In fact, I may even set you free. But all of that is going to depend on how well you cooperate."

Hanjour shook his head. It took him a moment to find his words. "You will never set me free."

"Why do you think that, Khuram?"

"Your country doesn't release people like me."

He had a good point, but Harvath wasn't going to concede it. "You'd be surprised what kind of an arrangement might be made," he said. "Of course, you would be working for us, but I think we're getting ahead of ourselves. Let me finish laying the ground rules. If you lie to me, I will know and I will put you back in the box. If I even think you are lying to me, I'll put you back in the box. If you give me an unsatisfactory answer at any time, I will put you back in the box. I know everything, Khuram. I just want to hear it in your words. Have I made myself clear?"

Hanjour nodded.

"Is it your wish then not to be put back in the box?"

Hanjour nodded again.

"Say it. Say *I don't want to be put back in the box.*"

The man saw the expression on the American's hard face and knew he was serious. "I do not want to be put back in the box."

"Say it again," Harvath ordered.

"I do not want to be put back in the box."

"Where are you going if you do not cooperate with me?"

"Back in the box," stammered Hanjour, his voice trembling.

"And who will put you there?"

"You will."

Harvath watched the recruiter's face. He was establishing a baseline in order to be able to read his microexpressions and catch whether, at any point, he was lying.

When Harvath was ready, he asked, "Who is Ahmad Yaqub?"

"Ahmad Yaqub?"

Harvath exploded off the wall. "That is not an acceptable response. That's a delaying tactic. For that, you're going back in the box."

Harvath walked over to the door, pounded on it, and yelled, "Bring me the box."

Hanjour began shaking. "Please," he implored him. "No box."

"You're doing it to yourself, Khuram. I told you what would happen if you didn't cooperate."

"I *will* cooperate. Please."

"Who is Ahmad Yaqub?" Harvath demanded.

"I do not know this man," said Hanjour.

There was an almost imperceptible twitch at the corner of his left eye.

"What is your name?" Harvath demanded.

"My name?"

"Yes. What is your name?"

"Khuram Hanjour."

No twitch.

"Who is Ahmad Yaqub?"

"I have told you. I do not know this man."

There it was again, the *tell*. Hanjour was lying.

Cowles entered with the Storm Case, placed it on the floor, and then exited the cell. Immediately, Hanjour began breathing faster. Just seeing the case was enough to trigger a panic attack.

Harvath walked over to the chair and pointed at the case. "I'm sure it felt like an eternity for you inside there. It wasn't. You weren't in there that long at all. This time, though, you will be. I have all the time in the world. I can lock you in that box and come back later tonight, tomorrow, or I can leave you in there for days.

"You'll feel like you're going to die, like you can't breathe, but I'm not going to let you die, Khuram. I am going to keep you alive so that your fear grinds down every nerve, every fiber in your body. You're going to go insane, but before you do, I promise, you'll tell me what I want to know."

Harvath dragged the case right next to his prisoner and opened the lid. The odor was horrible. It smelled not only of urine and feces, but of sweat and one hundred percent pure fear.

He moved behind Hanjour to unsecure him from the chair and the man said, "Please, no. *Please.*"

Harvath ignored him and reached for the first restraint.

"Ahmad Yaqub is a mujahideen from Saudi Arabia," Hanjour blurted out. "He is a member of Al Qaeda."

Harvath stopped what he was doing and slowly circled back in front of the recruiter. "How long have you known him?"

Hanjour paused to consider his response, but it appeared a legitimate attempt to recollect the exact information. "Five years."

No twitch.

"Where is Ahmad Yaqub based?" Harvath asked. "Where does he live?"

"Waziristan."

No twitch. Hanjour was telling him the truth.

"When was the last time you both communicated?"

Hanjour thought and then replied. "Sometime in the last six months."

"He paid you to recruit a team of men."

Hanjour nodded.

"No nodding," Harvath ordered. "Answer me."

"Yes. He hired me to recruit a team of men."

"For what purpose?"

"I don't know."

Harvath kicked the man's chair, hard. *"For what purpose?"*

"I don't know," Hanjour repeated. The outburst had startled him, but he didn't appear to be lying.

"He asked for engineers. Six students."

That was a new piece of information. *"Students?"*

"Yes, Ahmad Yaqub wanted engineering students," said Hanjour.

"Why?"

"Because it was easier to get them U.S. visas."

Harvath knew Levy was watching the feed of the interrogation in a room upstairs. He didn't need to look into the camera to tell her what to do; she would already be on a secure link back to Langley.

"Did you get the visas yourself?"

"Yes. I got the visas," Hanjour replied.

"What were their names?"

"I don't remember."

There it was, the twitch.

"You're lying to me," said Harvath. Pulling the hood from his back pocket, he prepared to pull it over the man's head and Hanjour began stammering again.

The recruiter rattled off a list of six names. Harvath listened and then made him do it again.

It appeared that Hanjour was telling the truth. Harvath, though, knew there was only one way to be absolutely sure.

CHAPTER 18

anjour lived beyond his means on Palm Jumeirah—an artificial archipelago built out into the Persian Gulf. It had been constructed in the shape of a palm tree with a trunk, a crown with seventeen fronds, and an outer eleven-kilometer crescent that acted as a breakwater. It had been dubbed the "eighth wonder of the world," and even by Dubai standards, was extremely ostentatious.

There was shopping, luxury five-star hotels, restaurants, sports complexes, mosques, a monorail, and even two U.S. 1970s F-100 Super Sabre fighter jets that had been stripped and sunk beyond the breakwater to form an artificial reef for residents to scuba-dive around.

Hanjour's sprawling apartment was located at Oceana, a gated community situated on the trunk portion of Palm Jumeirah. To facilitate their entry, Harvath had returned to the Arabian Courtyard with Hanjour's parking ticket stub. The valets were busy shuttling cars back and forth as guests checked in, arrived for dinner, or departed. No one suspected that the clean-cut Westerner was there to pick up a car that didn't belong to him. When the valet brought Hanjour's Mercedes around, Harvath tipped him and drove back to the safe house.

By the time he had returned, Hanjour had already been cleaned up and dressed in fresh clothes. They loaded the Storm Case in the trunk just in case. As long as Hanjour continued to cooperate, he would be spared a repeat of what had happened earlier. He sat in the backseat with his FlexiCuffed hands hidden beneath a gray sport coat. Cowles sat next to him. Upon his lap was a soft, leather briefcase. Inside, his left hand was wrapped around the butt of a suppressed 9mm Springfield XD pistol. Harvath had made it perfectly clear that if Hanjour tried anything at all, Cowles would shoot him in the genitals or the stomach, neither of which was a good way to die.

Anne Levy rode in the front passenger seat, her suppressed SIG sitting in the purse on her lap. Harvath kept his weapon tucked under his left thigh as he drove.

Traffic in Dubai was always a nightmare, especially at night. If it hadn't been for the heavy blue chrome tint applied to the Mercedes' windows, Harvath never would have trusted Hanjour to sit in the backseat. All it would have taken was for him to mouth *Help me* to someone in another car rolling alongside, and cell phones would have come out, the police would have been called, and all hell would have broken loose. It would have been very difficult for them to escape.

Glued to their back bumper was the black BMW with four very special CIA operatives. If anything happened, they were the counterassault team. Harvath's job would be to get Hanjour away safely. The men in the BMW would stay and fight.

With each intersection they approached, visions of what had happened in Karachi passed through Harvath's mind. He kept his eyes wide open and proceeded with an abundance of caution.

Finally, they arrived on Palm Jumeirah. Per their plan, the vehicles split. Harvath, Levy, and Cowles took Hanjour to Oceana, while the team in the BMW would remain nearby and on call.

A scanner read the special decal on Hanjour's Mercedes and automatically the Oceana gates opened. The process repeated itself at the underground parking entrance beneath his building. Hanjour directed them to a parking space and they exited the vehicle.

Harvath had been marking the positions of CCTV cameras since they had driven onto the property. He had seen two more since driving into the garage. There would likely be one in the elevator vestibule, maybe another in the elevator itself.

Per Harvath's suggestion, Cowles had placed a pair of sunglasses on Hanjour to make his face more difficult to read. Wearing sunglasses at night would also help reinforce their ruse.

As they got out of the Mercedes, Levy walked up to Hanjour's right side and slipped her arm through his. Cowles stood on the recruiter's left side and held on to Hanjour's arm as if trying to steady him. Harvath walked in front, weaving just enough to make it appear to anyone watching that they were a group of friends returning home from an evening of drinking. Any security personnel watching them via CCTV would think nothing of it. Dubai had the reputation of being the one spot in the Muslim world where Allah "couldn't see you." Everyone overindulged here— especially Muslims.

They used Hanjour's key card to access the elevator and ascend to his floor. His apartment was a corner unit with floor-to-ceiling glass windows. The view of the Dubai skyline was stunning, but they weren't here for the view. They were here for what Hanjour had in his office.

After they swept the apartment to make sure it was safe, they took Hanjour back to the master bedroom, which he also used as his office, and Harvath recited the list of things he wanted. Reluctantly, Hanjour led Harvath toward his king-sized platform bed. Beneath the mattress was a safe, whose door opened with the assistance of two pistons. Hanjour gave Harvath the combination.

As soon as it was open, Harvath began pulling everything out and handing it to Levy, who organized it along Hanjour's desk.

The man had been a meticulous, practically compulsive record keeper. Dates, times, amounts of money, clients he had worked for, the people he had recruited and placed, it was all there. The CIA was going to have a field day with this information, especially with the names of the six men Hanjour had recruited and dispatched to the United States. Those were the files he was most interested in seeing.

The data Hanjour had assembled lived on two laptops, multiple external hard drives, accordion files, manila envelopes, and ledger books. Harvath knew better than to touch any of the electronic data. Hanjour could have it buttoned down, ready to self-destruct if the correct password wasn't punched in within moments of the computer being booted up. Setting aside the electronic items, he and Levy focused on Hanjour's printouts and notes while Cowles kept an eye on their prisoner.

In one of the ledgers, Levy found what appeared to be payments to the six engineering students. After each were the initials AA. She was concerned it stood for American Airlines. "What does *AA* stand for?" she demanded.

"Al Ain. It's where the engineering students were recruited from."

Harvath was familiar with it. It was a town about seventy-five miles south of Dubai on the border with Oman. It was home to several universities and health facilities, as well as a falconry hospital Harvath had targeted in a previous operation when he was last in the UAE. "What about these other entries, below the names of the men you recruited for Ahmad Yaqub?"

"Those are family members of the men," said Hanjour. "As part of the arrangement, their families receive support."

Harvath had already grilled Hanjour back at the safe house over the attack. He claimed, and Harvath believed him, to know nothing about the details. He had been hired to recruit six engineering students and facilitate their entry into the United States.

"You told me that you helped secure student visas for the men," Harvath stated.

Hanjour nodded.

"For that to happen, they would have had to have been accepted for enrollment at American universities. Where's the list?"

"There is no list."

Harvath looked at him and then, removing the key fob for the Mercedes, tossed it to Cowles. "Go down and get the Storm Case from the trunk."

Hanjour held up his hands. "There is no list because they were not accepted to any American universities."

Harvath signaled for Cowles to wait. "If they didn't have letters of acceptance, how were you able to get them student visas?"

"There was an internship program they were particularly qualified for."

Harvath didn't notice Hanjour giving off any tells, but there was something odd about what he was saying. "From what you've already told me, there was nothing remarkable about these six men. They weren't hardcore jihadists and were mediocre students at best. What could they possibly be *particularly qualified* for?"

"All that mattered was that they were Muslims."

Harvath looked at Levy. None of it made sense to her either. An American internship program that recruited foreign students and based acceptance on whether or not they were Muslim? It was beyond ridiculous.

Looking back at his prisoner, Harvath asked, "Who sponsored this Muslim internship?"

Hanjour smiled. "NASA."

CHAPTER 19

Harvath couldn't believe it. *NASA?* The National Aeronautics and Space Administration had sponsored the visas of six would-be Muslim terrorists? America's visa program was absolutely screwed up, but *that* screwed up? How the hell could an agency of the United States government not only have imported six terrorists, but have actively sought them out? It was beyond insane.

He locked his eyes on Hanjour. He still didn't buy it. "Why would NASA create an internship program for foreign Muslim students?"

Hanjour shrugged.

Harvath was about to press him, when Levy spoke up. "I know why."

"You do?"

"A couple of years ago, there was an interview on Al Jazeera TV. It caused a lot of controversy back in the U.S. The director of NASA was being interviewed. It was during the previous administration. He said that when he took the NASA job, the President wanted him to do three things. I thought it was a joke when I heard it. The President said he wanted the NASA director to inspire children to learn math and science, expand international relationships, and at the top of the list, he

wanted the director to find a way to reach out to the
Muslim world to help them feel better about their historic contributions to science, math, and engineering."

"What the—?" Harvath began, his voice trailing off.
"Are you kidding me?"

Levy shook her head.

"No wonder NASA was forced to scrap the space
shuttle program. Raising Islamic self-esteem must be
an around-the-clock operation."

Harvath shook his head in disgust. Political correct-
ness was the biggest weakness in America's national security. The TSA was a joke, America refused to learn
from the Israelis, and now NASA had gone from ex-
ploring the reaches of outer space to soothing the in-
nermost reaches of the Muslim world's feelings. The
weakness that had been projected by the United States
was astounding. It was a wonder that it hadn't been in-
vaded yet. It would take years to repair the damage.

At least for now, Harvath had helped the country
take another step in the right direction. "We need to get
on the phone to the FBI," he said. "Have them swoop
in on NASA and round these guys up."

"You won't find them," Hanjour replied.

Harvath looked at him. "Why not?"

"Because it was a summer internship. They're gone
now."

"Gone where? Back to Al Ain?"

"Wherever their handler needed them. The internship program was just the means to get them their visas,
get them into the country, and get them acclimated.
Once the internship was over, NASA assumed they
would return home."

"Which they didn't," Harvath stated.

Hanjour nodded.

FedEx and UPS could track millions of packages a day, but the U.S. government couldn't track down foreigners who overstayed their visas. It was a disgrace. Coupled with the directive for NASA to help enhance Islamic self-esteem, Harvath couldn't help but wonder if there were politicians and bureaucrats intent upon hastening the country's collapse, which brought him back to China.

No matter what America's problems were, none of them would matter if America ceased to exist. Whatever the Snow Dragon attack was, it had to be stopped—by any means necessary.

He and Levy spent another forty-five minutes poring over all the materials, asking Hanjour repeatedly for clarification on his notes. Harvath asked for pictures of the six men he had sent to the U.S. Hanjour stated that they were on one of the laptops. When Harvath asked him for the "control files"—the dossiers he had built on each man—Hanjour also claimed those were on the computers. Until the NSA could go to work on them, those would have to remain beyond Harvath's reach.

Harvath pressed him on Ahmad Yaqub and the students. Hanjour asserted that he had communicated solely with Ahmad Yaqub. Once he had found and recruited the engineering students, he had guided their applications to the NASA program. Once they had been accepted, NASA had handled the visas.

Harvath learned that Hanjour had received six cell phones via messenger, which he assumed had been from Yaqub and which he had distributed to the students. They were to turn the phones on once they arrived in the United States, keep them charged, and await further instruction.

Hanjour claimed to have no idea what the telephone numbers were, what carrier the phones used, or if any pictures or instructions might have already been loaded on the phones. According to him, that wasn't his job and he hadn't wanted to know.

Once the phones had been handed out and the men had left for the U.S., Hanjour's only responsibility was disbursing the agreed-to sums to the men's families. The students had been made aware that if they screwed up, not only would the money stop, but their loved ones would be targeted. Whoever was behind the plot had been serious about a carrot-and-stick approach.

After wringing what they could from Hanjour, Harvath had a decision to make. He had no intention of letting the recruiter go. Maybe, at some point way in the future, he could be used as an asset, but right now—just like Ahmad Yaqub—he was headed for a dark cell and a hell of a lot more questions.

In the meantime, Harvath had to get everything from Hanjour's safe back to the United States. He wanted to be on a plane with it and on his way out of the United Arab Emirates ASAP. That would require a little bit of tap-dancing with the authorities, some diplomatic immunity, and a VIP big enough to take any attention off him and his less-than-fully-backstopped black passport.

He asked Cowles to remove Hanjour from the room for a moment. Once they were gone, Harvath turned to Levy and asked, "Does anyone owe you any favors at the embassy in Abu Dhabi?"

"A couple," she said. "Why?"

"I need you to call in a big one."

CHAPTER 20

Eric Tucker looked up at Fordyce and shook his head. Les Johnson was keeping watch while Tang spoke soothingly to the boy in Korean. It was a total cluster. The sun would be up in an hour. They had some serious decisions to make.

Running away, the boy had stepped into a hole and had broken his right leg. That had been the *pop* Fordyce had heard.

"See how it's all loose between the knee and ankle?" Tucker asked.

Fordyce looked down. Tuck had used his shears to cut up the length of the boy's right pant leg. The little boy was scared to death and in a lot of pain. "How bad?" Fordyce asked

Tucker shook his head once more and unsealed one of the two-hundred-microgram Fentanyl lollipops the teams carried. "Bad," he replied. "It looks like he's got a tib/fib fracture." He handed the lollipop to the boy and said to Tang, "Tell him to put this in his mouth and to suck on it slowly. Make sure he doesn't bite it. Tell him it'll help take away the pain."

Tang nodded and translated the instructions as Fordyce continued to study the boy's leg. He had played rugby at the Naval Academy and had seen some pretty bad bone breaks. And while he wasn't a corpsman, he knew a tib/fib fracture was pretty serious. The kid wasn't going to be able to walk on that leg.

Johnson shifted his eye from his rifle sight down to the boy. "What's the plan?" he asked. "What are we going to do with him?"

"First we're going to splint his leg," stated Tuck.

"And then what?"

"And then," Fordyce said, "we're going to see where he's from and what he knows."

Johnson shook his head. "Bad idea. Sun'll be up soon. People are going to come looking for him."

Holding the boy's hand, Billy Tang looked at Johnson. "So what are we supposed to do, bail? We'd be lucky to make the ridgeline by sunrise."

"Hold on," Fordyce interjected.

"We'd be exposed, in broad daylight," Tang continued. "Not to mention the fact that our ride won't be here until tomorrow night."

Johnson hadn't liked the CIA man from the get-go. Turning his attention back to his weapon sight, he repeated, "People are going to come looking for that boy."

He was right. Fordyce knew it. They all knew it, including Billy. But Tang was also right. They were stuck. The sun would be up soon. Even if they wanted to pull the plug, they couldn't. There was nowhere to go, not in broad daylight.

To make matters worse, the kid had probably left a trail behind him that even Helen Keller could follow. If someone did come looking for him, and they knew what they were doing, every broken twig and bent leaf of grass was going to lead them right to this spot.

The only way to prevent the team from being uncovered was to stop any search as soon as possible. To do that, they'd have to give up the boy. The drawback to that plan was that as soon as he began talking, the North Koreans would be after the SEALs and it would be Afghanistan 2005 and Operation Red Wings all over again. Fordyce wasn't going to let that happen.

"Les is right," Fordyce announced. "People are going to come looking for that kid."

There was something about the way he said it that Tang didn't like. "What are you suggesting?"

"His leg is already broken. We'll make it look like he also hit his head."

"We're going to kill him?" Tang exclaimed. "Dude, I've got a boy almost his age."

"And that's exactly who you should be thinking about," Fordyce ordered. "If this operation fails, your boy and millions of other children back home are going to get wiped out."

Tang turned his attention back to the little boy with the broken leg and began asking him questions.

"Tang," Fordyce insisted, but the CIA man ignored him. "*Tang*," he repeated. "Quit talking to that kid. That's an order. We've got to get this done and our trail scrubbed before the sun is up. Can you not fucking hear me?"

Johnson was closest to Tang, and pulling his foot back, he kicked him hard in the side.

Tang fell to the side, only to come up with his pistol. Leveling it at Johnson, he said, "You touch me again and I'll kill you."

Johnson was about to respond when Fordyce interrupted, "Tang, you've got two seconds to unfuck yourself. Put your weapon down."

Tang continued to eyeball Johnson and ignore Fordyce.

Johnson smiled. He could see something Tang couldn't. "You got him, Tuck?"

"I do," said Tucker, who had snatched up his own weapon and now had it pointed right at Tang's head.

"I'm giving you one last chance, Billy," Fordyce commanded. "Put that fucking weapon down, *right* now."

"We're not killing this kid," said Tang.

"That's not your call. Put your weapon down. Do it now."

"This kid has a sister," Tang stated as he continued to converse with the little boy.

"I told you to stop talking to him," Fordyce said. "It's only going to make it harder. This is the last time I'm going to tell you to put your weapon down, Billy. I *will* order Tucker to shoot you. Do you understand me?"

"I thought SEALs were honorable."

"Shoot him," Johnson said to Tucker.

"Shut up, Les," Fordyce commanded. "I'm in charge here. I give the orders." Focusing on Tang he said, "Billy, I'm going to count to three. If you do not put your weapon down, you're going to leave me no choice. One—"

The little boy, who seemed to know what was at stake, rushed off a string of sentences, intelligible only to himself and Tang. The boy was so emphatic, Fordyce paused his countdown.

As soon as the boy stopped speaking, Tang laid his pistol down. Johnson looked as if he was about to butt-stroke the CIA man with his rifle, but Fordyce raised his hand and signaled him to back off.

The look on Tang's face had them all wondering what the boy had just said. "What the hell did he say?" Fordyce asked.

"He says he knows why we're here."

"Bullshit," Johnson quipped.

Fordyce motioned for him to shut up. Looking at Tang, he said, "How the hell could he possibly know why we're here?"

"He's pretty bright," the CIA operative replied. "He figures we're here because of the Chinese."

"So?"

"So, he says that if we help his sister back in the camp, he'll tell us anything we want to know."

"Don't do it, LT," Johnson said. "We're just here to take pictures."

Fordyce looked at Tucker, who replied, "I'm with Les. This kid is going to get us all killed."

"You ever shot a kid before?"

Tucker shook his head.

Fordyce looked at Johnson. "What about you?"

Johnson looked away.

"I'll do it," Tang stated.

All eyes were now on him.

"If he has zero value, I'll do it," the CIA man reasserted.

"Billy, we don't have the time," Fordyce replied. "Start scrubbing the trail."

"And then what?"

"Then," Tang stated, "I'll either get you some intel, or I'll bring you the body of a dead little boy."

CHAPTER 21

While most government workers were fighting Beltway traffic on their way home or out of town for the weekend, President Porter had reconvened his national security team in the Situation Room.

"Let's start with the CIA," he said.

There were certain people in the room who didn't need to know who Harvath was, so CIA Director Bob McGee referred to him by his call-sign. "As previously discussed, Norseman succeeded in locating Khuram Pervez Hanjour. During the interrogation, Hanjour gave up the names of six engineering students he had recruited on behalf of Ahmad Yaqub."

"Do we know where these six engineering students are now?"

"The FBI is working on that."

The President looked at FBI Director Edward Erickson and raised his eyebrows.

"We have confirmation that they did in fact enter the country," Erickson replied. "They flew from Dubai to Houston via Emirates airlines."

"What do we know about the NASA internship program they were in?"

The FBI Director knew the President wasn't going

to like the answer, but there was no getting around it. "It was started under the previous administration and it really wasn't an internship as much as it was a goodwill summit."

"Meaning?"

"Muslim students would go through a bunch of feel-good exercises and leave with the impression that without Islamic contributions to science, there would be no U.S. space program."

"In other words," said President Porter, "it was a boondoggle."

The FBI Director shrugged. "From what I understand, there are legitimate Islamic contributions to science. Also, these were college and grad students and this was a summer program. It wasn't supposed to be difficult."

"Of course not. And in addition, I suppose everyone left with a certificate or a trophy of some sort?"

"Yes, sir."

Porter shook his head. "Do I even want to know what this cost the American taxpayers?"

"No, sir. You don't."

"What about the six students? Are they still at NASA?"

"No, sir," the FBI Director replied.

"Were they *ever* at NASA?"

"Yes, sir. After entering the country last May, they stayed for the duration of the internship and then departed."

"*Departed* for where?" the President asked.

"No one knows. Our Houston field office already has a team at the Johnson Space Center conducting interviews with anyone and everyone who might have had contact with the Al Ain Six."

"Al Ain Six?"

"All six of the engineering students came from Emirati universities in the city of Al Ain. It's just a shorthand we've developed."

"Let's make sure the press doesn't get hold of that. It sounds way too catchy."

"That wasn't the intent, but I understand, sir," the FBI Director replied. "I'll make sure it stops being used."

The President processed everything he had been told. "So, the program ends and everyone goes home, except for our six students from UAE. Is that correct?"

"Yes, sir."

"And we have no idea where they are now."

"Correct."

"Do we have photographs? That's part of the visa process, right? We fingerprint and retina-scan them upon entry into the United States, don't we?"

"Yes, sir, we do," the FBI Director answered. "And we have all of that." He nodded to the Situation Room tech, who put the photos up on the monitors. Under each man's picture was his name.

"Are we putting these pictures out to state and local law enforcement?"

"Not yet."

"Why not?" the President asked.

"Because when those pictures go to the state and local level, we have to assume they'll get leaked to the press. That could push them to launch the attack."

"Do we have any other leads?"

"Having their names and faces is a big leap forward from where we were twenty-four hours ago," said Director Erickson. "In addition to the interviews the Houston field office is conducting, we're trying to decide what to do about the man who ran the NASA Islamic internship program."

"Is he a suspect?"

"We haven't made the determination yet. When NASA recruited him, he was working for an organization that has had a very checkered past. Several of its board of directors have been indicted for terrorism-related funding."

"Why was NASA even talking to them?"

"They are the best-known Muslim advocacy group in the U.S., but they're not the cleanest, that's for sure. NASA's director told me that the wife of someone in the last White House knew somebody at the organization and it just sort of happened."

The President shook his head. You couldn't make this stuff up.

Before the FBI Director could continue, the Attorney General spoke up. "My office and the FBI have been discussing whether to interview the internship director or go to the FISA court, get a warrant, and dig around first."

"Your grounds for a warrant being?" the Secretary of State asked.

"That the internship director had to personally approve the candidates for the internship, that he communicated internationally in the process, and that six of the interns—who have been conditionally identified as being part of a terrorist plot—have overstayed their J-1 visas and cannot be located."

"Go for both," the President ordered. "Don't waste any more time. Get the warrant, gather as much intel as you can, and then bring him in for questioning. If you get any pushback from the FISA court, I want to know immediately. Understood?"

"Yes, sir," the Attorney General replied.

When the man remained seated as if he intended to stay for the rest of the meeting, the President pointed toward the door and said, "Go. Now."

The President had a brusque style when he felt things weren't moving fast enough. He hated inertia and believed in kicking people's rear ends often and hard in order to get things moving.

The Attorney General gathered up his documents and exited the Situation Room.

Looking at the remaining faces gathered around the table, the President said, "What else do we have?"

The CIA Director spoke up and all eyes turned back to him. "Before leaving the UAE, each of the engineering students was given a phone, told to keep it charged and to turn them on when they arrived in the U.S."

"Have we been able to track those?"

"We know when the men cleared customs and immigration control, so that gives us an arrival window and narrows the search. The NSA is compiling a list of every phone in and around the airport that was turned on during that time."

"Good," replied the President. "What else? Any problem with the Pakistanis?"

The Secretary of State shook his head. "Fortunately, no," he said. "It's like a hornet's nest over there, but nobody is pointing a stinger at us. Yet."

"Until they do, we're not going to worry about it. And if they do, I want you to speak to me first before responding. Understood?"

"Yes, Mr. President."

"And what's this issue with our ambassador in Abu Dhabi?"

"*He's* upset that he hasn't been fully read in on what's going on."

"*He's* upset? What did you tell him?" the President asked.

"I told him he didn't have a need to know and that you'd be glad to appoint a new ambassador if he didn't cooperate."

"Did that work?"

The Secretary of State nodded.

"Good. As long as Norseman makes it out of the UAE with everything, that's all we care about. When's he due to arrive?"

"It's a fourteen-hour flight, so they should arrive here around 0700."

The President looked at CIA Director McGee. "You've got a full crash team meeting the plane?"

"Yes, sir. Crypto, finance people, NSA, the whole nine yards. We'll dive right into the material as soon as he touches down."

"Good," the President repeated. Looking back at the FBI Director, he said, "Before you all hear the bombshell Treasury has uncovered, where's the Bureau in regard to the Chinese princelings?"

The FBI Director looked at his colleagues. "The Politburo Standing Committee is the most powerful body in China. It is composed of nine members. Of those nine, four have sons attending college or grad school in the United States, and one has a granddaughter.

"Because of who their fathers, and in one case grandfather, are, they have been flagged for special monitoring. Communications, rotating physical surveillance, that sort of thing. In light of the Snow Dragon revelations, the FBI has stepped up its monitoring of the princelings. We now have them under 24/7 surveillance. We're also monitoring all of their communications in real time.

"If China's attack is as bad as predicted, we believe the princelings will be moved, or given some sort of head start before it takes place. They could be our only canaries in the coal mine."

"I wouldn't put all my resources in just one basket," the Secretary of State cautioned.

"We're also watching Chinese embassy personnel and other high-ranking Chinese currently in the country," the FBI Director replied.

"Anything else?" the President asked, looking around the table. No one spoke. "As we all know, Gold Dust is a zero-communication op. We won't hear back from the team until they have been exfiltrated from North Korea. In the meantime, we have something else.

"Based upon the intelligence the CIA received, I asked the Secretary of the Treasury to look into another possible motivation for a Chinese attack. The Secretary has come back with some very disturbing information. Mr. Secretary?"

CHAPTER 22

Secretary of the Treasury Dennis Fleming looked like an aging bank president. He kept his gray hair short and neatly combed, wore gray suits, wingtip shoes, and muted ties. He took notes in pencil on a large, white legal pad. He was bullish on America and its prospects for economic recovery. The President's "Wild West, blow the gunk out of the system, trim all the fat to the bone, and let the pieces fall where they may" style was disconcerting to him, to say the least.

Where the President saw the economy as an Abrams tank that needed to be whacked with a gigantic wrench to get it going in the right direction, Fleming saw it as a Swiss watch that needed delicate adjustments. While the President's cowboy rhetoric and bold approach to problems was popular with a public beset with economic worries and a national identity crisis, every time Porter stepped up to a microphone, Fleming's heart seized in his chest. He was convinced that one of these times Porter was going to fly wildly off script and send the markets tumbling.

But President Porter had no script. He had a vision for returning America to greatness and either you were on board or you were tossed overboard. He made no secret of the kind of people he wanted around him.

That didn't mean, though, that the President sought only to surround himself with yes-men. He welcomed healthy debate and differences of opinion. But you had better be prepared to defend your position. And no matter what else, your policy ideas had to be informed by the same sense of America's continued potential that coursed through Porter's veins.

In the history of the world, Porter was fond of saying, there had never been a greater force for peace, stability, liberty, and freedom than the United States. Before America, the history of mankind had been one of tyranny, with the masses lorded over and controlled by the few. The United States had been established to protect the rights of the smallest minority that had ever existed— the individual. You could not work for President Paul Porter and not be fully dedicated to these ideals.

It was with those things in mind that Secretary Fleming had accepted the quiet assignment given to him by the President several days ago. In all honesty, he had thought the President was sending him on a wild-goose chase. The suggestion that something like what he had suggested could even exist was unthinkable before the threat by the Chinese. And while Porter might not have possessed a Ph.D. in economics, he did hold an MBA and he was an extremely intelligent man. Still, Fleming couldn't understand how the President had come to suspect what they now knew to be true.

Fleming had been cautioned to lay things out in a manner as easy to understand as possible. Though Porter encouraged his people to ask questions when they didn't understand something, he knew that when it came to economics, most people were in the dark and didn't want to flaunt their ignorance. "Assume they know a lot less than you," the President had directed him.

Keeping that directive in mind, Fleming accepted the remote from the Situation Room tech, cleared his throat, and began his presentation. "After Snow Dragon came to light, the President asked me to look into something. He was curious about the fact that the Chinese believed they would be able to land and establish permanent forces in the United States after an attack.

"What did this mean? The intelligence suggests that the Chinese are training some sort of specialized force in North Korea, but to what end? And why would they believe they would be able to put troops on American soil without any fear of international reprisal?

"The Chinese do not possess any specialty that would be uniquely needed in the aftermath of a catastrophic event. None. This left us with only two reasonable possibilities. One, that the attack is biological in nature and that they possess some sort of immunity to the causative agent. This type of scenario is obviously outside our area of expertise at Treasury, and is being considered by other, more appropriate national security parties here in this room.

"Which brings us to the second. Is it conceivable that China could make a legitimate, legal claim to the United States after a catastrophic terrorist attack?"

"Of course they can't," stated the Secretary of Defense.

Fleming raised his index finger in caution. "Up until this week, I would have agreed with you." He advanced to his first slide. "The national debt under prior administrations has been mounting at an alarming rate. "Skyrocketing" would actually be a better term. The bigger our government gets, the more money it needs to operate. In order to get that money, it has two choices. It can continue to raise taxes again and again on our citizens and risk a revolution, or it can borrow in relative quiet, out of sight of everyday Americans who don't pay attention. The federal government has chosen to do a crippling combination of both.

"While high personal taxes leave Americans with less money to invest and spend in the marketplace, high corporate taxes leave businesses with less money to hire employees and force them to move things like manufacturing and customer service call centers offshore in order for their products to be competitive.

"We saw the last administration increase the top marginal tax rate by 5 percent. The increase pulled billions of dollars out of American households and ended up being only enough to run the federal government for six days.

"We then saw this same administration, desperate to reverse its falling poll numbers, continue to stoke the embers of class warfare. There is no more anti-American, anti-democracy rhetoric than this. To turn neighbor against neighbor because of the size of one's pocketbook is to plow the ground and sow it with the seeds of socialism. In America, only opportunity is assured, not outcomes. Anyone who promises otherwise is acting contrary to the values upon which our Republic was founded.

"The bottom line is that the federal government was never intended to be the size that it has grown to. The Founders intended for it to remain small and for the majority of issues to be handled at the state level where citizens can be more easily involved and have their voices heard.

"But as the federal government has expanded, it has become its own living, breathing organism. You have all heard the President liken it to Jabba the Hutt from the *Star Wars* movies, sitting on his throne gorging himself all day and dispatching his henchmen whenever his existence is threatened. This is exactly what the federal government has become. It is like a giant octopus with razor-sharp tentacles, which lashes out whenever it feels threatened. We have seen the IRS, the NSA, the Attorney General's office, and countless other federal departments and bureaucracies weaponized and turned against the American people.

"Anyone with the temerity to suggest that the government be scaled back becomes an enemy of the state, targeted not only by its aforementioned tentacles but by a complicit, big-government media. It is worse than Louis XIV's claim *L'état, c'est moi*. It is no longer one person, but the entire government declaring that the state takes precedence over the individual. It has devolved into *L'état, c'est l'état soi-même*.

"Imagine a family that is completely out of money but that keeps signing up for more credit cards. It doesn't scale back its lifestyle but actually takes it to the next level, buying more expensive cars, summer homes, and luxury vacations abroad. It's a recipe for complete and unmitigated disaster. Yet damning the torpedoes, the government proceeds full speed ahead.

"And as it does, as the government continues to tax and grow and borrow and spend, the day of reckoning draws ever closer. The bill is already overdue and at some point, we will no longer be able to borrow the money we have been using to put off the inevitable. Simply put, our national debt is growing faster than we can pay for it. The laws of physics and economics are inescapable. No nation can keep spending money it doesn't have forever. But spend we do.

"The prior administration tripled the deficit and increased the national debt by over seventy-five percent. Within the next ten years, every penny from taxes will go just to covering the interest on our debt. We'll have to borrow money for *everything* else. Military spending, Homeland Security, you name it. And knowing this, who would be stupid enough to loan us any money?" Fleming asked as he advanced to his next slide. "This is where President Porter's thoughts come in.

"Forty percent of our national debt is held by the federal government and the Federal Reserve. Essentially we print money and move it from our left pocket to our right. The largest foreign holder of American debt, though, is China."

"Despite everything you've said," the Secretary of Defense interrupted, "that still doesn't mean that they can come in here and declare themselves owners of the United States."

"Again, a week ago, I would have agreed with you, but hear me out," Fleming replied as he went to the next slide. "In the 1990s, Mexico had a currency crisis, which the United States stepped in to help resolve. We propped up the peso with an influx of $20 billion. It was the largest nonmilitary international loan the U.S. had made since the Marshall Plan.

"There was a rumor that circulated at the time that the loan almost didn't happen. Some were very concerned that the Mexicans wouldn't be able to pay it back. Others were less concerned with whether the loan would be paid back than with what would happen if the Mexican economy completely collapsed. Would our southern border be overrun with economic refugees? Congress was dead set against the loan.

"A small D.C. think tank aligned with the administration at that time made a radical suggestion. Have Mexico collateralize the loan by putting up the Baja Peninsula. If Mexico defaulted, Baja would belong to the U.S. and become the fifty-first state. That idea was allegedly discussed and dismissed as 'too crazy.' The think tank then recommended Mexico secure the loans with oil and natural gas drilling leases. That idea was also dismissed. The administration was worried they could end up looking like they had taken advantage of 'poor little Mexico.'

"In the end, the then Secretary of the Treasury skirted Congress by tapping a Treasury Department emergency reserve fund and got the money to Mexico that way. The idea, though, of nations backing up their loans with something tangible had been planted."

Fleming clicked his remote and a new slide appeared. "I know the President doesn't like to blame the previous administration. We've all been told we have to play the hand we've been dealt as well as we can for the American people. But, it is important to note that the Congressional Budget Office warned the last administration that the nation's debt was unsustainable and their spending policies were presenting lawmakers and the public with difficult choices.

"They were told that if nothing was done, entitlement spending would double, the government would have less flexibility to respond to unexpected challenges such as economic downturns or wars, and the risk of another financial crisis was being greatly increased. All of these, they were warned, would cause America's lenders to demand super-high interest rates in order to continue financing our government's borrowing binge.

"The CBO's warning wasn't top secret. It was very public. Not only were the markets listening, but so were the Chinese. They knew that it didn't matter much who sat in the Oval Office. The United States government was a life-form committed wholly to itself. It would continue to borrow, spend, and grow. It would die of obesity before ever agreeing to be slimmed down to a manageable size.

"The previous administration used the Federal Reserve to keep interest rates artificially low so it could continue to borrow money, but the Chinese were not only wise to it, but also growing increasingly tired of this game. Apparently, they got to the point where they were no longer content to play along."

The Secretary of State looked at Fleming and asked, "What do you mean, *apparently*?"

"Your predecessor said it best. 'Our debt and deficits are unsustainable and will cause us to not only lose our influence, but prevent us from making the right decisions.' He was right and that is exactly what has happened.

"China stopped listening to us about their human rights violations, international partners no longer wanted to line up with us to take on threats like Syria, Iran, or North Korea, and country after country, including China, has been bucking to dump the dollar as the world's reserve currency.

"In short, much of the world no longer respects us, China in particular. In order to continue to loan us money, they began to demand a new premium, one more reflective of the risk they were taking."

"What kind of premium?"

"They wanted their loans backed up with more than just the full faith and credit of the United States government. They wanted the loans to be collateralized."

"With what?"

Fleming went rapidly through a series of slides.

"Everything. Oil and gas leases in Alaska and the Gulf of Mexico. Mining rights throughout the Rockies and the Mountain West. Timber. Farmland. Water rights. Shipping ports. National parks. For every loan we rolled over or issued anew, the Chinese demanded a concession."

"And the last administration gave in to this?"

Fleming nodded.

"Without congressional approval?" the Secretary of State, a former senator, asked incredulously.

"The bigger the government, the less the respect for the rule of law."

The Secretary of Defense jumped in to chastise the Secretary of State and former senator. "All that administration did was end-run Congress. The warning signs were there and plenty of people were screaming for you and your colleagues to do something. You and your pals, though, didn't want to 'alienate voters.' You all said, 'We'll fix it later'; that it had to begin at the ballot box. Well, here we are. Thanks a lot."

Normally, the President would have short-circuited this kind of pissing match, but all of it needed to be said. The Secretary of State was a good peacemaker, but peacemaking had its place and its price. Turning a blind eye to abuses of office when he was a senator wasn't making peace. It was capitulation.

"How is it even possible that this is the first time I am hearing about this?" the Secretary of State demanded.

Fleming looked at the FBI Director, who had been assisting him over the past week. Pulling a file from the folder in front of him, the FBI Director said, "There had been a whistleblower at Treasury. She was apparently ready to name names and went to a congresswoman she thought would be sympathetic. The congresswoman was sympathetic all right, to the last administration.

She ended up ratting her out in exchange for a bunch of special items she wanted the President to approve through executive order.

"The President's people then went after the whistleblower with a vengeance. It's not hyperbole to say they turned her life into a living hell. She was not a perfect woman by any means and they used everything they could against her. She has a handicapped son and they pulled the trump card. They threatened her pension and medical benefits. She folded on the spot."

The Secretary of State was irate. "I want to know who the congresswoman was and I want to know who on the President's staff was involved. This will not stand."

Now it was time for the President to get involved. Raising his hand he said, "We'll get to all of that, but now is not the time."

The Secretary of State backed down and Secretary Fleming reclaimed the floor. "During the congresswoman's reelection, the whistleblower approached her challenger and gave his campaign the full story. It was a very serious claim, which the campaign couldn't prove. Plus, she told them they couldn't use her name, so they didn't go public with it. They did, though, pass it along to the FBI. But when agents approached her, she denied she had made any of the claims."

"Why? Is she some sort of loon?" asked the Secretary of State.

"No, it was still under the previous administration and she was afraid they would come after her again. But with the new presidency, she's had a change of heart.

"The FBI Director and I met with her personally. In exchange for her cooperation, and eventual testimony, I offered to bring her back to the Treasury Department, plus give her a promotion. She hasn't made up her mind yet, but she has begun working with us.

"What we've learned is that several key figures from the think tank advising the administration during the Mexican peso crisis back in the 1990s were brought in under the most recent administration to advise President Porter's predecessor. We believe there was a second set of books being kept in relation to China. We're attempting to locate them."

The Secretary of State shook his head. "The lawlessness you're suggesting is unfathomable."

"And none of it will matter if the Chinese succeed in pulling off their attack. Which brings me to my summation. If everything we have learned is true, if the Chinese were able to get the United States to collateralize its debt obligations, and those obligations cannot be vacated—no matter what happens to the United States—then we know why the Chinese feel they'll be able to waltz right in here after a catastrophic attack and make themselves at home.

"With a ninety percent casualty rate, America as we know it won't even exist anymore and China will be holding the deed to the United States.

"As we talked about at the beginning, who is going to argue with them? They'll probably even send us aid and offer humanitarian assistance. But in the end, when America cannot repay its debts, because it has collapsed, they are going to stake their claim and take what they believe is theirs. If we do not stop them, this absolutely will be the end of the United States."

CHAPTER 23

Harvath had flown with some absolute assholes in his day, but the U.S. Ambassador to the UAE, Leslie Conrad, was one of the worst.

U.S. ambassadors serve at the pleasure of the President. After an election or a reelection, all ambassadors submit a letter of resignation. Some are accepted immediately, usually for the plum ambassadorships, while others are asked to remain in place until a new ambassador can be chosen. Conrad was one of those asked to stay put until the President could find his replacement.

Conrad had gotten his ambassadorship by being a big bundler and raising a lot of money for the previous president. He reminded Harvath of Peter O'Toole in *Lawrence of Arabia*. In addition to being a thorough Arabist who thought he knew the region better than anyone else—along with what America's foreign policy absolutely should be—his hair was too blond, his teeth were too white, and his skin was too tan for a man of his age and stature. Harvath chalked a certain amount of that up to his parents' having named their male child Leslie.

It was apparent that Ambassador Conrad had not voted for the current president and didn't think much of his foreign policy. Conrad also didn't seem to think much of his very own duty to his country. The ambassador resented being awakened in the middle of the night to be roped into some "cloak-and-dagger circle jerk," as he put it.

Initially, Conrad had refused to cooperate. Then the Secretary of State had gotten on the phone and chewed his ass. Even though Conrad had done nothing of note while serving in his post, he was passionate about the Foreign Service and wanted to continue in it. The Secretary of State had used that to push his ungrateful behind out of bed, out of his villa, and into the motorcade waiting for him outside in Abu Dhabi.

Harvath and Levy had gone through Khuram Hanjour's entire Palm Jumeirah condo and had stacked anything of potential intelligence value at the front door. Cowles packed all of it, along with the contents of the hidden bed safe, in a set of designer luggage Hanjour had in one of the guest bedrooms.

Driving Hanjour's Mercedes out of the Oceana complex, Harvath and Levy had met up with the CIA assault team parked nearby. They transferred the luggage and traded cars while Levy handed over Hanjour's key card and explained how to enter the building in order to retrieve Cowles and the prisoner. Harvath and Levy then set out for the ninety-mile drive up the coast to the U.S. ambassador's residence in Abu Dhabi.

What would have normally been an hour-and-a-half drive, Harvath completed in forty-five minutes as Levy worked on her cell phone the entire way. The State Department, as well as the CIA, maintained accounts with private jet companies around the world, and with that in mind, Harvath had made two requests. He needed the fastest plane they could get, plus Ambassador Conrad's cooperation in coming along for the ride. With a United States ambassador in tow, none of the other passports in the entourage, particularly Harvath's, would receive additional scrutiny. That went double for their baggage.

Harvath had suggested creating a phony family emergency back in the U.S. that would require Conrad to leave the UAE immediately. But without knowing Conrad's family situation, Harvath could make only a few general suggestions of how to handle things. Levy had taken it from there.

Levy relayed everything to her boss, Chuck Godwin—a seasoned CIA veteran—who then coordinated with CIA headquarters in the U.S. Langley pulled Conrad's file and decided to use the ambassador's aging mother in Carmel, California, as the source of the emergency.

After assembling the plan, CIA Director Bob McGee contacted the Secretary of State for sign-off. With the green light in place, Godwin was told to wake the ambassador.

Conrad was told that his "family emergency" would be cover for getting a U.S. intelligence operative and some highly sensitive documents and other materials back to the United States. The ambassador had asked what the documents and other materials were, but was politely told that the information was of national security importance and classified above his clearance. Conrad asked Godwin who the intel operative was and what he had been doing in the UAE without his knowledge, only to be told that was also classified above his clearance. That was when Conrad had lost it.

The best term Chuck Godwin could come up with to describe it was "hissy fit." The ambassador was incensed that a covert operation had been carried out in his backyard without his approval. He didn't like being kept in the dark. And not only had he been kept in the dark, but now the CIA wanted to rope him in as cover to help get whatever they had out of the country. He announced that he was not only "personally and professionally insulted," but had no intention of cooperating.

Chuck Godwin hated the ambassador's guts. He was a feckless dilettante who had bought his way into the ambassadorship and was doing it only because of his love of parties, not love of country. In his estimation, the ambassador was worthless.

So when Conrad pushed back on helping to provide cover for Harvath and transporting the luggage as his own, Godwin simply thanked him, stepped out of the room, and called the seventh floor back at Langley. Three minutes later, the Secretary of State himself had called the ambassador's home and begun to read him the riot act. Within a half hour, Conrad was in his armored Suburban headed to the airport. Harvath was there, too, riding shotgun and posing as part of the ambassador's security detail. Wherever the bags went, Harvath was going. He had been instructed not to take his eyes off them.

Conrad's staff alerted the Emiratis to the ambassador's family emergency, and the convoy was met at the airport by an Emirati official who sped them right out to the tarmac and their waiting Gulfstream G650. The passports were handled planeside and every courtesy was extended to the ambassador and his retinue.

When the crew offered to stow the luggage in the belly of the plane, Harvath explained that the ambassador preferred to have access to his bags during the flight. The crew explained where the luggage could be stored in the cabin and helped carry it up the stairs and into the aircraft.

The ultra-high-speed, ultra-long-range G650 was considered the gold standard of business jets. The wide, fold-flat, first-class-style seats as well as the walls were wrapped in white leather. The tables, cabinets, trim, and doors were bird's-eye maple. The thick, café-mocha-colored carpet sported a motif that looked like lines drawn with twigs in wet sand. The cabin had one divan that folded flat into a nice-sized bed. The ambassador made a beeline straight for it. Harvath and the other three passengers picked the remaining chairs and settled in.

Though Harvath had locked the zippers of the luggage with the TamperTell seals provided by Chuck Godwin, he knew you could still pierce a zipper seam with a ballpoint pen, get into the bag, look around, and zip the seam back together with no one the wiser. He didn't think the ambassador would be that vindictive, or that stupid, but he didn't know for sure.

His concern caused him to sleep fitfully, waking every time he heard something unusual, or sensed someone was near the luggage. It made for a long flight.

In the ultimate twist, Ambassador Conrad's fold-out bed was right next to the main lavatory. Every time his assistant or one of his security team passed by to go to the bathroom, it woke him up and Conrad shot them angry looks.

Harvath had no idea if the man thought he deserved to have the bathroom all to himself and everyone else should use the crew lav up front, or if he just resented people traipsing through "his space." He figured it was probably a little bit of both and took a perverse pleasure in seeing the ambassador being awakened each time nature called.

Listening to how he talked to his people, Harvath could see the guy was a bully. He had always hated bullies. He was glad he didn't have to work for the ambassador.

Conrad, though, didn't seem to realize or care that Harvath didn't work for him. When Harvath got up to use the restroom, the ambassador stopped him and proceeded to dress him down. "You're a pretty smug guy, aren't you?"

"Excuse me, sir?" Harvath replied.

"You heard me," the ambassador snapped. "You're a pretty smug SOB, aren't you? Who do you think you are?"

Harvath didn't care for the man's tone, but he kept his temper in check. "Mr. Ambassador," he said politely, "if you prefer I use the forward crew lav, I don't think they'll mind."

"*If you prefer I use the forward crew lav,*" the man mocked. "This isn't about the fucking lavatory. This is about you coming into my country and operating completely unauthorized."

"I wasn't aware that the UAE was *your* country, or that you were the only one allowed to authorize operations there."

"Don't get cute with me. You know what I'm talking about. You violated protocol."

Protocol. Harvath shook his head. "I'm just catching a ride back to the States, Mr. Ambassador. That's all."

"Bullshit," Conrad spat. "I want to know what you've been up to."

"Shopping, sir."

"*Shopping*, my ass. You think I don't know people? You think I can't make your piece-of-shit life difficult?"

"I am sure you could, sir," Harvath replied.

"Who are you to have me dragged out of bed in the middle of the night?" he demanded.

As he moved to the side a bit, Harvath noticed the drink caddy next to his bed. Someone had been getting into the bourbon.

"I'm no one, Mr. Ambassador," Harvath said as he proceeded to the lavatory.

As he reached for the knob, the ambassador grabbed his wrist. *Bad move.*

"I want some straight answers," Conrad ordered. "Do you understand me?"

Harvath's eyes flicked to the nearest member of the ambassador's security team. The man was pretending to be asleep, but he was watching the whole thing. Harvath shook his head as if to say *stay out of this*. The man acknowledged by rolling over in his seat to face the window.

In a flash, Harvath had slipped the ambassador's boozy grasp and now had him in a wristlock. Applying pressure, Harvath sat down on the edge of the bed and looked him square in the eye.

The ambassador grimaced in pain.

"Let me make one thing perfectly clear," said Harvath. "I don't work for you. If I show up in your country unannounced, it's because someone a lot more important than you is very worried about something. Does that make sense?"

Conrad was about to sneer at him until Harvath applied more pressure to the man's wrist. The ambassador started nodding like his head was on a spring. "It does. It does," he repeated.

Harvath eased up on the pressure. "Now, I know you've already been told this, but I'm going to repeat it. What I was doing in the UAE is none of your business. Do you understand that?"

The ambassador glared at him until Harvath made ready to press his wrist again.

"I understand," said Conrad. "Totally."

"Good," Harvath replied. "One more thing. You are an insult to the people you are supposed to be leading. In fact, you're an insult to anyone who has ever chosen a career of service to the United States. There are a lot of people out there risking a hell of a lot more than you to keep our country safe. When you insult the people working for you, you're insulting all of us.

"We do what we do because we believe in something outside ourselves; something bigger. If you're lucky enough to stay in the Foreign Service, and you ever get asked again to help a fellow American, your only answer is going to be *yes*. Do you understand me? Because that's your *fucking* job. Not throwing parties, not riding camels, not rubbing elbows with oil-soaked sheiks just so you have some cool pictures to show off. Your job is about serving the nation, *our* nation. Got it?"

Harvath cranked down on his wrist to drive the point home and the ambassador nodded even faster as tears formed at the corners of his eyes from the pain.

Standing up from the bed, Harvath prepared to let go of the man's wrist, but stopped. "By the way," he added. "If I ever hear of you bullying any of your staff ever again, Leslie, I'm going to come find you and I'm going to tear both of your arms out of their sockets. Are we clear?"

The man kept nodding until Harvath let go of his wrist.

After using the lavatory, Harvath returned to his seat. When he passed by the ambassador, the man was pretending to be asleep. He didn't look at Harvath for the rest of the flight.

When the G650 finally landed at Andrews Air Force Base, Harvath remained seated as the ambassador and his people deplaned. Bringing up the rear was the security agent who had pretended to be asleep while Harvath had dressed down the ambassador. He paused next to Harvath's seat and both men locked eyes. Harvath wondered if the Diplomatic Security Service agent was going to admonish him for his less-than-professional behavior.

Instead, the agent smiled and held out his fist. Harvath gave him a bump and the man deplaned. Nothing else needed to be said. Probably everyone at the embassy in Abu Dhabi had wanted to do what Harvath had done on this flight. Very few things are as uplifting as seeing a bully get punched in the nose.

Once the ambassador's team had deplaned, Lydia Ryan boarded. "Nice plane," she said. "How was your flight?"

"Center seat. Crying baby," Harvath replied as he got up and started passing the bags forward. "Give me some good news. Where do we stand on everything?"

Ryan moved aside as members of her crash team came aboard and accepted the luggage. "So far, we're a bust on the six engineering students. We don't have any record of them leaving the country, so we assume they're still here. The FBI is interviewing everyone who had any contact with them via the internship program."

"What about the phones? They were each given one and told to turn it on when they arrived."

"Lots of people turn on their phones when they land, especially at a busy international airport like Houston's. The NSA has compiled a list of all the phones turned on, in and around the airport, on that day. They're trying to winnow it down now."

"So other than that," Harvath replied, "we don't have anything. Nothing at all."

Until recently, Ryan had known Harvath only by reputation. Then she had worked with him. Bureaucrats and politicians were afraid of him precisely because of the traits that made him successful. He couldn't be put in a box and told what to do. He operated outside the box and wouldn't stop until he had achieved whatever task had been set for him. She had zeroed in on his fear of failure almost immediately. He was one of the most driven people she had ever met.

Ryan was about to say something when a member of the crash team poked his head back in the cabin and said, "We're good to go."

Ryan thanked him and turned back to Harvath. "You did a good job. A *really* good job."

Praise normally made him uncomfortable, and he brushed it aside. "Who's lead on everything now? Where's the investigation being coordinated from?"

"Your ride will fill you in."

"My ride?"

Ryan pointed out the window at a black Chevy Suburban. "Reed is here to pick you up. I'm going back to Langley. I want to turn our geek squad loose on the laptops and hard drives right away."

"Will you keep me in the loop?"

Ryan smiled. "Absolutely. In the meantime, get some rest. You look like shit."

Harvath smiled back and followed her out of the plane. Standing at the top of the airstairs, he watched as she descended. Her team had loaded the bags into a Sikorsky S-76 helicopter and its rotors were already churning the humid late-summer air. As soon as she had climbed inside and put her headset and seat belt on, the helo lifted off, its landing gear retracted, and the bird banked northwest for the short hop to Langley.

Walking down the airstairs, he thought about the intel Ryan was carrying with her. Tracking down Hanjour had been a success, but he wondered whether it would be the string that would unravel the entire plot. Nothing was ever easy in their business, and no one knew that better than Reed Carlton.

As Harvath crossed the tarmac to the black SUV, he hoped the Old Man would have good news for him.

CHAPTER 24

Well aware that his protégé would be wiped out from the long flight, Carlton had stopped and picked up coffee—black with two shots of espresso. He'd seen Harvath order it enough times to know that's how he took it when he needed a lift. As they drove off the base, he handed it to him.

"I've heard Ambassador Conrad is a real piece of work," he said.

Harvath peeled the lid off his cup and blew on the surface of his coffee. "He's a real piece of something."

The Old Man chuckled. "Well, you'll be happy to know that he isn't headed straight to the Four Seasons."

"No?"

"No. He's been ordered to Foggy Bottom. Whatever ass-chewing he got over the phone in Abu Dhabi, the Sec State wants to repeat in person."

Harvath took a sip of coffee before replying. "I think the Sec State is going to find the ambassador has a much improved attitude."

Carlton took his eyes off the road for a moment to look at him. "Why? What'd you do?"

"Nothing. Don't worry about it."

The Old Man doubted that, but he let it go. There were more important things to discuss. He needed to debrief Harvath and be walked all the way through the Karachi and Dubai operations.

For his part, Harvath wanted to know what they were going to do next. He was exhausted. He didn't want to rehash Karachi and Dubai, not now. Besides, the Old Man would expect written reports on everything anyway.

Nevertheless, Harvath understood this was how things worked. If they didn't do it while it was fresh in his mind, they might miss something. So as they drove, Harvath provided the Old Man with an extensive accounting of everything that had happened.

They discussed what had gone wrong and what had gone right. Occasionally, Carlton injected some Monday morning quarterbacking about how Harvath could have done things differently. The goal was to make him a better operative and Harvath understood that, but it didn't mean he agreed with everything the Old Man said. It had been a long time since Carlton had been in the field.

At the end of the day, Harvath had gotten the jobs done in Karachi and Dubai. That's all that mattered. He wasn't in the mood for advice on how he could make improvements. Right now, what he wanted to focus on was how to move forward.

Mercifully, they had just turned onto his road and were nearing his house. Not that the Old Man would have let him change the subject just because they had arrived at their destination. He and Harvath had a lot in common—neither of them stopped until he had everything he wanted.

Harvath saw the entrance to his driveway up ahead. Normally when he returned home, he was happy to be back. It meant that whatever job he had gone off to do was completed and he could relax. Those times when he couldn't relax, when he had seen terrible things he couldn't get out of his mind, he would engage in what he referred to as "Potomac therapy."

Grabbing a six-pack, or sometimes something stronger, he would head down to his dock. Watching the boats pass by, he would drink until whatever was bothering him no longer bothered him. Once it was locked in an iron box and shoved into the darkest corner of his mind, he would reengage the civilized world, ready for the next challenge its uncivilized inhabitants were preparing to throw at him.

Today, though, felt different. He'd been successful, but the task was far from over. Worse still, he had no idea what, if any, role he was going to have going forward. His trip had technically been a success, but it felt a lot like failure. There had to be more he could do.

As they rolled up to the gate, Carlton fished out his set of keys from his pocket and handed them to Harvath. The Old Man was one of the few people Harvath trusted with keys to his property.

Hopping out of the air-conditioned Suburban, Harvath was greeted with all of the sights, sounds, and smells that he associated with being home.

Home was a small, renovated eighteenth-century stone church known as Bishop's Gate. It stood on several acres of land overlooking the Potomac River, just south of George Washington's Mount Vernon estate, and technically belonged to the United States Navy.

The mothballed property had been contracted to Harvath on a ninety-nine-year lease for one dollar per year. It was a prior president's way of thanking him for his service to the nation. The Secretary of the Navy had agreed, finding it fitting that the house would be occupied by a U.S. Navy SEAL.

In typical Harvath fashion, he had been reluctant

to accept such a generous gift. It didn't matter that the President made the case that he'd be doing the Navy a favor by living in and maintaining the property. When Harvath politely refused, the President said, "Just go look at it and then make up your mind."

Harvath had driven out to Bishop's Gate with anything *but* an open mind. There was no way he could imagine himself accepting such largess. It didn't seem right. Then he drove up the long drive and his mind began to change. It was an incredible property.

Despite the fact that it needed lots of work, he began to envision himself living there. When he discovered the sign with the motto of the Anglican missionaries—*I go overseas to give help*—he knew he was home.

Even though this time he returned with the weight of the world on his shoulders, it still felt good to be home. Unlocking the gate, he swung it open and climbed back in the SUV.

Carlton parked at the top of the drive and the two men went inside. After turning off the alarm, Harvath fired up the air-conditioning and led Carlton back to the kitchen.

He opened up the windows to pull a cross breeze, and then looked to see what he had in his fridge. "Are you hungry?"

"I ate before I picked you up."

"How about something to drink?"

Carlton looked at his watch. He knew he wasn't being offered a soft drink. "A bit early, don't you think?"

"I'm still on Karachi time and I've been dying for a beer all week."

"Is that all you have? Beer?"

"Beer and debutante heroin," said Harvath as he pulled a six-pack and a bottle of chardonnay from the fridge.

Carlton gave him a look and asked, "When did you start drinking white wine?"

"It's not mine. Lara and Marco were here for a visit before I left. I've got juice boxes, too, if you want one."

The Old Man smiled. Harvath had dated some terrific women, but he really liked Lara and her little boy. It was a shame they lived all the way up in Boston. "Is that Lone Star beer?" he asked.

Harvath nodded, grabbed one for each of them, and put everything else back in the fridge. He opened the bottles, flicked the caps into the sink, and joined Carlton at the kitchen table. "Cheers."

The Old Man took his beer, clinked it against Harvath's, and returned the toast.

Harvath took a long swallow. There was nothing like a cold beer on a hot day. *Scratch that.* There was nothing like a cold beer on a hot day when you have been overseas dreaming of nothing but.

Carlton settled back in his chair. "I'm guessing you've got fifteen, maybe twenty minutes tops before you fall asleep on me. What do you want to know?"

Finally, thought Harvath, *answers*. "Everything. Let's start with who's in charge?"

"Our piece fell under CIA with DoD support. The Gold Dust op is DoD with CIA support. Everything in the United States is FBI and is being overseen by the Director of National Intelligence and coordinated out of the National Counter Terrorism Center."

"Where are they in hunting the six engineering students down?"

"From what I understand, they haven't reached out to state and local law enforcement because they don't want it leaked to the press. They're afraid that could accelerate the attack."

"Has anyone ID'd the mosque these guys might have attended while they were in Houston?"

"The FBI is working on it," said Carlton, "but they haven't found one."

"Do we know how pious they actually were? Did they frequent strip clubs? Did they drink alcohol? Did they drink alcohol at a strip club and say something to one of the strippers that could be useful?"

"Once again, that'd be the FBI. This is priority number one for them. They've been pulling agents from across the country and sending them down to Houston to conduct interviews."

"You and I both know that interviews may not be enough," said Harvath.

The Old Man nodded. "The President knows that, too."

"What's he prepared to do?"

"On the record? Everything that is necessary to prevent this attack from happening."

"And off the record?" Harvath asked.

"Off the record, he actually *means* it. Which means he's ready to use us."

"What about Sloane and Chase? Where are they?"

"On their way back from Karachi," said Carlton. "They'll be in tonight."

"And then what are we going to do?"

"We're going to pray."

"Pray for what?" said Harvath.

The Old Man took a long drink of beer. "We're going to pray that we catch a break. A big one."

They finished their beers in silence and then Harvath walked the Old Man back out to his SUV.

"I can't help but feel there's something we may be missing here," said Carlton.

Harvath smiled. "You always feel that way."

"So do you," he replied.

"That's only because paranoia is highly infectious."

This time, it was the Old Man who smiled. "If this was your operation, if you were running cells here with six engineering students out of the UAE, what would be your biggest concern? What would be the thing that kept you up at night?"

Harvath thought about the question for a minute before answering. "Usually, it's the little things that screw it all up. Most people lack discipline and because of that, they lose focus."

"You don't think engineering students have discipline?"

He shook his head. "I would imagine they do, but my concern would be their motivation. Why are they doing this? The control files we get off Hanjour's computer will tell us for sure, but I'm willing to bet this is all about money for them. This isn't about Islamic ideology."

"There were some pretty sharp, pretty well-educated guys among the 9/11 hijackers," said Carlton.

"But that was a martyrdom operation. They were recruited because of their ideology. Our engineering students were recruited because of their backgrounds."

"Okay, so if you were their handler, what would be the one thing you would worry most about them doing that could blow the operation?"

Harvath let the question percolate for a moment and then replied, "I think I may have an idea."

"What is it?"

"Come back inside and I'll show you."

CHAPTER 25

When Tai Cheng traveled to the United States, he preferred American Airlines. Their flight crews weren't as professional as the Asian or European carriers; they were too informal, too chummy, but he always developed excellent American contacts while flying in their first class. They tended to be men and women of means with wide circles of acquaintance. It was a boon for a Chinese intelligence operative always looking for ways to expand his human network. Being subjected to American English for the interminably long flight also helped get his mind in the game.

He was entering the country as he always did, as a Chinese entrepreneur named Bao Deng, traveling on a legitimate American green card issued by the United States government. It was his golden ticket. Never once was he detained, hassled, or given a second look.

The American green card had cost him, or more appropriately had cost the Second Department, only five hundred thousand dollars. Posing as a wealthy Chinese businessman, he had invested in a poultry-processing plant in rural Nebraska. That was all it had taken. In exchange for the investment, plus lawyers' fees and a little paperwork, his Bao Deng identity had been granted a green card and permanent resident status.

The only thing the Americans cared about was money. They would sell their worst enemy the keys to the castle as long as the price was right. It never ceased to amaze him how easily their national security apparatus could be circumvented.

After moving effortlessly through customs and immigration, he exited the Tom Bradley International terminal and headed for American Airlines' domestic operations in Terminal 4. He had passed through LAX so many times that he knew it like the back of his hand.

He cleared security for Terminal 4 and, towing his wheel-aboard bag behind him, walked down the concourse to the American Airlines Admirals Club. His contact would not arrive for another hour, so Cheng availed himself of a hot shower, a shave, and something to eat. As much as he despised America and its decadent culture, there were some things the Americans got right. Of course all of these things came with a price—far outside the reach of the everyday man or woman.

The bartender asked if Cheng wanted a cocktail or glass of wine to go with his meal. The intelligence operative declined. He never drank when he was on assignment, and seldom even when he was at home. It dulled the senses and made you susceptible to all forms of entrapment or attack. He had only made one recent exception—when he had learned of his wife's infidelity.

He should have anticipated it. Mi was a beautiful but weak woman. She had been a rising Chinese actress. Modeling jobs had led to bit parts in low-budget movies. From there the budgets had increased and so had the roles. She had graduated from playing the attractive girlfriend of mobsters and street thugs to roles of sensitivity, scope, and intelligence. But with fame had come temptation. In her case, it had been drugs, and drugs had been her downfall.

When Cheng had discovered her, she had hit bottom, twice, and was attempting for a third time to get back on her feet. Cheng was a handsome man in his own right, ten years her senior. He had seen all of her films. For him, it was love at first sight.

She had returned to her family in Nanjing. He had been there on business. She had stopped into her father's restaurant to speak with him. Cheng had followed her home and arranged to "bump" into her the next day.

They dated for a year and he came to see her in Nanjing whenever possible. He knew important people in the city and made sure favors were done for her family. A small-time criminal enterprise had been shaking down her father. When he learned about it, he brought a stop to it immediately. The family loved him. They had no idea what he did for a living, only that he was a businessman who traveled often and brought them wonderful gifts. If Mi had any suspicions whatsoever, she never voiced them.

Her heart had been repeatedly broken in her painful rise to fledgling stardom and all along her subsequent fall. It had been torn from her chest again and again. Eventually, she had learned it was safer to feign love than to actually succumb to it.

She had wanted to love Cheng, but she couldn't. It was as if the capacity to love no longer existed in her. She loved her family, though. That love had not been ground down and blown away. And they loved Cheng, or at least they loved what he did for them. In her way, she also loved what he did for them. But loving the deeds and loving the man were two different things.

There was something about him, something she couldn't put her finger on. She didn't want to call it evil, but she didn't know what other word to use. It was cold and dark. She caught flashes of it from time to time and it frightened her.

Sometimes she chastised herself for feeling that way. She had never seen any outward acts that could specifically be described as evil, but there was something burning just below his surface that she was certain wasn't good.

With her own heart a cold, dead thing that did nothing more than move blood through her body, she feigned love for Cheng. She did it for her family. She did it for herself. She still had her looks and Cheng wanted her. He was a good lover and he would provide for her and help protect and provide for her family. They dated and she agreed, with squeals of joy and the most passionate love scene she had ever performed, to marry him.

She had slept with so many two-bit producers, directors, and casting agents on her way up the ladder that she couldn't recall all of them. She could, though, remember the after-hours trips to the doctors. The ones with the cold, nondescript offices who would scrape the consequences of her thirst for fame from her womb. She remembered them all, especially the last one, the one who had arrived smelling of gin and who had rendered her barren. She would never forget him, ever.

She came to see it as a blessing. Cheng didn't want to have children and in a sad way, she saw it as a sign that they were meant to be together. Perhaps they were meant to start anew, to slingshot each other forward.

Cheng's home was in Beijing. He lived in the Chaoyang district near the St. Regis Hotel. He liked to be close to the action, he said, so he could entertain his clients when they came to the city.

On weekends when he was in town, he would take her sightseeing to the Temple of Heaven and the pearl market, or Hou Hai Lake and the Summer Palace. When he traveled, he encouraged her to go back home and be with her family, or to invite them to come to Beijing. He was incredibly generous, and she sometimes lamented not being able to love him. Her mother, so dependent upon his generosity, railed against Mi if she so much as gained an ounce between visits. They all expected her to stay as attractive as possible for her husband. There was no doubt the role she filled for her family. Her husband was the meal and she was the ticket.

She settled into an uneasy but somewhat predictable rhythm with him. When he was home, they never stayed there longer than was necessary to make love, grab some sleep, change clothes, and go back out. Cheng was a physical fitness fanatic. He involved her in none of his businesses, but he expected her to run and lift weights with him when he was in town, and to continue the practice without him when he was gone.

With or without clients, they ate at the best restaurants and danced at the best nightclubs. This was her favorite part. People recognized her, and Cheng proudly showed her off. She was glad to see what he was getting out of the relationship. She wasn't just a sex object—he could have slept with her without marrying her—she was a status symbol to him. In fashionable, fast-moving Beijing, she was an extension of him, a reflection of his worth. Only an important, successful man could land a woman like her.

Suddenly, her past no longer mattered. She began,

slowly, to think about the future. Cheng had begun talking about buying a house on a lake outside Nanjing—one that they could spend summers in. He talked about her father working too hard, that he should hand more of the business off to her brother so he and her mother could enjoy the warmer months along with them. It was like a fairy tale, and in that fairy tale the black ice that surrounded her heart was beginning to melt.

Of course she was a fool not to see what was happening. Cheng knew her better than she knew herself. He knew she didn't love him, not truly, and he had been looking for every single thing he could do to make her fall for him. He had quietly interrogated her parents, her siblings, and anyone who had known her as Mi the person, not Mi the actress. He spoke with two aunts and even an old schoolteacher. What made Mi tick? What were her fears and what did she dream about? He had tried to ask her, but she always told him she was happy, and that she had everything she could ever want.

The summer home near Nanjing had been a stroke of genius on Cheng's part. Even just talking about it produced a noticeable change in his wife, but he was convinced that there had to be more, something else he could do that would melt the rest of the ice and win her heart once and for all.

Amazingly enough, the best suggestion had come from someone at the Second Department—another intelligence agent. Cheng had overheard him talking about how his relationship with his wife had been faltering. He had tried, as best he believed any man could do, to listen and attempt to reconnect with her. He had wanted to do something big, put a score on the board that would keep him out front for a long time. He succeeded and had blown his wife away.

The men had eagerly gathered around him to learn how he had done it. "Simple," he responded. "I stopped treating her like my wife and started treating her like a target."

It was both disturbing and brilliant at the same time. Cheng had kicked himself for not having thought of it sooner. He paid more attention to and knew more about his intelligence assets than he did his own wife. It wasn't for lack of trying. For some reason, he just hadn't found that secret channel to her heart. He decided to flip everything on its head and treat her like he would any target he had been assigned. He wanted to know everything about her—where she went, what she did, who she saw, right down to what she thought. If he could do that, he would have the intelligence he needed to finally win her over completely.

In his rush to know his wife, Tai Cheng sped right by one of the most popular Chinese proverbs—one known even by every child—*be careful what you wish for*. And as he sped right by it, he crashed and burned.

The Chinese entertainment industry was littered with the mistakes of young actors and actresses. Some were so desperate for fame and advancement that they would do almost anything. Throw in drugs and a stalled or failed career, and "almost anything" became "anything."

When Mi had reached the "anything" stage, she had slept with multiple men to support her habit. Pictures had been taken, and unbeknownst to her a video had been made. That video had made its way into the hands of a Communist Party official who could not have shown up in her world at a worse time.

She had gotten her life together, she was trying to learn to love her husband, and she desperately wanted her marriage to work. Things were actually going her way. She was as close to happy as she could ever remember being. Then a snippet of the video showed up in an email. Her husband "never needed to know." "One time together" and the official would destroy the tape. She couldn't see any other way out. She didn't want to lose her husband. As stupid and wrong and deceitful as it was, she agreed to meet with the official.

They had met at a hotel while Cheng was out of town. It was to be a onetime thing. One and done. But it was only the beginning. The blackmailer called her for another meeting within a week.

In his desire to know his wife better, Cheng had violated the trust that should remain sacred between a husband and wife. He had spied on her. And it wasn't just spying. He followed her, bugged her cell phone, and hacked into her email account. That was how he had discovered the affair. That was when he had gone over the edge.

He sent Mi to her parents in Nanjing. He didn't tell her why. She was terrified. *Did he know? Was their marriage over? What would happen to her? What would happen to her family?* She had been given a second chance at life and she had screwed it up. No husband sent his wife away without warning or explanation unless something was very bad. She knew what it was. She knew why she had been exiled.

No sooner had Cheng gotten Mi out of their home in Beijing than he started drinking, heavily. No matter how proficient at meting out violence or death they might be, intelligence operatives were social by nature. Their business involved guns and knives and all sorts of black arts, but at its heart it was about people. You could not recruit and control people if you didn't understand them. In his way, Cheng understood his wife.

By spying on her, he had come to better appreciate her pain. His only regret was that he hadn't done it earlier. He blamed himself. He had plucked her from ignominy in Nanjing, polished her up, and brought her back out, all bright and shiny, to be put on display in Beijing. In a certain way, he had asked for what had happened. He had been prideful, boastful, a show-off. He had used his wife's allure to make him feel like more of a man. How could he expect that men wouldn't take notice of her? That's what he had wanted and that's what had happened.

He may have borne some responsibility for what had happened, but not all of it. The worst offender was the official who was blackmailing his wife. Cheng could think of no worse a character than a man who would prey on women, particularly someone else's woman.

It made no difference that the man in question was a high-ranking party official. He could have been on the PSC for all Cheng cared. His sin was unforgivable. There was only one way he could make restitution— with his life.

But before he died, Cheng wanted the man to repent for what he had done. While he could have beaten him into repentance and then death, Cheng wanted it to appear to have been an accident. The less people suspected, the less of an investigation would be conducted. The man was overweight, a drinker, and a heavy smoker. A heart attack wouldn't have surprised anyone, but that might elicit pity. He wanted people to shake their heads when they reflected on the embarrassing stupidity of his death.

Cheng waited until the official's family had gone to

Shanghai for the weekend and he was alone. When he came home from dinner and drinking, Cheng, pistol in hand, was waiting for him. The man was belligerent at first. He had no idea what was happening. He thought it was a robbery. Then Cheng explained who he was and why he was there. The blood drained from the party official's face completely. He was afraid, and with good reason.

Cheng forced the official to hand over the video of his wife. Then he forced him to open the email account he had used to solicit her. When that was done, Cheng directed the man to a small powder room off the kitchen.

There, a bottle of scotch and a glass sat on the sink. Cheng ordered him to fill the glass and drink it down. The man found it difficult. He was already drunk and gagged several times. Eventually, he succeeded. Cheng then told him to refill the glass and do it again.

As the man tried to get the smoky beverage down his raw esophagus and into his inflamed stomach, Cheng explained the price he would exact on the man's legacy.

Chinese culture was about its male heirs. The party official had been blessed with one boy. Cheng explained that the boy would spend the rest of his life paying for the sins of the father. Drugs and a murder weapon had already been planted in his apartment where police would find them. He had made sure the boy had no alibi. His life would be ruined and along with it, the family's reputation. Everything the party official had worked so hard for was about to crumble.

Enraged, the man charged, but Cheng was ready for him. He deftly parried the clumsy attack and spun him back into the bathroom where he stumbled and ran headfirst into the toilet. He lay on the floor not moving. Cheng felt for a pulse. He was alive, but unconscious.

Cheng picked up the glass and the bottle of scotch in his gloved hands and placed them on the island in the kitchen. He then retrieved the Styrofoam cooler hidden in the front closet, along with a bath towel and roll of painter's tape.

Standing on a stool, he sealed off the bathroom vent with the painter's tape and then rolled the block of dry ice from the cooler into the sink and turned on the faucet. He took a camera-phone picture of the man's position on the floor and then adjusted his legs so they would clear the door.

Removing the stool from the bathroom, he exited and pulled the door shut behind him, leaving the party official still unconscious on the floor. He stuffed the towel into the crack under the door and then sealed the rest of the edges with the painter's tape. After that, all he had to do was let the dry ice do the work.

While he waited, Cheng cleared out all traces of communication with his wife from the party official's computer. When enough time had passed, he unsealed the tiny bathroom and looked inside. The carbon dioxide from the dry ice had done its job. The man was dead.

Consulting the picture, Cheng positioned the body as it had been. He then stripped away the rest of the painter's tape from the vent and stuffed all of it, along with the towel, back into the cooler and set it near the front door.

For carbon monoxide poisoning to be believable, there had to be a source. Cheng walked back into the kitchen and, searching through the fridge, cupboards, and freezer, assembled an array of fatty, unhealthy foods—the same kind someone might want to cook up after a night of drinking—and set them on the counter next to the stove. He then turned on the oven and two burners, blew out their flames, and left the oven door open.

He waited to make sure enough gas would collect in the room. Once he was satisfied, he left the party official's home, returned to his life, and kept watch for news of the man's death.

When word did finally make it to the Second Department, it was just as Cheng had planned. It had been ruled an accident—death by stupidity, as many were calling it. He had been so drunk, he didn't realize his gas had been left on. Suffering from carbon monoxide poisoning, he had fallen, hit his head, and died.

Based on the man's reputation, no one was surprised. He became a cautionary tale of what lies at the end of the road to excess. When speaking of him, people simply shook their heads. No one remembered what, if anything, he had accomplished, only how ignobly he had died.

It was a fitting demise. Cheng chose to leave the son alone. He did not deserve to be punished for the monster of a man his father was. Cheng's battle with the party official was over, but his battle with himself had just begun.

He slipped into a drunken haze. He ignored his wife's attempts to contact him. He ignored his friends, and, most unforgivable of all, he ignored calls from the Second Department. Colonel Shi then came to see him personally. Cheng was a mess. When he wouldn't answer his questions, Shi began digging, starting with the man's wife.

Shi eventually put everything together, but Cheng

was in no condition to care. When the colonel asked him if he'd been behind the death of the party official, Cheng ignored him. That was the only confirmation Shi needed, and he ordered him to pull himself together.

That was the last he had heard from the colonel or anyone else, until Shi informed him he was going to America to carry out at least one operation, and possibly two. It wasn't a request. It was another order. And when it was explained what he was expected to do, Cheng had debated resigning on the spot. Such theatrics, though, would have been useless. He would have been given two very clear alternatives, comply or face a speedy trial and receive a bullet to the back of the head.

There was so much wrong with what Cheng had been asked to do that he didn't know where to start. Moving so quickly was dangerous. Doing things right took time. Unfortunately, time was something China did not have. The General Secretary, the Politburo Standing Committee, Colonel Shi, and General Wu were expecting him to move as rapidly as possible. They had, though, made one concession. Since Cheng knew the United States best, he would handle the details as he saw fit. They would not micromanage him from Beijing. All that mattered were his results.

Now, sitting in the American Airlines Admirals Club, he looked up from his *Wall Street Journal* and noticed a young man of Chinese heritage approach. He pointed to the seat on the other side of the power port next to Cheng. "My iPhone is almost dead. Is anybody sitting here?"

Cheng shook his head and motioned for the young man to sit down. He was carrying a small plate of carrots and celery. "Where did you get the vegetables?" Cheng asked.

The young man nodded back toward the bar area. They had just put them out, near the coffee station.

Cheng folded his paper, set it on the arm of his chair, and stood up. "Would you mind watching my things for a minute? I'm going to go get some."

"Sure thing."

Cheng went to the bar area, fixed himself a plate of vegetables, and returned. The young man had plugged his iPhone into the power port, plugged his earbuds in, and was now listening to music. Cheng slid the *Wall Street Journal* into his suitcase and ate his vegetables.

Twenty minutes later, the young man unplugged his iPhone and left the lounge.

Cheng waited for fifteen minutes and then followed. He stood on the other side of the concourse and watched as the young man boarded the flight to Omaha. Once the door had closed and the plane had taxied away from the terminal, Cheng retrieved the boarding pass that the young man had slid inside his *Wall Street Journal*.

After checking the name and departure time, he then sought out his gate and his new flight to Nashville.

CHAPTER 26

A re you getting all of this?" Les Johnson asked as he watched the buzz of activity through his binoculars.

About three square miles of the valley had been fenced like a large tic-tac-toe board with something going on in every square. In one, men were learning how to operate old tractors. In another, men on horseback were being shown how to herd cattle. There were pens with pigs, pastures with sheep, llamas, goats, and more cows, along with field after field planted with all kinds of crops.

A water wheel built along the stream powered a gristmill of some sort. Red-and-white-bladed windmills pumped water into troughs for the animals. American cars and trucks from the seventies and early eighties traveled along dusty roads, transporting hundreds of people and assorted supplies. If this wasn't the DPRK, it could have easily been a scene right out of the American heartland. Even the clothes looked American.

"I'm getting it," replied Jimi Fordyce as he took picture after picture.

"What the hell are they up to?"

"Farming," the little boy answered when pressed by Billy Tang. His name was Jin-Sang, but after all three

SEALs had called the kid *Ginseng* for the fourth time, Tang had given up trying to correct them.

Jin-Sang was eleven and looked eight years old only because he was so badly malnourished. Tang had offered the boy some of his peanut butter and he had scarfed it down and then looked to the rest of the group to see what else they might have to offer. He had huge eyes and an unbelievably frail body. It was no wonder to any of them that his leg had snapped so easily.

Though terribly underweight, the boy was indeed bright. He had lots of questions for Billy Tang, but Tang wasn't interested in sharing anything but pain meds and nourishment with the little guy. The American had his own questions.

The boy knew something bad had almost befallen him. He wasn't sure what the other three soldiers had intended to do to him, but he knew it was serious. He also knew it was Tang who had intervened on his behalf, even to the extent of pointing a gun at one of his comrades. While the boy didn't understand everything that was going on, he knew enough to know he needed to stay on Tang's good side.

"Where do you live?" Tang had asked.

"In the camp," the boy replied.

"The soldiers' camp?"

"No, the prison camp."

"Are you a criminal?" Tang asked.

Jin-Sang shook his head. "My father was. They brought us all to the camp."

"Is your father at the camp?"

"No," the boy said. "He is dead."

"What about your mother?"

Tears welled up in the boy's eyes. "She is also dead. They both died in there."

"You said you have a sister?"

Jin-Sang wiped away his tears. "Yes, but she is sick. She needs food, meat. I also make tea from the pine needles. They have vitamins."

Tang was aware of the tea North Koreans made from pine needles. It contained a ton of Vitamin C. "If you're a prisoner, what are you doing out of the camp?"

"I was born there."

"Born there?"

"Yes, my sister was five years old when my father was arrested and they brought us here."

"But how did you get out?" Tang asked him.

"I know the camp and I know the guards. The camp is not well maintained. As long as I bring them rabbits, the guards pretend I do not sneak out and I pretend there are no holes in the fence."

"Jin-Sang, look at me," Tang had insisted. "How long will it take them to notice you did not return last night?"

The boy shrugged.

"Have you ever gone out and not returned to the camp the same night?"

The boy shook his head.

"Will the guards come looking for you?"

The boy shrugged again. Tang was getting frustrated. He knew how evil the camps were. All of the prisoners, including the children, were taught to snitch on one another. Even family members were encouraged to turn one another in. Informants were rewarded with extra rations. "What about your classmates, your teacher? They'll notice you are gone."

"There is no school tomorrow," the boy replied.

If Jin-Sang was telling the truth, that was good news. But there was no way to verify his story. The kid was a little hustler, a survivor. He would say and do anything to get what he wanted—what he *needed* to live another day. That made all his statements suspect.

Even so, they had to find out what he knew.

"Why are the Chinese here?" Tang asked him.

"For farming."

"What about farming?"

"My sister is sick," said the boy. "She needs food and medicine."

"Focus on my question, Jin-Sang. Why are the Chinese here?"

Tears began in the boy's eyes again. "Please," he said. "My sister. She needs food, medicine."

Though Fordyce couldn't understand the words the boy was saying, emotion was universal. "What's he upset about?" he asked from behind his camera.

"There's a labor camp in the valley. He and his sister are prisoners. He says she's sick and that she needs food and medicine."

"If he's a prisoner in a labor camp, what's he doing out here?"

"Apparently, he's a good little trapper. He's bought off some of the guards by bringing back rabbits for them. They look the other way when he sneaks out."

"What's wrong with his sister?" asked Tucker. "What are her symptoms?"

Tang asked Jin-Sang and translated as the boy spoke. "Cough. Fever and night sweats. She has lost a lot of weight."

"Is she coughing anything up?"

Tang asked the boy and then looked at Tucker and nodded. "He says sometimes there's blood."

Even before the response, Tucker had already begun digging into his medical kit. He removed a surgical mask and handed it to Tang. "Explain to Ginseng that he needs to put this on and keep it on."

"Why?"

"Because it sounds like his sister has TB."

"Tuberculosis?" Tang replied as he explained to Jin-Sang what he was doing and then helped place the mask on the boy.

Tucker nodded. "Multi-drug-resistant tuberculosis is a shape-shifter and it's surging in North Korea. We're not taking any chances."

Jin-Sang said something and Tang translated. "He wants to know if we have medicine that will help his sister."

Tucker was about to answer when Fordyce interrupted him. "You tell him that before we talk about helping his sister, we need to know what's going on down there."

Tang relayed Fordyce's directive and waited for the little boy to respond. When he did, Tang said, "The Chinese are here for farming."

Fordyce set his camera down. "We got that point. But first of all, how does he even know what China is? They only teach these kids enough reading to understand how to operate sweatshop equipment. They never learn more than basic addition and subtraction."

"He says his father had worked for the North Korean government. He had been a trade negotiator. Not only spoke Korean, but English and Chinese, too. He fell out of favor and was accused of taking bribes. That's what led to the family's imprisonment. His father taught him where China was and that if he could ever escape, that's where he and his sister should go."

"So why didn't he? If he's able to get out of the camp, why hasn't he run?"

Tang waited for the boy to explain and then said, "Because the parents made the children promise to watch over each other. He wants to run, but his sister has been too afraid. Rather than leave without her, he's been staying to protect her."

The men respected the young boy's sense of honor.

"So his father taught him about China," Fordyce clarified. "What has he learned about the Chinese since they've been here?"

"He says they've been bringing through waves of farmers, thousands of them. They're also being given military training and have bullets that hurt real bad."

"What kind of bullets?"

Tang asked the boy to explain. When he was done, Tang replied, "It sounds like rubber ones."

"And they've been using them on the prisoners? What the hell for?"

"The Chinese have established multiple farms across the valley. Every couple of days, the guards select a group of prisoners and tell them that if they can successfully raid any of them, they will be given extra food. The Chinese are being trained how to defend their farms. That's why they're using the rubber bullets."

Tang paused for a moment before saying, "The Chinese are being told to envision the prisoners as starving Americans coming to steal from them."

Fordyce was repulsed by what he heard.

"He says," Tang continued, "that the Chinese farmers have even killed a few prisoners. Now, before each exercise, they are reminded not to attempt headshots, especially on the children. One of the kids Jin-Sang went to school with was killed by one of the rounds."

Fordyce shook his head. "Let's back up. Why *exactly* are the Chinese here? Does he know?"

The boy nodded and asked again about medicine and food for his sister.

"We're not doing anything for him, or his sister, until he tells us all he knows," Fordyce replied. "In fact, take that Fentanyl pop away from him. Maybe if his leg starts hurting again, he'll get more cooperative."

Tang looked at Fordyce. "Seriously?"

"As serious as a heart attack. We're running out of time on target."

"But he's just a kid."

"Listen to me closely, Billy. Maybe you've gotten used to operating by yourself in Indian country, but as long as you're on this team, you'll respect my command. Our orders are to gather as much intelligence as we can and get out. We're not here to open a children's hospital, dig a well, or build a new school. We're way behind enemy lines and the security of our country depends on what we do here. I will not allow this operation to fail because you can't do what needs to be done. Are we clear?"

Tang didn't like being spoken to that way. It mattered little that Fordyce was completely justified and that Tang had brought it upon himself. "We're crystal clear," Tang said, as he snatched the Fentanyl pop away from Jin-Sang.

As the startled boy looked at him, Tang launched into a series of angry questions in Korean. The boy would begin to answer, only to have Tang cut him off and either repeat the question or berate and browbeat the child. Tang's good-cop persona had completely evaporated. If Lieutenant Fordyce wanted him to play rough with an eleven-year-old, he would give him what he wanted.

The SEALs watched the exchange between Tang and Jin-Sang ebb and flow for a good fifteen minutes. Several times, the little boy was reduced to sobs.

When it was over, Tang handed him back the Fentanyl lollipop and pinched the bridge of his nose.

Fordyce waited until the quiet CIA operative opened his eyes before asking, "So?"

"You have no idea what this poor kid has seen."

"I'm sure it sucks. For right now, though, I only want to hear the details relevant to our mission. Got me?"

Billy Tang nodded. "The Chinese are here for both military and agricultural training."

"Two areas in which they far outpace the North Koreans. I don't buy it," Fordyce replied.

"From what I can gather, they aren't here to necessarily learn how to farm well, but to learn how to farm in extreme hardship. When the Soviet Union collapsed in the 1990s and agriculture-related subsidies to North Korea dried up, the North Koreans had to learn new methods very quickly."

"Yeah," said Tucker. "They *learned* how to starve. One million North Koreans died in that famine. That'd be like losing twelve million Americans. What could the Norks possibly have to teach anyone?"

"*How to survive*. How to survive with no pesticides. How to survive without commercial fertilizers. How to survive without electricity. How to survive without running water. How to survive with little to no fuel for generators or vehicles. How to breed and raise livestock under medieval conditions. How to ration much-needed supplies when they barely trickle in from abroad. And how to protect all of it from roving bands of angry, starving American citizens. That's what the North Koreans are teaching the Chinese."

"Do you believe him?" Fordyce asked.

"Do I think he's telling me the truth?" said Tang. "I think he would tell me anything if he thought it would help. But, yeah, I think he's telling me the truth."

"What about the nets? Those things are the size of football fields. We can see a lot of people coming and going, but what specifically are the buildings underneath them?"

"Jin-Sang has not been allowed in that sector, but his sister has. According to her, they have built a small American downtown, complete with storefronts, a restaurant, those kinds of things."

"Why?"

"For some reason, they think rural Americans are much more likely to survive the attack. They believe they will band together in small towns similar to what has been created here. Jin-Sang says the farmers may need to trade with them and may possibly recruit them as laborers. The town exists to teach them what they may encounter."

"What was his sister doing there? Was she a role-player?"

Tang nodded. "A role-player who speaks Chinese *and* English."

"The father taught her?"

Tang nodded again. "He saw it as a skill that could make her useful to the DPRK. Then they were arrested. He kept it up with her in the camp. Maybe it allowed them to secretly communicate, or maybe it just functioned as a way to hold on to something from their old life. It sounds like the father didn't put much effort into teaching Jin-Sang. Only words and phrases he thought might be helpful if they ever escaped to China."

"What about the attack?" Fordyce asked. "Does the boy know anything about it at all?"

"No, but he says his sister knows—a lot."

CHAPTER 27

FBI Special Agent Heidi Roe looked at the text that had just come across her BlackBerry. *Unbelievable.*

Her partner saw her shaking her head. "What's up?"

"Our task force officer in Nashville says Tommy Wong never got off the plane."

"You've got to be kidding me."

"I wish."

"What happened?"

"I have no idea," said Roe, "but I intend to find out. Are you good here if I duck out for a minute?"

Her partner nodded and Special Agent Roe stepped out of the conference room they had been assigned. It felt good to stand up and stretch her legs. They had been at it nonstop since arriving from Los Angeles. The FBI had brought their best people in from all across the country. They were in Houston to conduct interviews and follow up every single lead in relation to six Muslim engineering students who had gone missing and were suspected of plotting a mass-casualty terrorist attack on the U.S.

But just because the FBI had called for all hands on deck didn't mean other cases could be allowed to lapse. Roe and her partner had already been working on breaking the LA arm of a Chinese transnational criminal organization involved in narcotics and child sex trafficking. After identifying the major players, they had focused on members further down the food chain. Their hope was to find cause to arrest one of them, and then offer immunity if that person would become an FBI mole within the organization. Tommy Wong was the man they wanted.

They had placed Wong under loose surveillance and had been watching him for several months. They knew he was up to something. They just hadn't been able to put their finger on what that *something* was. To do that, they'd need to devote a lot more manpower to the surveillance. Roe had run it up the flagpole at the LA field office only to be told that without something more substantive, no additional resources could be assigned at this time.

It was a typical Catch-22. She knew the guy was dirty and her bosses knew he was dirty. He was too small a fish, though, to justify investing any more dollars in. But if they didn't invest more, they wouldn't get what they needed to roll him and move up the triad food chain. In her head, she understood the bureaucratic limits that she had to work under, but in her heart they still pissed her off. It was one of her biggest complaints about law enforcement. Cops and FBI agents had to operate by the rules. Bad guys were free to do whatever they wanted. Even with all the government's tools for eavesdropping, tracking, and surveillance, the bad guys still kept coming up with ways to stay ahead of them.

Roe, who had been an attorney before joining the FBI, understood the importance of law. Without it, freedom was impossible. She was amazed by how many

Americans, when asked what kind of system of government the U.S. had, would answer, "Democracy." America wasn't a democracy. It was a republic, and that was because of one thing—the law.

When each of her three kids started studying government in grade school, she made them watch a YouTube video called "The American Form of Government." She wanted them to understand why America was different and why their mom had joined the FBI and worked a lot of late nights and weekends.

The video began with Ben Franklin exiting the Constitutional Convention and being asked by a woman, "Sir, what have you given us?" Franklin's response? "A republic, ma'am. If you can keep it."

It then went on to describe the difference between a democracy and a republic. A democracy was where majority ruled. If a posse rode off after a horse thief, caught him, and voted fifteen to one to hang him, that was democracy. He would be hanged by the neck until dead.

In a republic, though, the sheriff arrives and tells the posse that they can't hang the alleged horse thief. He has to be returned to town where he will stand trial by a jury of his peers because that is what is dictated by law. In fact the word "republic" came from the Latin *res publica,* or the "public thing," meaning the law.

It took seeing the video for her kids to fully grasp that without law, there was chaos, and with too much law, there was tyranny. In order for the right balance to exist, the laws needed to be enforced and citizens needed to be vigilant stewards of the republic and strive to elect the most responsible leaders.

What the video didn't teach, and what she had tried to keep her young children shielded from, was the absolute evil that existed in the world. As an FBI agent she had seen horrors she hoped her children would never know about, much less experience. Man's capacity for inhumanity was boundless.

Roe had grown up in a solidly middle-class family with a mom, a dad, two siblings, and a cat, just outside Detroit. Her parents had taught her right from wrong and had encouraged her to become the best she could be. Their vision of the American dream was to see their children go farther in life than they had. Her parents had succeeded. Their daughter was happily married with a family of her own and she loved her job. When people screwed up, though, it made her angry.

Wong's purchase of a last-minute plane ticket to Nashville had immediately caught Roe's attention. There had been no phone or email contact with anyone in Nashville, and as far as they knew, Wong didn't have any friends or associates there either. It was completely out of character for him, which was why Roe and her partner had been so interested to see where he went and with whom he met. This could be the break they were looking for.

Pulling up the phone number in Nashville, Roe hit Dial and raised the phone to her ear. Moments later a man's voice answered on the other end.

"Detective Hoffman," the voice said.

"Detective Hoffman, this is Special Agent Roe."

"So you got my text?"

"Yes," she replied. "I got it, but I don't understand it."

"What don't you understand? Your guy didn't get off the flight."

"You're absolutely sure of that?"

"Positive."

"You were there, right?"

"I was there and your guy Tommy Wong wasn't. Trust me."

"You had the picture I sent and everything?"

Hoffman let out a condescending laugh. "Agent Roe, contrary to what a lot of folks might think, Nashville's a pretty cosmopolitan place. We get our share of Asian visitors. If I had a plane full of them, it might have been hard to spot your guy. This plane wasn't full of them."

"Were there any?"

"There were three—an old man in his seventies, a young girl in her twenties, and some middle-aged guy. There was no twenty-six-year-old matching the photo or description of Thomas 'Tommy' Wong. How positive are you that he got on the plane in the first place?"

As progressive as the FBI was, Roe had come up through the ranks feeling that she had to work twice as hard to prove herself as any male agent. She had a chip on her shoulder, but it was a small one. It manifested itself only when she thought she wasn't being treated with the proper respect. "I don't know how the Nashville PD does things, Detective Hoffman, but I wouldn't have asked you to be there if I didn't know for certain that Tommy Wong was on that plane."

"Did you see him get on?"

"No, but—"

"So you don't know *for sure* if Wong was on that plane, do you?"

Technically, Hoffman was correct, but Roe trusted and respected her LAPD colleagues. It was the same respect she was trying to extend Hoffman as a member of the Bureau's Nashville Organized Crime Task Force. Multiagency task forces were successful only if everyone did his job. She needed to win him over.

"You're right. My guys in LA might have screwed up," she admitted. "Are you still at the airport?" she asked.

"I'm on my way to the parking garage, why?"

"I need a favor. I don't like that your time was wasted. And I really don't like that we've lost track of Wong."

"What do you want?" Hoffman asked.

"How solid are your airport contacts?"

"They're not bad."

"Do you think you can get me a copy of the flight manifest and security camera footage of the passengers deplaning?"

"Probably. What are you going to do with it?"

"I'm going to use it as Exhibit A when I rip my LA people a new one."

"You can't do that without the footage or a manifest?"

"I could," Roe agreed. "But a picture is worth a thousand words. Besides, something doesn't feel right about this whole thing. I don't know what it is, but I want to see that footage for myself. Maybe there'll be another face I recognize."

"Give me forty-five minutes and I'll email you what I can. Okay?"

Roe smiled. "Thank you, detective. I really appreciate it."

The minute they hung up, she called her LAPD colleague.

Nancy Vargas answered on the third ring. "Vargas," she said, rolling the *r* and pronouncing her last name with a Spanish accent, despite being a fourth-generation Angelino.

"Nancy, it's Heidi."

"Hey. How's Houston?"

"Cloudy with a big chance of pissed off. What happened with Tommy Wong?"

"What do you mean?" Vargas asked.

"What happened at LAX?"

"Hold on a second. Let me find out."

Roe could tell that Vargas had taken the phone away from her ear and was holding it against her chest in order to mute her conversation. Though the sound was muffled, Roe could tell she was having a rather heated discussion with someone in her office.

When she came back on the line, Vargas said, "My officers confirm that they tailed Wong all the way to the airport and one of them watched him go through the security checkpoint. What happened?"

"What happened is that your people were supposed to confirm that Wong actually got on the plane."

"I know, but we're shorthanded and they got called out on another case. We figured if he made it through security, everything was good."

"Apparently, everything is not good. Our team in Nashville says he never got off the plane."

"Shit," Vargas replied. "He must have come back through after my officers left. I'm really sorry, Heidi."

Roe felt a migraine coming on.

"You guys were right. Wong's definitely up to something," said Vargas. "That was a hell of a ruse just to slip surveillance."

"A hell of an expensive ruse," Roe stated. "Why not just buy a cheap Southwest flight up to Oakland?"

"Your guess is as good as mine. In the meantime, you're in Houston, we're back in LA, and my guys dropped the ball. What can I do to fix this?"

Roe was about to respond when her other line

beeped. Pulling the phone away from her ear, she looked at the caller ID, then said, "Nancy, I'm going to have to call you back."

She didn't wait for Vargas to respond. Clicking over to the other line she said, "Special Agent Roe."

A woman's voice on the other end said, "Agent Roe, this is FBI headquarters in Washington. Please hold for the Director."

Moments later, FBI Director Erickson came on the line. "Agent Roe, this is Director Erickson."

Roe had met the Director only once, and then only long enough to shake his hand. She had never spoken with him personally. "Yes, Director," she replied. "What can I do for you, sir?"

"You and your partner have been working on building the Tommy Wong case out of the LA field office?"

Roe was stunned. Why would such a small-time case rise to the Director's attention? And why now? She was tumbling all the pieces in her mind, trying to make them all fit. Walking quickly back to the conference-room door, she tapped on the glass to get her partner's attention and wave him out into the hall.

"Agent Roe?" the Director repeated.

"Sorry, sir," she replied. "Yes, we're the ones who have been building the Tommy Wong case. May I ask why you're interested, sir?"

"I'll tell you in person. We're sending a plane for you now. In the meantime, I want to know everything you know about Wong."

"Does this mean we're off the Al Ain Six search?"

"No," replied Erickson. "In fact, we think you may be able to help speed it up."

CHAPTER 28

China had found its criminal organizations, particularly the triads, to be quite useful, especially as proxies abroad. No one had been more adept at leveraging them from an operational perspective than Cheng. They fulfilled a very important role within his U.S. network and he made sure they were well compensated—both financially and with favors back in China. They couldn't move the kinds of drugs, weapons, and human cargo that they did without very powerful political figures agreeing to look the other way.

Stepping off the plane in Nashville, Cheng wheeled his bag downstairs and purchased a shuttle ticket to the Opryland Resort and Convention Center. The buses departed at the top and bottom of each hour and took only twenty minutes to get to the hotel.

When the shuttle arrived at the resort, Cheng's fellow passengers walked inside, but he headed to the adjacent Opry Mills Mall. Built on the site of the former Opryland USA theme park, it was one of the largest shopping centers in the southeastern United States.

Cheng moved in and out of stores and back and forth through crowds of people, careful to avoid security cameras whenever he could. Once he was convinced he wasn't being followed, he ducked into a bathroom, changed clothes, put on a hat and sunglasses, and then exited the far end of the mall. He found the vehicle right where he had been told it had been left. Reaching behind the rear license plate, he removed the key fob and unlocked the doors.

The Lincoln Navigator had been driven down from Chicago. Opening the lift gate, he found a small duffle bag inside. He placed his carry-on bag and briefcase in the cargo area, and after grabbing the duffle, closed the lift gate and walked around to the driver's-side door.

He climbed in and started the SUV. Looking around to make sure no one was close enough to see, he then unzipped the duffle bag sitting on his lap. Inside were a suppressor, a Smith & Wesson M&P9 pistol, two spare magazines, and a box of ammunition. Satisfied, he zipped the bag back up, placed it on the floor behind him, and headed for the highway.

When he reached his hotel and checked in forty-five minutes later, the clerk handed him a FedEx box that had been delivered that morning. Cheng thanked the woman, accepted the box and his key card, and then headed up to his room where he locked the door and drew the drapes.

While the weapon and car had come from Chicago, the FedEx package was from a different and unrelated asset in San Francisco. Inside were an envelope full of currency and three sterile cell phones. He knew better than to turn any of them on. As soon as he did, there would be a record of the phone touching the nearest cell tower. He didn't plan on leaving any trails. There was a cord included and he plugged the first phone in to make sure that it was fully charged.

As he did this with the second phone, he removed

the envelope full of currency, counted the bills, and stacked them according to denomination. Out of all the tools intelligence operatives could wield, money was one of the most powerful.

Removing the Smith & Wesson M&P9 from the duffle, he disassembled it and made sure all the parts were clean and properly lubricated before putting it back together.

After plugging in the third cell phone to make sure it was topped off, he walked into the bedroom area to change his clothes.

Putting on a pair of khakis, a short-sleeved dress shirt, and a tie, he then stood in front of the mirror and combed his hair in a different style. He slipped on a pair of glasses and reviewed his appearance. Not only did he not look menacing in any way, he appeared to be some sort of midlevel bureaucratic functionary, which was exactly what he wanted.

Stepping over to the desk, he fired up his computer and refreshed himself with all of the details in Wazir Ibrahim's file. Once satisfied that he had everything committed to memory, he gathered up his briefcase, turned on the TV, and left his hotel room, hanging the *Do Not Disturb* sign on the door as he did.

Surveying the exits, he found one that led to a small smoking patio that wasn't monitored with a CCTV camera. Stepping outside, Cheng hopped over a low fence and walked around the corner to where he had parked the Navigator.

Traffic was heavy and it took him more than an hour to reach Wazir's neighborhood. It was typical of many of the poor, immigrant neighborhoods Cheng had seen across the United States—run-down four-story apartment buildings cheek-by-jowl with small, dilapidated houses. Yards were untended and filthy children ran back and forth unsupervised. The only thing residents seemed to care for were their cars and trucks, almost all of which had glittering rims, lift kits, and paint jobs you could see yourself in. Cheng shook his head.

He did a slow pass by Ibrahim's house. There were no signs of life from inside. He found a spot and parked halfway down the next block. Picking up his briefcase, he exited the SUV and walked back the way he had come.

Though he couldn't see them, he could feel eyes watching him. Old women behind curtains, cautious neighbors peering out to see who the stranger was.

Being Chinese made operating in the United States quite easy. Not many people saw him as dangerous, or even potentially dangerous. Being Asian seemed to automatically disqualify him as a threat. It was a prejudice that he played thoroughly to his advantage.

Arriving at Wazir's address, he walked up the cracked walkway to a set of uneven stairs to the front porch. He removed a business card from his pocket, pressed the doorbell, and waited. No one came. He leaned over and peered through the front window. *Nothing.* He leaned back and rang the bell again.

When no one answered, he opened the frayed screen door and knocked. He waited again, but still no one came. He moved back to the window and was about to use his car key to rap on the glass when he heard a voice nearby say, "She's not home."

Cheng turned to his right and saw a Hispanic man in his late twenties who had stepped out onto the porch of the house next door. "Pardon me?" Cheng replied in perfect English.

"Mrs. Ibrahim," the man said. "She's not home. She

went down to her sister's in Shelbyville. That's who you're looking for, right?"

Cheng smiled and walked to the edge of the Ibrahims' porch to better chat with the neighbor. "Actually, I'm looking for Mr. Ibrahim," he said. "Wazir."

"You're not here from Social Services?"

"No, I'm not."

Suddenly, the neighbor appeared more reserved. "Are you a lawyer?"

Cheng smiled even more broadly. "No. Insurance. Mr. Ibrahim filed a claim at work. We have an appointment to go over it."

"What kind of claim?"

"I'm sorry, but that's confidential."

"Are you really an insurance agent?"

Cheng handed him his card.

"Well, you may have to reschedule your appointment," the man said.

"Why is that?"

"Wazir's in jail."

That wasn't good news. In fact, it was very bad news. "Jail? Why would Mr. Ibrahim be in jail?"

The man jerked his head, indicating Cheng should leave the Ibrahims' porch and join him on his. When he did, the man said, "Mrs. Ibrahim had him arrested for domestic violence."

Cheng acted shocked. "Really?"

The neighbor nodded. "He beat her pretty good."

"When did this happen?"

"It's been going on for a while. Someone at the Community Center finally convinced her to file charges."

"No," said Cheng. "I mean, when did he get arrested?"

"A day or two ago, I think," said the neighbor. "I just got back and heard about it. No one is surprised. Wazir's a *pendejo*. A total dick."

Cheng let all of this sink in. "The Nashville police have him?"

The young man nodded. "He can't afford to bond out, so he's fucked until his trial."

The idea of Wazir Ibrahim sitting in jail and possibly coming to the conclusion that he should make a deal by giving up a plot much bigger than a wife-beating charge was very troubling. It was good Cheng had come. He just hoped he wasn't too late.

Thanking the neighbor, he left and returned to his SUV. He had to figure out a way to get to Wazir.

Going in as a visitor and warning him to keep his mouth shut would be dangerous. The same could be said for paying another inmate to deliver the message. It would take too long to set something like that up. That didn't leave him with a lot of options.

Cheng had slipped into two jails and a prison before, but all three of those had been in third world countries, not a heavily guarded, high-tech facility in a major American city. There was only one way he was going to be able to get to Wazir Ibrahim and that was to assist him in getting out. The sooner, the better. But he was going to need help.

He drove around until he found a business hotel with free Wi-Fi. Sitting outside in his vehicle, he opened his anonymous browser, took a deep breath, and ran everything through his mind. Cobbling together operations on the fly was a necessary part of fieldwork. Clear thinking was imperative. If you moved too quickly, many things could go wrong. The same could be said for moving too slowly. The key was striking the right balance.

Confident that he had come up with an exceptional plan, he opened his eyes. There were two things he needed. The first was a bail bonds operation.

He looked at several websites. Once he had found the one he wanted, he turned on one of the sterile cell phones and dialed Lumpy's Bail Bonds. He identified himself as Mushir Ali Mohammed of the Somali Friends Association of Nashville and explained that they had taken up a collection at their mosque in hopes of bailing one of their members out of jail. Cheng asked if the bail bonds agent could help. The man took Wazir Ibrahim's information and then asked him to hold for a moment while he checked the county court computer system.

When the agent returned to the line, he listed the charges against Wazir Ibrahim, as well as the bail amount. Cheng was relieved on both counts. The fact that Wazir was even eligible for bail meant that he hadn't yet tried to cut a deal. If he had, the FBI would be involved and there was no way they would let him walk—unless they were trying to set a trap.

Suddenly, that seemed all too plausible to Cheng. It was very much like the FBI to try such a sting. They could allow Wazir Ibrahim to bond out and then follow him to see what he did, where he went, and whom he talked to. Cheng would have to take extra precautions.

The bail would burn through most of his cash, but he had no choice. If he didn't pay the cost of the bond in full, plus the bond agent's fee, then collateral and residents with ties to the community would be required to act as cosigners. The fewer people involved the better.

After the bond agent finished explaining the process, Cheng asked how quickly Wazir Ibrahim could be released. "As soon as I walk across the street and sign the paperwork."

This was good news. Cheng thanked him and, after hanging up, removed the battery and disassembled the phone.

The only other thing he needed at this point was a middleman, someone he could use as a cutout to shield his involvement and add to the authenticity of his plan. If the Somali community in Nashville was big enough, that wasn't going to be a problem at all.

Cheng searched the Web again and, finding what he was looking for, pulled up the directions online. It was downtown, on Murfreesboro Pike.

Traffic was light and it took less than twenty minutes to get there. When Cheng arrived, his eyes were greeted by exactly what he had hoped to see—taxicabs. And as it was a Somali restaurant, he had no doubt about the ethnicity of the drivers.

He parked out of sight and came back to the restaurant on foot. It didn't take him long to find what he was looking for. The young Somali man was a flashy dresser. He wore pressed jeans, expensive basketball shoes, and a designer shirt. In his hand was a brand-new iPhone. He was louder than his colleagues, with a big smile and a bounce to his step. He thought highly of himself and liked to show off. This was exactly the kind of man Cheng needed.

As the Somali reached his cab, Cheng approached him and asked if he was free. The man nodded and Cheng climbed in back.

"Where to?" the driver asked.

Cheng asked to be taken to Music Row. He wanted

enough time to make small talk and feel the man out. Nodding, the driver started his cab, turned on the meter, and pulled away from the curb.

As they drove, Cheng learned everything he needed to know about the driver. He would be perfect.

When they arrived at Music Row, Cheng paid his fare and gave the Somali a hundred-dollar tip. The man was extremely grateful.

"If you need a taxi again," he said, scribbling down his cell phone number and handing it to his passenger, "call me."

Cheng took the number and smiled. "Actually, I have two important errands to run tonight. How would you like to make a thousand dollars?"

CHAPTER 29

The taxi driver had balked at only one thing, having his signature on the bail paperwork. When Cheng offered him an additional thousand dollars, the young man's reservations magically disappeared. Cheng had definitely chosen the right man for the job.

Cheng turned on the second cell phone and gave the driver the number in order to keep in touch. Once the bail agent had been taken care of, the taxi driver parked across the street from the jail and waited. He had only two questions. Where was he supposed to take Wazir Ibrahim and whom should he say was behind getting him out of jail?

Cheng knew Wazir Ibrahim was going to have a lot more questions than that. He kept his answers for the driver short. He told him to bring Wazir Ibrahim home. There was a restraining order in place to keep Wazir away from his wife, so Cheng made sure that the driver knew to tell Wazir that his wife had gone to her sister's. As far as who had gotten him out of jail and had sent a cab to pick him up, Cheng simply told the young Somali to describe him to Wazir. That would be all that was necessary. He doubted Wazir Ibrahim would ask any more questions after that.

The Snow Dragon operation consisted of six cells.

Each cell paired one of the engineering students with a battle-tested Somali who would act as muscle. The cell members reported to a handler who went by the name Henry Lee. Lee's real name was Ren Ho and he was a deep cover operative the Second Department had placed inside the United States more than thirty years ago. It was Lee who had informed Beijing when Wazir Ibrahim went missing. When the taxi driver described his benefactor, Cheng had no doubt Wazir Ibrahim would assume it was his handler, Henry Lee, who had bailed him out of jail.

Per their agreement, the taxi driver hailed Wazir Ibrahim when he walked out of the jail and then drove him on a long, circuitous route, while Cheng ascertained whether the FBI was following.

When he was satisfied that no one was tailing them, he returned to the Ibrahims' neighborhood, parked his car two blocks away, and broke into the house from the alley. He drew all the blinds and then texted the taxi driver that it was safe to bring Wazir home.

As the cab pulled up in front, Cheng sent his final text explaining where the driver could find the envelope containing the balance of his tip. Cheng then removed the phone's battery, sat down at Ibrahim's dining table, and waited.

There was a thin layer of dust on everything, and he wondered if Ibrahim's marital woes revolved around housekeeping.

He looked up as he heard Wazir's key open the front door. Stepping inside, the Somali man reached for the light.

"Leave it off," Cheng ordered.

Wazir obeyed the instruction. Closing the door, he removed his shoes as he peered into the semidarkness. "Is that you?" he asked.

Cheng reached over and gently nudged a small dimmer switch behind him. A light over the table began to glow and softly illuminated the dining room.

Wazir Ibrahim stopped halfway there. "You're not Henry. Who are you?"

"I'm Henry's boss. Come here and sit down," said Cheng.

He looked nervously from side to side. "Why isn't Henry here?"

"You disappeared, Wazir. No one knew what happened to you. We were worried."

"But why are you here and not Henry?"

"Because Henry is a manager. He doesn't do search and rescue. I do."

"You're the one who got me out of jail?" Wazir asked.

Cheng nodded. "I need to know what happened and what you told them. All of it."

"It's time for prayers. May I pray first?"

"You can pray in a moment. Right now, I need you to explain everything that happened. I need to know exactly what the police know."

Wazir took a deep breath and began to recount his tale. "Because we are refugees and receive government assistance, we are required to meet with a social worker. Our social worker convinced my wife to file charges against me."

"For beating her."

The Somali was not remorseful in the least. "Yes. If my wife does not obey me, I am entitled to beat her."

"Did you admit that to the police?"

"No."

"Good. What else happened while you were in custody?"

Wazir lowered his head.

Cheng tensed. It was obvious Wazir had done something he was ashamed of. "What else happened while you were in custody?"

"Some men I know brought girls to Nashville."

"What men?" asked Cheng.

"Somali men, from Minneapolis."

"What kind of girls did they bring?"

"Young girls, pretty girls."

Cheng's feelings of unease continued to grow. "How old were these girls?"

Wazir refused to look at him. "I don't know," he said.

"Look at me, Wazir. And don't lie to me. How old were these girls?"

The Somali man slowly looked up and met the man's gaze. "They were very young."

"*Too* young?"

Wazir turned his eyes back down to the ground. "Yes," he replied.

"And the police know this?"

"They asked me a lot of questions about it."

Cheng kept his demeanor cool. "What did you tell them?"

"Nothing. I assumed that if they had evidence, they would have presented it."

It was a good point. If they had anything related to charge him with, they would have. As it stood, he had been charged only with spousal abuse.

"Did you say anything at all to the police about Henry Lee or what you have been working on?"

"No."

"Nothing that could even possibly make them suspicious about anything else?"

"No," he repeated.

Despite his protestations, Cheng made Wazir take him through every moment of his ordeal—from his arrest until he walked back into his home. He wanted to know every question the police had asked him, every response he had given, if he had been held in a communal cell, what other prisoners he had talked to, all of it. It went on for over two hours.

Sometimes he gave the same answer, other times his answers changed. Sometimes it was three underage girls he had communed with, sometimes it was "just" two. At first he was held in a solitary cell, then he said there were only four people, and then he said he was in a cell with at least ten other men. Wazir Ibrahim had a hard time keeping his facts straight. This troubled Cheng considerably. The Somali's word was unreliable at best.

"If you're worried that I said anything to the police about Henry Lee or what has been planned, I didn't," Wazir assured him. "Even though I could have."

"And *what* exactly could you have told them?" Cheng asked. Wazir Ibrahim knew very little about the attack. After the NASA internship ended, Henry Lee had brought all of the cell members together to train for one week near his ranch in Idaho. They had only gone over the mechanics of what was expected of them. The canisters they had used were dummies. None of the cell members knew what would be inside them.

"I need money for a lawyer," Wazir responded. "A good one."

Now he wants money for a lawyer? Though Cheng wanted to reach out and strike him, he restrained himself. "First, Wazir, let's talk about what you think you know."

"I know about the canisters," the Somali said.

Cheng smiled. "Of course you do. You trained with them."

"But I know what's going to be in them."

"Really? And what's that?"

With his finger, Wazir drew a word on the tabletop in the dust between them.

Cheng was stunned. How the hell had this stupid Somali pieced it together? Maintaining his steady mask, he laughed and said, "My goodness. That's something. It's not correct. In fact, it's quite fantastic. Why would you think something like that?"

If it had been a guess, it was a well-informed guess. "Because I know."

"How do you know?"

"The engineering student I trained with said something."

"Said something when?" Cheng pressed.

"After the training, as we were all leaving. He said he had been thinking about it, and that's what he believed was going to be in the canisters."

"Did he share this *hypothesis* with the others?" He drew out the word 'hypothesis' to feign how absurd he found the idea.

Wazir Ibrahim shrugged. "What are we going to do about getting a lawyer for me?"

Cheng used his sleeve to erase the word that had been written in the dust. "Everything will be okay," he said.

"So you will get me a lawyer?"

"We may even be able to get the case dismissed."

"Really?" Wazir said hopefully. "How?"

"Don't worry about it. You are important to us. We need you. We'll make this go away."

"I have your word?"

Cheng nodded. "You have my word."

Wazir smiled. He looked as if the weight of the world had been lifted from his shoulders. "May I pray now?"

"Of course, just don't turn on any of the lights."

The Somali thanked him and excused himself from the table. After washing his hands and feet, he returned to the living room, where he rolled out a small rug and began his prayers.

Cheng watched. He was familiar with the routine. He had seen it many times. The last time was in China's Uighur region when he had watched Ismail Kashgari perform it.

When Wazir Ibrahim knelt on the rug, Cheng quietly stood from the dining-room table and slipped into the living room. He counted how many times the Somali had bowed to Mecca. As Wazir rose for the third time, Cheng stepped behind him, wrapped the garrote around his neck, and pulled the wire tight.

It was like slicing butter with a piece of piano wire. There was a spray of blood and the Somali's body flailed wildly for several seconds before collapsing. Wazir wasn't as strong as Kashgari, but his desire to live had been just as powerful, and just as pointless.

Stepping away from the body, Cheng retraced his steps through the house, making sure he had not left any fingerprints anywhere.

An hour and a half later, via an encrypted email, Cheng provided Colonel Shi with both an update and a recommendation. It took less than twenty minutes for Shi to respond.

The colonel okayed Cheng's next move, but required him to make one other stop before leaving Tennessee. Cheng didn't like it, though he had little choice but to comply.

CHAPTER 30

Harvath had tried to get some sleep as soon as Carlton left, but he was too keyed up. He shared the Old Man's concern that they might be missing something and he wanted to think. Exercise always cleared his head so he changed into shorts, threw on a T-shirt, and went for a long run.

The sweat rolling from his pores and the burn in his legs felt good. The steady pounding of his feet along the shoulder of the tree-covered road had relaxed his mind.

The game of intelligence was a lot like assembling a puzzle with the lights out or the top of the box missing. Two pieces might feel as if they "should" fit together perfectly, but in reality they couldn't be further removed from each other. You had to be very careful about what kind of assumptions you made.

As he ran, Harvath had gone through the bits and pieces of intelligence they had amassed so far, trying to see the bigger picture. *How did it all come together? What was the attack?* No matter how hard he had pushed, he couldn't get it to come into focus. He was frustrated and it made him angry.

Returning home, he grabbed a quick shower, changed clothes, and went out to pick up some food. He knew he needed to get some rest, but the further he could push it off, the more helpful it would be to battle his jet lag. In fact, the more sun he could get on his skin, the faster he would reset his body clock back to D.C. time.

It took him about forty-five minutes to run his errands. Returning home, he put away his groceries and carried his lunch down to his dock. While Potomac Therapy normally involved some sort of an alcoholic beverage, this time he only brought a bottle of water. He wanted his mind clear.

He sat there for a long time, eating and watching the summer boats pass by. He thought about Lara, the woman several years his junior whom he was dating up in Boston. Friends who had seen her picture called her the "underwear model" because of her striking resemblance to one of the Victoria's Secret women. Friends who had actually met her, though, called her perfect for him.

He had never dated a woman with a child before. This was completely new territory. He wasn't just building a relationship with Lara; he was also building a relationship with her little boy, Marco, and he cared for them both very much. It was daunting, but it felt right.

Sitting there with the late summer sun blazing down on him and the water lapping at the pier, he enjoyed letting his mind wander. When he was on an op, he couldn't afford to think of anything but the mission. He had to wall off everything back home. If he didn't, he wouldn't be able to focus. And when operators were unable to focus was when bad things happened.

When his lunch was eaten and his bottle of water empty, he walked back up to the house. Retrieving his laptop from his office, he set it on the kitchen table while he brewed some coffee. As soon as it was ready, he poured himself a large mug, sat down at the table, and opened his iTunes app. Scrolling through, he selected Parliament's album *Up for the Down Stroke*.

With coffee to keep him awake and some of his favorite funk music to keep him company, he began to hammer out the written debrief the Old Man was expecting.

By the time his after-action reports on the Karachi and Dubai ops were complete, all the coffee in the world would no longer have been able to keep him awake. Dragging himself upstairs, he stripped out of his clothes and fell into bed.

When a muffled ringing of bells beckoned from a distance, it felt as if he had been asleep for only ten minutes. It sounded like a church tower had been covered with a heavy blanket. The more he tried to ignore the bells, the closer together and more insistent they became.

As he slowly shook off the fog of his deep, dreamless black sleep, he realized it wasn't church bells he had been hearing but rather the old-school telephone ringtone he had assigned to Reed Carlton. He began to reach for his nightstand and realized he had left his cell phone in the pocket of his shorts on the floor.

Leaning over the side of the bed, he found the phone and activated the call.

"Time to move," said the Old Man. "Briefing at the White House in an hour. I'll meet you at the West Wing entrance."

With that, Carlton ended the call.

Harvath looked at his watch. What felt like only ten minutes of sleep had actually been several hours.

Getting out of bed, he walked into his bathroom and turned on the shower.

He stood under the hot water just long enough to get soaped up and then threw the temperature selector all the way to cold. He forced himself to stand there for a full sixty seconds.

He had heard it referred to once as a "Scottish shower," but regardless of its origins, it was the equivalent of three cups of coffee. Nothing woke him up or sharpened his mind faster.

He shaved, taking care not to cut himself by going too fast, threw on a dark suit and tie, then hopped into his Tahoe for the drive up to D.C.

When Harvath arrived at the White House, he was cleared at the West Gate and waved in. He parked his SUV near the West Wing entrance and met the Old Man, who, as promised, was waiting for him inside.

"The President doesn't want either of us saying anything in this meeting. We watch. We assess. And we discuss afterward. Understood?"

Harvath nodded and followed Carlton down to the Situation Room, where they took the last two remaining seats. FBI Director Erickson was just beginning his briefing. The flat-screens in the room showed the face of a young Asian man in his twenties.

"The man you see here," said Erickson, "is Thomas Ming Wong, better known as Tommy Wong. Wong is a member of a Chinese transnational criminal organization called 14K. Based out of Hong Kong, 14K is the third-largest triad in the world. They make their money from a variety of criminal enterprises including arms trafficking, the heroin and opium trades, money laundering, prostitution, child pornography, smuggling, and counterfeiting.

"Special Agent Heidi Roe of our Los Angeles field office was spearheading an investigation into Wong when new information about the six missing Muslim engineering students came to our attention. Agent Roe?"

Roe, who had been sitting near the middle of the Situation Room, stood and said, "Thank you, sir. 14K is one of many criminal enterprises that the FBI is focused on. Earlier this year, the LA field office targeted Tommy Wong as a likely candidate to be turned and used against 14K's Southern California hierarchy and hopefully all the way back to China.

"As we have been made aware, each of the six engineering students was given a cell phone, told to turn that cell phone on when they arrived in the U.S., and to await further instructions. Thanks to the diligence of the National Security Agency, we think those cell phones have been successfully identified. All six phones received one phone call each, were turned off, and were never used again. Based on the metadata collected by the NSA, the point of purchase for each of the phones has been identified.

"All six were purchased within Los Angeles County. Upon being given this information, agents from the LA and San Diego field offices visited the six stores involved. Of these, four had some sort of security-cam system. Only three, though, had retained their footage going back to the date in question."

Roe pressed her remote, the screens split in three, and the footage rolled. "As you can see, in two out of the three we get a very good view of who is buying the phones."

"Tommy Wong," said the Secretary of State.

"Correct."

"So we believe Wong bought the phones and then shipped them to the recruiter over in Dubai?" asked CIA Director McGee.

"Yes," Roe replied.

"Do we know who called the six engineering students?"

"It was also a phone used only once and was purchased from a store in Salt Lake City, Utah. Agents from the Bureau's SLC field office visited the store, but no security camera footage was available."

"Still," said the Sec State, "this is a huge breakthrough. Where's Wong now?"

"Up until this morning we knew exactly where he was. Then he disappeared."

"What do you mean?"

"Yesterday, Wong purchased a last-minute airline ticket to Nashville, Tennessee. This morning, LAPD officers followed him to LAX and watched him pass through security. The Bureau's Nashville office arranged to have a Nashville PD detective who works on several of our task forces be at the airport when Wong landed. The last-minute travel had piqued our interest and we wanted to see what Wong was up to. The only problem is Wong never got off the plane."

"What happened to him? Did he even get *on* the plane?"

"He got on a plane, all right, just not this plane."

"What does that mean?"

Roe advanced to her next clip, which showed footage from several different security cameras. "After clearing security at LAX, Tommy Wong proceeded to the American Airlines Admirals Club where he purchased a day pass, hung out for less than an hour, and then boarded a plane for Omaha."

"Omaha?" The Chairman of the Joint Chiefs said. "Why?"

"So that this man," Roe replied, advancing to her next clip, "could travel to Nashville on Wong's ticket."

CIA Director McGee looked at the Secretary of Homeland Security. "How many times have we talked about this? Anyone can switch boarding passes once they're behind security."

The DHS Secretary didn't want to discuss it. He knew it was a flaw in the system. He also knew the airlines had screamed bloody murder every time they tried to get them to start checking IDs at the gate again. "Talk to Congress, Bob. I'm on your side. I personally don't care if it triples boarding times."

McGee shook his head. "Wait'll some bomb maker checks a bag and then switches boarding passes with some patsy who thinks she's getting a few hundred bucks just to take a flight to Miami."

The bomb would still have to make it past all the baggage-screening mechanisms, but the point was taken. The boarding card system was a problem. The DHS Secretary nodded in agreement.

"This is footage of the passengers deplaning the LA to Nashville flight that Wong should have been on. The man you see here," said Roe as she paused her presentation and zoomed in, "entered the United States today from Shanghai and was supposed to change planes at LAX for Omaha.

"His name, at least the name we have on file for him, is Bao Deng. He is allegedly a Chinese businessman who holds an American green card and owns part of a poultry-processing plant in Nebraska."

"Is there any known connection between Wong and Deng?" asked the Secretary of State.

"None that we have been able to make so far."

"What about CIA?"

"Nothing," replied McGee. "But it wouldn't be the first time a nation-state has used a criminal organization to assist with its activities."

"So who's the bigger fish here? Who should we be more concerned with? A triad member who buys phones for terrorists or a Chinese businessman who switches places with him at the airport?"

"The FBI wants both of them," Director Erickson asserted. "And to answer your question, you don't fly a guy all the way from China just to be a decoy. Tommy Wong is a street thug with no tradecraft. If he'd been properly trained, he wouldn't have been caught on camera buying those phones."

"Good point," said the Secretary of State.

"Do we have any leads to either of their current whereabouts?" asked the DHS Secretary.

Erickson nodded to Roe, who continued her presentation. "Both our Omaha and Nashville offices have been fully mobilized and additional assets are being sent in. For the moment, all we have is the footage from the airport CCTV systems. Upon arriving at their respective destinations, both men boarded hotel shuttles and disappeared."

"What do you mean *disappeared*?" said the Secretary of State.

"Tommy Wong took a shuttle to the Super 8 motel, two miles from Omaha's Eppley Airfield. The Super 8 doesn't have any external cameras. He got off the shuttle but didn't check into the motel. FBI agents spoke with management and staff, showed them Wong's picture, and no one fitting his description has been seen by anyone other than the shuttle driver."

"What about this Bao Deng?"

"We have a little more there, but not much. Based on CCTV footage from the Nashville airport, after Bao Deng deplaned, he went to the baggage level. There, he bought a ticket and took a shuttle to the Opryland Resort and Convention Center about twenty minutes away.

"Just like Tommy Wong and the Super 8 in Omaha, Opryland has no record of a Bao Deng checking in. In case he was using an alias, agents showed his picture to management, desk clerks, and staff. The only person who could positively ID Deng was the shuttle bus driver. He states he has no idea where Deng went once all of the passengers got off the bus.

"The Opryland Resort, though, does have external CCTV cameras and allowed our agents to review the footage. Deng can clearly be seen debussing and then entering the nearby shopping mall called Opry Mills. But sifting through the mall's security footage has been a nightmare. Opry Mills is one of the largest malls in the southeastern United States and has over two hundred stores. It was very crowded. We're talking thousands and thousands of people.

"There were a couple of times Deng appeared on camera, but because he had his carry-on bag with him, we think he may have changed clothes. The mall is a mix of retail and outlet stores. If Deng also disguised his luggage by using some of those oversized outlet store bags, he may have slipped out an exit looking like a normal shopper.

"We have agents going through every piece of the footage frame by frame. Maybe we'll get lucky, but we're not pinning all of our hopes on it."

"What about the poultry plant in Nebraska Deng was invested in? Are you checking there?" asked the DHS Secretary.

"Yes, sir," Roe replied. "We are not leaving any stone unturned. We're placing additional agents at Nashville's and Omaha's airports, train stations, and bus stations. Bao Deng and Tommy Wong have had their names and photos added to the no-fly list, but with a 'contact the FBI before any action' flag. We expect to have more for you by the next briefing."

With that, Special Agent Roe took her seat and the President went around the table asking for updates from the rest of his national security team. Ten minutes later, the President adjourned the meeting.

As the attendees filed out of the room, Director of National Intelligence Johnson, CIA Director McGee, and FBI Director Erickson remained seated with the President. Once the door with its pneumatic lock had clicked shut, Harvath and the Old Man moved forward and took seats at the conference table.

The President looked at them and said, "We've got a few other developments that weren't included in the briefing. Let's go over those first."

CHAPTER 31

DNI General George Johnson slid two briefing books across the table—one to Harvath and the other to the Old Man. "Whose idea was this Facebook thing?" he asked.

Carlton cocked his head at Harvath and said, "It was his idea. He deserves the credit."

"It was pretty clever and may be the break we've been looking for," said Johnson. "According to the NSA, all six of those engineering students have a Facebook account. None of them have been posting to their accounts. Total radio silence. Except," he said, pausing and looking at Harvath.

"They're still tuning their radios in and listening," said Harvath, recalling what he had brought the Old Man back into his house to discuss.

"Bingo."

"Can you be more specific?" the President asked.

Johnson ceded the floor to Harvath, who replied, "Facebook, sir, is huge in the Middle East. Asking six young men to refrain from posting is a big deal. With the right carrot and stick you could probably get them not to post. But what I was wondering was whether they would be able to stay off Facebook altogether. Would they 'sneak' on just to look? Just to check in and see what their family and friends were up to back home?"

"And that's what they've been doing?"

The DNI nodded and pulled up a map of the United States on the monitors. "One account has been accessed multiple times from Seattle, another from Las Vegas, another from Des Moines, one from Dallas, one from Baltimore, and, surprise, one from Nashville." As he named each city, he tapped a key on his keyboard, which highlighted it and then popped up the corresponding engineering student's picture next to it.

Johnson then zoomed in on Nashville and showed where the Facebook account was being accessed from. "This is an example of how our engineering student is accessing the Internet from different locations offering free Wi-Fi."

"If these were my guys," said Harvath, "I wouldn't allow them to operate a motor vehicle. There's too great a chance that they would come into contact with law enforcement that way. I would have them in a lower-middle-class neighborhood in each city, lying low. To get to those Wi-Fi spots, they'd either have to walk, ride a bike, or take public transportation."

"Which means we can start drawing circles around each one, see where they intersect, and then start tightening the net," replied FBI Director Erickson. "This is significant."

Harvath looked back to the DNI. "What about the handler? Whoever is in charge of these guys has to be aware of their Facebook accounts. He'd be watching to make sure they stay off and don't post anything."

"That one was a little bit harder to track down, but the NSA found him. He's using six different accounts—one dedicated to each engineering student's Facebook page."

"Where is he located?"

"He's using different free Wi-Fi locations in Idaho, specifically within a couple of hours' drive of Boise. Truck stops, coffee shops, he never uses the same spot twice. Boise is interesting because three weeks after the NASA internship ended, all six engineering students used the free Wi-Fi at the Greyhound bus station in Boise to check their Facebook accounts. All six, all on the same day."

"Do we have any idea what they were doing in Idaho?" Carlton asked.

"I'll bet you a month's pay," said McGee, "they were training. Pretty rugged and rural up there. They wrap up their training, the handler drops them at the bus station, and they all jump online to see what's been going on back home since they've been off the grid."

Harvath agreed. "We need the CCTV footage from the bus station, as well as every single ATM, traffic, and security camera from that area. Plus, we'll need all the locations where we believe the handler has been."

"We're on it," said Erickson.

"Besides possibly training, do we have any other idea why they might have picked Idaho?" McGee asked.

"We're not sure," General Johnson replied. "A couple of years ago, a Chinese company was looking into building what it called a 'self-sustaining city' about fifty miles south of Boise, but nothing ever came of it."

"What do you mean, 'self-sustaining city'?" the President asked.

"They have these in China. They call them 'technology zones.' Everything is self-contained, even their power plants and the housing for workers. They don't need much of anything from the outside. Some company owned by the Chinese government called the China National Machinery Industry Corp. began lobbying the Idaho governor a couple years ago to be allowed to build a thirty-thousand-acre 'technology zone' with homes, retail centers, and industry. It would include a $2 billion fertilizer plant as well as a facility that would mass-produce solar panels, all to be built just south of the Boise airport, which would be used for all of their air freight."

"Did anything come of it?"

"According to the governor's office, it was just preliminary. The delegation also approached several other states proposing similar technology zones."

"All near major airports?" asked the President.

Johnson nodded.

"Knowing what we know now," stated McGee, "it sounds like these could have also functioned as self-sustaining forward operating bases for their landing forces."

The President nodded and turned to the FBI Director. "Let's talk about the other item that wasn't included in the briefing."

"We believe we know where in Nashville Bao Deng is," said Erickson.

"Where?" Harvath asked.

Pulling up a satellite image onscreen, he said, "FedEx delivered a package this morning to a Residence Inn by Marriott in the Cool Springs area near Nashville. It was addressed *Hold for Hotel Guest Mr. Bao Deng.*"

"How did you find that?"

"NSA uncovered it."

Harvath didn't bother asking what NSA was doing

combing through FedEx's shipping receipts. "Where did the package come from?"

"An unattended drop-box in San Francisco. Billing info is from a prepaid credit card," said Erickson. "We have agents out there looking into it."

"Do we know what was in the package?"

"No. Only that it was a standard shipping box that weighed in under five pounds."

"Is he registered at the hotel?" Harvath asked.

The FBI Director nodded. "He checked in this afternoon."

"Do you have people sitting on it?"

"Yes. We don't believe he's there right now, but we have it under surveillance."

"Pull it back," Harvath said.

"What?"

"Pull your people back. As far as possible."

"Why?" Erickson responded.

"Because if you don't, this guy *absolutely* will spot your surveillance teams."

"How do you know that?"

"With all due respect, Mr. Director, when I get sent halfway around the world by my government, it's not because someone needs help slicing birthday cake. This guy will know what to look for."

The FBI Director held up his hand. "First of all, you're assuming he's a professional."

"I'm not assuming anything," Harvath replied. "Based on what we've already seen, Deng has proven that he *is* a professional. The question is, why is he here? Has anyone looked into when he bought his airline ticket?"

The Director looked through his notes and found the information. "Two days ago."

"Last-minute. Just like Tommy Wong," said Harvath. "That's a huge risk. They know we scrutinize last-minute purchases. He would have needed a cover story in case immigration asked him anything at LAX. You should tell your people to triple-check any stories they come across at his poultry plant."

"What kind of stories?"

"An accident, a failed piece of machinery, a client backing out of a major deal. That sort of thing."

The FBI Director made a note on his pad.

"Why do you think he took the risk?" the President asked.

Harvath thought about it for a moment. "Everything should be on autopilot at this point. You don't do anything that risks exposing the operation unless something has gone very wrong. I think that's what's happened. Something has gone upside down and the Chinese have sent in a pro to straighten it out."

"What do you think it is?"

"I think the Nashville cell is probably compromised."

"*Compromised* how?" asked McGee.

Harvath shrugged. "You know this game as well as I do. It could be anything. Did someone get cold feet? Is the cell being blackmailed? Do they need to get rid of a body? Did a key piece of equipment fail? Whatever it is, it isn't good news for them. But if we handle this right, it could be good news for us."

Silence settled over the room as the directors for National Intelligence, CIA, and FBI all turned and looked at the President.

The President looked at Harvath. "In your estimation, what do we need to do to handle this right?" he asked.

Harvath studied each of the faces gathered around the table. "Off the record?"

President Porter nodded.

Looking over at Carlton, Harvath asked, "How soon do Sloane and Chase land?"

The Old Man glanced at the Situation Room clock and said, "Twenty minutes."

CHAPTER 32

FBI Director Erickson didn't like a single thing Harvath had proposed. His entire plan was dangerous, outside the law, and just too damn risky. He offered to put all of the resources of the FBI at his fingertips, but Harvath said *no*.

In Harvath's estimation, he not only knew the enemy better than Erickson, he also knew the Achilles' heel of the law enforcement system. He had the utmost respect for the FBI, particularly its Hostage Rescue Team, which was world-class, but he knew what would happen if Erickson and his G-men succeeded in capturing Deng.

They would hold off on Mirandizing him in the hopes that the High Value Detainee Interrogation Group, or HIG, could squeeze the information they needed out of him. HIG had been created by the previous administration to interrogate terrorism suspects immediately after arrest in order to gain intelligence that would head off an attack and help round up accomplices.

HIG teams were staffed with FBI, CIA, and DoD personnel, as well as linguists, professional interrogators, and terrorism analysts. All of them were good, solid, experienced people, but all of them were bound by a very specific set of rules. Harvath wasn't bound by anything.

If Deng was half the professional he appeared to be, even the best HIG team wasn't going to get anything out of him. But he was putting the cart in front of the horse. Before HIG could question Deng, the FBI would have to apprehend him.

You could be the best dogcatcher in history, but it wouldn't amount to much on the day you had to catch a panther. When that happened, you wanted somebody around who not only knew how to track a big cat, but knew how to think like one—somebody who knew what to do just in case the panther turned the tables, and began tracking you.

More important, you wanted someone who understood the number-one rule of tracking a top predator—there are no rules. That's what made a panther a panther and that's why the President wanted Harvath to go to Nashville.

By the time he arrived at Reagan National, Sloane and Chase's plane had already been diverted from Dulles and touched down. They met up at Signature Flight Support, a fixed-base operator, or FBO as it was known, on the general aviation side of the airport. Bob McGee had arranged for Harvath and his team to use one of the Agency's Citation Longitude business jets.

While Sloane and Chase used the courtesy showers in the Signature building, Harvath unloaded his Tahoe. In addition to the bug-out and overnight bags he always kept loaded and ready to go in his vehicle, he also had a Truck Vault.

The Truck Vault was a strongbox bolted to the cargo area with two lockable sliding drawers, which turned his vehicle into a rolling armory.

Sloane and Chase had flown home clean. The weapons they used in Karachi had stayed in Karachi. If they had been caught trying to get guns out of Pakistan, they would have been arrested, and it wouldn't have taken long for the ISI to link them to the death of their agents and the kidnapping of Ahmad Yaqub. As they had been working with no official cover or sanction, Sloane and Chase would have been looking at heavy prison time. They left all of their gear with a trusted CIA operative who was happy to have it.

Harvath set an empty Blackhawk load-out bag on top of the Truck Vault and began filling it up. Into the bag went his LaRue 14.5" PredatOBR rifle and his Remington 870 Express tactical shotgun. He grabbed his .45 caliber H&K USP compact pistol, a Glock 21, a Glock 17, and a RONI conversion kit that would turn the 17 into a short-barreled rifle.

He threw in a Taser X26P, a set of night vision goggles, flashlights, walkie-talkies and earpieces, an extra Benchmade folding knife for Sloane and one for Chase, as well as plastic restraints, holsters, ammunition, his Otis cleaning kit, and extra magazines.

With his bug-out bag over one shoulder and his overnight bag over the other, he extended the handle of his load-out bag and wheeled it behind him into the building.

Signature Flight Support was known for always having fruit, fresh-baked muffins, cookies, and popcorn. Harvath grabbed an apple and a bottle of water.

He had just taken his first bite when Sloane Ashby appeared. She was wearing jeans, trail runners, and an Under Armour shirt.

"An apple, huh?" she said. "I guess guys your age really have to watch their weight."

"Fuck you," Harvath replied through a smile and a mouth full of apple.

"Gotcha. Listen, about my hostile work environment complaint? How does Tuesday look for a sit-down with HR?"

Harvath gave her the finger and grabbed another apple.

"Allahu Snackbar," Sloane said, lampooning the terrorist battle cry of *Allahu Akbar*, as she studied the counter full of treats. She made a show of picking the two biggest cookies and then filled up a bag with popcorn.

Harvath shook his head. Ashby was a wiseass and it was one of the many things he liked about her. Despite the difference in their ages, they had a lot in common—the same healthy disrespect for authority, the same determination to succeed at any cost, and the same wise-guy sense of humor. They were two peas in a pod. So much so that Carlton had given Harvath a very stern warning—*no dating*. The last thing the Old Man wanted was a romance to develop between them. He had been perfectly clear what the repercussions would be if that happened.

Even though Harvath thought Sloane was "cute"—a word he used continually because he knew she hated it and it got under her skin—he kept their relationship platonic.

He admired her skills and saw her as a teammate; someone he could mentor. In fact, he believed she'd probably end up being an even better operator than he was. She was born for the work and everything about her made her perfect for it. The Old Man had always been a scary-good judge of talent.

Chase Palmer was the other operator Harvath figured would outpace him. General George Johnson, the Director of National Intelligence, had uncovered Chase while heading the Army's Intelligence Support division, also known as "The Activity."

Johnson had a career full of experience with clandestine operations. He had seen men rise and fall, come and go, but he had never seen an operator like Chase. There was a row of locked file cabinets at the Pentagon stuffed with accounts of his exploits at the Unit. There was also a coterie of career soldiers, or *Chairborne Rangers* as they were derogatorily referred to, who resented not only Chase's talent and meteoric rise but also his above-average intelligence.

His star was burning white-hot right about the time he ran afoul of a drunk two-star general and knocked him out. It didn't matter that the general was asking for it both by being overly aggressive with a female soldier and by exhibiting conduct unbecoming an officer. Word spread quickly. Chase had embarrassed the two-star, who was bound and determined to make Chase pay. That's when General Johnson had stepped in.

Johnson spoke with the Unit and they agreed to "share custody" of Chase. It gave Chase the best of both worlds, and he very much enjoyed the arrangement. But just when he thought it couldn't get any better and he was preparing to reenlist, Reed Carlton had come along. He was a difficult man to say no to.

Before Chase knew it, he had given up his house at Fort Bragg, had bought a new car, and had taken a splashy condo in D.C. Carlton was opening up an incredible new world to him and he could already tell he had a lot to look forward to. And with his sense of humor, he fit right in.

Joining Harvath, Chase looked at Sloane's cookies and said, "A moment on the lips, forever on the hips."

Harvath chuckled as Sloane gave them both the finger. As she did, the copilot stepped inside and told them the plane was ready to go.

CHAPTER 33

The flight to Nashville would take a little over an hour and the FBI would have a car waiting at the airport for them to use. Harvath had requested something with a big trunk, as well as rope, plastic sheeting, and several other things Director Erickson would probably rather not have known about. Harvath also asked him to arrange a safe house, preferably in the middle of nowhere, with lots of acreage and no neighbors.

He had watched the man write everything down and was sure that as soon as the instructions had been relayed to the field office in Tennessee, Erickson would burn the list. He was a decent man who played by the rules. The way Harvath handled business obviously made him uncomfortable. Not because he couldn't stomach violence, but because he believed in the rule of law and the concept that Americans should hold themselves to a higher standard than their enemies.

It was a noble notion and one that Harvath wanted to live by as well. The trouble was, it was something that no nation could afford to cling to without having a Plan B. When your enemies succeed because they aren't constrained by rules, at some point you have to either accept defeat, or tear up the rulebook. Harvath had pretty much played by the rules while he was in the Secret Service. The President at that time had joked that it was like staking a pit bull to a chain in the backyard. No matter how mean he looked or how loud he barked, there were some people who wouldn't be deterred.

Take that same pit bull, though, unchain him and let him go, and it was a different dynamic altogether. The pit bull might bite the wrong person someday, but if he was well-trained enough, you wouldn't lose sleep over something that *might* happen. You actually might sleep much better knowing he was on duty. That was how President Jack Rutledge had seen Harvath then and how President Paul Porter saw him now.

Onboard the plane, Harvath and his team stowed their gear, chose their seats, and buckled up. They had been given priority clearance for takeoff.

Once the plush Citation Longitude was airborne, Harvath accessed the pressurized luggage compartment behind the lavatory and retrieved his load-out bag. He wanted to clean and check the weapons as they went over what the plan was going to be.

"And if he's not there?" Sloane said as she broke down the LaRue rifle. "What then?"

"Then we're going to let ourselves in, take a look around, and let ourselves out."

"What about wiring the room?" Chase asked.

Harvath shook his head. "I don't have that kind of equipment. The Bureau is sending one of its top guys, but he won't get in until later tonight."

"It had better be a top guy," Sloane interjected. "If he doesn't do a first-class job, and Deng finds something, that's it. We're blown."

"I agree. That's why I'd rather follow him and see where he leads us."

"Understood," Chase replied as he tried the action on Harvath's Remington. "How long are we going to let him walk around before we grab him?"

It was a difficult question. Time was a double-edged sword. The longer they followed Deng, the more they might learn from him. The flip side was that the longer they followed him, the greater their odds of losing him. The biggest factor, though, was that every minute that they weren't interrogating Deng was one minute the terrorists were closer to pulling off their attack. Usually, as the clock was winding down, you wanted to score as soon as you could. Putting up some Hail Mary right at the buzzer wasn't an act of professionalism; it was an act of desperation. Sometimes, though, a Hail Mary was all you had.

Harvath didn't intend to let it come to that. "We're going to watch him for as long as we can. I'll let you know when it's time to roll him up."

That answer seemed to satisfy Chase and the team went back to checking the equipment before restowing it in the load-out bag.

Because Sloane and Chase hadn't had to share a plane back home with a pissy ambassador, they had slept a lot better than Harvath. Despite a little bit of jet lag, they announced they were ready to hit the ground running.

When the Longitude touched down, it taxied to the general aviation area of Nashville International and a local Signature Flight Support FBO. An impressive array of high-end jets was lined up outside. Nashville hosted a lot more than just country music. The city was booming in high tech, biotech, health care, publishing, and finance. Harvath knew more than a few Tier 1 military operators, as well as intel people, who had purchased homes and land in the Volunteer State.

Inside the Signature building, an envelope had been left at the desk under one of Harvath's aliases. Opening it, he found a set of keys for a blue Ford Taurus sedan parked outside.

The team exited the building and Harvath popped the trunk. Inside were all the items he had requested. Pulling out his phone, he texted the Old Man that they had landed and that everything was a go.

Next, he called the FBI agent whose card had been left in the envelope. Special Agent Dennis Urda had been designated the team's local liaison.

While the FBI's main Tennessee field office was in Memphis, it operated satellite offices, referred to as "resident agencies," in other cities, such as Clarksville, Cookeville, Columbia, and Nashville.

Urda was the number-two agent in the Nashville office, and he answered his phone on the second ring. "Special Agent Urda." He spoke with a slight New York accent.

"Agent Urda, this is Scot Harvath."

"Did you find the car?"

"Yes. We just arrived at the airport. Thank you. Can you give me a situation report?"

The Residence Inn by Marriott in Cool Springs was situated in a mixed-use office park. In addition to high-rise office buildings, there were single-story buildings that housed retail businesses, including bars, restaurants, and a yoga studio.

When Harvath had insisted the FBI pull back their surveillance, he had agreed that they could covertly set up in any of the office buildings, but he didn't want them in the parking lot or the hotel itself. He had also insisted that none of the agents move around the area on foot. Experienced operatives could smell law enforcement from a mile away. Unfortunately, pulling back had limited what the FBI could see, especially at night.

"Lots of what we would consider normal hotel traffic," said Urda. "No obvious signs of our guy."

"What about his room?"

"The TV is on, the *Do Not Disturb* is still on the door, and the drapes are still pulled."

"Okay," Harvath replied. "You've got my cell number. Call me if anything changes. We're headed your way now."

Urda agreed to call Harvath if anything changed and they ended their call.

Turning to Sloane and Chase, Harvath said, "No matter what happens, we absolutely take this guy alive. Understood?"

His two operatives nodded and Harvath signaled for everyone to get in the car. As they did, a sense of foreboding swept over him. He silently hoped that they had made the right decision by coming to Nashville.

CHAPTER 34

Jimi Fordyce looked Billy Tang square in the face and said, "Are you crazy? Not only no, but *hell* no. There's no way I'm authorizing that."

"What if I told you I wasn't asking for your authorization?"

"You're going to get us all fucking killed," Johnson stated.

Fordyce held up his hand to calm his teammate down and kept his attention focused on Tang. "I'm not letting you jeopardize this mission, Billy. The answer's *no.*"

"But what if his sister does know something?" said Tang.

"What if she doesn't?"

"Then we'll know for sure. Isn't that better than wondering *what if*?"

"Completing our mission is what's better, period."

Tang looked at him. "And our mission was to gather as much intel as possible. This *is* possible."

"No," Johnson said. "It's insane."

Fordyce waved him off again. "If you go down there and you get caught, you're going to bring an army down on us. I won't have that."

"The key word here is *if* I get caught. They're not

going to catch me. Do you know how many times I have snuck in and out of the DPRK?"

"I don't know if you have a huge set of balls, or you really are just crazy, but you're talking about fences, armed guards, and prisoners who are conditioned to snitch. You know damn well if they see a strange face, they're going to find the nearest guard and raise the alarm in the hope of getting an extra half-ration of cabbage soup."

Tang shook his head. "It's a labor camp. Those people are being worked to death. You think they sit up all night playing Mah-Jongg? By the time I slip in there, they'll all be asleep."

"Except for the guards," Fordyce replied.

"You saw the map Jin-Sang drew. The part of the fence he sneaks through is less than a hundred meters from the infirmary. He says the guards don't patrol that area as often."

"And 'the check is in the mail' and 'I'll still respect you in the morning,'" Johnson snarked.

Tang ignored him. "If it's too hairy, I'll pull the plug. Believe me, I have no desire to spend the rest of my life in a place like that."

"No," Fordyce repeated.

"Damn it, Jimi. That girl may hold the key to unlocking the entire thing. When conditions on the ground change, the op parameters have to change."

"We get in, we get what we can, and we get out. Those are our parameters. Nothing has changed."

"If I got up right now," said Tang, "and began to walk down into that valley, what would you do? Shoot me?"

"No," Fordyce replied. "Tuck would."

Looking up from his rifle, Tucker smiled.

"And then I'd shoot you again," said Johnson. "Just to make sure."

"Bullshit. I don't think any of you would shoot me."

Johnson shouldered his rifle. "Let's find out. Start walking."

"Nobody's walking and nobody's shooting," Fordyce ordered. "At 2100, just as planned, we ruck up and retreat back over that ridgeline. We work our way down the other side, meet up with our ride, and head back to the coast."

Tang looked over at Jin-Sang. "What about him?"

"We're going to feed him one last time before we go, give him some pain meds, and then gag him and tie him up. I've got a signal mirror in my kit. We'll tape it to him. By the time there's enough sun in the valley, we'll be long gone."

"They'll torture every last piece of information out of him."

"Which is why you're going to ask him some questions about the terrain northwest of here and if there are any rail lines. Make them think that's the direction we're going."

"You don't think they'll double their coastal patrols and put everything they have in the air?" Tang asked. "They'll look northwest, all right, but they'll look in every other direction, too. Talk about kicking the hornets' nest."

"What are we supposed to do?" Johnson asked. "We know this kid. We know his whole life story. Now you want to kill him?"

"No, I don't want to kill him," Tang asserted. "We can bring him with us."

"You *are* fucking crazy."

"Why? If we can get him to the rally point and into

the truck, Hyun Su can get him into South Korea. There are special organizations there that will take him in."

Fordyce shook his head. "One minute you want to sneak into a DPRK labor camp, the next you want to carry a kid with a tib/fib over a mountain."

"Wrong. I want *you* to carry him over the mountain," said Tang. "I still plan on talking to his sister."

"Tuck should have shot you last night when he had the chance," said Johnson.

"Enough," ordered Fordyce. Looking at Tang, he said, "Billy, we're not taking this kid and you're not going to talk to his sister. I can't be clearer than that. Start packing up your shit. That's an order."

"You can't leave him here," said Tang.

"Watch me."

"Jimi, they'll torture him and they may even decide to make an example out of him for sneaking out of the camp. They could execute him."

"He should have thought about that before he snuck out."

"Look at him," Tang insisted. "He's a fucking kid and he's starving. What would you do?"

"It's not my fight," Fordyce replied.

"Not your fight? You're a Navy SEAL, for Christ's sake. You're a good man. All three of you are. I *know* that. I also know that we're different than the North Koreans. Life means something to us. Freedom means something to us. We can save this boy. We *have* to save him. And as far as his sister is concerned, if she has even one piece of intel that can help protect our country, I'm willing to do what it takes to get it."

Fordyce began to interrupt, but Tang motioned to be allowed to finish. Fordyce allowed him to speak.

"I have enough red herrings, fake backstories, and outright deceptions planned that *if* I got captured, and that's a big *if,* I could keep the North Koreans chasing their tails for months. By the time they untangled everything and figured out that I was American and not South Korean, you'd all be long gone," said Tang. "I wouldn't compromise this operation."

"Not at first," replied Fordyce. "But they'd torture you, too, and eventually, you'd tell them everything."

"Of course. No one can hold out forever."

Lieutenant Jimi Fordyce looked long and hard at both of his SEALs, but he didn't need to ask Johnson or Tucker what they thought. They were his brothers. He could read their minds.

Looking back at Tang he said, "I'd better not regret this. Okay, let's map out how we're going to make it happen."

CHAPTER 35

Colonel Shi studied the report on his screen. He was not happy with what Cheng had discovered in Nashville.

Ren Ho had personally approved each of the Somalis for the operation. He should have been able to anticipate that Wazir Ibrahim would be a problem. Cheng had done the right thing by eliminating him. Ibrahim was a disaster waiting to happen. On the other hand, Mirsab, the engineering student who had been paired with him, was a different problem.

One of the greatest difficulties of dealing with educated people was that they made educated guesses. It had been assumed that the engineering students would ask questions, and Ho, posing as their handler, "Henry Lee," had been instructed what to tell them.

The devices they would be assembling had been smuggled into the United States in pieces. In their training, they had been given a wiring diagram, several innocuous components, and a battery. There was no way that they could figure out what they were being asked to build. When the students did ask what it was, Ho delivered his prepared response.

Because of all the secrecy, the students naturally assumed they were participating in something illegal. They each came from a very poor family and the money being sent home was more than they would earn in a lifetime. That alone should have cut off any questions, but the Second Department had wanted the engineers to be told what to think, rather than trying to figure things out on their own.

What Ho had conveyed was that they were creating a "temporary Internet" that would act like a network of nationwide cell towers. With it, a series of incursions into corporate computer systems would be conducted and never be traced. The fact that the targets were corporations, the item to be stolen was data, and that the network was untraceable had satisfied all of the students. All, it appeared, except for one.

When it came time to practice launching the attack, Ho provided dummy containers for the devices and stressed the importance that they all launch at the same time. If they didn't, he warned that the network would not be fully functional, and their plan would collapse. That's why the students had been issued partners. The Somali men were there not only as an extra set of hands to help transport and assemble the equipment, but also to handle any problems that might arise en route to or during the launch.

Once their task was complete they would all rendezvous with Ho in Boise, receive their final payments, and be provided with routes to return home.

It was a solid, plausible explanation, but somehow their Nashville student, Mirsab, had discovered the real purpose of the devices. What Shi put down to an educated guess may have been just that, or it may have just been wildly lucky. Either way, the colonel wanted to know how Mirsab had arrived at his conclusion and, more important, if he had shared it with anyone. It was bad enough he had shared it with Wazir Ibrahim, but if he had been foolish enough to reveal it to the other engineering students or, heaven forbid, someone outside the operation, drastic measures would need to be taken.

Based on the seriousness of Cheng's report, Shi had some difficult decisions to make.

As he pored over maps of the United States, as well as the most recent weather reports, he transmitted a message to the PLA's hacking unit in Shanghai with instructions. They were already standing by and he wanted to make sure they had the latest information, as well as his precise instructions. It was important that every participant be on the same page.

The biggest question plaguing Shi was, *Was Nashville salvageable?* What they were planning had never been done before. Like the mythical Snow Dragon itself, the attack was designed to stretch from tip to tail across the United States. The efforts of each cell were designed to overlap, and they had run contingency scenarios to account for losing up to half of the cells, but no one knew for sure how successful the attack would be if even one of the cells was taken offline. If the dragon was incomplete, would its fire still burn as hot?

There was, of course, no way to know for sure. They were in the realm of the hypothetical. Formulas, diagrams, charts, and assumptions were of no use now. Their time had passed. Shi had made a command decision and Tai Cheng had been given his orders. At this point, all Colonel Jiang Shi could do was wait. It was all in Cheng's hands now.

CHAPTER 36

Cheng sat outside and watched. He had no idea who Mirsab was fraternizing with in his apartment. The engineering student had been instructed to keep to himself and mind his own business. It was apparent, though, that he had ignored those orders. It made Cheng wonder what other orders Mirsab had chosen to ignore. Cheng had no choice but to sit and wait until Mirsab's guests had departed.

When the procession of four men filed out an hour later, Cheng stayed where he was until they had driven away. Then, he got out of his vehicle and entered the building.

The hallway smelled heavily of mildew and the carpeting was stained. He approached Mirsab's door and knocked.

Thinking one of his guests must have left something behind, the man opened his door with a smile while saying something in Arabic. Then he saw Cheng.

"May I help you?" he asked, switching to English.

"Henry Lee sent me," Cheng replied.

The look on Mirsab's face went from carefree to concerned in a fraction of a second. Slowly, he stepped back and said, "Come in."

As Cheng entered, he swept the room with his eyes.

It was spartanly furnished and what furnishings there were looked as if they had been there for decades.

Mirsab kept a clean home. There were no dishes in the sink or on the counter in the small, open kitchen. It didn't smell of garbage or spoiled food. In fact, it smelled much better than the hall.

In terms of personal effects, there weren't many Cheng could see. There were some Arabic-language magazines on the coffee table, along with a laptop and a Qur'an. A prayer rug had been rolled up and tucked away in the corner of the living room.

"Who were those men?" Cheng asked.

"What men?"

"The men who just left. The ones you thought had come back when you answered your door in Arabic."

Mirsab cast his eyes toward the floor. "I met them at a mosque. I am part of their prayer group."

Cheng snapped his fingers to get the engineering student to look him in the eyes. "You are not being paid to go to a mosque and there is only one group you are allowed to belong to. That's our group. Is that understood?"

"Yes, sir."

"Sit down," Cheng said, pointing at the small dining table. When Mirsab was seated, Cheng took the chair across from him and set his briefcase under the table.

"Why has Mr. Lee sent you? Is it time?" the engineering student asked.

"Soon," Cheng assured him. "In the meantime, I have come to check on you."

Cheng was highly adept at reading people. It was part of what made him a successful intelligence operative. Already, he could sense several things about

Mirsab. Adopting a relaxed posture, and a calm, even tone, he asked, "How have you been?"

"I have been lonely," the man instantly admitted.

"Lonely?"

"Yes," Mirsab replied. "I have never been away from my family for this long."

"Have you made any attempt to contact them?"

He shook his head. "No. It is forbidden."

So was fraternizing with others, but Cheng put that aside for the moment. "I know it is difficult, but you will see them again soon and they will be proud of you. The money is already helping them and it will continue to help them as long as you live up to your agreement."

"Yes, sir. I understand."

"Good. Now, let's talk about the men I saw leaving here. How long have you known them?"

"Not long. A couple of weeks," said Mirsab.

"Why did you go to the mosque?"

"To pray."

"You can't pray here?" Cheng asked.

"It's lonely. I wanted to pray with other people."

"Are you being paid to pray with other people?"

"No, sir," the engineer replied.

Cheng feigned a smile. "Mirsab, you need to think of your family. You are being well paid. Is there food in your kitchen?"

"Yes, sir."

"Does your toilet work? Is there water for you to bathe?"

"Yes, sir."

"Does your air-conditioning work? Does the roof keep you dry?"

He cast his eyes downward again. "Yes, sir."

"Look at me, Mirsab," said Cheng. He waited until

the young man looked at him before continuing. "You are free to go out to a park, to go to a movie. You may listen to music. You may watch TV. You may read your Qur'an. You may use your computer as long as you follow the rules. I don't think we have unduly burdened you, have we?"

"No, sir."

"In fact, I think we have been quite good to you. Haven't we?"

"Yes, sir."

Cheng studied him. "What do these men from the mosque know about you?"

Mirsab shrugged. He was a short man, only about five-foot-five, and pudgy. When he shrugged, skin rolled like a shar-pei. His habit of staring at the floor only added to the likeness of a guilty dog.

"I'm not angry," said Cheng. "But I need to know. What did you tell them?"

"I told them I was an engineering student."

Internally, Cheng tensed, but he didn't outwardly betray his concern. Instead, he maintained an appearance of calm and waited. Another part of being an effective intelligence operative was being comfortable with silence.

"I told them that I was in the process of transferring to Nashville Community College, but not until the next term. I told them I was just taking classes online at the moment."

It was a decent lie, thought Cheng. *Plausible.* Mirsab hadn't shot too high by claiming attendance at a school like Vanderbilt, and the part about taking classes online would explain why he spent so much time in his apartment. But while it was a passable cover story, he should have never placed himself in a position to have to use one.

His loneliness was troubling. He was too needy. With all of the distractions America had to offer, the fact that Mirsab couldn't tolerate being by himself spoke to deeper issues—none of which Cheng had the time or the desire to address.

"What else did you tell these men?" Cheng asked.

"Nothing, I swear."

"Did you tell them where you are from?"

"No," Mirsab replied, before changing his answer. "I mean, yes."

"Which is it?"

"They know I am from the Emirates, but I lied about what village."

Cheng's displeasure was growing. "What else?"

"Nothing, I swear."

That was the second time he had given that answer and Cheng didn't believe him. The man was a weak link. While he didn't think Mirsab had blurted everything out, he only needed to have said just enough. If one of the men in his prayer group had been an FBI informant or, even worse, an actual FBI agent, there was no telling what damage might have already been caused. All it would take was Mirsab not to remember one of his lies or to go halfway down a conversational road he hadn't intended. Cheng could only hope the other cell members were not this dysfunctional.

"Mirsab, I want to talk with you about the project," said Cheng. They didn't use the term "operation" with the cell members, it sounded too military, too much like terrorism. If any of them were ever interrogated by authorities, the Second Department wanted the entire thing to sound as much like a criminal enterprise as possible. "Do you understand what it is we are trying to do?"

Once again, Mirsab looked at the floor. "Yes."

"Look at me," said Cheng. "What is it you think the project is?"

"I don't think anything. I just want it to be over so I can go home."

"Mirsab, before I came to see you, I paid a visit to Wazir Ibrahim. Do you remember what you told Wazir you thought was in the canisters?"

The engineering student nodded.

"We explained to you what our project is, so why would you think any different?" asked Cheng.

"Because the canisters we trained with were too heavy."

The intelligence officer smiled. "Did you share this concern with the others?"

Mirsab shook his head.

"Good," replied Cheng.

Pulling the suppressed M&P pistol from his briefcase, he then shot the Emirati right between the eyes.

CHAPTER 37

Normally when it came to surveillance, you were left trying to make lemonade out of truckloads of lemons. In this case, though, they had caught a partial break right off the bat.

Harvath's first goal had been to isolate Deng's room. He didn't want any hotel guests above, below, or on either side. Fortunately, only the rooms above and below were occupied. Offering those guests upgrades, the manager moved them to another part of the hotel. She then blocked out the rooms on either side of Deng in the computer so that they'd remain empty.

The room across the hall was also unoccupied and that's the one Harvath wanted. When he and Sloane entered the lobby with their bags, the manager met them at the front desk and checked them in. Despite the fugitive drama unfolding in her hotel, she remained calm and professional.

She provided Sloane with key cards to their room and then handed Harvath an envelope with an override card that would open any guest room or other key-card-controlled door on the property.

Harvath thanked her and he and Sloane headed toward the elevator. As they did, Chase entered the hotel and approached the front desk. The manager met him there and led him back to her office where he could watch the CCTV feeds unseen. For as big a building as it was, they could have done with a lot more cameras, but the limited number they had was better than nothing.

Harvath and Sloane got off the elevator on the third floor and followed the signs to their room. They appeared to pay no attention to Deng's door, though they paused long enough for Harvath to listen while Sloane pretended to look for the room key. All he could hear was the television. The *Do Not Disturb* sign was still hung from the handle. There was no telling if Deng was inside. That was the first issue Harvath planned to address.

When Sloane finally produced their key card, she opened the door and Harvath followed her in.

He quietly reminded her not to turn on the lights. Sloane understood. They would be using the peephole to watch Deng's door. If their room was backlit and one of them stepped up to the hole, they might give themselves away.

Setting her bag down, Sloane stepped into the kitchen area and turned on the small light under the microwave above the stove. Then, walking into each bedroom, she turned on the en suite bathroom light. It would give them enough light to operate by, but not enough to indicate when one of them was standing at the door.

Harvath unpacked his gear and handed a radio and earpiece to Sloane. Once he had his set up, he walked into one of the bedrooms and hailed Chase down in the manager's office.

"All clear here," he replied.

Harvath told him to stay alert and tucked his radio

in his pocket. Returning to the living room, he set his phone on vibrate, made his LaRue hot, and propped it near the door. Sloane readied her Glock and then stepped into the bedroom to rack a round into the shotgun. There was no other sound like it in the world. The last thing she wanted to do was give away their presence with a loud *schik-schak*.

The FBI had had the hotel under surveillance for only a matter of hours. Before Harvath had asked them to pull back, they had paid a visit to the manager and gone through all of the CCTV footage. They had seen Bao Deng check in and get on an elevator up to his room, but he hadn't appeared on camera again after that. As far as they knew, he was still in his room. If so, *What was he waiting for? Who was he waiting for?* Those were the questions on everyone's minds.

The list of possible answers was endless—he was waiting for someone to make contact with him, he had a meeting but it wasn't until well after midnight, he was here to make sure the Nashville cell carried out its assignment. There were countless reasons an intelligence operative might hole up in a hotel room. There also was another possibility—Deng might not even be in the room. He might have used the hotel simply to receive his FedEx, and once he picked it up, had covertly left the premises. That was the first thing Harvath wanted to ascertain.

Turning on the TV, he sent Sloane to the peephole, called the front desk, and asked for the manager. When she got on the phone, he told her they were ready to go and explained what he wanted her to do.

The housekeeping crew had already gone home for the night. What's more, the hotel had a strict policy of respecting their guests' *Do Not Disturb* signs. If Deng had stayed at the hotel before, he might very well know both of these things. Sending a maid to his room for turn-down service could make him suspicious. That wasn't something they wanted.

As Harvath waited, he listened as the manager picked up another phone and dialed Deng's room. The sound of it ringing could be heard from across the hall.

It rang several times and finally went to voice mail. When it did, the manager left the message Harvath had instructed her to leave. It was time for the next step.

The manager had been reluctant to place one of her staff in harm's way. Harvath had reassured her that he and his partner would be right across the hall, watching the entire thing. While he could have sent Chase, all it would have taken was one question about the hotel that he couldn't answer and Deng would have been on to him. That, in Harvath's opinion, was an even more dangerous risk. The hotel engineer would be fine.

A couple of minutes later, Sloane signaled that she could see the engineer in the hallway. Walking up to Deng's door, he knocked loudly, saying, "Engineering."

When there was no response, he pulled out his key card, opened the door, and once again announced himself.

Removing a rubber wedge from his pocket, he propped the door open and walked inside. If he saw Deng, the hotel engineer had been told to explain that the room below had water dripping down and he had come to investigate the possible source of the leak. The engineer was only inside for a few moments before stepping back into the hall and knocking on Harvath's door.

"Nobody's there," he said as Sloane opened up.

"Thank you," she replied. "We'll take it from here."

Handing the engineer back his wedge, Harvath stepped inside Deng's room while Chase monitored the CCTV feeds downstairs and Sloane stood in their doorway to keep a lookout.

There was no food in the fridge, no dishes in the sink, nor in the dishwasher. The bed had not been slept in. The shower had not been used. Some clothing hung in the closet. An empty suitcase sat with its lid open on a luggage stand. As far as Harvath could tell, it didn't contain any hidden pockets or false panels.

The empty FedEx box sat next to the wastepaper basket under the desk. Harvath studied the shipping label, but it provided no clues to what had been inside. On top of the desk was a wall charger for a cell phone. That was all that he could see sitting out in the open.

He now moved much more methodically through the room, looking anywhere and everywhere things could be hidden. He looked under tables, opened air vents, unzipped cushions, slid the fridge out from the wall, and took the lid off the toilet tank. He removed drawers, outlet covers, and light fixtures, putting each item back afterward exactly the way he had found it.

When he left the room and closed the door behind him, he looked at Sloane and shook his head. "Suitcase and some clothes, that's it."

"Which sounds like he'll be back at some point."

Harvath stepped into their room. "Probably," he repeated. "But if he sneaks back in, we're going to have to be watching that hallway, or none of us will know."

There was no easy way to conduct the surveillance. Someone had to stand at the door, stare out the peephole, and wait. In a word, it sucked. But surveillance normally did. They had decided to go in half-hour shifts. Harvath offered to go first.

After radioing down to Chase, he pulled out his phone and sent a quick SITREP to the Old Man and Agent Urda. Then he took his place at the door.

Sloane grabbed the remote and sat down on the couch. They'd had the news on, but searching through the program guide, she found a romantic comedy she liked and switched over to that. Harvath rolled his eyes. Sloane ignored him.

While Harvath wasn't a big romcom fan, having something going in the background helped break up some of the monotony. After his half hour was up, he handed over the surveillance to Sloane.

They had bought snacks on their way in and he grabbed a bottle of water and a granola bar before sitting down on the couch.

Picking up the remote he searched the program guide to see what else was on. He just wanted to zone out for a little bit and didn't care for Sloane's movie. He was in luck as *Black Hawk Down* was on. As soon as he changed the channel, she flipped him the bird.

He smiled and put his feet up on the coffee table. Opening his granola bar, he began to eat.

When his cell phone vibrated, he looked down to see the Old Man had sent him an update. None of the FBI interviews at the Johnson Space Center had been able to produce any actionable intel and the CIA's interviews with the engineering students' families in the Emirates had also come up empty.

The one piece of good news was that some employees in the free Wi-Fi locations the terrorists had used in Seattle, Dallas, and Baltimore had remembered seeing them. It wasn't much, but it was a start.

Everyone had been hoping that the engineering students had been undisciplined, and that when they had used the same locations for free Wi-Fi, it was because those were the closest to where they were living. Harvath acknowledged the Old Man's message, set his phone on the arm of the couch, and closed his eyes.

When he opened them and looked at his watch, he saw that he had slept through his shift. "Why didn't you wake me up?" he asked.

"Old people need naps," said Sloane.

Harvath smiled and got off the couch. "You know what? You're going to make a great first wife someday."

Returning his unopened bottle of water to the fridge, he grabbed a tall Red Bull and took his post at the peephole.

"Touché," Sloane replied, before hailing Chase over the radio for a SITREP.

All was quiet downstairs, so she settled in on the couch and changed the channel back to watch the end of her romantic comedy. Harvath had no grounds to complain. She had given him the gift of extra sleep.

After a couple of lines of stupid comedy dialogue, though, he smiled when she clicked back over to *Black Hawk Down*. They really did have a lot in common.

Listening to the movie as he peered out the peephole, Harvath could picture all of the scenes in his head, he had seen it that many times. The operation never should have gone as wrong as it had. Too many lives were lost on that op. Every branch of the military had studied it. The greatest insult that could have been paid to those who had died that day would have been to not have learned from their sacrifice.

When his shift was up, Sloane handed him the remote, told him the movie *Commando* was coming up, and then, mimicking one of Arnold Schwarzenegger's lines from the film, added, "I eat Navy SEALs for breakfast."

"The line is 'I eat *Green Berets* for breakfast,' *not* Navy SEALs," Harvath corrected. He offered to repay her kindness by taking the next shift, but she wouldn't hear of it.

"I've got my second wind," she said.

Harvath didn't want to risk falling asleep again and was halfway to the fridge for another Red Bull when his cell phone vibrated. It was Special Agent Urda.

"This is Harvath."

"I think we know where Deng is," said Urda. "Or at least where he was recently."

"That's fantastic. Where?"

"There's a brew pub on the corner. I'll be parked outside. Meet me there in five minutes."

CHAPTER 38

Urda dispatched one of his agents to share watch with Sloane and another to sit with Chase in the manager's office. Knowing they were both backed up, Harvath left the hotel and met up with the FBI man at the Cool Springs Brewery on the corner. He was a tall, solid guy in his late forties who looked like he had probably played football in college.

Once they were on the highway and confident that they hadn't been followed, Urda activated his lights and siren.

He exited the highway east of downtown and navigated through a low-income neighborhood of weed-infested yards and houses that were falling apart. Flashing blue lights and the powerful white lights of evidence lamps two blocks up told Harvath they were in the right place.

Urda showed his credentials to a Nashville PD patrol officer, who waved them through, and he grabbed the nearest parking place they could find. Yellow crime scene tape blocked off one of the houses, and crowds of onlookers were being held back across the street.

Walking up to one of the detectives, Urda identified himself and asked for a man named Hoffman.

"Hey, Mike!" the detective shouted. "You've got a visitor."

A muscular man in a tight suit stepped away from a group of evidence technicians and came down the walkway. Urda shook hands with him and then introduced Harvath.

"Detective Mike Hoffman," he said, shaking Harvath's hand.

"Mike works with the FBI's Nashville office on a lot of our cases," Urda explained. "He's the detective who agreed to be at the airport to follow Tommy Wong."

"Except we ended up with somebody even worse," he replied.

"What exactly happened here?"

"Follow me," said Hoffman. "I'll show you."

After they signed in, with Harvath giving a fake name and agency, they were issued paper booties and told they could go inside. The techs were done collecting samples and everything had been photographed. The body had not yet been removed.

Hoffman stood back as he approached the front door and allowed Harvath and Urda to go in first. More portable evidence lamps crowded the living room, bathing it in hot, white light. The scene was horrific. Blood was everywhere. The FBI man stood with the Nashville detective as Harvath did a circle around the body and studied the room.

"Somali?" he asked.

Hoffman nodded. "Wazir Ibrahim. Thirty-one years old. He was a political refugee who moved to Nashville a couple years ago."

"Is there a big Somali population here?"

"We're not Minneapolis, but we've got our share."

Ibrahim was in a kneeling position, slumped over forward, with his throat cut clean through.

"Any idea what the murder weapon was?" Urda asked.

"We're thinking it was possibly a straight razor," replied Hoffman.

"Or a garrote wire," said Harvath as he bent down and studied the wound.

"He really bled out, didn't he?" stated the FBI man as he looked at the large pool of blood across the carpet. "What's he kneeling on? A prayer rug?"

Harvath nodded. "It looks like the killer came up behind him and did him while he was in prayer."

"Which we're assuming means that Wazir Ibrahim knew his killer. He knew he was in the house, and was comfortable enough to pray in front of him, or maybe even with him."

"Big mistake," Urda replied.

"No kidding."

Harvath stood behind the body and mimicked garroting Ibrahim, in order to get a feel for how everything went down. "So what's your connection to all of this?" he asked Hoffman.

"One of the task forces I'm on is focused on child sex crimes. We've been working a child prostitution ring run by a Somali network. Ibrahim's name had come up, but we didn't have enough evidence to charge him. A couple days ago, he got popped for beating his wife.

"I got called in and we tried to sweat him for details about the sex ring. As soon as we started talking about it, he clammed up and asked for a lawyer. He got his bail hearing, but couldn't afford to bond out, so he sat in lockup."

"Where's the wife?" Harvath asked.

"She has family south of here in Shelbyville. The social worker recommended she stay with them for a while. Her brother-in-law came back up to get some more of her things. He's the one who discovered the body. And before you ask, the wife and the brother both have airtight alibis."

"Okay, so how do we know this is connected to our guy?"

"Because when officers collected statements, the next-door neighbor, a Mr. Enrique Vasquez," said Hoffman, referring to his notebook, "stated that an Asian man had come looking for Ibrahim earlier today. The man claimed to be from the warehouse Ibrahim worked at. Said he was here about an insurance claim. I spoke to Ibrahim's boss. Wazir never filed any insurance claim and the company carrier never sent anyone out.

"The guy gave the neighbor a business card, but it was bogus. Obviously, something's going on, so I started thinking. What are the odds that two Asian gentlemen switch boarding passes for a flight to Nashville on the same day some Asian guy with a bogus cover story is sniffing around a murder scene just hours before the murder happens?"

"Probably not a coincidence," offered Urda.

Hoffman nodded. "Which is why I put together a photo lineup and included one of the stills of your guy Deng from the CCTV footage at Nashville International. Guess which one the neighbor picked out?"

"Deng."

"Yup. Says he's positive, except the guy he saw banging on the front door today had glasses."

"What about the brother-in-law? Does he know anything?"

"No. He and Wazir didn't really have a good relationship. We showed him the photos, too, but he didn't recognize anyone."

"Have you had a chance to question the wife?" Harvath asked.

"Not yet," said Hoffman, "but we're working on it. She's on her way back to Nashville now."

"So who bailed Ibrahim out of jail?"

"His bond was put up by a local operation called Lumpy's. The agent who did all the paperwork said he had a phone call claiming to be from the director of some Somali benevolence association. The caller allegedly stated that he had heard Wazir had been locked up, but didn't know any of the details. He stated his mosque had taken up a collection to help him.

"The bond agent pulled up the info in the county system and relayed it to the caller. He told him what the rap was and how much it would cost to get him out. A while later, some Somali showed up with the entire thing in cash, plus the bond agent fees, and that was that, Ibrahim got sprung."

"Do we know who the Somali that showed up with the money is?"

"He's a taxi driver," Hoffman replied. "We've got detectives with him right now. He says some Asian guy paid him three thousand dollars to drop off the bail money, sign the paperwork, and drive Ibrahim back here."

"Which makes him one of the last people to have seen Wazir Ibrahim alive," stated Urda.

"And he's scared shitless, believe me. The detectives have put the fear of Allah into him. He's been totally cooperative."

"Have they given him the photo lineup?"

"They did," replied Hoffman. "Same results. He picked Deng right out, but also said he was wearing glasses."

Urda looked at Harvath. "So Deng switches boarding passes in order to come to Nashville, bail this Somali out of jail, and kill him. Why? Who is this Ibrahim guy?"

Harvath drew closer to the pair so that no one could overhear their conversation. "He's got to be connected with the Nashville cell somehow. Why else send Deng all the way here from China?"

The FBI agent nodded. "But if this was just about whacking some guy, why not pay one of the U.S.-based triads to do all of this? Plus, if you're going to croak him the same day you arrive in town, what's with the hotel room? Why hang up your clothes as if you're planning on sticking around?"

They were excellent questions and ones Harvath didn't immediately have the answers to. He was about to ask Hoffman something else when the same detective from earlier stuck his head in.

"Hey, Mike," he said. "It looks like we have a partial description of the suspect's vehicle."

"Talk to me," Hoffman demanded.

"An officer canvassing the neighborhood talked to some residents about a block down. They said they saw an Asian man with glasses driving a black SUV this afternoon. He parked down by them and walked up the block in this direction."

"Do we know what kind of SUV?"

"Either a late-model Mercury Villager or a Lincoln Navigator," the man replied. "I want to give them the photo lineup to see if they pick out your guy. Do you have it here?"

"No. It's in my car on the passenger seat. Go ahead and grab it. Let me know what they say," said Hoffman.

The detective flashed him a thumbs-up and left the house.

Special Agent Urda turned to Harvath. "What do you want to do? Sit on the hotel and hope he comes back, or put out a *Be on the Lookout* and rope in Nashville PD and the state police?"

"This guy *is* a murder suspect," Hoffman added. "If one of our officers rolls up on him, they deserve to know who they may be dealing with."

Hoffman was right and so was Urda, to a degree. The cops and state police needed to know that there was a dangerous suspect on the loose. The search also needed to be expanded beyond the hotel.

Harvath relented. "I'll go along with the BOLO, but we need to limit it. Nothing over the radio. I don't want somebody on a news desk with a scanner picking any of this up."

"We can send it via the mobile data terminals in the patrol cars."

"Go ahead and do it, then," said Harvath.

If Bao Deng's only reason for coming to the United States was to kill Wazir Ibrahim, he would already be on his way out of the state, and possibly even out of the country by now.

But something told Harvath that there was more to it. Much more.

CHAPTER 39

The self-storage lot had been chosen well. It was a mom-and-pop operation on a quiet road without a lot of traffic. It was the exact type of location Cheng would have chosen himself.

Driving the lanes between the rows of outdoor storage units, he studied the numbers. When he found the one he was looking for, he brought his vehicle to a stop parallel to the door and killed the engine.

He had already done one slow loop around. No one was there. He was completely alone. Stepping out of the Navigator, he walked around behind it and over to the storage locker door. He double-checked the number against the slip of paper in his hand—26. He was at the right spot.

With a small flashlight, he searched the frame of the metal roll-up door until he found it. It was a clear, tamperproof decal no one would have noticed had they not been looking for it. It was still intact, telling Cheng that no one had entered the storage unit since the items had been placed inside. Turning his attention to the heavy, high security combination lock, he rotated the five wheels on the bottom into place and the lock released.

Removing it from the hasp, he bent over and pulled the door open high enough to slip underneath. At the back of the unit were several boxes, two of them about a foot wide and almost five feet tall, all stacked upon a faded wooden pallet. He approached the boxes cautiously. Using his car key, he sliced the tape and opened each box to verify the contents and make sure everything was there.

He began with the tallest box and worked his way through the pile. Except for the heavy metal cylinders, everything was contained in its own hard-sided storage case. There was one case in particular that Cheng did not want to open. He took little comfort in the assurances Colonel Shi had given him that it was perfectly safe. After removing its locks, he lifted the lid and looked inside. He had been shown a picture of it before leaving China, but somehow he had thought it would look different. Instead, it just sat there looking rather benign. It was amazing to think that something of that size had the potential to end so many lives.

Closing all of the lids, he relocked the cases, and placed them back into their cardboard boxes.

He had a roll of packing tape in the SUV and he returned to get it. Opening the Navigator's rear door, he reached across the seat for the plastic bag containing his supplies. As he did, he heard a car nearing. Unless it was someone retrieving a boat to go fishing in the morning, it wasn't a good sign.

In an instant, Cheng made his decision. Leaving the bag, he stepped onto the backseat and then grabbed the roof rack to pull himself up. After quietly closing the Navigator's door from above, it was a simple step onto the metal roof of the storage unit.

He lay down on his stomach, slid back several feet from the edge, and waited.

When the car came down his lane, the first thing he

noticed was that it didn't have its lights on. *Another bad sign.* He removed the suppressor and threaded it onto the barrel of his Smith & Wesson.

No sooner did he have it affixed to the front of the pistol than a bright searchlight began sweeping both sides of the lane below. *Was it some sort of private security service, or was it the police?* He doubted a private security service would drive around with their headlights off. Their job was to present a visible presence in order to deter crimes. It had to be the police.

The vehicle came to a stop a couple of car lengths behind his SUV. Cheng lay completely still. He thought he discerned the muted squawk of a police radio coming from an open window.

It was an unfortunate circumstance. Cheng didn't look down his nose at police officers. He admired them. They had a very difficult job, which required a tremendous amount of courage. Whoever was down there was simply unlucky. They had shown up in the wrong place at the wrong time. *Or*, he wondered, *were the authorities on to him?*

Did they know he had switched boarding passes and that he had killed two men since arriving in the United States? Were they looking for Bao Deng, or worse, Tai Cheng? Was this random, or was it something more? There was no way to tell.

None of it mattered, though. Not with what was inside the storage unit. No one could be allowed to see that.

He listened as one of the vehicle's doors was opened. He then waited for a second. It never came. Whoever was down there was alone. Cheng prepared to act.

He visualized the officer's position by listening to

his boots on the asphalt. The officer probably had a
flashlight, maybe even one mounted to his weapon. He
would have seen that the storage unit door was partially
open, but he would check the Navigator first to make
sure no one was inside.

Using his forearms, Cheng crept to the edge of
the roof and peered over. It was indeed the police. He
could see the officer, behind the SUV. He had a flashlight in one hand and his pistol in the other. He had
been squatting, shining the light beneath the partially
open roll-up door.

Straightening up, he now began to back away. When
he reached for the microphone at his shoulder, that's
when Cheng fired.

He depressed the trigger twice in rapid succession.
The pistol bucked in his hands, punctuated by two
muffled spits. Each of the nine-millimeter hollow-
points found its mark, killing the officer instantly.

Hopping down from the roof, Cheng checked to
confirm that the man was dead. He was. The back of his
head was blown away and one of the rounds had exited
his left eye.

Cheng needed to move quickly. When the officer failed to report back in, backup would be sent, if it
wasn't already on the way.

Climbing down from the roof, he stepped to the
police cruiser and popped the trunk. It took him only
a second to find what he needed. Returning to the officer, he removed his radio and threw it on the Navigator's front passenger seat. He then dragged the corpse
out of the way and reentered the storage locker.

There wasn't enough time to load everything, so he
made a beeline for the most important item, the one
that absolutely could not be left behind.

Picking up the box, he carried it back to the SUV, opened the tailgate, and slid it into the cargo area.

Closing the tailgate, he started the Navigator and pulled it forward. After climbing out, he backed the patrol car into the storage unit, so that the bumper of the cruiser was pressed up against the boxes stacked upon the pallet.

Flipping open the cruiser's gas tank cover, he unscrewed the cap and, taking the top off one of the flares he had retrieved from the trunk, wrapped it in a rag and shoved it into the opening. Next, he dragged the body of the dead cop into the unit and placed him behind the wheel.

With everything ready to go, he ignited his second flare, tossed it on the backseat of the squad car, and exited the storage locker.

Rolling down the steel door, he replaced the padlock, slid back into the Navigator, and drove away from the storage facility.

CHAPTER 40

After questioning Wazir Ibrahim's neighbor, Vasquez, Harvath, and Urda followed Hoffman toward his office downtown. Nashville PD had brought the Somali cab driver in for further questioning and Harvath had several of his own he wanted to ask.

They were halfway there when an explosion erupted in the distance behind them and a roiling fireball climbed into the night sky.

"What the hell was that?" Harvath exclaimed as he turned around to look.

Urda watched the blast in his rearview mirror. "I don't know, but it was big. Gas leak?"

Harvath had no idea, but he didn't like the timing.

Two minutes later, Hoffman flipped his lights and siren on in front of them.

"Now what?" said Harvath.

Urda shrugged just as his cell phone rang. It was Hoffman, and he put him on speaker: "Did you see that explosion?"

"Affirmative."

"Radio says it came from a self-storage facility where a Nashville metro cop was investigating a suspicious black Lincoln Navigator."

Harvath could feel his heart rate pick up. "What caused the explosion? Was the Navigator rigged?"

"No idea. Dispatch lost contact with the officer. Stay on my bumper. We're going to turn around."

The two cars took advantage of a break in the median, U-turned, and, with Urda now also under lights and siren, sped toward the fire. When Harvath looked over at the FBI agent's speedometer, he saw that they were doing well over eighty miles an hour.

As Hoffman made it to the exit, he barely slowed down. Using the shoulder, he flew up the ramp, only feathered his brakes, and took a hard left into the intersection. Urda followed right behind.

They crossed over the highway and headed toward the source of the explosion. Up ahead were multiple emergency vehicles making their way in the same direction. The sound of screaming klaxons filled the air.

Hoffman blasted through two red lights and kept going. Suddenly, a blazing fire could be seen up ahead.

Four squad cars were already on scene. Leaning against one of the vehicles was an injured Nashville PD officer who was pressing a bloody bandage against his head. From the looks of him, he must have been close when the blast detonated. That was the first person Harvath wanted to talk to.

Urda pulled his car off the side of the road, just past the main entrance of the storage lot. He didn't even have it in Park before Harvath had thrown open his door and jumped out.

The bloody officer's nameplate read *Edmondson*. "What happened?"

The cop looked at Harvath and then over at Urda's sedan with its flashing lights. Figuring Harvath was some sort of law enforcement, he said, "Sergeant

Gerads was investigating a suspicious vehicle. When dispatch couldn't raise him, they called for any nearby units to respond. I was about a mile away. I pulled up just as the explosion happened."

"What exploded?"

"I don't know," the officer said.

"Where's Gerads?"

"I don't know."

"How about the vehicle? The black Navigator he was investigating?" Harvath asked.

"I didn't see anything except the explosion."

The officer's head, face, and upper body looked as if they had been raked with shrapnel. Behind them, fire trucks were now turning off the road and moving quickly into the lot.

"Where were you when the explosion happened?"

Officer Edmondson lifted his head and pointed to his patrol vehicle inside the lot. Even at this distance, Harvath could see that it had sustained some pretty serious damage. It looked like it had been hit by an IED. The man was lucky to be alive.

As Urda approached, Harvath looked at him and said, "Get on the phone to Quantico. Tell them to scramble a forensics team and get them here as quickly as possible."

"Will do," said Urda, as he pulled his cell phone from his pocket.

Harvath walked up the drive to join Hoffman, who was standing at the keypad for the open gate. The facility resembled a trailer park that had been turned upside down and set on fire. There was furniture, personal effects, and all sorts of debris everywhere. It was going to take months to figure out what belonged to whom.

"The Fire Department wants everyone to stay

back," the detective stated. "They don't know what other explosive items may be stored in some of these units."

Over the chaos, Harvath heard the sound of rotors. Looking up, he saw a police helicopter. It was sweeping the area with its powerful Midnight Sun spotlight. Hoffman held up his handheld radio so that he and Harvath could listen. As the pilot held the helo in hover, the tactical flight officer ran the searchlight and also studied his FLIR to direct firemen to the hottest part of the fire.

There were six rows of storage units, four of which were burning. Harvath pointed toward the business office at the edge of the sixth row and said, "Gather up as many officers as you can and meet me over there. If any of them have breaching tools, tell them to bring them."

"What are you doing? The fire chief said—" Hoffman began.

"I know what the fire chief said," Harvath replied. "Just do it."

Hoffman nodded and went to round up officers as Harvath ran toward the office. With every step, the temperature from the fire seemed to go up by ten degrees. By the time he reached the glass front doors, his face was flushed and the hair on his arms was beginning to singe.

He tried the doors, but they were locked, so he looked on both sides to see if there was another way in that was open. There wasn't. When he came back around to the front, Hoffman was there with four officers, none of whom had any breaching tools.

Speaking to the nearest cop, Harvath said, "Give me your ASP."

The officer complied, and with a snap of his wrist

Harvath extended the collapsible baton. Turning his head to the side, he swung hard and shattered the glass in the right front door.

He reached inside, unlocked it, and pulling both doors wide open, kicked down their rubber-capped stops.

Pointing at the handcarts arrayed on one wall of the lobby, he gave instructions. "I want every file cabinet out of here as quickly as possible."

As the cops rushed for the handcarts, Harvath said to Hoffman, "You and I will grab the computers and any DVRs they may be using to store security footage."

Hoffman nodded and the pair charged inside.

Beyond the lobby with its front desk and packing supply area was the office. It was a mess. There were papers everywhere. None of the cops knew where to start. Harvath told them to take all of it. A suspicious black Navigator, a massive explosion, and a missing police officer. Deng had been here. And he had been here for a reason. Harvath wanted to know why, and he hoped that something in the paperwork would tell him.

Despite the heat and the danger of the rapidly encroaching fire, the officers removed stacks of documents, file cabinets, and boxes filled with even more files. While Hoffman pulled out the computers and spirited them to safety, Harvath located the storage facility's DVR.

When everything that could be removed had been removed, Harvath took one last look inside. He sifted through desk drawers and cabinets looking for external drives, or any other items that they might have overlooked. Satisfied that he had gotten it all, he used his empty hands to carry out as many of the owners' personal effects as possible. Despite the best efforts of the firemen, the fire was still spreading and the office wasn't going to make it.

Hoffman looked at the pile of everything they had managed to save. "What do you want to do with all of this?"

What Harvath wanted to do was to stick his hand into it and pull out exactly what he was looking for, but he knew he'd have a better chance of getting hit by lightning or winning the lottery.

Sorting through massive amounts of data, searching for patterns, wasn't his forte. But he knew someone who was excellent at it.

Harvath looked at his watch. "I'm going to bring in a specialist."

CHAPTER 41

The man who stepped out of the Gulfstream G450 suffered from a condition known as Primordial Dwarfism. It was an extremely rare affliction, affecting fewer than one hundred people worldwide. What the man lacked in physical stature, though, he more than made up for in intelligence.

He was a genius when it came to algorithms, and he was a computer hacker par excellence. His friends called him Nicholas. His enemies, which included most of the international intelligence community, referred to him as the Troll.

Sold to a brothel by his soulless parents, he had been subjected to a monstrous upbringing. No child, much less one who wasn't expected to reach three feet tall or live past thirty, should have to endure the inhuman cruelty he had experienced.

But Nicholas had survived. And what's more, he had learned to thrive. His sharp mind was his greatest asset, and he had wielded it like a scalpel. Keeping his ears open and his mouth shut, he had picked up all sorts of information from the rich and powerful men who passed through the brothel. Once he understood that it wasn't knowledge that was power, but the application of it, his life had completely changed.

Some called what he did blackmail. He, though, liked to think of it simply as leverage. As his power had grown, so had his bank account. He became a master at the purchase, sale, and theft of black market intelligence. Intelligence agencies hated him and the powerful feared him. He had come a long way from the brothel in Sochi along the Black Sea.

He had also come a long way from his cutthroat days of intelligence theft. He still plied the dark digital arts, but with his thirtieth birthday a decade behind him, he had longed for something more. A perpetual outcast his entire life, he had wanted to become part of something bigger and more important than himself. Scot Harvath had provided him with that opportunity.

Descending the airstairs, Nicholas was accompanied by two enormous white dogs—Argos and Draco. Weighing more than two hundred pounds each, the twin beasts stood over three and a half feet tall at the shoulder. They were Caucasian sheepdogs, better known as Russian Ovcharkas, a favorite of the East German border patrol, as well as the Russian military. Fast, fiercely loyal, and ferocious when threatened, they were the perfect guardians for a man who counted among his enemies some of the most powerful and dangerous people in the world.

The dogs were as wary as their owner. Like a pair of devout sentinels, their eyes scanned everything and everyone in the private hangar. When they lighted on Harvath, they trotted over to him and placed a head beneath each of his hands.

As a sign of trust and affection, they leaned against him. It was like being pressed between two pickup trucks. He patted both of them until Nicholas clucked with his tongue against the roof of his mouth for them to return to him. Immediately, the dogs obeyed his command.

Harvath took in the sight of the little man. He looked healthy. He was tan and though he had spent the summer letting his hair grow longer, his beard was still neatly trimmed. It was a sign of his virility and something he was very proud of. Sufferers of Primordial Dwarfism were not known for being able to grow beards. He had spent a small fortune attempting to beat his ailment, trying all sorts of remedies and scientific treatments. He liked to think that the facts that he had outlived his life expectancy *and* had managed to grow a beard were signs that he was actually winning the battle.

Harvath had never seen Nicholas as engaged and as positive as he had been since coming to work for the Carlton Group. In addition, Nicholas now had a woman in his life. Something to do, someone to love, and something to look forward to. The man had discovered the three keys to happiness. Harvath was happy for him.

The large, private hangar the jet had taxied into had been converted into a gargantuan war room. The filing cabinets from the office were all lined up, boxes and piles of paper sat on folding tables, and desks had been brought in with power strips connected to long extension cords that ran across the floor of the hangar to various outlets.

Nicholas's eyes focused on all of it. Taking in a deep breath, he sighed and said, "Paper. How provincial."

Harvath understood. Nicholas preferred to work in the digital realm. He did, too. Even so, if there were answers in those files or on the computers, between the two of them, they would find them.

"Are those my research assistants?" he asked, pointing to an older couple sitting in the glassed-in hangar office.

Harvath nodded. "Mr. and Mrs. Logan. They own the self-storage company. I'll be helping out, too."

The little man shook his head. "It's going to be a long night."

While Nicholas had been in flight, Harvath had interrogated the Somali cab driver. Bao Deng had indeed been his customer, there was no question about it. But other than what he had already told the police, the Somali didn't know anything else. He was a dead end, so Harvath had decided to focus on the storage facility. Now that Nicholas had arrived, they were able to get to work.

Where Nicholas was mathematical, Harvath was visual. Thus, they came at the problem from two different directions. Like two teams tunneling through a mountain from opposite sides, they hoped to meet in the middle and find their answer there. Mrs. Logan worked with Nicholas and her husband worked with Harvath.

Harvath had a lot of questions, starting with the CCTV footage. According to the Logans, they used an inexpensive, wireless camera system. It came with an Internet app that allowed them to remotely check in on their facility from home. From time to time it was known to drop offline and could be fixed only by someone in the office rebooting it manually. Despite those facts, Harvath had doubted it was a coincidence that it had picked tonight to go down again.

His next question had to do with the specific layout of the self-storage facility. Mr. Logan located an old survey of the property in one of the file cabinets, brought it over, and laid it on the table he and Harvath were using.

Based on the blast damage, the Fire Department had approximated the general vicinity of the blast. Harvath circled that cluster of storage units as his ground zero and started there.

"What information do you have on these?" he asked.

"Twenty-six, twenty-seven, thirty-six, and thirty-seven."

Mr. Logan walked back to his file cabinets and began searching for the paperwork. Though he and his wife kept some things on computer, he preferred pen and paper. Every rental agreement required a signature and he had kept copies of everything.

"Are there any unusual customers that stand out in your mind?" Harvath asked as the man conducted his search.

"You see all sorts of people in the storage business. 'Unusual' is kind of a loose term."

"How about suspicious?"

"We get our share of those, too," said Logan, a pair of reading glasses perched on the end of his nose as he combed the files. "We always have to watch out for people using the units for illegal activities. Sometimes, people will take one of these deeper units to hide a stolen car until it can be chopped up. Sometimes they even do the chopping inside, late at night. That's why we make sure the police have the gate code, so they can patrol any time they want."

Harvath remembered seeing the keypad. "Does everyone use the same code?"

"No. Each customer gets their own unique code. That way, if they don't pay their bill, we can freeze them out. We put an additional lock on their unit, too."

"Do you keep a record of when the gate is accessed?"

"We do. It feeds to our computer system."

Harvath looked at Nicholas, who was sitting across one of the desks from Mrs. Logan. "I'm on it," the little man said.

"The other thing we have to watch out for is people trying to cook meth," Logan added. "I wouldn't be surprised if that's what caused the explosion. Chemicals stored in one of the units."

Harvath doubted it. It would take a lot of chemicals to cause an explosion that size, but anything was possible.

After locating the agreements for the four units, Logan returned to the table and handed them over.

Harvath placed them in a grid and looked at the names on the top sheets. "Ring any bells for you?"

Logan turned each of the rental agreements to the last page and laid them in a row. Each contained a photocopy of the customer's driver's license. As he studied them, Harvath asked Mrs. Logan to come over and look at them, too.

"Nothing?" Harvath asked after several minutes.

Both of the Logans shook their heads.

Harvath looked at the third photo in their impromptu lineup. He could barely make the guy, Todd Thomas, out. "Why is this one such poor quality? It looks like a copy of a copy."

Mr. Logan picked it up and examined it more closely. "I don't know, but it wasn't done with our Xerox machine."

"How do you know?"

He picked up the other applications, looked at their dates, and said, "Because our machine's in excellent condition. We bought it new and barely use it. Besides, look at the other copies. They're fine."

Harvath looked for himself. Logan was right. The two agreements that had been processed before the blurry Thomas photo were crystal clear, as was the one that came after.

"I've never heard of a Xerox machine just having a bad day."

Mrs. Logan drew her husband's attention to something on the Thomas agreement by tapping the bottom of the page.

"What is it?" Harvath asked.

"We didn't take this application," Mrs. Logan said. "Donald did."

"Who's Donald?"

"Don is our manager," replied Mr. Logan, shaking his head. "He's a nice young man, but he doesn't always have the greatest eye for detail."

"My husband is being generous," Mrs. Logan interjected. "He means Donald is lazy. Half the time I lose sleep at night wondering if he remembered to lock up, or if he left all of the lights burning."

"Do you know where he is now?" said Harvath.

"Probably at home asleep."

"Do you have his number? I'd like to talk to him."

Mr. Logan nodded and fished a worn address book from his breast pocket. As he searched for the number, Harvath waved Urda over and asked him to run the names and driver's license numbers of the clients on the four storage unit agreements.

Urda wrote them all down and then stepped to the front of the hangar to make his call. When Mr. Logan had found the page with his manager's phone number, he held it up for Harvath to see.

Pulling out his cell phone, Harvath punched in the number.

"When Donald answers, just tell him that there was a fire and we're trying to locate one of the customers whose unit was damaged."

Mr. Logan nodded and Harvath handed him the phone.

CHAPTER 42

The call with Donald lasted about fifteen minutes. Did he remember the customer who had rented unit 26, Mr. Todd Thomas? He did.

"Why?" asked Harvath.

"I've got cousins in Kentucky named Thomas," said the manager. "I joked that maybe we were related. He didn't think that was funny."

"Why didn't he think that was funny?"

"Probably because he's Asian and I'm not."

Bingo, thought Harvath. "Would you recognize him if you saw him again?" he asked, snapping his fingers to get Nicholas's attention.

"Maybe," Donald replied.

"Do you have access to a computer?"

"For, like, the Internet and stuff?"

"Yeah," said Harvath. "For, like, the Internet."

"I've got my phone."

"Okay, hold on a second."

Harvath muted the call and asked Nicholas if there was somewhere he could post the picture of Bao Deng so that Donald could look at it.

"Ask him if he does Snapchat," the little man replied.

"I don't want to use Snapchat and have it on their server. I want us to keep control."

Nicholas gave Harvath a URL and told him he'd have Deng's picture posted in a moment.

As they waited, Harvath asked the manager about Mr. Thomas's photocopy. Donald explained that while most customers filled out a rental agreement while standing at the front desk, Thomas had shown up with his already completed. Along with it, he had also included a copy of his driver's license.

"Did you ask to see his actual driver's license in order to verify it?" Harvath asked.

"Of course," Donald replied. "But everything matched up. I could read his address, date of birth, all that stuff, so I figured why make another copy? Go green, right?"

Harvath shook his head. There was so much they could have done with that photograph.

Nicholas flashed him a thumbs-up, indicating that Deng's picture had been posted, and Harvath gave Donald the URL.

After a moment, the manager placed his phone back against his ear and said, "That's not him."

"You're sure?" Harvath said. "Take a look again."

"I don't need to look again. The Thomas guy was much older than the guy in your photo."

"How much older?"

"I don't know," Donald said, thinking. "Fifties. Sixties maybe."

"Is there anything else you can remember about him? Any other distinguishing features? Tattoos? Scars?"

"Not really. He was just kind of a plain dude."

"Do you remember how tall he was?"

"Shorter than me. Definitely. Maybe five-foot-seven."

Harvath made another note. "How about what he was driving? Did you get a look at his car?"

"Nope. Never saw it."

Harvath asked a couple more questions before thanking the man and disconnecting the call. As he did, Urda came back over.

"That Todd Thomas Tennessee driver's license is bogus," the FBI agent reported.

Harvath wasn't surprised. His mind was now going a million miles an hour. He asked the Logans if they would be kind enough to return to the hangar office and wait there. He didn't want to discuss anything further in front of them.

Once they had gone, Nicholas said, "So, who's our new mystery Asian man?"

"I think it's probably safe to call him Chinese," stated Urda.

Harvath nodded. "Agreed. And if this new guy, *Thomas*, rented a storage unit in Nashville, we should assume he rented units in the other cell cities, too."

Urda already had his cell phone back out. "Under the same name?"

"If it were me," Harvath replied, "I'd use a different name with different ID for each one. I wouldn't want someone like me connecting the dots."

"So what should the field offices in the other cities be looking for?"

"We've got a male Chinese, in his fifties or sixties, around five-foot-seven, who has used the alias Todd Thomas. With a name like that, he may be trying to not have the paperwork reflect anything Chinese, so that's something to look for. We know when he rented the Nashville storage unit, so that gives us a date to work backward and forward from. I'd also look for anyone who walked into a self-storage facility with a copy of his or her driver's license already in hand."

There was something else about that photocopy, something that bothered him, but Harvath couldn't place it.

"What else?" Urda asked.

"I'd focus on mom-and-pop operations in quieter, somewhat secluded areas near each city."

"Without cameras?"

"If those exist, sure. I've got a feeling, though, that cameras don't bother this guy. In fact, they might be a plus. Once he hacks his way in, he's got a way to remotely monitor all of his units."

"Anything else?"

"No. I think that's it. For now."

"Wait," said Nicholas, who had been clicking away at his laptop. "There may be one additional item."

He had asked to see the Thomas paperwork, especially the payment information. "Did you get a hit on the credit card?" Harvath asked.

The little man nodded as he peered at his screen and wrote something down. "It looks like he used a high-value, prepaid credit card for the storage company to draw his monthly rent from. Short of someone paying with cash, that's one of the top things I'd be looking for."

"Got it," said Urda. Taking his checklist, he strode back toward the front of the hangar to update the team at the National Counter Terrorism Center.

Harvath turned his attention back to Nicholas. "Were you able to access the facility's keypad log?"

"I was, but a big chunk of data from tonight has been erased."

Harvath wasn't surprised about that either. "Whoever knocked the CCTV footage offline could have accessed the keypad data."

"What do you think he had in that storage locker?" Nicholas asked.

"Something that made a very big bang."

"You don't think the bang was the explosion of the police car they found?"

"No. I think Deng was doing something at that unit when the cop showed up and he killed him. Maybe he used the police car as a fuse to start a chain reaction. There was definitely something else in there."

"Any clue as to what?"

Harvath shook his head. "My guess is that it had something to do with the attack. Maybe a bomb of some sort. I think Wazir Ibrahim, the dead Somali, was involved and maybe got compromised, so Deng was sent in to kill him."

"What about the engineer accessing Facebook from Nashville?"

"Ibrahim is dead. A police officer is dead. And a storage unit went up in a big fireball. Right now, I don't think it looks too good for that engineer."

Nicholas opened another window on his laptop. "Well, he hasn't accessed his Facebook page recently, so you may be right."

"Or I could be completely wrong. Maybe Deng was sent to kill the Somali and take his place. Maybe he and the Nashville engineer have gone operational and torching the storage unit was intended to buy them enough time to do whatever they need to do. I don't know."

That was what was so frustrating. They were steps behind, playing catch-up in a game that was only getting faster.

"What do you need me to focus on next?"

Harvath looked at all of the materials that had been

driven to the hangar and organized into sections. Then he looked at Nicholas sitting behind his computer. What made the most sense was to set him loose on what he did best.

"I want you to find me whoever took that CCTV system offline and erased those keypad entry logs."

CHAPTER 43

Lieutenant Fordyce accepted Billy Tang's rifle and set it against the rock next to him. "For the record," he whispered, "this is still a really bad idea."

Tang nodded. "Yeah, I know."

Fordyce looked over his shoulder at the ridgeline in the distance. Tucker and Johnson would almost be at the top with Jin-Sang by now.

Looking back at the prison camp, he adjusted his rifle and tried to make himself comfortable. Comfortable, though, was a highly relative term. He wasn't going to feel truly comfortable until they had gotten the hell out of this godforsaken country.

"In and out," he ordered Tang. "Five minutes tops and not a second longer."

"Understood," the CIA operative agreed.

He was dressed in his peasant clothing with his suppressed nine-millimeter pistol concealed underneath. From his shoulder hung Jin-Sang's canvas bag. It would give him a way to carry what he needed, as well as a place to hide his night vision goggles once he got there. It would also, he hoped, be a sign to the sister, reaffirming that he had been sent by Jin-Sang.

Fordyce watched through his rifle scope as a guard

walked slowly by the fence, stopped for a moment, and then moved on. Just beyond was the infirmary where Jin-Sang's sister, Hana, had been relegated. According to the little boy, neither the official camp doctor nor the prisoner charged with assisting him remained there overnight. If a patient died, so be it. The only things of value the doctor bothered locking up were the medicine and his office. Tang packed his lockpick set just in case.

"Guard's gone. Time to move," Fordyce whispered.

"Whatever happens," Tang replied as he stood, "don't do anything stupid just to save my ass."

"Don't worry. We don't do stupid."

With a smile, Tang took off for the fence. Inside, his heart was already pounding against his chest. He had done a lot of dangerous things over his years of sneaking into North Korea, but this was hands-down the most dangerous.

He had quizzed Jin-Sang about mines, trip wires, and other measures that could be around the perimeter, but the boy had told him none of that existed. "Then how do they keep the prisoners in?" he had asked. "Fear," was Jin-Sang's response.

All of the prisoners believed that the fence was electrified. It wasn't. The small stream that ran through the valley barely generated enough electricity to power camp necessities. Running a lethal voltage of current through the fence was something the prison establishment decided it couldn't afford.

Despite all of the boy's assurances, when Tang got within one hundred meters of the fence, he chose his steps very carefully. Through his night vision goggles, he could make out the lightly trod path that ran parallel to the fence. It was at the spot where it cut in that Jin-Sang had told him he would find the hole.

As he moved, Tang made sure to lift his head up every once in a while to scan the interior of the camp for guards, as well as other prisoners. Everyone was a potential alarm ringer. As Jin-Sang had said, the camp operated completely on fear.

Where the path curved to the right, Tang saw the warped part of the fence. It was held together with two pieces of narrow wire—one above and one below. The hole wasn't huge, but it looked just big enough for him to squeeze through. So far, everything the little boy had told him had been spot-on. The next question was whether he had been correct about the electric current.

When the team had asked Jin-Sang why there were no visible lights in the evening, he said that this was a phenomenon of the Chinese. Whatever hardships they were expected to face in America, lack of electricity was allegedly one of them.

Approaching the fence, Tang crouched down near the opening, reached into his canvas bag, and withdrew his "testing stick." Fordyce had snapped a piece of metal off his Leatherman tool, which Tang had then lashed with surgical tape to a plastic syringe given him by Tucker, the corpsman. Tang had pulled the plunger, which allowed the syringe to ride on the end of a stick to give him a little distance. It was like having a screwdriver with a long, insulated handle. If the fence was live, the current would cause an arc when the fence was touched by another piece of metal.

Tang made ready and then extended his testing stick toward the fence. His body tensed as the metal made contact, but it was only a psychological reaction. Nothing happened. Just as Jin-Sang had said, the fence wasn't hot.

He pulled the syringe off the stick, took off his

night vision goggles, and dropped everything into his bag. Unwinding the two pieces of wire holding the fence closed, he crawled through and then quickly put everything back as he had found it.

By design, there was absolutely no cover between the fence and the infirmary. It made it easier to identify and shoot prisoners who were trying to escape. That was just one of the many reasons Fordyce hadn't liked the plan. But the die had already been cast. Billy Tang was inside the wire and now it was time to move.

His dark clothing, the moonless night, and the complete absence of searchlights and perimeter lighting helped to make Tang *almost* invisible. He covered the ground to the infirmary as fast and as quietly as he could, then pressed himself up against the outer wall. It was a cold, one-story building built of concrete.

He listened for several moments as he took deep breaths and waited for his heart rate to slow. There were no noises coming from inside. He couldn't hear anything outside either. Not even the nighttime creatures seemed to want to be anywhere near this place.

Fordyce had wanted Tang to carry a radio, but he had refused. If he got caught, the North Koreans would immediately know that he wasn't working alone. He was willing to risk his own life, but not theirs, not so needlessly. It was yet another thing about the plan Fordyce hadn't liked. Nevertheless, he had agreed.

With his breathing and heart rate steadier, Tang ducked below the windows and crept toward the infirmary's front door. Jin-Sang had described the layout to him as best he could. His sister, Hana, was isolated, but she wasn't alone. There were other patients inside the building. If any of them became suspicious of him and raised the alarm, he was cooked. It was Les Johnson, the SEAL he had pointed his gun at, who had made a simple but brilliant suggestion: "Mask up."

It made perfect sense. It was an infirmary. Hana's condition sounded like TB. The doctor and assistant probably wore surgical masks around her, as well as around any other patients with similar conditions. The problem, though, was that the doctor would be dressed in military garb and the assistant in a prison uniform. Neither of them would be dressed in the clothes of a North Korean farmer.

Tang, though, had no choice and hoped that his mask and an authoritative bearing would be enough to bluff his way through and cow any prisoner into believing he had a right to be there.

He was also hoping that the presence of the Chinese, along with their North Korean advisors, had been disruptive and odd enough to condition prisoners to accept the out-of-the-ordinary. It was a long shot, and he knew it, but it was the only shot they had if he was going to make contact with Hana.

Placing the mask over his face, Billy Tang crept the final distance to the door, took one more deep breath, and prepared to slip inside.

CHAPTER 44

The old wooden door was unlocked, just as Jin-Sang had said. As Tang opened it, the hinges groaned in protest. It was a terrible sound; like someone moaning in pain. He debated whether to close it, but knew that an open door would attract attention. Lifting up on the handle, he helped alleviate the pressure on the hinges and the door closed more quietly than it had opened.

Even through his surgical mask, the inside of the infirmary smelled terrible. The only thing sterile about the place appeared to be its décor. The bare, concrete walls were unadorned and the floors were stained. With what, Tang could only imagine, but he had a pretty good idea.

Based on the streaks that started at the door and led down the hall toward what must have been an examination room, there had probably been countless prisoners beaten, tortured, and then dragged bleeding into this building. The DPRK treated farm animals better than it did its prisoners. The smell, mixed with thoughts of the horrors this building had seen, turned his stomach.

The first door Tang passed was labeled *Doctor* and was locked up tight. The next was marked with the

Korean characters for *Storage* and was also locked. The third room was an empty exam room. Considering that the guards, the prison officials, and their families used the infirmary, it was stunning how substandard and filthy the place was.

By smell alone, he knew that he was nearing the ward. Above the smell, he could hear coughing, lots of it. Tang was glad to be wearing a mask.

The North Korean idea of "isolating" Hana from the other patients had been to separate her bed with three sheets hung from the ceiling. The sheer incompetence of even the doctors in the DPRK never ceased to amaze him.

Stepping behind the sheets, he saw her. The sixteen-year-old looked more dead than alive. Her arms were covered with lesions, her breathing was labored, and her chest was covered with the bloody sputum that she had been coughing up. Despite all this, there was an angelic quality to her expression that broke his heart. The idea that a five-year-old could be locked up in a labor camp for what her father had done was beyond inhuman.

Coming closer, Tang looked for the scar beneath her right eye. It was there, Jin-Sang explained, that an angry foreman had once struck her with a pipe for not working fast enough.

Having confirmed it was Hana, Tang removed a small digital camera from his bag and turned it on. The circumstances weren't even close to optimal for filming a video, but he would have to make do.

Hana's eyes were half-open. Billy Tang knelt next to her bed so he could whisper in her ear. Taking her hand, he asked in Korean if she could hear him. Slowly, she turned her head to look at him.

There was neither shock nor curiosity in her eyes; just a shallow glassiness. Tang was worried that the TB might have already affected her brain.

"Jin-Sang sent me," he whispered. "Look, he gave me his bag to show you."

He held up the bag so Hana could see. Her face remained expressionless, but he felt her give his hand a subtle squeeze.

"Jin-Sang is safe."

The girl squeezed his hand again.

"Hana, I am a friend. I can help you. But I need you to help me."

Billy Tang knew he was making a ridiculous proposition. You didn't have friends in a DPRK labor camp, not in the traditional sense. You didn't even have family, not really. Everyone was a source of competition for food and a potential turncoat who would sell you out for an extra ladle of soup. No one trusted anyone in the camps. Jin-Sang, though, seemed different. Tang hoped Hana was, too.

He had programmed his camera to its low light setting and now depressed its Record button. He took a quick establishing shot of Hana and her circumstances and then brought the camera in close, more concerned at this point with what she said than what she looked like saying it.

Before splitting up from the other half of the team, a thought had struck Tucker, the corpsman. If what the Chinese were planning was biological in nature, the North Koreans might have agreed to infect some of the prisoners with it in order to make the training even more realistic. Tucker had warned him that the surgical mask, especially if he got close to the girl and it wasn't TB she was suffering from, might not be enough to protect him. He tried not to think of that as he hovered only inches from her face.

A fit of coughing overtook her and Tang moved to the side to avoid the bloody droplets that were being choked up out of her lungs.

When the fit had subsided, he gently repositioned her head so that she was staring up at the ceiling. She didn't need to look at him. It was more important that he be able to whisper his questions in her ear.

"Hana, I can help get you out of here. I can help you escape. I can take you and Jin-Sang to China just like your father wanted. But first, I need you to tell me why the Chinese are here."

As the words formed on her lips, Tang leaned in and brought the camera close to her mouth so its microphone could pick up every word.

It was difficult for her to take in enough air to breathe, much less to speak. Tang could barely make out what she said.

"Farming?" he repeated.

Hana squeezed his hand and managed another word.

"Fighting," Tang repeated. "Farming and fighting."

The sixteen-year-old acknowledged with another squeeze.

"Where will they go once they have trained to farm and fight?"

Her response sounded like the air being released from a half-deflated basketball. "America."

"Do you know where in America?"

The girl had been only five years old when she had been condemned to the camp. Anything at all she knew about the United States would have come strictly from her parents, or what she had picked up being a role-player for the Chinese.

When she didn't reply, Tang repeated the question.

"Farms," she whispered. "Villages. No cities."

The four words sent her into another spasm of coughing. Even though he was eager to ask his next question, he had no choice but to wait for it to pass.

This fit went on longer than the previous one. With each body-racking series of coughs, life seemed to ebb from her body. It was as if her soul was leaving one piece at a time.

Once the seizure had subsided, Tang noticed her breathing was more labored than before. He could hear bubbles of the bloody moisture rattling and popping in her lungs. It sounded like a dying rattlesnake shaking its tail in one final act of defiance. Tang had taken a handful of tactical medicine courses, but it didn't take an expert to know that Hana was dying.

He took her hand back in his with a warm, loving grasp. It was the same way he held the hands of his own children when they were sick. Except that unlike their colds and occasional flus, he knew this was something she was not going to recover from.

"Hana," he said. "What kind of attack are the Chinese planning?"

He waited, but again there was no response.

Repeating the question, he leaned in closer, but there was still nothing.

"Hana, Jin-Sang says you know how China will attack America. Tell me."

The air gurgled from her lungs along with an almost unintelligible response. "China. Take Jin-Sang to China."

"I will take you *both*," Tang replied. "But you have to tell me. What did you hear?"

"I cannot go to China."

He needed her to focus. "Hana, do you know what kind of attack the Chinese are training for?"

As the words struggled from her lips, Billy Tang leaned in even closer. But then he heard something else. Something close. It was the sound of the groaning hinges on the infirmary's front door.

CHAPTER 45

Before his mind had even fully processed what his ears had heard, Tang's body reacted. There was no good place to hide. The bed was too small for him to crawl under and there was no other furniture to offer any concealment. If the lights came on, he was in trouble. If a flashlight was aimed at the sheets, he was in trouble. In fact, there was only one way he could possibly get out of this.

Switching to the other side of the bed, he knelt as he had done before, like a priest praying over a dying parishioner. There was more than a little truth to the metaphor, as Hana's breathing was coming in shorter and more rapid gasps.

All of the rabbits and all of the pine needles on the Korean peninsula wouldn't have been enough to save her now, no matter how badly Jin-Sang wanted it to be so. Little did he know, but by going out in search of what his sister needed, he himself had been provided with a once-in-a-lifetime opportunity—a chance for freedom and an American Special Operations team to see that he would get it.

Helping Hana get it, too, had been part of Tang's plan; a part that he hadn't shared with Fordyce or the other two SEALs. Had she been strong enough to be moved, he'd had every intention of moving her, even if he had to carry her himself. If any of the SEALs had guessed that was his intention, none of them had let on. No one had discouraged him. In fact, that very well could have been part of why Fordyce had agreed to the plan in the end and was waiting outside the camp's perimeter. Why go in and talk to the girl and not share the golden ticket with her as well? Whether the team was carrying one child or two, what difference would it make?

Of course, Tang knew that Johnson and Tucker had a head start, which made a big difference. Nevertheless, he had intended to liberate Hana as well.

The DPRK's labor camps had been around twelve times longer than the Nazi death camps, but unlike the hue and cry over why the Allies didn't bomb German rail lines in the 1940s, no one today—not even with undeniable satellite imagery—was calling for the shutting down of North Korea's camps. Tang had vowed that if he ever got the chance to help even one prisoner, he would take it.

But while Jin-Sang was going to make it, Hana wasn't. She would know freedom soon enough, but it wouldn't be of the earthly kind.

Tang now strained his ears to discern how many were headed his way. The footfalls were heavy and deliberate. That meant either guards or infirmary personnel.

He heard door handles being rattled. At first he thought it might have been someone checking to make sure everything was locked up, but the intensity was too much, desperate even, and didn't make sense.

The footfalls drew closer and Tang readied himself for what would come next. He ran through his mind how long it would take to get from the infirmary door to the hole in the fence and then to Fordyce's position.

Though he would never wish death on anyone, he prayed for Hana to slip away. If she survived, if he was wrong and she recovered, the torture facing her from what he was about to do would surely result in her death. Listening to her, though, he could hear the distinct sound of guppy breathing. She was definitely dying. Even if Tucker had been here, there wasn't anything he could have done for her. Tang took selfish solace in that thought.

As the footfalls neared, Tang was able to discern that there was only one person making his way through the infirmary. Was it a parent coming to check on a sick child? Maybe a family member had waited until the staff was gone in order to steal the medicine a loved one needed?

While stealing was a death penalty offense in the camps, as a husband and father, Billy Tang had no doubts that there were certain things worth dying for.

But it didn't matter who was coming, or why. Whoever it was, he was a threat. Children were one thing, but adults were something completely different. Adults were most definitely a threat.

Despite that snap realization, Billy Tang didn't fire his weapon the moment the booted footfalls stopped, just feet away from him, and the sheet was snatched back.

Instead, he looked up and saw a Chinese military officer, his left hand wrapped in a bloody towel of some sort. His Korean was excellent. "You, there," he barked. "I need help. Right now."

The soldier must have believed Tang was the doctor's assistant.

"Please go to the exam room. I will be right with you," Tang replied.

The soldier drew his pistol. "You will be with me *now*. Let's go."

Tang's hand was wrapped around the butt of his SIG beneath Hana's blanket, his finger on the trigger. He could have shot the officer, but if he had missed and the man got off a shot of his own, the guards would come running. Letting go of his weapon, he decided to leave it under the blanket.

Standing up, he gestured for the officer to follow. The man stepped back as Tang passed and then fell in behind him.

They walked into the exam room and Tang told him to sit on the table.

"What happened?"

"What do you think happened?" the Chinese officer snapped. "An accident."

He was arrogant, but Tang let it pass. "What kind of accident?"

"I cut myself."

Tang set down Jin-Sang's canvas bag and approached the table.

The officer looked at him. "Do you have proper medical training?" he demanded.

Tang nodded. "I studied in Pyongyang and was a practicing physician before circumstances brought me here."

The answer seemed to satisfy the man, who had made no comment on the way Tang was dressed. He likely had no idea how things operated in the camp, much less the infirmary. The fact that he had shown up in the middle of the night seeking medical assistance confirmed it.

"I was demonstrating something with my knife," the officer said. "It slipped and I cut my hand. Badly."

"I'm going to need to take a look."

"Don't you want to turn on the lights?"

Tang forced a smile. "They don't trust us with lights."

The officer grunted as Tang unwound the bloody cloth around his hand. "Here," he said, fishing a small flashlight from his pocket with his good hand. "Use this."

"Are you allowed to use flashlights?" Tang asked as the officer clicked it on and handed it to him.

"This is an emergency. Besides, do you think we're sending our people without flashlights?" he replied with a grimace. "If so, you're as stupid as the Americans."

The CIA operative smiled. "You are indeed embarking on something exciting and worthwhile."

The Chinese officer paused and looked at him. "What would you know about it?"

"Me?" Tang replied. "Nobody talks to me unless they have a problem. All I know is what the rumors are around the camp."

The Chinese officer seemed to relax. "Tell me about the rumors," he said. "*While* you're seeing to my hand."

A good intelligence officer was adept at putting people at ease. If you were a good listener and could get them talking, it was amazing what you could pick up.

"Let's see what we've got," Tang said as he removed the final layer of wrapping. The cut was bad, and blood instantly began pulsing from the wound.

"We're going to need to slow the bleeding," he said, placing the bloody cloth back against the man's hand. "Hold this and keep pressure on it."

The officer had no choice. Holstering his pistol, he used his good hand to press down upon the cloth.

"You're going to need stitches," Tang explained. Stepping to the cabinets along the wall, he found one that wasn't locked. There was no medicine inside, but there was an almost empty bottle of antiseptic and some clean bandages. Tang removed them and made a show of preparing a tray.

He was fully aware that his five minutes were now up and that Jimi Fordyce had undoubtedly seen the Chinese officer enter the infirmary. Even so, he felt the opportunity was worth the risk.

He wished he could activate the camera in his pocket and record the conversation, but that was as good as begging to be shot. One electronic chirp and everything would be over.

"Make sure to keep pressure on the wound."

The officer was in pain, but seemed intent on continuing the conversation. "I am," he said. "Now tell me about the rumors."

Tang wondered if the man had a background in intelligence and was himself gathering information. "The guards talk about the mock American town," said Tang. "They're jealous. All of them want to go to America with you. They say they dream about pizza and milk shakes."

The officer shook his head. "There won't be pizza and milk shakes there for a long time. The guards will be better off here."

Tang looked up from his tray. "But we've had political prisoners who have been to America. All they talk about is the food."

"Only the Chinese will have the food."

"Interesting," he replied, turning his attention back to his tray.

The officer looked at him. "What do you mean, *interesting*? You don't believe me?"

"I'm sorry. You know better than I."

The great thing about arrogant men was that they thought they were smarter than everyone else and often liked to lecture.

The Chinese man laughed. "How much do you know about America?"

"Not much."

"Well, let me tell you about the United States. It is not only decadent, it is completely reliant upon technology. If you remove their technology, they die."

"*Die?*" repeated Tang.

"Yes," the officer replied. "They *die*. None of them are prepared to take care of themselves. They believe that their stores will always be open and stocked with food, that their pharmacies will be stocked with drugs, that water will continue to flow from their taps, that their heating, their air-conditioning, and even their civil order will continue in perpetuity, no matter what happens."

Tang approached with some clean bandages and swapped them for the bloody cloth. "But how do you *remove* a nation's technology?" he asked.

"With a very powerful weapon developed by your country."

"The DPRK?"

The officer changed the subject. "How many stitches will my hand need?"

He tried to lift the clean bandages to examine it, but Tang stopped him, "You need to keep pressure on it."

The man relented and reverted to the previous subject. "Are you familiar with your country's nuclear tests?"

Tang nodded. "Yes, they were a glorious success.

There were many television programs about them. The West and the Americans fear us because of our military strength."

The officer laughed and shook his head. "The West made fun of your nuclear tests. They said that they weren't serious. That the yield was too low."

"The yield?" the CIA man said, trying to appear uninformed enough that the Chinese man would keep talking. "I don't understand. The TV programs said—"

"The television programs are propaganda. So were the tests. The yield was never intended to be any larger than it was."

"I don't understand."

"Of course you don't. Just like the Americans. Everyone believed the DPRK was testing conventional weapons. They were not."

"They were not?" Tang repeated.

"No. They were testing something very unconventional."

"A weapon that can remove a nation's technology?"

The Chinese officer smiled. "*Now* you're beginning to understand."

"But doesn't a nuclear weapon remove everything? Not just the technology?"

"You're a somewhat educated man," the soldier said. "You should know about electromagnetic energy."

Tang's heart stopped in his chest. Now he understood what Hana had been mumbling when the Chinese officer entered the infirmary.

"I know how doctors use it, but not how soldiers would," he replied. "Is it a missile fired from a ship? Or is it dropped from a plane?"

The soldier suddenly decided he was done chatting.

"You're right. These things are beyond your under-standing. Enough talking. Focus on my hand."

Tang wanted to press the issue, but he had already been inside the camp too long. If he didn't leave, there was a good chance Fordyce would come in looking for him and there were a million and one ways that could end up badly.

Wheeling the tray over, Tang reclined the table and asked his patient to sit back.

The Chinese officer, though, was having second thoughts. "I think I would rather see the real doctor."

"That would not be a good idea."

"Who are you to question my request?"

Tang pantomimed the doctor drinking alcohol, and the officer got the point. "Oh," he said. "I see."

"Please," Tang offered, encouraging him once more to lie back.

"Do you have anything for pain?" the soldier asked.

"I might," he replied, stepping back to the cabinet.

Turning, he saw the Chinese officer swing his feet up on the table and lie back. The table had been set up along the wall so the patient faced the door, not the cab-inets. Tang was behind him.

"Can you please remove the dressing and tell me if your wound is still bleeding?" he asked.

The soldier did as he was told. "Still bleeding," he replied.

When he next heard Tang's voice, the CIA man was over his right shoulder.

"You're going to feel a little pinch," Tang said. He had already pulled out his Otanashi noh Ken knife.

Before the Chinese officer knew what had hap-pened, Tang had come up behind the exam table, clapped his hand over his mouth, locked his head back, and slid the blade into his neck.

Like a butcher's knife going through a piece of birthday cake, it moved through the soft tissue without any resistance. It wasn't the first time Tang had done this.

The trick was sliding the blade in just above the base of the neck behind the Adam's apple, between the trachea and the esophagus. If you hit vertebra, you had done it wrong. Bone would stop even the sharpest of knives.

But Tang didn't hit bone. He had done it correctly. With practiced precision, he rolled his wrist, sending the entire blade out the front of the officer's throat like a fillet knife.

The man clutched and gurgled as blood sprayed from his severed carotids. With his trachea transected, his lungs began to fill with blood. There was blood everywhere, except where the man needed it most—going to his brain. Within seconds, he was dead. Billy Tang now had to move as fast as he could.

Returning to Hana, he stepped behind the sheet to find that she had expired. He tried to console himself with the thought that at least Jin-Sang would make it, but the entire team had a lot of ground to cover before they could consider themselves safe. Retrieving his pistol from beneath her blanket, he reached over and closed her eyelids. She had finally escaped the camp.

With the canvas bag over his shoulder, he kept his weapon hidden and headed for the front door. He stopped only long enough to take a picture of the Chinese officer and tear the unit patch off his uniform. Closing the exam room door, he used his picks to lock it, and then broke them off in the lock to make it harder to open in the morning.

He slipped the remaining lockpick tools back into his bag and then stood at the front door listening. He heard nothing from outside. Careful to lift the door so as not to groan the hinges, he opened it just wide enough to exit and then pulled it soundlessly shut behind him.

Tang retraced his footsteps, making sure to duck below the window line, and stopped at the rear of the building. Taking one last look around, he counted to three, and bolted for the fence.

CHAPTER 46

Cheng didn't need to see the explosion at the Nashville storage facility to know that it would be seen and heard for miles. Hidden in the cardboard boxes were two large cylinders of hydrogen. They would create an incredible blast and better still, an incredible mess.

He had always believed that if you were going to make a mess, you should make the biggest mess possible. The more the authorities had to sift through, the longer it would take them to figure out what had happened. Anything that gave him more time was good. There was a lot of unfinished business yet to be done.

The first thing on his list was to get rid of the Navigator. The police would be looking for it.

The safest and fastest thing for him to do was to steal a vehicle from a long-term parking lot. He hoped that by the time anyone knew a car had been stolen, he would have already abandoned it and moved on to something else. He headed for Nashville International where he located an older Toyota Corolla and went to work on it.

Once he had it started, he transferred his belongings into the trunk and exited the lot. Steering onto the highway, he plotted a course north for Kentucky. After

Louisville, he picked up I-71, which would take him north toward Cincinnati and from there, Columbus.

He knew driving late at night was dangerous. With fewer cars on the road, the odds of being pulled over for a minor or even nonexistent traffic violation increased exponentially. Nevertheless, he chose to push through. He wanted to have mapped out his target and to be there when their doors opened in the morning. He also needed to send an update to Beijing. If he could also squeeze in even half an hour of sleep, he would be better able to focus on everything he needed to achieve.

He arrived in Columbus shortly before dawn. Using the last of his sterile cell phones, he called a Chinese asset named Wei Yin and gave him a code word. When he arrived at Yin's home in Dublin, a suburb just outside Columbus, the paunchy, middle-aged Ph.D. with glasses and thinning hair was waiting for him. He was sitting in a darkened downstairs window. As Cheng pulled into the driveway, Yin pressed the garage remote, the door opened, and Cheng drove in. Yin then pressed the button again and closed the door behind him.

They said few words. They were not friends. Theirs was purely a business relationship.

Yin was rusty and uncomfortable. He had not provided sanctuary for a Chinese operative in twenty years. His primary function in the United States was espionage. As a research fellow at the Battelle Memorial Institute, a leading science and technology development company, he had access to a wide array of sensitive and important American projects.

Forgetful of what the specific protocol was, Dr. Yin fell back on his upbringing. He offered his visitor tea and something to eat. Cheng accepted both.

As the doctor cooked a traditional Chinese breakfast, he used Yin's computer to "link surf" the Web. He knew how the NSA's sophisticated algorithms worked and he was careful not to conduct key word searches about what had transpired in Nashville that might be picked up and flagged. He merely clicked from one link to another, trying to zero in on what he wanted.

From what he could tell, the authorities didn't appear to know who was behind the death of the police officer or the storage facility fire. That, or they weren't making anything public.

There was also no mention of the murder of Wazir Ibrahim or Mirsab, the engineering student assigned to the Nashville cell. While that was a good sign, he was wise enough to know that just because the information was not in the press didn't mean the authorities were unaware. He would have to proceed with an abundance of caution. Disguising himself wouldn't be a bad idea either, especially considering everything that had happened in Nashville.

He knew the CCTV system had been taken offline, so there would be no record of his having been there, but the officer's behavior still bothered him. It was too aggressive, almost as if he suspected something bad was happening. Perhaps Cheng was making too much of it, but he didn't think so. He was worried that somewhere, dots were being connected.

After breakfast, Yin asked what else the visitor needed. Cheng wanted to lie down for a few minutes, then to shower and change. There had been no time to return to the hotel in Nashville for his belongings. Not that it mattered. There was nothing in the room, nor in his suitcase, that was incriminating. He planned to contact the hotel, check out over the phone, and have them FedEx the bag to the poultry plant in Nebraska. Then, all he would need was a new vehicle. That was where Yin had come in.

Cheng was to collect the princelings and transport them to the Second Department's asset known as Medusa. To do that, he was going to need an appropriate vehicle. He wanted a low-key minivan, preferably white or silver, with tinted windows. He would be covering a lot of ground over the next thirty-six hours and the vehicle had to be completely reliable.

After Cheng had showered and changed into the clothes Yin provided, the research scientist drove his visitor past multiple Columbus used car lots until the man identified the vehicle he wanted. When the lot opened forty-five minutes later, they test-drove it, and Yin bought and registered the van using one of the false identities and the cash he maintained in case of emergency. Cheng instructed him to submit a request to the Second Department for reimbursement.

More an academic than a field operative, the mild-mannered Yin had been anxious to be rid of his surprise guest the moment he had arrived. After the van had been purchased, his visitor told him he would be responsible for disposing of the stolen Toyota sitting in his garage. Yin wasn't looking forward to driving it to a bad part of town and leaving it running, in hopes that someone else would steal it, but if that's what was required of him, that was what he would do. Anything to hurry the visitor on his way. This was more intrigue than Yin cared for and he would be glad to put it all behind him.

Cheng, though, had demanded one more thing. It was eleven hours from Columbus to Boston, and he expected Yin to do the driving.

Having Yin drive would allow him to sleep and

keep his timetable moving forward. His body clock was already upside down from the time difference between China and the U.S. If he didn't rest, he could very well make a fatal mistake. He needed to be sharp.

Cheng was not happy to have been sent to collect the PSC's precious little princelings. He had never met a single one of them who wasn't spoiled and arrogant, but those were his orders. He would do as he had been commanded. It was exactly what he had told Yin when the man tried to make excuses about why he couldn't drive him to Boston.

Cheng had been quite terse. His stress levels were mounting. There would be multiple radiological sensors along the East Coast. Allegedly, the shielding for the device he was carrying was 100 percent effective. The technology had been developed by the Americans, and stolen by the Chinese, to protect spacecraft from radiation. Colonel Shi had attempted to reassure him that they never would have been able to get the devices into the United States in the first place, much less keep them hidden, if the containers were not perfectly suited to their task.

It was easy for Shi to downplay his concerns. He was safely ensconced back at the Second Department in Beijing. He didn't have to drive around with the device in his trunk.

They had driven cautiously, but not overly so. Yin had set the minivan's cruise control appropriately and they stopped only for gas or to use a rest-area bathroom.

Despite his fatigue, it had been difficult for Cheng to fall asleep. His mind kept running through all of the things he had to do and how he would have to handle any contingencies. It was only through sheer force of will that he finally silenced his thoughts and was able to get some sleep.

When they arrived in Boston, Cheng asked Yin to conduct a few errands for him and then he let him go. He had kept him in the dark on everything, except the destination. Yin had no idea why he was in the United States, why he needed the minivan, what was in the large, hard-sided case, or what he was doing in Boston. It was better that way for both of them.

Cheng had encouraged him to pay cash for a bus ticket, return to Columbus, and forget everything that had transpired since his phone had first rung. He watched Yin get in a cab and disappear.

Once he was gone, Cheng got back in the minivan and headed for Boston's South End. After finding a parking spot, he climbed into the back and, using the bicycle locks Yin had purchased, secured the device to the tie-down eyelets in the cargo area.

He packed his laptop and the other items he didn't want to risk leaving behind in the backpack he'd had Yin pick up and stepped out of the minivan.

Locking the doors and turning on the alarm, he put the hood of his sweatshirt up, threw the backpack over one shoulder, and walked toward Chinatown.

CHAPTER 47

It's called Unit 61398," said Nicholas as he sat back from his computer screen and rubbed his eyes. "It's one of the PLA's best hacking groups. They're based out of Shanghai."

"You're sure?" Harvath asked.

"As sure as I can be without tipping them off that we're on their trail."

Harvath leaned back in his chair. They were all exhausted and had caught only bits of sleep here and there. With the Chinese engaging in such risky behavior and the speed with which things were escalating, everyone was convinced the cells had likely gone operational, and whatever the attack was, it was imminent. If they didn't catch a break soon, it was going to be game over. Nicholas's finding was not what Harvath had been hoping for.

What Harvath wanted was a path to the handler—the person who had been watching the engineering students' Facebook accounts from somewhere in Idaho. He had hoped that it would be the same person who had hacked the CCTV system and keypad log from the self-storage facility. That would have been a nice way to tie the strings together, but now he realized why it had been a foolish hope.

One person could never watch one storage facility around the clock, much less six. If, of course, that's what was going on. Had Harvath had the resources the Chinese did, it was how he would have set things up. The Chinese had a billion people. They could easily afford the manpower to watch the hacked storage facility feeds and make sure that nobody was tampering with their units. He also had no doubt that their hackers could bump systems offline and erase any evidence that one of their operatives had been someplace. It made a lot of sense. It also made him think of something else.

"If the FBI is able to track down other storage facilities, how are they going to get close enough to the actual units without the PLA being able to see what they're up to?" he asked.

Nicholas thought about that for a moment. "I suppose we could do the same thing right back at them and knock the cameras offline."

Harvath shook his head. "Maybe that'd be plausible for one location, but anything more than that and they'd get suspicious pretty fast."

"But suppose we're right. Suppose that's where they're hiding whatever it is they plan to use in the attack. What do we care at that point?"

"That's a big supposition. Suppose it's wrong. Suppose that's only where one piece is. Suppose it's a piece they can replace from somewhere else."

Nicholas nodded. "Good point."

"What about looping the footage?"

"You'd need clean footage for the interior cameras."

"Meaning?" Harvath asked.

"Meaning they'd have to be looking at something static. There couldn't be cars and things like that going past in the background. If they notice the same car or bicycle go by twice, that's it."

"But it *could* be done."

"Anything's possible," said Nicholas, "but how do you transition from a live picture to a looped one without somebody noticing?"

"You interrupt the signal somehow. Turn it off and then turn it back on."

"You want to hit their headquarters in Shanghai? That'd be one heck of an operation. It would take months to plan."

"Who says we have to hit them there?" replied Harvath. "It's like two cans and a string; we just clip it at our end. But I don't think it could just be the CCTV feeds in question. It would have to be a whole bunch of stuff. So much stuff, in fact, that it dwarfs our stuff."

"Are you talking about turning the Internet off?"

"We don't have to turn it off. We just jiggle the switch. Can that be done?"

"Not with this," Nicholas said, pointing at his laptop.

"But it *can* be done."

"Not only can it, it has been done."

Harvath looked at him. "It has?"

"Not too long ago, in fact. Back in January, almost all of China's 500 million Internet users got bumped off the Web for eight hours. We're talking half of the world's Internet users. It's been called the greatest failure in the history of the Net."

"What happened?"

"China has this vast cyber snooping and censoring system nicknamed the Great Firewall of China. Its goal is to control all of the digital traffic coming in and going out of the country. They use it to squash dissent and root out any antigovernment sentiment. The Chinese have even employed it to jail journalists and dissidents.

"Sites like Facebook and Twitter have been blacklisted. Even Bloomberg.com and the *New York Times* have been blocked."

"Why Bloomberg and the *NYT*?"

"Because," said Nicholas, "despite some particularly procommunist people at the *New York Times*, the Gray Lady still publishes unflattering stories about China's leaders. China doesn't like that."

"I'm sure they don't," Harvath replied. "But how did the Great Firewall cause the outage?"

"If you imagine it like an old-fashioned switchboard, all the cords got plugged into one hole. Somebody screwed up and sent three-quarters of China's Internet traffic all to one location. Ironically enough, that one location was the servers of an Internet hosting company based in Cheyenne, Wyoming. It was an epic failure."

"And you think we could replicate that?"

"I think with the help of the computing power of one U.S. government agency in particular, I might be able to put together something similar. There's just one problem," said Nicholas.

"What's that?"

"The NSA vowed a long time ago they would never let me inside any of their facilities."

"You let me worry about the NSA," said Harvath. "I want you to start figuring out exactly how you're going to handle the Great Firewall."

"You have a lot of faith in the FBI. We don't even know if they're going to be able to find any of the storage units, much less find them in time."

"They'll find them. Trust me. That's what they do.

In the meantime, start packing. I want to be wheels up within a half hour."

The Logans had already been sent home, surveillance of the Cool Springs Marriott had been handed back over to the FBI, and Chase and Sloane were now sacked out on the couches in the hangar office. No one held out much hope that Deng was coming back to the hotel, not after everything that had happened. In fact, Harvath doubted that the man was even still in Tennessee.

They had turned over every imaginable stone. Even that gnawing discomfort Harvath had had about the photocopied driver's license had finally clarified itself. He asked himself how, if he had been renting storage units under different aliases in different cities, he would have done it. The exercise had shaken an idea loose. It was a tiny needle in a big haystack, but it wasn't impossible, so he had passed the idea on to the Old Man.

"Where are we going?" Nicholas asked.

"Back to D.C."

CHAPTER 48

The National Counter Terrorism Center was located in a stone and glass complex near Tysons Corner. It was part of the Office of the Director of National Intelligence and as such, fell under the responsibility of DNI General George Johnson.

The NCTC brought together experts from all of the alphabets in the soup, including the FBI, CIA, DIA, NSA, and DHS. Their goal was to prevent terrorist attacks on the United States as well as American interests abroad by making sure all available intelligence was being shared and no clues were being overlooked.

Entering the main building, Harvath saw Nicholas without both of his dogs for the first time. Reed Carlton had made an exception for the animals at the Carlton Group offices. It was a private business and he could make that call. He had explained to Nicholas, though, that federal buildings were a completely different story and that at some point, his job would require that he visit one of those buildings. When that happened, he wouldn't be able to bring Argos or Draco.

Nicholas, being Nicholas, had, within twenty-four hours, both dogs officially recognized as certified service animals. Old habits died hard and Harvath could only wonder whom he had blackmailed, and with what, to secure the designation. Carlton, though, had had no idea.

The minute he saw the enormous dogs outside the NCTC with their bright red vests emblazoned with the words "Service Animal," and patches proclaiming *Working Dog* and *Don't Pet Me Please, I'm Working*, he lost it.

Without missing a beat, Nicholas removed a card from a zippered pocket on Draco's vest and handed it to him. On one side was written the corresponding portion of the Americans with Disabilities Act that applied to service animals and on the other was written, "If you have been handed this card, you have very likely already violated the Americans with Disabilities Act."

"You're not even American," Carlton countered.

"I'm still protected," said Nicholas, his hand on Draco's shoulder.

No one was sure if he meant protected by the ADA or by the dog. Harvath figured it was probably both.

Carlton wasn't in the mood. It was a con, and he didn't like it. There were people with legitimate needs for service animals. Nicholas, in his opinion, wasn't one of them. But with so many returning service members now using service animals, federal agencies were used to seeing dogs in their buildings. Granted, they were breeds like German shepherds or golden retrievers, not monsters the size of Nicholas's Ovcharkas.

The Old Man caved and they came to an agreement. "You can bring *one* of your *service* animals," he said, making air quotes around the word "service."

With the issue settled, Argos returned to the Carlton Group offices with Sloane and Chase while the rest of the team walked past the flagpole and its puzzle-piece surround, and into the main building.

By the looks on many of the faces inside, one would

have thought that the circus had come to town. The huge dog accompanied by a man less than three feet tall was certainly part of it, but the true draw for the employees of the NCTC was the two highly accomplished and highly respected warriors in their midst. There wasn't a single analyst who didn't harbor superspy fantasies of killing and capturing bad guys. From the Cold War to the War on Terror, Carlton and Harvath were two of the best operatives the nation had ever fielded.

At the moment, though, that wasn't how Harvath saw his skills. No matter how many pieces they had been able to uncover and put into place, none of them felt as if they were making a difference. They weren't any closer to stopping the attack. Part of him was glad to be at the NCTC trying to figure things out, rather than at the White House having to answer to the President.

After Harvath got Nicholas settled with the NSA people, he and Carlton headed for the NCTC's Operations Center.

With its spiral staircases, sleek workstations, glass conference rooms, enormous flat-panel monitors, and loftlike vibe, the Ops Center was the nexus of America's counterterrorism effort and looked like a Hollywood set designer had put it together.

General Johnson had been alerted that Harvath and Carlton were on their way in and had delayed his pre-presidential briefing. Waving the pair into the main conference room, he directed them to two chairs near the head of the table and then nodded for the FBI Director to begin.

His jacket was off and his sleeves were rolled up. Harvath had seen the man only at the White House, where he was always buttoned up. "First, let's start with Nihad Hamid, the director of the Muslim internship program at NASA," he said, referring to his notes and getting right into the briefing. "As most of you know, once the FISA court approved our warrant for surveillance on Mr. Hamid, we went after his phone, computers, banking records, all of it. We also brought him in for interrogation.

"Hamid claimed he had never heard of Khuram Hanjour, the recruiter out of Dubai. But when he was shown the files of the six engineering students from the UAE, he became very nervous.

"As soon as our interrogator saw that, he began to push him on it. As it turns out, many of those internship slots weren't necessarily awarded on merit. Several of the board members at Hamid's organization, the Foundation on American Islamic Relations—"

"Wait," Harvath interrupted. "FAIR is involved in this?"

"Yes. You know them?"

"All too well. I thought that shill organization was disbanded after their offices got bombed a couple of years ago."

"No such luck," said the Director. "Three of their board members put the word out in the Arab world that for the right 'contribution,' they could guarantee acceptance into the NASA internship. Hamid went along with it. As best we can tell, Khuram Hanjour used a cutout to pay FAIR fifty thousand per engineering student. The transaction went through a Hawala in Northern Virginia."

"Where are the board members now?"

"We have them in custody and the Attorney General is drawing up the indictments."

"Did they know they were abetting terrorists?" Harvath asked.

"I watched feeds of the interrogations," the Director replied. "Are these men corrupt? Absolutely. They tried to get money out of everyone. But we don't think this was designed to help get terrorists into the country. That won't change the facts of the case, though, especially if an attack is successful."

"Where's the Bureau with pinpointing the locations of the engineering students?" General Johnson asked.

"We've got plainclothes agents staking out the different Wi-Fi locations they've used, and we've got additional agents covertly combing all the neighborhoods. Short of putting up flyers or going house-to-house, we're at full capacity. At some point, the President is going to have to allow us to release the names and photos to local and state law enforcement."

"Which, as we've already discussed, if it leaks to the press could trigger the attack."

The FBI Director shook his head. "And if we don't bring local and state LEOs in and an attack *does* happen? Who's responsible for that?"

Johnson put up his hands. "I get it. We're damned if we do and damned if we don't. The President, though, has made his position clear on this."

"With all due respect, General—and you know I like the President—he's wrong. Look at the 9/11 hijackers. They bumped up against the cops. These guys might, too. But it'll only matter if the police know to be on the lookout for them."

"The President says *no*. Not until we've exhausted every other available avenue."

"You went statewide in Tennessee for Bao Deng," the Director challenged.

"First of all," Johnson replied, shifting his gaze to Harvath before returning his attention to the Director, "I didn't make that call. Somebody overstepped his bounds. Secondly, we had him as a legitimate murder suspect."

"So let's put the six engineering students on the radar for having overstayed their visas then."

The DNI thought about that for a moment. "They should already be in the ICE database."

"Which won't mean a thing for the cells in Seattle, Dallas, or Baltimore."

"Why not?" Carlton asked.

"They're sanctuary cities," the FBI Director explained. "They don't take action against illegal immigrants. Oftentimes their police departments are told flat-out not to work with the Feds and not to cross with their databases. Just flagging these guys for having overstayed their visas wouldn't have any impact at all. That's why the Bureau wants them tagged as terrorists."

The Old Man shook his head.

"How about Deng, at least?" Harvath asked. "Why don't we go nationwide on him for the murder in Tennessee?"

"And if one of the national newscasts picks it up?" said Johnson.

"What if the White House reached out to the head of each network in advance?"

"To tell them what? That we have a suspected Chinese intelligence agent coordinating a massive terrorist attack, but don't say anything?"

"No. It would have to be something that put them on a moral meathook so large that they couldn't flop off it," Harvath replied.

"Like what?"

"How about an assassination plot?"

The FBI Director shook his head. "You're one administration too late. The mainstream media hate the current president."

"Who says we have to go with the current president? We can use his predecessor. That's even better. They loved him. We'll make it a journalistic act of conscience for them to keep quiet."

Johnson looked at the FBI Director. When he nodded and indicated that he was good with it, the DNI said, "Okay, I'll run it by the President."

"Which leaves us with Boise," said the Director as he looked once more at his notes. "There we've got at least a little good news."

"The bus station where the students all accessed the Wi-Fi network?" Harvath asked.

"That's the one. We pulled the CCTV footage for the entire day and have been able to identify each of them, when they got there, what they did while they were there, and what bus they got on."

"What about how they got there?" asked Carlton. "Did someone drop them off? Do we have a license plate? Anything?"

"They were staggered and came at different points throughout the day. Two of them overlapped, but just barely and they never made contact at any point. And as far as *how* they all got there, we're still trying to piece that together. There's no smoking gun, no truck that pulled up in front and dropped them all off.

"I've saved the best discovery, though, for last." Picking up the remote for the monitor at the front of the conference room, the FBI Director activated a string of short CCTV clips. "Recognize the man in the blue jacket?" he asked.

Harvath studied the images on the screen. "That's Wazir Ibrahim."

"We concur. He apparently paid cash and bought a ticket to Nashville on the same bus as our Emirati engineering student, Mirsab Maktoum. Here's a split screen of each of them getting on the same bus, though not together.

"Interestingly enough, five other men, who all look to be of Somali descent, also paid cash for tickets that day. Guess what buses they were on?"

"Every bus that one of our engineering students was on."

"Precisely."

"What about CCTV footage from the stations in the arrival cities?" Harvath asked. "Have you pulled those to see who picked them up or where they went once they got there?"

"We've had agents going over the footage, as well as looking for any footage from other cameras radiating out from the bus stations. As it stands now, all of them appear to have just walked off and disappeared into each of the cities."

Harvath was about to ask if the bus drivers or any of the passengers had been identified and interviewed when there was a knock on the conference room door.

It was the FBI Director's assistant. He was holding up a file folder and the Director motioned for him to come in.

Walking over to his boss, he handed him the file, said something quietly in his ear, and then left the room.

Harvath wondered if they had finally located Tommy Wong. It turned out to be something even better.

Opening the folder, the Director quickly scanned the contents and then said, "I think we may have just caught a very big break."

"What is it?"

"We think we have located three more of the storage units."

CHAPTER 49

While the FBI coordinated their strike teams, Harvath and Carlton commandeered one of the conference rooms and asked Special Agent Heidi Roe to join them.

"What do you know about Somali criminal enterprises?" Harvath asked her.

"I know the biggest thing they seem to be into is importing narcotics, most particularly a substance known as khat, and that they also dabble in prostitution."

"What about terrorism?"

"Well, both the Bureau and the Agency have been concerned about all the young Somalis in the U.S. who have been traveling back to Africa to receive training and fight in the jihad there. Everyone's predicting that it's only a matter of time before we see them bring those skills back here."

"What do you think the chances are that's what we're seeing right now?" Harvath asked. "The engineers were recruited for their engineering skills and the Somalis were recruited for their *terrorism* skills, let's say."

"Skills at what, specifically? Martyrdom?"

"Maybe."

"Why did they go to Idaho, then?" asked Roe. "To learn how to martyr themselves?"

"Depends on the method. The 9/11 hijackers needed to learn how to fly airplanes to complete their martyrdom."

"Not all of them."

Harvath nodded. "That's true. Some were simply muscle."

"But when you think of Somalis, is muscle the first thing that comes to mind?" Carlton asked.

"No. Not really."

"You think jihadi, right? A shaheed who martyrs himself," said Carlton.

"A jihadi can be a fighter. It doesn't have to be someone who intends to martyr himself. Maybe that's why they were brought in."

"Let's back up a second," said Roe. "What do we know with a fair amount of certainty? The engineering students were brought to the U.S. specifically because of their engineering expertise. Let's assume they're needed to build or assemble something. Let's call it a bomb."

"Okay," Harvath replied.

"They needed to be imported because, for whatever reason, the Chinese can't find that kind of labor here."

"Or because they want this to look like an Islamic attack."

"Right, the whole unrestricted warfare plan. Okay, so you have your bomb assemblers. They're Muslim, from the UAE, and let's assume religious. Given that the Chinese are behind everything, let's also assume that they've planted, or will plant, enough clues to make the case that the men were affiliated with Al Qaeda."

"Which their families will deny," said Carlton, "the same way many of the 9/11 hijackers' families denied the connections."

"Except this time, the families will be telling the truth," said Harvath.

Carlton nodded, and Roe continued. "So the UAE part makes sense. In fact, let's assume that as long as the engineers were from somewhere in the Arab world, they'd fit the bill. How do the Somalis then fit in?"

"That's what I've been trying to figure out," said Harvath. "If you want this to really look like Al Qaeda, why not use Arabs, or Yemenis, or even Pakistanis?"

"Too hard to get?"

"Jihadis are a dime a dozen."

Roe tapped her pen on the conference room table. "What would make Somalis special?"

"As far as Wazir Ibrahim was concerned, he had already been living in the United States for a couple of years."

"So he was somewhat established," said Roe as she wrote it down. "He knows the customs, he has a job, and he's married."

"He's also a fucking dirtbag who beat his wife and was likely involved in a child sex ring."

"Which his handler was obviously not aware of," said Carlton.

Roe looked at him. "Why do you say *obviously*?"

"Because you wouldn't want that guy in one of your cells. Too high-risk. Eventually a knucklehead like that is going to run afoul of the cops."

"So what's that tell you about his handler?"

"That there were some pretty significant things about Wazir Ibrahim that he didn't know."

"And why wouldn't his handler know those things?"

"How much time do you have?" the Old Man asked her. "The handler could have subbed Ibrahim in at the last minute. Ibrahim could have been a very good liar.

Ibrahim could have had a medical condition that only manifested itself on odd-numbered Thursdays of every other month. The list is endless."

Carlton reminded Roe of her grandfather. He could be irascible as well, but he was also very smart. "Ockham's razor," she pressed. "What's the simplest answer?"

"The simplest answer is that the handler just didn't do his due diligence."

"Okay, let's go with that. Why? Why, with something this important, would the handler not do his due diligence?"

Harvath sensed that she was getting under the Old Man's skin, but he liked the way her mind worked. She was highly analytical. She was also right and it was forcing them to think harder.

"You wouldn't cut corners," said Harvath. "Not on something like this. You absolutely would do your homework."

Roe looked at him. "So what's your explanation?"

"I think Wazir Ibrahim is the template. He's a long-term sleeper. You wouldn't have wanted him to be here on an overstayed visa. They would have brought him in another way—as a political refugee or something like that. That's how tens of thousands of Somalis have gained access to the country. The United States has one of the largest collections of Somali expatriates in the world.

"So the Chinese could have had a recruiter in Somalia who groomed sleepers and helped move them into the U.S. immigration pipeline. I would use Wazir Ibrahim as the nexus. Look at where he was from in Somalia and who immigrated around the same time he did and we might find the other men in that CCTV footage from Boise."

It was a good point and Roe wrote it down. "So whoever recruited him may not have known about his proclivities?"

Harvath nodded. "I know the Bureau is contacting all of its Somali informants, but I'd reach out to Detective Hoffman back in Nashville, too. See if he can uncover anyone in that Somali trafficking ring who recognizes any of the faces in the bus station footage. Have him check with Wazir Ibrahim's widow as well. She may know something about his trip to Boise that could prove helpful.

"Speaking of which, have your teams in Boise had any luck with that additional item I suggested that they look for?"

Roe nodded. "I don't think a warrant like that has ever been issued before. We got one, though, and I think your idea of roping in the police chief and the mayor was smart, especially for dealing with the smaller businesses. Everyone has cooperated so far."

"Do we have an ETA?"

"Everything is getting piped to the NSA. They're running the algorithms as they get the data."

"What about Tommy Wong?" Harvath then asked.

"Still nothing."

"What about the other members of the 14K triad back in Southern Cal? Maybe they know something."

"If they do, none of them are talking," Roe replied. "We've put their phones into heavy rotation and we're monitoring their email accounts, but the FBI only has so much manpower. We can't sit on them 24/7."

"I understand," said Harvath, who looked at the Old Man. "Has Anne Levy had any success running down any contacts of the students back in the UAE?"

Carlton shook his head. "Zip."

Harvath glanced at his watch. Even though they had located only three of what was believed would be five storage units, the President had given the go-ahead to move on them. They were located in Las Vegas, Dallas, and Des Moines.

The NSA had nixed the idea of launching an attack against the Great Firewall of China, and for good reason. Just because the PLA's hacking unit in Shanghai appeared to be watching the CCTV feeds of the storage facilities didn't mean that no one else was. In fact, as the NSA began to build on what Nicholas had uncovered, they believed there was another source dipping into the feed. And that source wasn't in China.

It was decided that a widespread Internet disruption originating within the United States was the only way to deal with the issue. The risks were discussed with President Porter, and after addressing a handful of national security as well as private sector issues, he gave his approval.

Plainclothes FBI agents in Las Vegas, Dallas, and Des Moines helped covertly evacuate customers at the facilities as three separate ruses were enacted to evacuate any nearby homes or businesses in each city. No one had any idea what was in the storage units, or if they were booby-trapped.

As soon as the customers had been removed from the facilities, the NSA began compiling the footage they would use for their loops. Two of the facilities, though, had cameras that picked up part of the road traffic near their entrances.

Because of the public safety concerns, traffic was being diverted away from all of the facilities in question. The NSA decided to roll the dice and pulled the entrance camera footage from two previous nights off those facilities' DVRs. After making sure no one was seen entering during any of the lengths they intended to use, they tested everything multiple times and then let everyone know they were ready to roll.

Once the strike teams were in place, the go code would be given and the simultaneous, three-city operation would launch.

DNI Johnson and the FBI Director had gone to the White House to be with the President in the Situation Room, along with the rest of his national security team. Harvath and Carlton had decided to remain at the NCTC, so they could continue working until the op launched.

Now, noticing the time, they exited the conference room and walked out onto the Ops Center floor.

CHAPTER 50

The floor of the Ops Center fell eerily silent and the tension was palpable. The large flat-screens that hung from the second-story catwalks displayed a variety of images. Aerial drone footage showed the storage facilities from above, while the cameras mounted on the team members' helmets gave on-the-ground POVs. The same secure images being viewed inside the NCTC were also being beamed to the Situation Room at the White House.

The only sounds on the floor came from the overhead speakers and the disembodied voices of Ops Center Command—the NCTC mission commander seated at the largest workstation on the floor—and the strike team leaders in Las Vegas, Dallas, and Des Moines.

"Deadbolt Four, this is Ops Center Command. Do you copy, over?"

"Ops Center Command, this is Deadbolt Four. We copy, over."

"Roger that, Deadbolt Four. Stand by. Over."

"Roger that, Ops Center Command. Deadbolt Four is standing by. Over."

The conversation was repeated two more times as Ops Center Command reached out to the remaining team leaders to make sure they were in place and ready to go.

"Smokestack, this is Ops Center Command. All teams are in place and ready to roll. Over."

There was a pause and then the voice of General Johnson came through the speakers overhead from the White House Situation Room.

"Ops Center Command, this is Smokestack. You are cleared for launch. Repeat. Ops Center Command is cleared for launch, over."

"Roger that, Smokestack. Ops Center Command is clear for launch. Over."

Even though Harvath wasn't on the ground with the strike teams, he knew what it was like, and he could feel his pulse quickening.

"Cellophane, this is Ops Center Command," said the voice as he hailed his counterpart at the NSA. "You are clear to commence operations."

"Roger that, Ops Center Command. Cellophane is clear to commence operation. Stand by."

Everyone in the room watched the images of the CCTV feeds from the storage facilities. Seconds later, they were replaced with an error message.

"Ops Center Command, this is Cellophane. Grizzly is down. Repeat. Grizzly is down. Stand by."

"Copy that, Cellophane. Grizzly is down. Ops Center Command standing by."

Seconds later, the CCTV cameras came back online.

"Ops Center Command, this is Cellophane. Bag tie. Repeat. Bag tie."

The camera feeds had been commandeered and the looped footage was now successfully playing.

When NCTC personnel had confirmed to the mission commander that the NSA had successfully looped the feeds, he said, "Roger that, Cellophane. Ops Center Command confirms bag tie. Repeat, Ops Center Command can confirm bag tie. Over."

"Good luck," replied the voice from the NSA. "Cellophane out."

It was time to send in the strike teams.

After checking all of the feeds, the voice said, "Deadbolt teams, this is Ops Center Command. Prepare to launch. Over."

"Deadbolt Four, copy that."

"Deadbolt Five, copy that."

"Deadbolt Six, roger that."

"Deadbolt teams, this is Ops Center Command. On my mark. In three. Two. One. Deadbolt teams, go."

There was a chorus of "Go! Go! Go!" from the team leaders as they leaped out of their vehicles and poured into the storage facilities.

The strikes played out almost identically across the screens. In Dallas and Des Moines, the units directly behind the storage units in question were tackled. In Las Vegas, because it was a lone row, the unit next to the unit in question was tackled.

First, nuclear, radiological, chemical, and biological levels were taken. When nothing registered, bolt cutters were used to snap off the padlocks. Once the doors were opened and levels were taken again, boxes, furniture, or whatever else was in the way was moved so that operatives could gain access to the common steel wall separating the units.

Standing on a ladder, an operative with a very small drill bored a hole through the partition near the ceiling, and a small "sniffer" was fed through. When no threats were detected, it was pulled out and a tiny fiberoptic camera was fed in.

Harvath, along with everyone else at the NCTC, watched as each of the fiberoptic feeds came up on the monitors. They all showed the same number of boxes, identically stacked.

Roe, who was standing next to Harvath, said, "Bomb parts?"

"Definitely doesn't look like baseball cards."

One by one, the team leaders reported in, requesting permission to go to the next phase. As they did, Ops Center Command gave them authorization.

The next phase involved clearing everything away from the shared wall so that a portable X-ray machine could be wheeled in. As soon as the machines were in place, they began scanning what was on the other side.

The X-rays were bracketed by two telescoping arms, which could be raised and lowered to provide the greatest range of images possible. The pictures they sent back were quite interesting.

There were two extra-large metal cylinders that reminded Harvath of helium tanks, what looked like a rolling metal toolbox with drawers, some boxes filled with clothes or some sort of folded material, another box that appeared to contain firearms and ammunition, and then a series of different boxes that the X-ray machines couldn't penetrate. They read as solid black.

The Old Man raised his eyebrows. "Lead-lined?"

Harvath nodded. "Yup. Not good."

"Are you thinking radiological?" Roe asked.

"Yup. And like I said, not good."

"Agreed."

They watched as the teams backed out of their respective units and went over to the target units themselves.

After failing to register any nuclear, radiological, chemical, or biological signatures on the outside, the teams began meticulously mapping the seams of the door frames. Deadbolt Five was the first to catch something.

"Ops Center Command, this is Deadbolt Five. Over."

"Trip wire?" Roe asked.

"Maybe," Harvath replied. "Or a tamper indicator."

"Go ahead, Deadbolt Five. Over."

"Are you getting this picture off my helmet cam? It's on the right-hand side of the frame, about sixteen inches off the ground? Over."

"Roger that, Deadbolt Five. Over."

It was a small, clear decal. Had they not been looking for it, they never would have seen it.

"Ops Center Command. This is Deadbolt Four. We've got one, too. Over."

"Deadbolt Six to Ops Center Command. Same thing here. Over."

"Tamper seals," said Harvath. "Lets the bad guys know if anyone has been in their unit."

Using a mild substance, the teams carefully removed the seals and marked the spot on the frames with chalk. They then went back to searching for anything else that might warrant special attention before making their entry.

"Ops Center Command, this is Deadbolt Four. Over."

"Go ahead, Deadbolt Four. Over."

"Are you getting this lock via my cam? Over."

"Roger that, Deadbolt Four. Looks like a five-wheel combination padlock, brand name is Squire. Over."

"Deadbolt Five has the same lock here. Over."

"Same lock for Deadbolt Six. Over."

"Ops Center Command. This is Deadbolt Four. I haven't seen one of these before. Do we have any information on this lock? Over."

The plan had been to pick the locks, not snap them off with the bolt cutters. This way, if they wanted, they could put everything back the way they had found it.

"Deadbolt Four. This is Ops Center Command. We've pulled a schematic here. It appears you're looking at a Squire SS50C. It's a high-security padlock manufactured in the United Kingdom. Their website calls it the strongest combination padlock on the market. At least a hundred thousand combinations. Over."

"It's highly attack resistant. Any suggestion on how to get into it? Over."

Before Ops Center Command could reply, the agent was hailed by an entry agent on one of the other teams. "Deadbolt Four, this is Deadbolt Six. Over."

"Go ahead, Deadbolt Six. Over."

"The locking cam engages on the inside of the shackle, but the high shoulder design won't let you work a regular steel shim all the way into the opening. Over."

"Roger that, Deadbolt Six. Any idea of what will work? Over."

"Use a zipper shim. Feed them in from each side until they bottom out on top of the locking cam. Then grab the tops with two small vise grips and push down. It should overpower the internal spring on the locking cam and pop it open without damaging the lock. Over."

"Copy that. Stand by."

Three minutes later, Deadbolt Four radioed. "Bingo. Lock has been removed."

Deadbolt Teams Five and Six chimed in with similar successes right after. It was time to go to the next phase.

With the padlocks removed and the door frames mapped, the strike teams retreated and a robot in each city was sent to make entry.

It took a certain degree of finesse, but via each robot's articulated arm, their controllers were able to get the rolling metal doors raised high enough for the machines to slip in underneath. None of the doors were booby-trapped.

From inside, the robots sent back images very similar to those that had been seen earlier. Careful not to jar the stack of cardboard boxes, each controller had his robot pick up a box, transport it outside, and set it down. A human being was going to have to take it from this point.

Wearing advance bomb suits, Explosive Ordnance Disposal specialists with each team thoroughly studied the first box, took readings, and then very carefully opened it up. Inside was another box. This one was filled with what looked like brand-new, uninflated weather balloons.

"I think I now know what's in those cylinders," said Harvath.

"Helium?" Carlton replied.

"No. Hydrogen."

CHAPTER 51

B oston's Chinatown was on Beach Street and near Boston Common. It was the only authentically historic Chinese area left in all of New England and it had been the perfect place for the Second Department to establish a safe house.

With more than thirty thousand people per square mile, Chinatown was one of Boston's most densely packed residential areas, and 70 percent of the people living there were Asian. If you were Chinese and wanted to disappear, this was the place in which to do it.

The five princelings Cheng had been sent to retrieve were scattered among three schools. One was at Princeton in New Jersey. Another was at Yale in Connecticut. And the remaining three were at Harvard, here in Boston.

Because of who they were, they had all received highly specialized training in China. It focused on escape and evasion, more commonly referred to as E&E. They learned not only how to detect surveillance, but how, when necessary, to escape it. They learned how to avoid kidnapping and what to do if in fact they ever were taken. They trained with the best and were expected to take their lessons seriously.

An emergency bug-out plan had been established

for each princeling. When a certain phrase was transmitted to them, it would trigger the plan.

Each had been given a specific destination in Boston's Chinatown. They were to leave their cell phones plugged in, turned on, and in their dorm rooms. Their laptops and any other electronic items were also to be left behind. That would make it much more difficult to track them.

Upon leaving their dormitories, they were to assume they were being followed and to take appropriate countermeasures. They were taught to stay calm and to not appear aware of any surveillance whatsoever.

After conducting their surveillance detection route, or SDR, each had been assigned a variety of options for how to reach their destination. The princelings at Harvard had it the easiest as Chinatown was right in their backyard. The students from Princeton and Yale had a greater distance to travel and Cheng had transmitted the activation message to them first.

He had done so using Facebook, tapping into established accounts of "friends" they had back in China, who were nothing more than Second Department operatives who kept the accounts active for just such an eventuality. Once the codes had been transmitted, it was up to them.

For the moment, Cheng tried to remain optimistic that their training and common sense would prevail. Princelings, though, tended to be spoiled. As a result, they often developed an overinflated sense of self-worth and entitlement. In short, they were wholly unreliable. They were also a pain in the ass.

Cheng had been very clear with Colonel Shi that he

would not stand for anything less than complete obedience from them. He didn't care who their parents were, or in the case of the youngest princeling from Harvard, who her grandfather was. His job was to get them all safely out of the United States. For that to happen, they would need to follow his instructions, every instruction, to the letter.

The colonel agreed and trusted Cheng to do what he thought was best. He did caution him, though, that today's princeling could be tomorrow's Politburo Standing Committee member.

Shi was correct, but that did little to lessen Cheng's loathing for China's politicians. He tried to put it out of his mind. As long as the princelings obeyed his commands, everything would be fine.

With the van secured in the safe house garage, Cheng cleaned his weapon, replenished his funds from a cache hidden beneath the kitchen floor, and prepared a medical kit, just in case any of his charges became ill or was injured during their trip.

The next thing he had to do was reconnoiter the nearby locations where each of the princelings would be arriving. The Second Department referred to them as "entry points." In an optimal scenario, he would be moving the princelings into the safe house at a rate of one every twelve to forty-eight hours. Tonight, though, he would have to move much quicker. He didn't like having to do things quickly. So much could go wrong.

Even though the entry points were only a handful of blocks from the safe house, it was still a highly complicated process. Having to move one princeling every hour would only add to the difficulty.

If their tradecraft had failed and any of them were being followed, that added a whole additional layer.

Using Chinatown, especially on a busy night, put the odds in his favor. But nothing was a sure thing, especially when the FBI was involved. He was alone and had no backup. Everything would have to be executed flawlessly.

Unit 61398 had tapped into security cameras around Chinatown, creating an overwatch grid he could monitor from his laptop. It wasn't perfect. There were numerous blind spots. But it was better than nothing.

With his safe house checklist complete, he exited the building and began to explore the neighborhood.

As he walked, he mentally mapped every face, every parked car, and every location for a potential ambush. Within two hours, he knew the area as well as if he had lived there for two years.

It was a surreal sensation knowing that all of the life around him was about to come to an abrupt and painful halt.

CHAPTER 52

Navy SEAL Lieutenant Jimi Fordyce had a million and one questions he wanted to ask, but he settled on the first one that had come into his mind: "Dude, what the fuck happened in there?"

Billy Tang's hands and sleeves were stained with blood. "Some Chinese officer cut himself. Came in looking for the doc. I got to practice medicine without a license."

"Did you smoke him?"

"I had to."

"Shit," Fordyce muttered.

"The body's locked in the exam room. Nobody's going to find him until the morning."

"Are you hurt?"

"No," said Tang. "I'm good."

"Did we get what we needed?"

Tang nodded and handed Fordyce the patch he had taken off the dead Chinese soldier.

"What's this?"

"A scalp. Let's get moving and I'll tell you the rest."

"Wait," said Fordyce as he tucked it into his pocket. "What about Ginseng's sister?"

Tang shook his head. "She didn't make it."

Though nothing had been discussed, much less agreed to, Fordyce had half-expected to see Tang come bolting out of the camp with the girl in tow or over his shoulder. After everything their family had been through, those children deserved a happy ending. But happy endings in North Korea were in exceedingly short supply.

After retrieving their packs, they chose their path back up over the mountain as carefully as they could, but they needed to move quickly. The side trip to the infirmary had already cost them and Tang's being forced to spend extra time inside had only put them further behind schedule. If they were not at the rendezvous location on time, Hyun Su would leave without them. Those had been his orders.

At the top of the ridgeline, they found some concealment and stopped to take their first break. It had been a grueling climb and both men were sucking wind. Fordyce activated his radio and sent one click, followed by two more. A moment later, his message was answered with a single click. Tucker and Johnson were halfway down on the other side waiting for them.

Though both men were still heaving, Fordyce gave them only a minute more before signaling that it was time again to move.

The way down was no less dangerous than the way up. Gravity was like a dull narcotic tugging at their tired bodies, offering to help them get down the mountain faster if only they'd give in. Fordyce knew all too well that if they sped up, their chances of injury would go through the roof. They had made it this far without incident and he intended to see the entire team back to the coast and to their extraction in one piece.

Hitting the loose scree, they lost their footing several times. Recovering was like catching a pencil rolling off a desk. If you didn't react immediately, the opportunity was gone. Both Fordyce and Tang took one good stumble each, the momentum of coming downhill only adding to the difficulty of pulling out of the fall. By the time they reached the tree line, their mouths were dry, their bodies were covered in perspiration, and their legs were on fire. But they had picked up some of their lost time. Fordyce signaled another rest break.

Activating his radio, he transmitted a different series of clicks and then waited. Moments later, he received a response and began scanning the terrain beneath them.

When he picked up the tiny orb of infrared light through his night vision goggles, he tapped Tang on the shoulder and pointed to where they were headed. Three and a half minutes later, they were again on the move.

Arriving at Johnson and Tucker's hide, the team members fist-bumped as Fordyce and Tang shrugged off their packs and sucked down a ton of water from their Camelbaks.

"How is he?" Fordyce whispered once he had gotten enough of his breath back.

Tucker looked at Jin-Sang and then back at the lieutenant. "He's pretty doped up. That ride back is going to suck for him."

Fordyce remembered how many potholes they had hit and how uneven the roads had been. It was a rough ride without a tib/fib fracture. Tucker was smart to have upped the little boy's pain medication.

"What the fuck happened?" Johnson asked, staring at Tang's bloodstained clothes. "Cut yourself shaving?"

With the bite valve of his water bladder between his teeth, Tang smiled and said, "Actually, cut somebody else shaving."

"Who was she?"

Tang flipped him the finger and Johnson smiled. It was one of the first moments of camaraderie between the men.

As Fordyce filled them in on what had happened, he showed them the patch Billy Tang had taken from the dead Chinese officer.

"You *are* a crazy motherfucker," Johnson said to the CIA man. "Good job."

"What about the sister?" Tucker asked.

Tang shook his head. "You were right. TB. She was never going to make it."

"Did you?" the corpsman asked, alluding to another reason there might have been blood on his hands.

"No. When I went back to her bed to get my SIG, she had already passed."

"Are you going to tell him?" he asked, tilting his head toward the little boy.

"Not now," Tang replied. "The less pain he feels, physically *and* emotionally, the better off this operation is going to be."

That was the smart play for right now and Tucker nodded his head.

"What kind of intel did the sister have?" Johnson asked. "Was it worth it?"

It was, and Tang kept his explanation short. Johnson and Tucker were stunned, but not surprised. Everyone, particularly those in the military and intelligence communities, knew that an attack of the type and magnitude the Chinese had planned was only a matter of time.

Shouldering their packs, Tucker took point, followed by Fordyce and Tang, who carried the makeshift stretcher with Jin-Sang. Johnson brought up the rear.

It was much easier going and they made it to the

bottom without any falls or twisted ankles. Once there, they hid themselves and waited.

Five minutes after the agreed-to rendezvous time, Fordyce looked at Tang and pointed to his watch. The CIA man had no idea why Hyun Su was late and could only shrug in response.

When five minutes turned to twenty, and then to a half hour, Fordyce pulled out his map and began refreshing himself with the details of their contingency plan.

There was a river twenty klicks away. If they followed it downstream another ten kilometers, they would come to a mining camp that had its own rail line. Anything headed east would shave off half to three-quarters of the distance they needed to travel to get to the coast.

"Fuck that," Johnson said. "It'll take forever with the kid."

"I'm open to any better ideas you may have," Fordyce replied.

Pointing down toward the road, Johnson said, "We'll wait until somebody comes along and then jack 'em."

Fordyce shook his head. "Nobody travels this road. We could be here for weeks."

Just then, the growl of a diesel engine could be heard climbing uphill in their direction.

Johnson raised his eyebrows.

"Sounds like our ride," said Tang.

"What if it isn't?" Johnson asked.

Fordyce looked over at Tucker. "Tuck, how clean a shot do you have?"

"It depends. What do you want me to hit?"

"The driver."

Tucker shook his head. "Lot of branches between here and there."

"Be ready to take a shot. If that isn't Hyun Su's rig coming up that hill, you're cleared hot."

"Roger that," said Tucker as he leaned into the butt of his rifle.

They all listened as the growling got closer. Whatever was coming, it didn't sound like Hyun Sun's truck.

"Coming into range," said Tucker as he flipped off his safety and began applying pressure to his trigger. "Three seconds."

When the truck came into view, it was obviously not Hyun Su's.

"Send it," said Fordyce.

"Wait!" Tang interjected. "Don't shoot."

"What the—" Johnson began to say.

"It's Hyun Su," replied Tang, handing his binoculars to Fordyce. "Look. It's him."

"He's right," said Tucker, easing off his trigger.

Fordyce looked through the binoculars. "Where's the truck he used to get us here?"

Leaving his rifle and the rest of his gear, Tang stashed his pistol beneath his tunic and prepared to receive the truck. "I'm going to go find out."

With the SEALs covering him, Tang walked down to the side of the road, staying hidden by the tree line for as long as he could.

When he arrived at the vehicle, Hyun Su had already leaped out of the cab and was busy opening the doors in back.

"Where have you been?" Tang asked.

"My truck broke down."

"Where'd you get this one?"

"I borrowed it."

Tang looked at him. "By 'borrow,' do you mean you stole it?"

"Do you want me to take it back?"

"No," the CIA operative replied as he signaled it was safe for the team to come out of the woods.

Hyun Su watched as they came, carrying the little boy on the stretcher. "Where'd he come from?"

"We *borrowed* him," said Tang.

When Hyun Su opened the doors in back, the cargo area was completely empty. There were no boxes, no fake cargo to hide the team behind.

"What if we get stopped?" Tang asked.

"Then you'd better have a lot of whiskey and *Playboy* magazines."

The CIA operative translated for Fordyce as the team climbed up into the truck. Once they got Jin-Sang in and Tang had changed into a fresh tunic, they closed the doors and got their show back on the road.

As Hyun Su drove, he detailed what had happened and what he had had to do in order to secure another vehicle. Even though it was a smaller truck, with no faux cargo and a much less healthy engine, it was a godsend and Tang complimented the young smuggler on his resourcefulness. As long as it got them where they were going, everything might be okay.

Hyun Su avoided asking Tang anything about his assignment. He knew better than that. Even if he had asked, the CIA operative wouldn't have told him. They did, though, talk about Jin-Sang. It was obvious from his clothing that he had been in a labor camp. It was also obvious from the mask, the stretcher, and the splint fashioned around his leg that he wasn't in the best of shape.

Tang explained to Hyun Su that he needed to get

the boy across into South Korea as soon as possible. As they drove, they discussed options and began to formulate a plan.

Tang was already projecting further than just getting the little boy into South Korea. What he knew and what he had seen was highly valuable. Very important people at the Agency were going to want to debrief him. But then what? Who was going to take responsibility for him?

Tang thought about his own family, how they often discussed the horrors of North Korea, and while not particularly religious, how they prayed for the people there. Would his wife and children open their home, and more important, their hearts, to that little boy? The adjustment wouldn't be easy for any of them, especially Jin-Sang.

The prisoners who did manage to escape often had difficulty fitting in. They carried a tremendous amount of survivor's guilt and could be antisocial, even suicidal. Tang, though, felt Jin-Sang was different. The little boy understood the importance of family, and even though his had been taken from him, perhaps, in time, he could learn to love a new family. With those thoughts in mind, Tang leaned back and closed his eyes.

The CIA operative had no idea how long he had been asleep. The dramatic slowing of the truck jolted him awake. Immediately he reached for his SIG Sauer in the door pocket as his head swiveled from side to side.

"What is it?" he asked. "What's going on?"

Hyun Su pointed up ahead and replied, "Checkpoint."

"*Checkpoint?* I thought there weren't supposed to be any checkpoints on this road."

"There's one now."

Tang swore under his breath. Opening the rear window of the cab, he rapped on the cargo area to alert the SEALs that there was trouble and then sat back down.

"What do you want me to do?" Hyun Su asked.

"Just stay calm and let me do the talking."

CHAPTER 53

The checkpoint seemed to be manned by an unnecessarily large detachment of six heavily armed police officers.

Everyone in North Korea was on the take. And while it was likely a shakedown operation meant to solicit bribes from smugglers who plied the country's rural roads, Tang didn't like it. Their presence, on this road of all roads, could easily represent something else. *Had the dead Chinese officer been discovered already? Had the camp finally noticed Jin-Sang's disappearance? Did the police know that their truck had been stolen?*

As Hyun Su brought the vehicle to a stop, Tang reminded him to keep his eyes down and remain deferential. They had been through these kinds of "checkpoints" together before and they knew how they operated.

The senior officer, a man about Tang's age, stood with a pistol in a leather holster and his hand out in an officious *stop* gesture. The North Korean police reminded Tang of the Gestapo. The ones in the countryside seemed more prone to the spit and polish, rules and regs, than those in the city, who were a lot more lax about their duties. For some reason, police in the countryside were quasi royalty and they lorded it over all of the rural inhabitants.

Bowing obsequiously, Tang stepped out of the

truck, canvas bag in hand. "Yes, sir. Thank you, sir," he repeated in Korean.

"What are you thanking me for, you moron?" the officer demanded.

"The roads are safe," he said, bowing again to the officer and then to his men. They all carried AK-47s and shared the same bored look. "You and your men have done a very good job. Very good."

"What's in your truck?" the officer demanded.

"Goose feathers!"

"*Goose feathers,*" the policeman repeated. "You must think we're stupid."

"No, sir. No, sir. Very intelligent indeed. And a man of good taste!"

A grin appeared on the cop's face. "What makes you say that?"

"You look like a whiskey man to me," said Tang.

As he reached into his bag, several officers brought their rifles up. They weren't as blasé as they originally appeared.

Slowly, he removed the bottle of Jack Daniel's and held it up for the police commander to see.

The cop stepped forward, accepted the bottle, and addressing his men, said, "There seems to be a very good living to be made in goose feathers."

Several of the men chuckled. The ones with their weapons raised remained expressionless. Tang was starting to get the feeling that this crew was more than a little dangerous.

"What else do you have in that magic bag of yours?" the policeman asked.

The CIA operative smiled and fished out three *Playboy*s, but kept them clasped to his chest. "Something only real men, refined men, could appreciate."

Slowly, Tang turned them around and showed him. There was a chorus of approval from the policemen who had just been chuckling.

The commander accepted the magazines and tucked them under his arm.

Tang smiled.

The commander looked at him. "That's it? That's all you have? A bottle of whiskey and a few magazines?"

"Please, sir. We are just trying to get home."

"Sure you are," the police officer said with a smile. "So are we. What else do you have?"

Tang produced the cigarettes.

"Aha!" the commander cheered. "I knew it! Hand them over."

Tang did as he was told.

"Now, if only you could pull a hot meal from that bag, our evening would be complete."

"If I could," Tang said, "what kind of meal would you want?"

The police commander was suddenly frozen in thought. When he spoke, it was with an entirely different tone. "You have an unusual accent," he said. "Where are you from?"

The CIA operative had worked hard on his dialects, but he knew they weren't perfect.

Tang cited an obscure province near the border with China and said, "I know, I speak strangely. I was deaf for most of my childhood. Measles. At sixteen, some of my hearing returned, but not enough. I was unable to join our illustrious military because of it or become a fine police officer like you gentlemen."

The man looked at him, unable to decide whether he believed his story.

Tang returned to the subject of food, something every North Korean fantasized about, even policemen.

"What hot meal would you like to see me remove from my bag?" he asked again. "Please, be creative."

The police commander smiled once more and after thinking for a moment replied, "Duck. And barbecued pork."

"Excellent choice," said Tang. "How about grilled beef with vegetables, too?"

"And rice."

"Of course. Lots and lots of rice."

Never losing his smile, the police commander stated, "I'm now hungry, very hungry. I hope for your sake, as well as your colleague's, that you have all of these things and more remaining in that very little bag."

"But of course I—"

The commander held his hand back up in the *stop* position, interrupting him.

"Because if you don't," he said, "then there had better *only* be goose feathers in the back of your truck and they had better be going to someone very, very important."

Tang bowed, respectfully conceding the point. And from his bag he produced a small roll of currency, secured with a rubber band.

"Make sure to buy your men dessert as well," the CIA operative said as he handed over the money.

The commander removed the rubber band and thumbed the currency. "You certainly travel well-prepared."

"And as I said, you and your men do an excellent job of keeping the roads safe."

"It is our duty and we strive to do our best."

Tang's nervousness was beginning to abate. He had gone through these kinds of checkpoints before. The transaction was almost complete. A little more chitchat and then he and Hyun Su would be sent on their way.

"Before you go," the police commander continued, "I think we should inspect your cargo. I have never stopped a truck full of goose feathers before."

The CIA operative maintained his cool. Nodding at the items the commander had been given, he said, "You already have the best parts of the goose, sir. Please leave me the feathers so that my family will be able to have food in their bellies tonight as well."

The commander was done being flattered. With a quick jerk of his head, he sent his men to conduct the inspection. Pointing at Hyun Su, he ordered, "Out of the truck. Now."

The smuggler complied, but slammed his door as he climbed down.

The policeman took it as an act of disrespect. "You're angry. Am I keeping you from something?"

Hyun Su bowed to the commander and then turned to Tang and exploded at him. "You idiot! I told you we should not take this road. I told you! I told you!"

"Quiet!" the police commander bellowed.

Tang doubted the SEALs needed any further warning that trouble was at hand. But if they did, Hyun Su's slamming of his door and yelling would have done the trick.

"Let's go," the commander said, directing everyone to the rear of the vehicle.

When they arrived at the back of the truck, Tang implored the police officer one more time.

"Enough!" the man ordered. "Open it up!"

Tang bowed and grabbed one of the doors, as Hyun

Su grabbed the other. Then, throwing the lever, he and Hyun Su stepped back and opened the truck.

The shooting started instantly.

Fordyce, Johnson, and Tucker fired in fast, controlled bursts. *Head, chest. Head, chest. Head, chest.* Brass shell casings rained down and bounced onto the floor around them.

Only two officers were able to return fire. One drilled a hole through the roof of the truck. The other drilled a hole through the head of the officer in front of him.

When the shooting stopped, it was Navy SEALs six, North Korean police zero.

The SEALs leaped out of the truck to examine the carnage.

Picking up the unbroken bottle of Jack Daniel's, Johnson handed it to Tang. "Like they say—pigs get fed, but hogs get slaughtered."

Tang accepted the bottle and then retrieved the *Playboy* magazines, his cigarettes, and his currency. "What are we going to do about this mess?"

Fordyce studied the landscape. "We can't leave them here. Not on the road like this. We've got to find someplace to get rid of them."

Tang spoke with Hyun Su, who suggested a smaller road about five kilometers ahead that wound into the forest. Fordyce agreed.

They backed up the van the policemen had been driving and loaded their bodies inside. Then the SEALs climbed back into their truck.

Tang drove the van and monitored the radio. No one was looking for the officers, and probably no one would for some time.

When they reached the turnoff, Hyun Su drove

about a mile and a half up the winding road, pulled onto the shoulder, and stopped. With the van already filled with blood, it was pointless to try to stage something. By the time it was found, the team planned to be long gone anyway.

That didn't mean, though, that they wanted to leave it looking like a military-style assault. After taking the officers' watches, wallets, and weapons, they tossed the *Playboys* in the van, poured Jack Daniel's on the corpses, and left the bottle near the commander.

Whether the North Koreans would ever figure out what had really happened didn't matter. Six well-armed police officers had been killed. That story would spread far and wide, and would scare the hell out of every cop, soldier, and government official in the country.

Piling back into the truck, everyone was on edge, especially Fordyce. Trouble had a way of compounding itself, and they had a lot of ground yet to cover.

CHAPTER 54

Unpacking the storage units was an agonizingly slow process, but without knowing what was inside each box, they had no other choice.

Harvath had explained to Carlton why he believed the cylinders contained hydrogen and not helium.

"Helium doesn't explode. That's why they use it for weather balloons now. Hydrogen, though, does explode. But it also provides much greater lift. If they're trying to float bombs of some sort, hydrogen would be dangerous, but it would make sense. Plus, seeing that explosion in Tennessee, it's not hard to imagine that something highly flammable like hydrogen was involved."

"Why would they want to *float* bombs?" the Old Man wondered.

"You could get around, or *over*, a lot of security that way."

"But you'd be at the mercy of the wind. You couldn't control where the bomb landed."

"Maybe you wouldn't have to," Harvath replied. "If these were designed to be airburst weapons, all you'd have to do is arm them and launch them."

"From places like Des Moines and Nashville? Why

not do it over major population centers like Los Angeles, Chicago, or New York?"

"Maybe it doesn't matter."

"Hold on," Carlton said. "Even if these weren't bombs, let's say they were biological dispersal devices, you would still need them to release their payload over major population centers. Remember the intel saying there'd be a ninety percent mortality rate within a year?"

Harvath nodded.

"Let's say it's not biological, but radiological, and it is a bomb of some sort. It still needs to be over a major population center. I don't get it."

"What if it's neither?"

"My answer's the same even if the device is chemical."

"We keep looking at this as if the device itself is what's going to kill people. What if we're wrong?" Harvath said. "What if it's something else?"

"Like what?"

They were standing next to the workstation Special Agent Roe had been assigned to and Harvath asked her to pull up a map of the United States on her computer. Once she had, he asked her to highlight the six cities associated with each cell.

"These cities form a chain across the country," he said.

"And?"

"And what if six devices were not only launched at the same time, but detonated at the same time?"

Roe layered concentric blast radius circles above each city until they were almost touching and the country was blanketed from coast to coast.

"Now," said Harvath, "what if this wasn't chemical, biological, or even radiological, but electromagnetic?"

Suddenly, the color drained from Carlton's face. "An EMP weapon."

Harvath nodded.

"Everything would stop," said Roe. "There'd be no electricity, no running water."

"No 911. No police, no fire, no ambulances," Carlton added.

"No Internet. No grocery store deliveries. No deliveries for pharmacies and hospitals. No heat. No air-conditioning. No fuel. No machines to harvest crops. No trucks to deliver them to market. There would be complete and utter chaos. Anarchy. Our entire country would collapse within weeks."

"That's got to be it," the Old Man said. "That's got to be what they have planned."

Harvath pointed up at the flat-screens and the situations unfolding in Las Vegas, Dallas, and Des Moines. "What they find in there will tell us a lot."

"In the meantime, we need to let General Johnson and the President know what we now think this is." Looking then at Agent Roe, Carlton asked, "Can we get these feeds in the DNI's conference room?"

"I'm sure you can," she replied. "I'll have someone set it up."

The Old Man thanked her and signaled for Harvath to follow him.

As they arrived at the conference room, Nicholas and Draco were coming from the other direction. Harvath held the door open for them and motioned for Nicholas to be quiet as Carlton picked up the Secure Telephone Unit and dialed the White House.

After he had relayed the information to General Johnson and hung up the STU, Nicholas was nodding. "It makes perfect sense."

"But we've only found three storage units. Four if you count Nashville," the Old Man said. "Even if we do find units in Baltimore and Seattle, how do we know we have all the devices? How do we know there aren't more sleepers out there?"

It was an excellent point. Only by completely dismantling the entire plot would they ever know for sure. But to do that, they would need to do more than just uncover a few storage lockers. In fact, Harvath was already convinced that whatever device might have been in the Nashville storage unit, Bao Deng had taken it with him before he had burned everything else to the ground. There was no way he would leave something like that behind.

Harvath was just about to say as much when he saw Agent Roe running toward the conference room.

"What's up?" he said as she came rushing in.

"Boise," she replied, out of breath. "You nailed it. Todd Thomas. We've got him."

"You've got him?" Nicholas said.

"Not him, but the Xerox machine he used."

"How?"

Roe looked at Harvath.

"The man using the Todd Thomas alias showed up in Nashville with a just passable photocopy of his driver's license," said Harvath. "As long as he was standing in front of you and showed you his real license to compare to, you'd accept it. There was no reason for the storage facility manager to make another copy. We now know he did the same thing in Vegas, Dallas, and Des Moines. That's what got me thinking.

"If I was going to do this, I'd use a grocery store Xerox machine or one at a small pack-and-ship place and I'd practice. Once I had it to the point where you could read the info but my photo was just dark and out of focus enough, I'd whip out all my other fake IDs and make copies on the spot."

"And copy machines have hard drives," Nicholas said approvingly.

Harvath nodded. "They keep a record of everything. All you need is a cable and the right software to access it. Which is what we asked the FBI to do. They looked for public copy machines in and around Boise, paying specific attention to those closest to the free Wi-Fi locations the handler used to access his Facebook accounts. They downloaded as many hard drives as they could find and that data was fed to the NSA."

"Who then used one of their algorithms to sift the data and look for matches of the blurry driver's license photos?"

"Exactly," said Harvath as he turned back to Roe. "What do we know?"

"The copy machine was in a small pack-and-ship place in downtown Boise called Going Postal. They offer PO boxes, shipping services, that kind of thing," Roe replied. "The hard drive had copies of the driver's licenses used at the storage units we already know of, plus a license from Washington State and one from Maryland. Now that we've got those aliases, we're pretty confident we'll be able to track down the storage units in Seattle and Baltimore."

"How many licenses total were on the machine for this guy?"

Roe smiled. "Seven. Just like you suspected, he practiced with a local, Idaho driver's license first. We've already run it. Unlike the others, this one is legit. It belongs to a fifty-seven-year-old naturalized American citizen of Chinese birth named Ren Ho. He lives in

Indian Valley, Idaho, about two hours north of Boise. We're doing a full workup on him now and the FBI has already scrambled an HRT team. DoE is also sending a NEST team."

Harvath looked at Carlton. "We need to be there, on site, as soon as they grab him, so we can do the interrogation."

The Old Man nodded. "Who do you want to take?"

"Sloane and Chase, plus Nicholas for anything we find computer-related."

"Done. Anything else?"

"Stephanie Esposito."

"The Agency's China analyst?"

"I want someone who knows the culture," replied Harvath. "Who can speak and read Chinese."

"I'll call the President and DNI and brief them right now."

Scribbling down his email address and cell phone number, Harvath handed them to Agent Roe and said, "As soon as we're in the air, I'll check my inbox. Please send everything you've got to that address."

"Will do," Roe replied. "Stay safe."

"I'll try," he said, and then, looking at Nicholas, nodded toward the door. "Let's go."

CHAPTER 55

Four out of the five princelings had done a good job. They had practiced excellent tradecraft and had not brought any surveillance with them into Chinatown. The fifth princeling, though, had been atrocious. Not only had she dragged a tail along behind her, but she had also brought her cell phone.

Cheng could forgive her for the tail; even the best operatives made mistakes. The phone, though, was unforgivable. From the moment he had first picked her up on the surveillance cameras, she had been either talking or texting. She was oblivious to the things going on around her. It infuriated him, because if she had chosen to ignore this part of the protocol, she had likely ignored everything else she had been taught. *The arrogance. This was not a game.*

The restaurant was noisy, crowded. It was filled with boisterous American Chinese. There was a fish tank with cloudy water. Everything smelled like crab.

Cheng watched to make sure the rude waiter had given the note to the right person and then he slipped into the handicapped bathroom.

When she knocked, he unlocked the door and stood back. She was wearing knee-high boots, a short skirt, and a flimsy top. Stepping into the small space, she kicked the door closed behind her and shot daggers at him.

"Lock it," he said.

Her cold gaze was averted only long enough to turn and do as he had asked. When she turned back around, he reached out and wrapped one of his hands around the back of her neck.

"Give it to me," he demanded in Chinese.

The daggers were gone. Her eyes were now wide with fear. She didn't like his hand on the back of her neck like that. "Give you what?"

He was done playing games. He ran his free hand over her body until he found it. She had tucked her iPhone in her bra and he brushed roughly against one of her breasts pulling it out.

"Hey!" she exclaimed.

"Shut up."

"My grandfather will—"

Cheng tightened his grip around her neck, forcing her to look at him. "Listen to me, princess. We are not in Beijing. I don't care who your grandfather is. I'm in charge. Do you understand me?"

The young woman didn't reply, so Cheng squeezed even tighter. When she nodded, he released his grasp.

"Do you know that you have an FBI agent following you?"

The girl rubbed her neck, hoping he had not bruised her. "I didn't see anyone."

"Of course not. You were too busy talking and texting on your phone."

"Where is he?"

"Shut up and pay attention," he snapped.

Pulling out one of the new, prepaid phones he'd had Wei Yin purchase when they had arrived in Boston, he handed it to her. "Take this. Then I want you to go back into the restaurant, sit down, and order dinner. When this phone rings, you will pick it up and you will do exactly as I tell you. Is that understood?"

The young woman shrugged.

He was ready to grab her by the neck again. "This is not a game, Daiyu. This is very serious. Do you understand me?"

"I guess," she replied. "Now give me my iPhone back."

"No," he said, unlocking the door. "Time to go."

As she stepped past him, the daggers were back.

"Enjoy your dinner. I'll call you soon."

He watched her disappear down the hall and back into the restaurant. He didn't need to look for the FBI man. He was out there somewhere.

Exiting the restaurant, he turned off the iPhone and then tossed it down a storm drain. *Stupid, arrogant girl.*

Back at the safe house, he checked on the other four princelings. They had eaten and were watching a Chinese DVD. He'd been loath to leave them alone, but he'd had little choice. To their credit, they had behaved themselves. Even the smokers had done as he had asked and had limited themselves to smoking in the bathroom with the window cracked. He had no desire to draw undue attention to the safe house, or to his charges. As soon as he could bring Daiyu in, they'd be able to get some sleep, and then they would be on their way.

The FBI agent, though, was now an issue, and there were only two ways to deal with him. Either Cheng could come up with a suitable distraction to help Daiyu slip away, or he'd have to pick the right spot and put a bullet in the back of the man's head. While a bullet in the back of the head was a lot easier to accomplish, it brought with it a host of new problems, not least of which was the possibility of a police dragnet if they found the body before the Chinese had been able to flee.

He couldn't risk it. He'd have to find a way to help her shake the tail without the agent's knowing he'd been spotted. The easiest way to do that was to pick a business that had multiple entries and exits.

After changing clothes, he left the safe house and found a small store where he bought Daiyu sweatpants, a sweatshirt, and a Boston Bruins baseball cap. Just changing her appearance was going to go a long way toward helping her disappear.

Next, he walked over to Avenue De Lafayette to explore the Hyatt Regency Hotel. It was a large, busy building with a restaurant, a café, and, most important of all, many ways in and out. It would be perfect. There was even a lobby bar from which he could take in everything as she entered.

As soon as he had mapped out how it would all unfold, he removed his sterile cell phone and called her at the restaurant.

"Do you know the Hyatt Regency Hotel?" he asked.

"Yes," she replied. "I know it."

"Ask for the check then. Once you have paid, don't do anything differently. Just walk to the hotel. Forget the man is there. Don't look over your shoulder, don't acknowledge him at all. Understand?"

"Yes, I understand," she said.

Cheng decided it would be better to keep her on the phone and talk her all the way in. If anything, it would help keep her calm and prevent her from doing something stupid.

It didn't take long before she announced that she

could see the hotel up ahead. Soon after that, she was outside and coming through the front doors. Cheng told her to walk straight to the main elevators, come up to the lobby level, and then take the guest elevators to the fifth floor. He would meet her there in the south stairwell.

Looking over the lobby, he watched as Daiyu arrived and did exactly as he had instructed. He then waited for the FBI agent in order to see what he would do. Cheng had figured the man would park himself on a chair somewhere in the lobby and wait for her to come back down. Cheng was wrong.

Seconds later, the agent arrived, but with two other agents in tow. This was not good. Cheng needed to act fast.

There was no time to wait for the elevator. In fact, the sooner he got out of the lobby, the better. Keeping his head down, he moved to the stairwell, opened the door, and began taking the stairs two and then three at a time.

When he reached Daiyu, he grabbed her by the arm and ordered, "Move. Now. Up. Go!"

On the seventh floor, he steered her out of the stairwell and down the long, carpeted hallway. At an ice machine station, he directed her into the little room, pulled out the clothes he had purchased for her, and said, "Hurry. Put these on."

Daiyu motioned for him to turn around. Considering how she was dressed and how she had behaved, he wasn't fooled by her false modesty. "Make it quick," he stated, turning his back.

When she had dressed in the sweatpants and sweatshirt, he had her tuck her hair up under the Bruins cap and then looked at her. *Good enough.*

Shoving her other clothes behind the ice machine, he stole a glimpse into the hallway to make sure it was safe. There was no one there.

Taking Daiyu by the wrist, Cheng moved quickly toward the stairwell at the other end of the hall.

When they got there, he opened the door and stepped onto the landing, but his heart caught in his chest. There were voices and the sound of heavy footsteps coming up toward them.

"What is it?" Daiyu asked as he backed out of the stairwell and silently closed the door.

"Trouble."

They moved even faster now, back toward the stairwell they had originally been in. Cracking the door, Cheng listened and didn't hear anything. It sounded safe until he heard the squelch from a radio. There was only one thing left to do.

Backing out of the stairwell, he dragged Daiyu behind him, his eyes scanning the wall for what he wanted. When he found the fire alarm, he activated it.

Instantly, strobe lights began flashing and the ear-splitting wail of the alarm filled the air. Seconds later, guests began to stick their heads out of their rooms, unsure what to do next. Was there a fire? Was it a mistake?

Turning to Daiyu, Cheng said, "Stay close to me. Don't say a word and don't let go of my hand."

The young woman nodded and Cheng led her back to the stairwell. Before he opened the door, he gave her a final reminder to be as quiet as possible. When she nodded, he opened the door and checked to make sure that whoever had been beneath them with the radio had not yet made it to their floor.

Convinced that it was safe, as long as they went up, he drew her into the stairwell and began climbing.

By the time they reached the tenth floor, hotel guests were already streaming in from the floors above and heading down in a torrent of robes, work-out clothes, and pajamas. It was exactly what Cheng wanted. It would be impossible for the FBI agents to identify the masses of people flooding down to the lobby and out onto the sidewalks.

Stepping onto the tenth floor, he searched until he found the service elevator and then pulled Daiyu into the vestibule. Depressing the call button, he removed his pistol, affixed its suppressor, and though he already knew the weapon was hot, checked to make sure a round was chambered.

The young woman stared at it aghast. "What's that?"

"A rice maker," Cheng replied as he retained his hold on the pistol and concealed it with the plastic bag her sweats had been in.

She resented his insolence. "You do not have my permission to shoot anyone."

The remark made him smile. "I don't need your permission. You're not in charge here."

"But my grandfather—" she began.

He shot her a stare that cut her off midsentence. "I told you. We're not in Beijing and I don't care who your grandfather is."

"You'll be made to care," she replied.

"Perhaps. But until then, you're going to keep your mouth shut and you're going to do what I say or you won't live to see your grandfather again."

The young woman folded her arms across her chest and refused to look at him.

Obstinacy. That was fine by him, especially if it shut her up. And as long as she followed orders.

The elevator arrived, they stepped in, and Cheng

selected the basement level. The hotel had underground parking and he planned for them to slip out via the side entrance on Chauncy Street.

He watched each floor blink by, ready for the worst should the doors open and they be confronted with a threat. Nothing happened. Even the hotel guests had stuck to the stairwells.

Arriving at the lower level, they exited the elevator into a long service corridor lit by bright, overhead lighting.

"This way," he said.

They followed the deserted corridor to a door that read *Garage, Exit Only, No Reentry*, all of which were fine by Cheng.

The alarm was still blaring as he leaned against the crash bar and pushed the door open with his hip. There was no sign of movement anywhere in the garage. They had almost made it.

"We're going to walk up the ramp and out onto the street," he said. "Keep your eyes down and stay close."

Crossing the garage, Cheng kept his eyes peeled. Already in his mind, he was planning what he would do once they were outside. They would take a left on Chauncy, move away from the hotel to Summer Street, and start carefully working their way back to Chinatown and the safe house.

At the top of the ramp, Cheng stuck his head out, looked both ways, and then led Daiyu onto the sidewalk. The sound of approaching police cars and fire engines could be heard in the distance.

The street was lined with parked cars. It was a very long block with a CVS and a Macy's at the end, and no other streets or alleyways branching off before then.

They had only made it about twenty feet when a

man shouted, "Bao Deng! FBI! Stop right where you are!"

The federal agent hadn't called out to Daiyu. He had called out to Cheng, specifically, and had addressed him by his alias. Somehow, the Americans were on to him. He had been left with no choice. Pushing Daiyu to the ground, Cheng spun, raised his weapon, and began to fire.

The FBI man's pistol jumped twice in his hands, accompanied by two loud reports, before it fell silent and he dropped to the ground, dead.

There had been only one agent, but there were very likely more on the way. Cheng pulled Daiyu back to her feet.

"Move!" he ordered her.

She looked at his left shoulder and gasped. "You're bleeding."

"I told you to move."

Prodding her toward Summer Street, Cheng ignored the pain in his arm and assessed what he would have to do next. Boston was no longer safe, and sleep was out of the question. In fact, the United States was no longer safe. They needed to get on the road and get to Medusa as soon as possible.

CHAPTER 56

The first asset to arrive on station was a surveillance drone, which circled far above the home of Ren Ho. The small ranch, consisting of the house, a barn and several outbuildings, and horses and other assorted livestock, was on the edge of the Payette National Forest.

The terrain was such that a full-on, daylight assault was impossible, so Harvath had suggested something else.

Nicholas wasn't crazy about using one of his dogs as a prop. And the idea was only made worse by the fact that he wouldn't be allowed to be there when everything happened. But considering there was no other option, he'd given in.

Special Agent Roe had forwarded all of the information the Bureau had compiled on Ren Ho to Harvath in-flight. They had his naturalization information, his tax returns, and a limited amount about his business dealings. According to the FBI, he was a manufacturer's rep who paired American companies with factories in China. He had been married at one point, but divorced and the wife had moved back to China. They had a college-age son, who held dual citizenship and appeared to be living with the mother back in Shenzhen.

Roe had included a State Department travel history in the file and told Harvath that the NSA was working to gather any intelligence it could from Ho's phone, email, and credit card histories. The CIA had come up completely empty. There was nothing in their files on anyone named Ren Ho.

Shortly before landing, Roe called the plane back and gave Harvath a full rundown on what had happened in Boston. An FBI agent had been following one of the princelings, a girl named Daiyu Jinping. She had eaten dinner alone, which was unusual for her, but what was even stranger was that she had been talking and texting nonstop on an Apple iPhone, but after going to the restroom at the restaurant, the behavior not only stopped, but she had returned with a completely different phone.

Because of the heightened alert, the agent following her reported the suspicious behavior to his superior. The superior then reached out to the other surveillance teams. All of them had been convinced that their subjects were in for the night. A check on the princelings' cell phone locations had confirmed their assumption. Finally, someone at the FBI called for physical confirmation and one by one, the surveillance teams began to report that the subjects were missing. The phones were plugged in and turned on, but no one was home. Panic quickly spread.

Extra agents were immediately sent to back up the man following Daiyu Jinping. When she entered Boston's Hyatt Regency Hotel, some agents gave chase, while others went to the security office to monitor the CCTV cameras. Rolling back the footage, they wanted to see if anyone had gotten on the elevator with Daiyu or passed anything to her in the lobby.

They didn't see anyone, but they did see a man who

entered one of the stairwells shortly after the FBI appeared in the lobby. Rolling back the footage a little further, they pinpointed when the man had entered the hotel and were able to piece together everything he had done. He had avoided all of the cameras—all except one near the cash register in the bar. Within minutes of transmitting the image back to the Bureau, the agents had a confirmation. It was Bao Deng.

But no sooner had the man's identity been confirmed than the fire alarm had been activated. It was an obvious ruse, but it complicated things tremendously for the FBI. They had called for additional backup, including Boston PD, but none of it had arrived in time.

One agent remained in the security office to monitor the CCTV feeds, while the others tried to locate Deng and the princeling. With all of the guests trying to evacuate the hotel, it was like fighting against a wave of salmon swimming upstream.

Then, Bao Deng had been spotted on CCTV with another figure in a service corridor on the lower level. The agent in the security office rightly pegged figure number two as Daiyu Jinping and fed out a description of what she was wearing and where the pair was headed.

As they came up the garage ramp and exited the hotel, they were accosted by the first FBI agent able to get to them. There was a gunfight. The agent was killed and Deng and the princeling disappeared.

It was bad news on many levels. Not only had a federal agent lost his life, but all of the princelings had now successfully slipped their surveillance. Harvath was willing to bet Bao Deng hadn't been sent to Boston just to pick up Daiyu Jinping. He very likely had something to do with the other four Chinese students' falling off the grid.

Leaving the cell phones plugged in and turned on meant that they didn't want anyone to notice they were gone. That was the most troubling part about all this. Eventually, their absence was going to be noticed. Apparently, though, by that time it wouldn't matter, which could only mean one thing. The attack was about to happen.

When the Carlton Group's jet landed in the resort town of McCall, Idaho, about thirty miles northeast of Indian Valley, an FBI command center had already been established at the airport.

A helicopter would transport Harvath, Sloane, Chase, and Nicholas's dog, Argos, to a ranger station in the Payette National Forest. The ranger knew where Ho's ranch was and was fairly certain he could get them right up to the property line and drop them off without their being seen. From there, they would be on their own.

The plan was for the helicopter to return to the airport to pick up a team of HRT shooters, while everyone else, including local law enforcement, would approach in SUVs via two unpaved roads.

Harvath had only two rules—nobody did anything until he gave the go-ahead, and Ren Ho was to be taken alive at all costs. Once the radio codes were established, gear was parceled out, and everything was settled, they launched.

While Argos might like Harvath, he didn't like being separated from his owner. According to Sloane, he had exhibited the same nervous behavior at the NCTC when Nicholas had taken Draco inside and she and Chase had taken him back to the Carlton Group offices.

Harvath tried to reassure the enormous animal by scratching his neck and behind his ears. Eventually, the beast put his head down on his huge front paws and seemed to relax.

Chase looked at Harvath and said via his headset, "That dog is going to hate your guts by the end of the day."

Harvath shook his head and looked out over the rugged landscape. He had always thought Idaho was one of the most beautiful states in the Union. It contained lots of space with very few people to bother you. If he was right, and the Chinese were planning to collapse the U.S. with a series of EMP devices, Idaho was definitely one of the places he would consider making his stand. If you had prepped enough in advance, and didn't have any major medical conditions that required hospital visits, you could probably ride it out somewhat comfortably.

The helicopter pilot radioed the ranger station once they were in range and then, after circling the clearing to get a visual, flared and came in for a landing.

Opening the door, Harvath hopped out first, followed by Argos and then Sloane and Chase. Once they had retrieved their gear from the cargo compartment, they retreated a safe distance away and flashed the pilot a thumbs-up.

It took only a moment for the giant bird to lift off and fade from sight beyond the soaring pines. Once it was gone, the thundering sound of its rotors was replaced by something else—total silence. It was amazing how quiet the forest could be.

The ranger introduced himself and led the team to his SUV. On the hood, he had laid out a detailed topo map. He explained where they were, where Ho's ranch was, and the route he would be taking to deliver them to the drop-off point.

"You all ready to go, then?" the ranger asked.

Chase looked at Argos and then at Harvath. "What do you say, Dr. Doolittle?"

"Help me get him in the truck," Harvath replied.

Walking around to the back of the SUV, they opened the tailgate and coaxed Argos to jump inside. Once the dog was in, Harvath leaped up and joined him. He had the dog lie down and then took his giant head in his lap.

"All right, let's do it."

Chase removed a tube of Derma Bond—the medical equivalent of Krazy Glue—and Sloane produced the small stone they had selected at the airport.

Nicholas had shown her the sensitive pocket of tissue on the dog's paw, between the pads, and that's where she placed the stone. Pinching the lips of the pocket together, careful not to get any on her fingers, she held everything in place as Chase covered it in Derma Bond. As they did that, Harvath tried to keep the big dog distracted.

Argos looked over at Sloane and Chase once or twice, but didn't seem to be terribly interested in what they were doing. He was more interested in the attention he was getting from Harvath.

When it was done, Sloane nodded and then she and Chase closed the hatch and climbed into the SUV with the ranger. For the duration of the ride, Harvath's job was to keep Argos's mind on anything but that paw.

CHAPTER 57

The ride down from the ranger station took a half hour. As they neared the spot where Chase was going to be dropped off, they did a final radio check.

When the ranger brought the SUV to a halt, he pointed to a stand of trees and said, "Fifty yards in is the creek. You'll hear it before you see it. The path is on the east side. Can't miss it."

"Got it," Chase replied. Gathering up his ruck and his rifle, he opened the door. "See you all down there."

"Don't get lost," said Harvath.

Chase smiled.

Once he had closed the door, the ranger put his truck in gear and drove Harvath and Sloane to their drop-off point. Their approach would be a little more difficult.

When they arrived at their spot, the ranger pulled over and cut his ignition. Coming around to the back of the vehicle, he waited for Sloane before opening the hatch.

She checked the glue on Argos's paw and then flashed Harvath the thumbs-up. "It's all dry," she said.

Harvath told the dog to stay as he climbed out of the back. He didn't want Argos jumping down onto that paw. It was going to be uncomfortable enough walking on it as it was. He didn't want to compound it for him.

With Sloane and the ranger helping, they lifted Argos out of the back and set him down. It only took him a few steps to realize there was something aggravating the bottom of his right front paw.

"All right," said Harvath. "Let's get going before he decides he wants to sit down and start chewing on it."

The ranger headed toward the trees and they followed.

The forest floor was soft and made it easier on Argos, but Harvath could already see he was starting to favor his paw.

Soon enough, they arrived at the edge of the tree line. The ranger held up his hand for them to stop, and everyone listened for a moment. Except for the sounds of the forest, it was completely quiet.

"This is as far as I go," he said. "About three hundred yards down from here is where the property begins. There's an old logging road. Follow it downhill and it'll take you right to his front door."

Harvath and Sloane thanked the ranger and watched as he walked back up through the trees to his SUV.

Removing the radio from his backpack, Harvath unfolded the antenna and established comms with the command center back at the airport. While Sloane kept Argos busy, Harvath gave the team at the airport a brief situation report. Once Chase radioed in that he was in place and the coast was clear, Harvath signed off and packed up the radio.

After doing a final weapons check, he and Sloane headed for the logging road.

About halfway to the ranch, Argos had gone from favoring his paw to a slight limp. By the time the ranch came into view, the limp was pronounced and unmistakable. Even though Harvath knew it wasn't intense pain, he hated having to put the dog through it. Nevertheless, Argos was tough and kept moving.

As they walked, Harvath scanned for cameras. He didn't see any, but he could sense they were being watched, so he and Sloane played their act to maximum effect.

Every fifty to a hundred yards they stopped, Harvath bent down to examine the dog's leg, and then they would start up again. By the time they came in sight of Ho's ranch house, Harvath was convinced the man had seen all of it.

On cue, they saw a figure leave the house, climb into a Gator side-by-side utility vehicle, and strike off in their direction.

The key to any successful con wasn't getting people to put their faith in you. It was making them think that you had put your faith in them. The quickest way to do that was to ask for a favor.

Posing as hikers who had lost their way was a lame con. But add an injured dog to the scenario and suddenly things became a lot more believable, especially in a heavily rural area. Farmers and ranchers understood animals. They also lived by the code that compelled them to assist others in need. The favor in this case was obvious.

"Here he comes," Harvath said.

Sloane had noticed him, too, and nodded in response.

Because their radios were hidden in their backpacks, they had to trust that Chase, dug in where no one could see him, was also watching everything unfold through the Schmidt & Bender scope atop his .50 caliber Barrett

M107A1. If they came under attack, he was their first line of defense. In fact, they were counting on Chase disrupting any potential attack before it happened. According to the drone footage, though, there was only one person at the ranch.

Harvath wasn't willing to bet everything on a drone, but its camera and infrared imaging had been very clear. In any case, they would have their answer soon enough.

As the Gator drew closer, Sloane raised her arm and waved. Harvath stopped walking. This was as good a place as any to make their stand. Argos leaned against him, taking his weight off his sore paw.

"Good boy," Harvath said, giving him a pat. "You're almost done."

If Ren Ho had been expecting trouble, he certainly didn't act like it. The unassuming Chinese man was dressed in jeans, a denim shirt, and a pair of work boots. His Ruger Mini-14 Ranch Rifle wasn't on the seat next to him, but rather in the Gator's overhead rack.

As he neared the two hikers and their dog, he slowed to get a good look at them, before pulling alongside and bringing the side-by-side to a stop.

"You're trespassing," he said. There was no greeting, no preamble. "My signs are all clearly posted."

"Our dog went after a moose," Harvath replied. "It took us two hours to find him. We didn't know where we were until we saw your signs."

"Well, now you do," he said curtly. "This isn't a rest area."

"Something's wrong with our dog," Sloane interjected. "We're sorry to be on your property, but we need to get him to a vet. Can you help us, please?"

Climbing out of his Gator, Ho asked, "What's wrong?"

Sloane smiled at him. "Thank you so much. It's his right leg."

"What kind of dog is he?"

"Russian sheepdog," Harvath said, stepping away so the man didn't feel too crowded or threatened.

"Is he friendly?" Ho inquired, bending down to examine Argos's leg. "He's not going to bite me, is he?"

"He's a pussycat," Sloane said, getting closer. "My boyfriend, on the other hand, is the one you need to worry about."

Boyfriend was the go code she and Harvath had settled on. Noticing a pistol under Ho's shirt, she had decided it was time to act.

Sloane brought her boot back and kicked Ho in his left side so hard she broke three of his ribs. As the man fell over, away from the dog, he gasped for breath and went for his gun. Harvath, though, was faster.

Whipping out his Taser, he made sure Ho was not in contact with Argos or Sloane and then let him ride the lightning. He pressed the trigger and the barbed probes deployed, hitting him in the chest, followed by a surge of electricity that interrupted his neuromuscular system.

As soon as he was down, Harvath tossed the Taser to Sloane and subdued Ho. He relieved the man of his 9mm Keltec PF9 pistol, FlexiCuffed his hands behind his back, and then patted him down.

Satisfied that he didn't have any other weapons on him, Harvath placed a piece of duct tape over his mouth and a hood over his head. Then, breaking out his radio, he gave the rest of the team the code to move in.

"Swing Arm," Harvath said over the radio. "Repeat. Swing Arm."

CHAPTER 58

With Ho trussed up in the bed of the Gator, Harvath and Sloane watched as the big Bell 412EP helicopter disgorged the HRT team. They cleared the ranch house first, then the barn, and then the rest of the support buildings. One of the buildings was a long metal structure stacked high with pallets of food, medicine, clothing, and assorted supplies. The head of the HRT team called it the mother of all doomsday caches.

Once everything had been deemed safe and HRT had given the all clear, a string of SUVs sped onto the ranch. First out was the NEST team, who conducted an extensive search of the property for any radiological or nuclear materials. As they did, Harvath went into the house and conducted his own search. He wanted to learn as much as he could, as quickly as he could, about the man he was about to interrogate.

The home's décor was pretty much what Harvath assumed it would be—bland and middle-of-the-road. It was a mixture of Ho's life in China and his life in Idaho. There was a calendar on the wall in the kitchen featuring Chinese cities and a painting above the worn couch in the living room depicting two American

Indians, a father and son, hunting deer. There were no posters of Chairman Mao in the den, no *Communist Manifesto* on the bedroom nightstand. The house was remarkably unremarkable. Which was exactly what the home of a deep-cover operative working in a foreign nation should be. But there were interesting touches that spoke to Ho the man.

The kitchen, while drab and out of date, had gourmet cookbooks and expensive small appliances, like a high-end KitchenAid mixer and a top-of-the-line Cuisinart food processor. His spices were from Dean & DeLuca and he appeared very fond of expensive Bordeaux wines. In the living room, he had an impressive collection of French jazz and Brazilian bossa nova records. Ho appeared to be a man of taste.

He also appeared to be a family man who loved his son very much. There were many pictures of him throughout the house, several taken right at the ranch. Some of the photos were from vacations he had taken with the young man over the years. There were photos of them at the Golden Gate Bridge in San Francisco, the Space Needle in Seattle, the Willis Tower in Chicago, the Empire State Building in New York City, and the Alamo in San Antonio. Ho could be seen with his arm around his son or the two high-fiving and laughing. It was a completely different face from the one the man had shown outside to the two hikers who had stumbled upon his private property.

It was also the only leverage Harvath would need. He radioed for the Agency's China expert, Stephanie Esposito, to be sent into the house.

After explaining what he wanted Esposito to do, he set up the video camera and radioed Sloane and Chase to bring Ho inside.

They sat him on the couch and removed his hood as well as the duct tape from across his mouth.

"What's going on here?" Ho demanded. "I'm an American citizen. Who are you? What do you think you're doing?"

Harvath introduced himself by one of his aliases. "Mr. Ho, my name is Tim Rudd. I represent the United States government. I am going to save us both a lot of time. As a spy, you were taught to deny everything and launch counteraccusations. But I expect your immediate and full cooperation. You will answer all of my questions honestly and you will answer them the first time I ask. If you do not follow these rules to the letter, let me show you what's going to happen."

Harvath snapped his fingers and Esposito stepped out of the kitchen with her cell phone. She dialed a number in China and put the call on speaker. When a man answered, Esposito spoke to him in fluent Mandarin.

"You have the boy in your sights?" she asked.

"Yes," the man replied.

"Describe him."

Using her camera phone, Esposito had taken pictures of the photographs Ho had around the house of his son. She had then emailed them to a colleague in Beijing.

The man not only gave a detailed description of what the boy looked like, but invented what he was wearing and described that as well. He then asked for permission to "take the shot."

Esposito looked at Harvath and translated.

Harvath shook his head.

Esposito relayed the message, told the man she would call back, and disconnected the call.

"Mr. Ho," said Harvath. "I'm only going to make this offer once, so please listen very carefully. We have everything. We have the storage units. We have the devices. We have the weather balloons. We have the engineering students recruited by Khuram Hanjour from the UAE. We have the Somalis, too. Of course, we need to discount what happened in Nashville, but you know all of that. We have all the locations you used to monitor the cell members' Facebook accounts. We even have the Xerox machine in Boise you used to photocopy your fake IDs. So here's my offer. Are you listening?"

Ho nodded.

"Good. We want you to come to work for us."

"And if I say no to you, will you kill my son?"

"Yes, but that's only the beginning."

"Then you'll kill me?"

Harvath shook his head.

"Of course not," Ho replied. "This is America. I'll get a trial first and then you'll execute me."

"I won't lie to you, Mr. Ho. There are those in my government who want to see you executed. In fact, there are those who would pin a medal on me if I shot you right now."

"So why don't you?"

Harvath changed the subject. He wanted to establish rapport with his prisoner, but he also needed to establish a baseline for his interrogation in order to discern if Ho was lying. "I noticed your albums."

"What about them?"

"My mother was a big Charlie Byrd fan. Do you have any of his records?"

"I do," Ho said reservedly. "A record he did with Stan Getz."

Harvath nodded his head for a moment, seemingly

transported. "I remember Getz. My mother's favorite song was 'The Girl from Ipanema.' She used to play it over and over. All the time."

"Why are you asking me about records?"

"Because, Mr. Ho, you strike me as a refined man. I also assume that you're a good father and that you care about your son. Whatever choices you have made, he doesn't deserve to die."

Ho shook his head. "No, he doesn't. He's a good boy."

"Like I said, if you don't cooperate, they're going to kill your son. You, though, will not be executed. You'll be sent to a top-secret detention facility in the Upper Peninsula of Michigan where the only thing worse than the unbearably cold winters are the unbearable, mosquito-infested summers. You'll be subjected to extremely hard outdoor labor every day, as well as solitary confinement.

"Within your first week, you'll wish you had been executed. Within your first month, you'll start trying to figure out ways to escape. Within your first year, you'll realize that the only escape you'll ever achieve is through death.

"And on a side note, I've seen your kitchen. You know what good food is. The dogs at this facility eat better than the prisoners. You can't even call what they serve food. The men they send there are animals. They don't possess your level of refinement. The utter absence of any comforts whatsoever will make life there harder, bleaker. There are no Amnesty International or Red Cross visits there. They aren't even aware the facility exists.

"It is designed to impose a punishment *worse* than death. And to top it all off, you'll be alone with your thoughts and the knowledge that all of it, including the death of your son, could have been prevented."

Ho stared at him blankly—completely unsure of what to do.

Harvath let the silence linger for several moments before asking, "Wouldn't you do anything to save your son?"

The man nodded.

"Then accept the offer, Mr. Ho. Come work for us."

"If I work for you, I'm as good as dead."

"If you work for us," said Harvath, "we can protect you. I give you my personal guarantee."

"Can you protect my son? Can you get him out of China?"

Harvath looked at Stephanie Esposito, who nodded. He then turned back to Ren Ho. "Yes, we can. But first, you and I are going to have a very in-depth conversation. If at any point you lie to me, our deal is off. Is that understood?"

"I understand," Ho replied.

Harvath began with questions he already knew the answers to. "What is the codename for your operation?"

"In Chinese, it is called Xuě Lóng. Snow Dragon."

"How many cells are there?"

"Six."

"How many members in each cell?"

"Two," Ho replied.

"Where are the cells located?"

"Seattle, Las Vegas, Des Moines, Dallas, Nashville, and Baltimore."

Harvath kept his eyes locked on the man's face and asked, "How did you enlist the cell members?"

"We used recruiters. One in Dubai and one in Mogadishu."

"Who is Tommy Wong?"

"He's a triad member in Los Angeles."

"Which triad?"

"14K," said Ho.

So far, all of his answers had been correct and truthful. Harvath had not noticed any microexpressions that would suggest the man was lying.

"The engineering students from the UAE all arrived in the United States by which city?"

"Houston."

"What was the cover used to secure their visas?"

"An internship with NASA for Muslim students," Ho replied.

"Each of them carried a cell phone. Where did these phones come from?"

"Tommy Wong bought the phones and shipped them to me. I got them to the recruiter in Dubai, who then gave them to the students before they left for the U.S."

Harvath was now ready to start asking other questions.

"Who is their handler?"

"I am," Ho answered.

"Where are your control files on the cell members?"

"On my computer. In the den. The password is Samba477823//*."

"And the hardcopies?" Harvath asked.

"Under the last stall in the barn. Beneath the hay is a trapdoor that leads to a storm cellar. All the files are there."

Harvath looked at Chase and said, "Take the HRT breachers with you to the barn. Make sure none of it is wired. Let me know what you find."

"Roger that," Chase replied as he stepped out of the room.

Harvath didn't want to start messing with any of Ho's computers, not if he didn't have to. Nicholas could do just about anything, but the NSA would have the best chance of sucking all of the data out of them. At the very least, the hardcopies of Ho's files should contain contact information for each of the cell members.

Turning back to Ho, Harvath was about to ask him another question when his cell phone, as well as Sloane's, chimed at exactly the same time. It was the tone they used for emails from the Old Man. Harvath didn't take his eyes off Ho. If the email was important, Sloane would let him know.

Scanning the brief message, she stepped over and whispered in his ear, "The Bureau found the remaining storage units in Seattle and Baltimore. The Old Man wants to know if there are any others. That's priority number one. Once you have that, he wants Bao Deng. He wants you to find out who he is, where he's going, and how we can get to him."

Harvath nodded and focused his full attention back on Ho. Choosing his words carefully, he moved the interrogation in a new and dangerous direction.

CHAPTER 59

In the time that they had been inland, the weather forecast had gone from bad to worse. Nevertheless, Lieutenant Fordyce looked at Billy Tang and said, "I'm putting my foot down."

"Fuck putting your foot down, LT," Johnson interrupted. "I'm going to put my foot up his ass." Pointing his finger right in Tang's face he said, "You and Jin-Sang are coming with us."

The CIA operative didn't know what he appreciated more, Johnson's insistence, or that the SEALs had finally started calling the little boy by his correct name.

"Listen," Tang replied. "You guys need to think about yourselves. That storm's coming. Look at how much wind we've got, and we're not even at the coast yet. You're going to need to double-time it to make your pickup."

"You let us worry about the pickup, Billy," Fordyce said.

"You're going to rappel down that rock face with him and then swim him out in those swells? He's so drugged up, we won't be able to get him to hold his breath long enough to get down to the ASDS. That's just stupid."

"I told you before, we don't do stupid."

The CIA operative looked at the men. "I was wrong when I said I *thought* SEALs were honorable. You *are* honorable. But this isn't open for discussion. You guys need to get back. It's imperative."

"You're right. This isn't open for discussion."

Tang held up his hand. "Hyun Su and I can get him into South Korea. It's going to take a few days, but we can make it happen. As long as Tuck gives me enough meds to keep him comfortable, everything will be okay. As soon as we get to Seoul, I'll take him right to the embassy. They'll want to debrief him and they've got an excellent medical team there. Besides, you can't bring a kid who's been exposed to a potentially drug-resistant form of TB onto a submarine."

Fordyce looked at him. "Are you finished?"

Tang stood there, unsure of how to respond.

Fordyce didn't wait for an answer. "One of the dumbest things you can ever attempt," he said, "is to tell a SEAL what he *can't* do. We'll let the medical officer decide on quarantine protocols. But we came in as a team and we're going out as a team. I don't give a fuck if the North Koreans *suspect* we were here. They're so paranoid they suspect everyone. Now, you either learn how to follow my orders, or this time I *will* have Tucker shoot you. Is that clear?"

The CIA operative had no idea how the SEALs were going to pull it off, but he trusted them. Shaking his head, he smiled and resigned himself to the fact that they were all leaving together.

Fordyce put his index finger behind his left ear and bent it forward, indicating that he was still awaiting a response.

"Sir, yes sir," Tang replied, throwing in a crisp salute.

"You damn well better salute me. It's the least you

can do for the ass-chewing I'm going to get. Now, let's talk about how we're going to roll this out."

The water was worse than any of them had anticipated. The incoming storm had picked up considerable strength and was roiling the sea with chop. Fordyce's brilliant plan was looking much less brilliant by the second.

Tucker and Johnson had argued over who would stay behind with Billy Tang and Jin-Sang. It would take two people to move the little boy and there was no way they were going to leave Billy alone. As the corpsman, and one hell of a gunfighter, Tucker won the argument. Johnson, though, was a stronger swimmer, and Fordyce was glad to have him as his swim buddy for the trip out to the ASDS.

Hyun Su brought them all the way to the coast and made two drops. The first was half a klick in from the cliff the team had climbed less than seventy-two hours ago. After loading Tucker up with extra magazines, Fordyce and Johnson bailed out of the truck and Hyun Su continued. He would drop Billy, Jin-Sang, and Tucker on a strip of beach two kilometers north.

The sound of the truck receding into the distance was replaced by the sound of waves pounding against the rocks at the bottom of the cliff.

Roping up, Fordyce and Johnson double-checked their gear, stepped out over the edge, and rappelled down. As he watched the waves crash below, Fordyce knew he had made the right choice. It would have been a nightmare trying to get Jin-Sang out this way.

At the bottom of the cliff, they rechecked the integrity of their drysuits, put on their swim gear, and did a final assessment before getting wet.

Timing the waves so as not to get battered against the rocks, they picked their moment and jumped.

It was a grueling swim, made just as difficult by the waves as by the current, which was as determined as it had been on their swim in to pull them off course.

They swam using GPS as their guide. Once they reached their GPS point, Fordyce switched to a hand-held acoustic locator to pinpoint the minisub. As soon as they were above it, they oxygenated their lungs, then took a deep breath and dove beneath the surface.

Feeling their way along the structure, they came up into the ASDS through the moon pool in its belly. Johnson climbed out first and Fordyce handed their gear up to him.

Once the gear was secure, Fordyce gave the pilots a new set of orders. After the moon pool was locked off, the pilots retracted their anchors and headed up the coast toward the beach.

As the minisub made its way through the water, Fordyce and Johnson unpacked its lone combat rubber raiding craft. They were going to do this down, dirty, and in a hurry. It wasn't going to be pretty, but it was the only option they had.

When the ASDS arrived off the beach, the pilots deployed the anchors and cleared Fordyce and Johnson to launch. Opening the moon pool, the two SEALs kicked everything into high gear.

Outside the minisub, they began inflating the CRRC and rose with it to the surface. The swells were even worse now, but Fordyce and Johnson focused on the task at hand.

Marking their location on GPS, they attached the outboard engine, and moments later were moving.

The waves pounded the crap out of them as they

headed toward the beach. Riding prone up front, weapon out ready to engage the enemy, Fordyce took the worst of it. It felt they were under the water more than they were on top of it.

By the time they hit the beach, Tucker and Billy Tang were already out of their hide and coming at them with Jin-Sang.

Fordyce knelt in the sand to cover them as Johnson spun the craft around. As soon as he had it pointed back out to sea, the men laid Jin-Sang inside. Tang joined him and then Tucker and Fordyce helped get the boat into deeper water before leaping in themselves and taking their positions forward. Johnson rolled the throttle and the CRRC shot off into the waves. They had been on and off the beach in the blink of an eye.

The ASDS had its comms antenna up and Fordyce radioed the pilots via UHF that they were on their way back.

By the time they hit their GPS point, the minisub had already surfaced.

They entered via the top hatch. Tang went in first, accompanied by a ton of water as a wave crashed right on top of them. As carefully but as quickly as they could, Johnson and Tucker handed Jin-Sang down to him. The ASDS was bobbing like a cork and it was difficult for Tang to maintain his balance. When the boy was safely inside, Johnson flashed Fordyce the thumbs-up and began feeding gear to Tucker, who had already climbed into the hatch.

Once the CRRC was stripped, the two remaining SEALs scuttled it with their knives and let it sink as they dropped through the hatch and closed it above them.

As soon as everything was tight, they gave the pilots

the word to get moving. The sooner they were out of North Korean waters and back on the USS *Texas*, the better all of them were going to feel.

Fordyce looked over at Jin-Sang. Tucker had placed a new mask on him and had wrapped the boy in a dry Mylar blanket. He was out of it, but not so out of it that he couldn't sense the relief of the men around him. Slowly, Jin-Sang lifted his hand and flashed Fordyce a thumbs-up.

The SEAL returned the thumbs-up and then began thinking of everything they needed to report back to Washington as soon as possible.

CHAPTER 60

Tai Cheng exited the van and looked out over the flat, turquoise water. A soft breeze moved the fronds of the palm trees along the beach. He had never been to this part of the United States before. He had seen it only in pictures.

His shoulder hurt like hell and he was exhausted, but they had made it. He was thankful to have had the foresight to pack a medical kit. The bullet wound to his shoulder had required repeated bandage changes.

They had overnighted in truck stops, staying off the roads from ten in the evening until five in the morning. It had added fourteen hours to the journey, but had dramatically reduced their odds of being pulled over. Cheng had gathered up the princelings and had made it out of Boston without being apprehended. All he had to do now was see them the last 120 miles to Havana, or the "Plantation," as the Second Department referred to China's intelligence station there, and his assignment would be complete.

Little Torch Key was a small island in the lower Florida Keys about thirty miles before Key West. It was so quiet the Dolphin Marina didn't even have a restaurant, just a small bait-and-tackle shop with a gas pump and cold drinks. Cheng couldn't have chosen a better rendezvous location if he had tried.

He was dressed for an afternoon of fishing, as were the rest of the princelings. They had purchased the clothing outside Fort Lauderdale, along with sunscreen, snacks, and an enormous cooler in which he had hidden the device.

Colonel Shi had warned Cheng to be careful around Medusa. The man held no loyalties except to himself. He would throw everyone overboard, including his crew, if it meant saving his own skin. He was lazy, which the colonel attributed to too much alcohol or too much sun, and he had very little honor. In other words, a *typical American*. But he was an exceptional smuggler and knew the waters from the Keys to Cuba like no one else. "Keep him sober and keep him focused," Shi had advised.

Cheng found the fishing yacht berthed exactly where he had been told it would be. It was a forty-five-foot Bertram with dual fighting chairs and an array of radar communications equipment. Cheng was particularly glad to see the radar array. If there was even a hint of trouble from the ship's captain, Cheng planned on his own kind of mutiny. Without hesitation, he would throw the man and his crew overboard and complete the journey without them. He had come too far to be undone.

Walking up to the vessel, he took the first mate and "hostess" by surprise. She was stocking beverages in a small fridge on the aft deck. As she bent over, the mate was rubbing himself against her. They were both white, sunburned trash.

The mate was a lean, muscled man with teardrop tattoos near his left eye and a host of other body art that suggested he had seen the inside of a prison more than once. She was petite, with greasy hair, a bikini top, and jean shorts. At the small of her back was what Americans referred to as a tramp stamp.

Cheng cleared his throat to get their attention. They were shameless. Neither seemed to be embarrassed to have been caught in such lewd behavior.

"Skipper!" the lean man shouted. "Charter's here!"

It took a moment for the captain to appear, which led Cheng to believe the man had probably been in the head. Whether the visit was alcohol-related or not, Cheng had no idea at this point.

The captain was grizzled and sunburned just like his crew. The word "redneck" flashed into Cheng's mind. It looked as if the captain had not seen the sharp edge of a razor for several days. He wore a tacky button-down short-sleeved shirt and a pair of swim trunks. A gold ship's-wheel medallion hung from a chain around his neck. In his left hand, he clutched a half-smoked cigar and a can of light beer. The man reeked of alcohol. Shi had been right to warn him.

"Don't just stand there, moron," the captain barked at his mate. "Help these people aboard."

Cheng could already tell this was going to be a long voyage.

The crew helped the party aboard, and after the captain had given them a brief tour and explained where everything was, including the life jackets, he fired up the twin Man 800s, the mate untied the vessel from the dock, and they shoved off.

As they got under way, the hostess offered them welcome drinks. When one of the princelings asked for a scotch and two others asked for beers, Cheng scolded them in Chinese. They settled for Cokes instead.

Cheng didn't care for the man the Second Department had codenamed Medusa. He sat up on the fly bridge, piloting the yacht, alone and aloof. There was no depth to him whatsoever. This was obviously all about the money. Cheng had no doubt that the man would indeed sell them out if it served his purposes. He made sure to keep a very close eye on him.

The hostess and the mate were another issue altogether. They were continually touching or passing too closely in order to rub against each other. Cheng hated Americans more than he could possibly express and couldn't wait to get to Cuba.

They had just entered open water when Cheng heard the engines throttle back and the boat begin to slow.

"What's going on?" he demanded. "Why are we slowing down?"

"We're not slowing down, chief," the mate said. "We're stopping."

"No, we're not."

"Yes, we are," the captain said as he climbed down from the bridge and began grabbing fishing poles from the racks mounted to the side of the boat.

Cheng stepped right up to him and got in his face. The smell of booze was overwhelming, yet Cheng didn't budge. "You're not being paid to take us fishing," he ordered. "You're being paid to take us to Cuba."

Medusa looked at him, his cigar clamped between his teeth, and replied, "Relax. You're going to get to Cuba. In the meantime, we're going to make sure we look like a fishing charter. If we don't, I promise you we're going to have trouble."

Turning to the princelings, the captain then asked, "Anybody want to try for sharks?"

There were several nods from the young Chinese

men, so the captain said to his mate, "Let's toss out some chum."

After the fishing poles were placed, the captain climbed back up to the bridge and began piloting the boat parallel to the Keys, not south toward Cuba. Cheng wasn't in the mood.

Climbing the ladder, he whistled to get the captain's attention. "You're wasting time. I'm sure there are plenty of fish en route to Cuba."

"And you're pissing me off," the captain replied, placing his cigar in the ashtray. Looking past Cheng, he yelled to his hostess, "Angie, bring me a rum runner."

"Aye, aye, skipper!" the slutty woman responded from below.

Cheng had had enough. "Let me explain something to you."

"No," the captain interrupted, "let me explain something to you. I know what I'm doing. This is my boat, my rules. You need to relax."

"I'll relax when we get to Havana."

"You need a drink," he replied. "Angie!" he yelled down to his hostess again. "Get our guest a drink."

"What I *need*," said Cheng, "is for you to explain exactly how this is going to go. I don't want any surprises."

Rolling his eyes, the captain snatched up his cigar, chomped down on it, and yelled for his mate. "Jimmy!"

"Yes, skipper?"

"Come up and take the wheel. I need to review the nav charts with our guest."

"Aye, aye, skipper," the mate said, and as he waited for Cheng to step down from the ladder, he motioned to one of the students to take his place, dig in the bucket, and keep tossing out the chum. Once Cheng had moved, the captain climbed down and the mate was able to climb up.

"Heading?" he asked.

"South," the skipper replied, locking eyes with Cheng. "Our guests are in a hurry."

"Aye, aye, Captain," the mate said.

Cheng hated the nautical-speak, he hated their boorishness, and he hated that his fate and the fate of his mission were in the hands of these idiots. He wanted to place bullets in all of them.

To add insult to injury, he saw the captain lose his balance as they entered the salon. The man recovered quickly, but it hadn't escaped Cheng's practiced eye.

"What can I get you to drink?" the hostess asked. "Rum runner?"

"No," Cheng snapped. "No more alcohol, for anyone."

The hostess looked at the captain, who waved the retort away. "Give us a minute, will you, Angie?"

The woman stepped out onto the rear deck with the princelings and closed the glass door behind her.

"My crew work for me, not for you," the captain then said. "You don't tell them what to do."

The man had stepped on Cheng's last nerve. Pulling out his pistol, he grabbed Medusa by his shirt, yanked him closer, and placed the barrel right under his nose. It sent bolts of pain through his injured shoulder, but it was a necessary show of force to earn the man's respect. "Until we safely arrive in Cuba, this is my boat, and all three of you are my crew. Is that clear?"

The captain put up his hands, palms out, and replied, "Crystal clear."

"I want you to sober up. Is that also clear?"

"I'll have Angie put on coffee."

"Good," Cheng said, letting him go and reholstering his pistol beneath his shirt. "Now, I want you to show me our route, as well as the contingencies. Heaven forbid anything should happen to you, I want to make sure the rest of us will make it."

"Heaven forbid," the captain repeated, fully grasping the threat that had just been made. "Let me get Angie started on the coffee."

He waved the hostess back in and pointed Cheng toward the bedrooms, one of which functioned as his office with all of his charts.

"No," Cheng insisted. "After you."

Shaking his head, the captain turned and led the man down the narrow companionway.

His office was dominated by a large map table with barely any space to maneuver around it. He signaled for Cheng to enter, but Cheng opted to step only halfway in and lean against the door frame.

"Suit yourself," said the captain.

He turned up the marine radio so he could listen in on the traffic and then selected a map from one of many hung upon a rack bracketed to the wall.

Splaying the map on the table, the captain grabbed a pencil as well as a protractor, and was about to indicate where they were in relation to Little Torch Key when he heard a noise from the hallway and saw the panic in Cheng's eyes.

CHAPTER 61

The roar of the shotgun blast was deafening, even out on the aft deck where the princelings were watching the frenzied sharks gathered off the stern.

Immediately, the mate, Jimmy, cut the engines and when the students looked up at the bridge, they saw him looking at them with a pistol in his hand. Angie, the hostess, appeared in the salon with a sawed-off shotgun. From behind her, the captain came dragging the bloody body of their chaperone—the man who had collected them in Boston and was supposed to get them to Cuba so they could fly home. The man had never told them why, only that it was life and death, and that they were not to question his orders. While he bought their food or gassed up the van, they all whispered that it had to be because China was finally going to war with the United States.

The scene was beyond shocking. The men gasped. Daiyu screamed. The corpse was covered in blood and almost his entire face was missing. None of them had ever seen such a grisly sight.

If it weren't for the clothing and the bits of jet-black hair that remained, they never would have even recognized him. Daiyu Jinping knew it was him, though.

She could see the bandage beneath his shirt, on his left shoulder.

"Listen up!" the captain ordered, dragging the corpse onto the deck and dropping the legs with a thud. "There's been a change of plans. Angie is going to hand each of you a cell phone. I want you to call your families back in China and tell them you've been kidnapped. In the draft folder of each of those phones are wiring instructions along with a price. If your family pays, there'll be no problem. If they don't, then this is what'll happen."

The captain nodded at Jimmy, who came down from the bridge and tucked his weapon into his waistband. Together, they bent down, lifted the body, and threw it off the back of the boat. The sharks immediately went to work, tearing it apart.

"Tell your families they have one hour."

The captain took the shotgun from Angie, who then removed five fully charged iPhones from a bag and passed them out to each of the horror-stricken princelings. They watched the sharks rip at their chaperone's flesh and were unable to look away.

"The cameras on those phones don't work, by the way," said the captain, attempting to break the spell of the sharks, "so don't get any bright ideas. Tell them your situation, send them the wiring instructions, and hang up."

Looking at his mate, the captain then said, "Let's take a little cruise, Jimmy. Not too far out. I want to make sure we remain within cell service, so our bank can let us know as soon as that money starts rolling in."

"Aye, aye, Captain," the mate said as he bounded back up to the bridge and fired up the engines.

"Angie," the captain called to the hostess, "I think I'd like that rum runner now."

"Anything you say, Captain," the young woman replied as she disappeared inside to fetch his drink.

The faces of the young Chinese were a mixture of shock, fear, and contempt. The captain smiled and motioned for each of them to hurry up and make their calls. One by one, they all started to dial home.

As soon as the calls had been placed, Angie collected the phones and the students were herded into the salon. After their hands and feet were bound, they were ordered to sit on the floor. While Jimmy piloted the yacht, Angie sunned herself on the rear deck and the captain sat in a comfortable chair near the students, shotgun across his lap, sipping his drink and watching satellite TV.

Forty-five minutes later, the mate slid down the ladder from the bridge, stuck his head in the salon, and said, "Captain, come quick. We've got a problem."

Several of the princelings looked up hopefully.

"Angie," the captain yelled, "get in here and keep an eye on them." Handing her his shotgun, he added, "If they move or make a sound, shoot them. *All* of them."

"Aye, aye, Captain," she replied and fixed the students with one of the coldest stares they had ever seen. The woman was obviously no stranger to violence and meant business. Not a single princeling made a sound.

From where they sat, with their backs against the couch, they could see out the opposite window. On the horizon a bright orange dot had appeared and was coming closer.

Soon enough they could not only see the U.S. Coast Guard chopper but hear the pounding of its rotors.

When it was almost overhead, there was a voice from

the helicopter's loudspeaker. "This is the United States Coast Guard. Drop your weapons and halt your vessel."

From outside, the students heard two shots, and they exchanged terrified glances.

There were two more shots and then suddenly the engines went dead.

"You! Inside the vessel," the voice boomed over the PA once more, "come out with your hands up!"

"Do as they say, Angie!" the captain yelled. "Do it now!"

"No!" she screamed back.

The helicopter could be heard repositioning outside and suddenly a heavy rope hit the aft deck. Seconds later, men in tactical gear with submachine guns slid down and stormed the salon and bridge.

The hostess tossed aside the shotgun just before being slammed to the floor by the Coast Guard team. Wrenching her arms behind her back, they FlexiCuffed her as two men raced forward to check the rest of the yacht.

A chorus of "Clear! Clear!" rang out as they searched each room and then returned to the salon. As they did, their colleagues entered and threw both the captain and his mate to the floor and made them lie, facedown, with their hands FlexiCuffed behind them.

Within fifteen minutes, two U.S. Coast Guard ships were on scene. Once the Chinese students had been transferred over to one of them, that vessel turned and headed back for land.

It was then that the head of the tactical team cut the boat's "crew" loose.

"You boys play rough," said Sloane as she rubbed her raw wrists.

The Coast Guard officer smiled. "You should have seen those kids' faces. They were freaked out."

"That's nothing," Chase replied as he sat up. "You should have seen their faces when we chucked that John Doe to the sharks. They'll never look at shark fin soup the same again."

"Don't drop that," Harvath said as two team members prepared to transfer the cooler containing the Nashville EMP device over to their vessel.

Standing up, he walked into the galley, removed his phone from the drawer, and called Nicholas, who was back at the NCTC working with the NSA.

"Did the Chinese buy it?" he asked.

"Hook, line, and sinker," Nicholas replied. "When those kids phoned home, Chinese intelligence began tracing the calls immediately. Not long after that, Ho's phone started ringing. Because Medusa was his asset, they blamed him for everything getting screwed up."

"Good," said Harvath. "As soon as we're ready to allow the princelings to call home, I want Stephanie Esposito listening in. Let's make sure we see this thing across the goal line."

"You got it. Anything else?"

"Yeah, tell Ren Ho he's one step closer to getting his son back."

"Will do," Nicholas replied. "Good luck interrogating Bao Deng, or should I say Tai Cheng?"

"Tell the Old Man I'll call him once we have something."

With that, Harvath disconnected the call and walked down to the master stateroom. Lying on the bed naked, except for his briefs, was Tai Cheng.

After Sloane had stepped into the gangway and Tasered him, Harvath had hit him with a syringe full of ketamine. They had dragged him into the master state-room where they stripped off his clothes, including the bandage on his shoulder, put a piece of duct tape over his mouth, and hog-tied him with FlexiCuffs.

After dressing their disfigured, dark-haired John Doe corpse from the Miami morgue and splashing it with pig's blood, Sloane fired a blank shotgun round and Harvath dragged the mutilated body out for the princelings to see.

As the middleman between the Second Department and the smuggler known as Medusa, Ho had indeed been helpful. He had provided more than enough intel for the FBI to arrest the boat's owner and its crew.

Ho had in fact cooperated every step of the way, including giving up the locations of all the cell members in each city and explaining how the EMP devices worked. He had even detailed how they had been smuggled into the country and who had been involved. He had explained how China's military intelligence division worked, who had been involved with Snow Dragon, and who had conceived of it. He talked at length about Colonel Jiang Shi and his mantra that they would turn out the lights and America would be made to bow to China.

Ho was an intelligence jackpot, and Harvath had been completely honest when he had said that for his cooperation, the man would get his son back.

Harvath had also been completely honest when he had promised Tai Cheng that he would see to it that he got to Cuba. But instead of Havana by boat, he'd be flying from U.S. Naval Air Station Key West to the GITMO detention camp at U.S. Naval Station Guantanamo Bay.

CHAPTER 62

Two Weeks Later

Harvath had balked at the idea of being picked up in a limousine, but the powers that be had insisted. It was out of his control, so he gave in and went along with it.

As he watched the world pass by outside his window, he reflected on everything that had happened. Cheng had been difficult to break, but he *had* broken, and once he did, Harvath had handed him over to the team at GITMO. Based on what the princelings had told their families, the PSC and therefore the Second Department believed that Cheng had been shot and fed to sharks in the waters off Florida. The intelligence he provided would be extremely valuable to the United States.

As Harvath had sent the GITMO team Ahmad Yaqub, Khuram Hanjour, and Tai Cheng all in the space of a week, the lead interrogator had thanked him and then suggested he take up some sort of hobby, fishing, for a while. The President, on the other hand, had other plans for him.

Harvath had marveled at how President Porter had handled everything. Combined with the intelligence gathered by the SEALs in North Korea, the President had assembled an airtight case against the Chinese.

Though he was outraged that any administration would secretly issue collateralized bonds and keep it from the American citizens, he had found a loophole.

The Chinese had conducted an act of war against the United States. Their goal was to force America's collapse so that China could collect on the resources it so desperately needed. The President found it only fitting that America's debt to the Chinese, all of it, be nullified. The Chinese were apoplectic, but there was absolutely nothing they could do about it. They had lost legitimacy and they had lost face. The President intended to press his advantage for every economic and diplomatic benefit he could reap.

For its role in helping to develop the EMP weapons, knowingly delivering them to the Chinese, and allowing Chinese soldiers to train for an American invasion on their soil, the President imposed crippling concessions on the North Koreans.

President Porter was particularly moved by the story of Jin-Sang, the little boy the Gold Dust team had rescued from the North Korean labor camp. In addition to a multitude of demands on the DPRK economically and militarily, President Porter had forced the North Korean government to accept all types of inspectors, including the IAEA, Amnesty International, and the Red Cross. It was that or face total annihilation.

Before the President had even picked up the phone to inform the Chinese and North Koreans of the consequences of their actions and the restitution they would be forced to make, he had consulted with America's allies. Each of them knew that the same plot could have been carried out against their country, and they stood shoulder to shoulder with the United States, agreeing to back them on anything they chose to do. It was good for them to be reminded of who their friends and enemies were from time to time. They seemed to get the two mixed up on a disturbingly regular basis.

As for the Chinese, the United States had one final demand. And until that demand was satisfied, the princelings would remain as guests in the United States.

Colonel Jiang Shi stepped to the window and watched the snow that had begun to fall outside. The seasoned logs in the fireplace snapped and popped as they gave off a bright orange flame. The opulent mountain retreat did little to lessen his dislike of China's political class.

The General Secretary and the rest of the PSC blamed him, of course, for the failure of Snow Dragon. He had thought about fleeing. He had money, contacts. Yet he knew eventually they would find him. While it wouldn't be Tai Cheng, it would be someone just like him. Someone born with a predator's instinct who knew nothing but the hunt. It would have been pointless to run. So he had gone to work, waiting to be summoned, waiting for a speedy trial and a bullet to the back of his head, with the bill sent to his wife. But neither the trial nor the bullet ever came.

As it turned out, the General Secretary and the PSC were more concerned about coming up with a trump card, something they could give the Americans that would stave off the inevitable. They didn't care what it was. They would throw any other country to the wolves in order to save themselves. Shi had never seen them so convinced that the Americans would unite the world against them in war.

The Second Department worked around the clock,

trying to develop a plan. On top of figuring out a way to avert war, contingencies were being made in case they did go to war. It was in this arena that the PSC wanted Colonel Shi focused. Despite the failure of his Snow Dragon operation, they had finally come to appreciate his talent in unrestricted warfare. If war were to come, the PSC, the PLA, and the Second Department needed a concise plan for how to win it. The stakes had never been higher, especially as the PSC was convinced that the new American president was so incensed that he fully intended to launch a full-scale nuclear attack.

That was why Colonel Shi had been invited to the PSC's mountain retreat. The Chinese had agreed to unconditionally release the Americans from their debt obligations, but that hadn't been enough. The United States had a bloodlust that couldn't be sated. China needed a plan, a brilliant plan, and Jiang Shi had been told to have multiple options for them by the time they arrived.

Turning from the window, Shi walked to the fireplace and added another log. His dinner sat on the table. He hadn't had much of an appetite, but knew he needed to eat.

Sitting down, he placed the elaborately folded napkin in his lap. As he did, he noticed a small, wooden gift box had been placed underneath.

He opened the box and inside was a tiny figurine. It was a snow dragon that had been hand-carved from a small piece of ivory. With it was a crisp, white note card.

Shi's name had been beautifully written on one side in Chinese characters. Part of him wondered if this was a symbol of recognition from the PSC for everything he had done, or perhaps from the General Secretary himself—a man known for giving such exquisite gifts.

Turning the card over, Shi felt his heart stop as he read words just as beautifully written, but in English:

America bows to no one.

Before Shi had any idea what was happening, Harvath had swung the garrote wire over the man's head, pulled back as hard as he could, and crossed his hands.

Colonel Jiang Shi struggled as the blood spurted from his neck, but only for a moment. The last thing he saw as he died was the snow falling just outside his window.

As Harvath exited the retreat and walked downhill to the limousine the PSC and the General Secretary had provided, he removed his cell phone and texted the President:

The Snow Dragon is dead.

ACKNOWLEDGMENTS

In an author's life, there are so many important people to thank when a new book is published, and I always start with you, my incredible **readers**. Thank you for all of your support and all the great word-of-mouth you generate. I could take out billboards around the world and they would never have the power of when you turn to a friend, colleague, or a family member and say, "You have to read this Brad Thor book . . ." I cannot thank you enough for being the best ambassadors a writer could ever have.

Without amazing **booksellers**, you wouldn't be holding this in your hands. I am very grateful for all they do to sell my novels and introduce new readers to my work every day. Wherever you buy my books, please know that you are interacting with a very special group of people.

James Ryan, **Rodney Cox**, and **Sean F.** are exceptionally talented men who have never once let me down personally or professionally. No matter how hard a challenge I throw at them, they always come back with the perfect solution. Thank you, gentlemen, for your professionalism, your patriotism, and your friendship.

Pete Scobell, **Jeff Boss**, **Peter Osyff**, and **Jon Sanchez** are not only a terrific group of men, but they contributed overwhelmingly to the verisimilitude of this novel. My thanks to them go far beyond their selfless contributions herein. America is a better place because of them.

An additional thank-you goes out to good friends **Chad Norberg**, **Frank Gallagher**, **Jeff Chudwin**, **Robert O'Brien**, **Steve Adelmann** of Citizen Arms, who created the Hoplite carbine, **Tony Williams**, Government Sales Manager at Aimpoint, **Steve Tuttle**, Vice President of Communications TASER International, Inc., and two other friends who are also two of my favorite must-read authors: **James Rollins** and **J. L. Bourne**.

I would also like to thank knife designer **James Williams** of CRKT, **Heidi A. Fedak** of Gulfstream Aerospace Corp, and **Nate** of Grumpy's Bail Bonds in Nashville.

There are others who contributed to *Act of War,* but who, out of security concerns, have asked that their names not be listed here. To them, and all the men and women with whom they work, I say thank you for your assistance and for your selfless service to our great nation.

The characters **Stephanie Esposito**, **Jimi Fordyce**, **Lester (Les) Johnson**, **Anne Reilly Levy**, and **Heidi Roe** were so named in the novel because of generous contributions made to worthwhile causes in their honor. I hope everyone enjoys how the names were used. My thanks to all involved for their generosity.

Great publishing happens because you have an outstanding team. From the phenomenal **Carolyn Reidy** and the extraordinary **Louise Burke**, to the marvelous **Judith Curr**, I am with the <u>absolute best</u> in the business. Thank you to everyone at **Simon & Schuster** for all that you have done and continue to do for me.

At the center of my amazing team is the most incredible editor and publisher an author could ever have, the remarkable **Emily Bestler**. There is a reason we have been together since Day 1. She is not only the best at what she does, she is also an absolute pleasure to work with. She always has my back, and for that I am eternally grateful. Thank you, Emily.

My magnificent publicist, **David Brown**, is a force to be reckoned with. He is not only one of the nicest men you will ever meet, he is also one of the hardest-working and most dedicated. David, thank you for everything.

In addition to David, the tremendous **Cindi Berger** and **Cara Masline** of PMK continue to help us shatter records with each book we publish. Thank you, ladies.

If you're very fortunate, you get to go to war with an army you love—and that's definitely the situation in my case. At **Simon & Schuster**, it is my pleasure to say thank you to everyone at **Emily Bestler Books/Atria** and **Pocket Books**, including **Michael Selleck**, **Ben Lee**, **Kate Cetrulo**, **Megan Reid**, **Irene Lipsky**, **Lisa Keim**, **Valerie Vennix**, **Ariele Fredman**, the **Emily Bestler Books/Atria** and **Pocket Books sales team**, including **Gary Urda**, **John Hardy**, and **Colin Shields**, **Jeanne Lee**, and both the **Emily Bestler Books/Atria** and **Pocket Books Art Departments**, **Al Madocs**, and the **Emily Bestler Books/Atria Production Department**, **Chris Lynch**, **Tom Spain**, **Sarah Lieberman**, **Desiree Vecchio**, **Armand Schultz**, and the **Simon & Schuster audio division**.

I am pleased to announce that upon completion of *Act of War*, I signed a new contract with **Simon &**

Schuster and that you will be seeing a lot more of Scot Harvath well into the future.

That contract happened because of **Heide Lange** of **Sanford J. Greenburger Associates**. Heide is the best literary agent on the planet, and I have learned more about publishing and business from her than I could ever hope to learn in two lifetimes. She is a brilliant negotiator, a fabulous advocate, and the dearest of friends.

Rounding out Heide's team are the awesome **Stephanie Delman** and **Rachel Mosner**. I thank you and everyone else at SJGA for all that you do, day in and day out for me. You are all very much appreciated.

Out in Hollywood, my longtime friend and extraordinary entertainment attorney, **Scott Schwimer**, continues to work his very special kind of magic. Thank you for everything, Scottie.

At Thor Entertainment Group, **Yvonne Ralsky** continues to be an absolute genius, who brings creativity and ingenuity by the truckload. We are in the most exciting phase of our company to date and you are a huge part of that. Thank you, YBR.

Happiness in life is all about three things— something to do, someone to love, and something to look forward to. The most important component to me is having someone to love. It was my gorgeous wife, **Trish**, who encouraged me to pursue my dreams of becoming an author. It was also Trish who brought our two incredible **children** into this world. A life without love is a life not fully lived, and that makes me so thankful for my family. They keep me grounded and happier than I ever believed possible. Thank you for all you put up with while I am writing. I love you all more than you will ever know.

In closing, let me say that I am constantly striving to create new and more exciting ways to add to your enjoyment of my novels. Please consider signing up at BradThor.com for my fast, fun, easy-to-read monthly newsletter, where I offer exclusive contests, prizes, bonus content, and special features that bring the locations in my novels to life.

Thank you for all of your support. I'll see you with a new adventure soon!

Emily Bestler Books

Proudly Presents

CODE OF CONDUCT

by

BRAD THOR

Read on for the riveting opening of
Brad Thor's pulse-pounding new thriller
Code of Conduct . . .

"If you must break the law, do it to seize power."

—Julius Caesar

PART I

A Murder of Crows

PROLOGUE

When word leaked that the President had been taken to the Bethesda Naval Hospital for observation, panic set in. If the President of the United States wasn't safe from the virus, no one was.

Scot Harvath swerved around the car in front of him and sped through the intersection as the light changed. The traffic was worsening. Quarantine rumors had sent people rushing to stores to stock up.

"We don't need to do this," the woman sitting next to him said.

What she meant was that *he* didn't need to do this. He could leave, too. He didn't have to stay behind in D.C.

"I've already talked to Jon and his wife," he replied. "You'll be safe there."

"What about you?"

"I'll be okay. I'll join you as soon as I can."

He was lying. It was a white lie, meant to make her feel better, but it was a lie nonetheless. They were already talking about shutting down air traffic. That's why he needed to get her out tonight.

"What if we're overreacting?" she asked.

"We're not."

Lara knew he was right. She had seen the projections. Even the "best case" numbers were devastating. The cities would be the hardest hit. Hospitals were already at surge capacity, and were being overrun by otherwise healthy people who had convinced themselves they were showing one or more of the virus's symptoms. It was beginning to make it impossible for real emergencies like heart attacks and breathing problems brought on by severe asthma to be seen. And it was only going to get worse.

Cities, towns, and villages from coast to coast scrambled to figure out how they would continue to deliver essential services, in addition to dealing with the staggering number of bodies if the death toll reached even half of what was being predicted. In a word, they *couldn't*.

As they succumbed to the virus or stayed home to protect their own families, fewer and fewer first responders would be available. Soon, 911 call centers would go down. After that, water treatment facilities and power plants. Hospitals, pharmacies, and grocery stores would cease operating—the majority of them looted and burned to the ground. Chaos and anarchy would reign.

The only people who might hope to survive were those who had exercised some degree of caution and had prepared in advance. But even many of them would not be spared. Because riding alongside death and its pale horse was another force that would prove just as devastating.

Suddenly, two blue-and-white Department of Homeland Security Suburbans spun around the corner and came racing toward them, their lights and sirens blaring.

Harvath jerked his wheel hard to the right to get

out of their way. Even then, he came within inches of being hit before the DHS vehicles swerved back into their lane.

Lara turned in her seat as they sped past. "Jesus!" she exclaimed. "Did you see that? They almost hit us."

The chaos had officially started.

Before he could respond, his cell phone rang. "Good," he said, after listening to the voice on the other end. "We're ten minutes away."

Disconnecting the call, he pressed harder on the accelerator and told her, "The plane just landed. Everything will be ready by the time we get there."

Nearing the private aviation section of Reagan National, they saw a sea of limousines and black Town Cars. He wasn't the only one who had seen the writing on the wall. Those who could get out were getting out now.

Not wanting to get tied up in the parking lot, he pulled to the side of the road near the entrance and hopped out to get Lara's bag.

Opening the rear of his Tahoe, he plugged his combination into one of the drawers of his TruckVault and pulled it open.

"I already have my duty weapon," Lara said. "Plus my credentials and extra ammo."

She was always armed. He knew that. Removing a small, hard-sided Pelican Case, he handed it to her. "Just in case," he said.

Lara popped the latches and flipped open the lid. "Sat phone?" she asked.

Harvath nodded. "If this gets worse, the cell phone network won't stay up for long."

"Is my cell even going to work up there?"

"Once you leave Anchorage, you might as well turn

it off until you get to the lodge. There's no cell service there, but you can make calls over their Wi-Fi."

Removing the battery cover, he showed her where he had taped the number for the sat phone he kept in his bug-out bag. If everything failed, the sat phones would be their fallback.

Closing up the Tahoe, he picked up her bag and walked with her to the Signature Flight Support building. Inside, it was pandemonium.

Wealthy families jostled with corporate executives to speed the departure of their jets. There were mountains of luggage and, from what he overheard, a vast array of destinations—Jackson Hole, Eleuthera, Costa Rica, Kauai—likely second or third home locations where they hoped to ride out the storm.

Harvath spotted their copilot, who took Lara's bag and the Pelican Case and walked them out to the jet.

Harvath didn't want a long good-bye. He wanted them in the air as quickly as possible.

Wrapping his arms around her, he kissed her. It felt detached, distant. His mind had already left the airport. It was on to the dangerous assignment that lay in front of him.

"It's still not too late," she said.

It was and she knew it.

"You need to get going," he replied, giving her one more kiss as he broke off their hug.

"See me onto the plane."

It was too loud on the tarmac to hear the chime, but he felt his phone vibrate in his pocket. Pulling it out, he read the message. Now he really needed to go.

"I can't," he said, kissing her one last time. "Let me know when you get there."

With that, he turned and walked back to the Signature Flight Support building.

As soon as he was inside, he called the person who had texted him. "Are you positive about this?" he asked.

"One hundred percent," the voice on the other end responded.

"How long do I have?"

"Could be hours. Could be days. What are you going to do?"

"What would you do?" Harvath asked.

"Get my affairs in order and hope it's painless."